The Other Middle East

The Other Middle East

An Anthology of
Modern Levantine Literature

FRANCK SALAMEH

Yale UNIVERSITY PRESS/NEW HAVEN & LONDON

Published with assistance from
the foundation established in memory of Amasa Stone Mather
of the Class of 1907, Yale College.

Yale University Press books may be purchased in quantity
for educational, business, or promotional use. For information,
please e-mail sales.press@yale.edu (U.S. office) or
sales@yaleup.co.uk (U.K. office).

Set in Minion type by Newgen North America.
Printed in the United States of America.

Library of Congress Control Number: 2017942329
ISBN 978-0-300-20444-5 (hardcover : alk. paper)

A catalogue record for this book is available
from the British Library.

This paper meets the requirements of ANSI/NISO Z39.48-1992
(Permanence of Paper).

10 9 8 7 6 5 4 3 2 1

To my Levantine great-grandmother,
who lived in five cultures and wielded five languages when most
children of her generation across the Mediterranean could barely
manage one; to a dignified literate lettered woman traveling in an age
of literacy restricted to men; to an exquisite *Sitt*—a Grande Dame—
who always asked me for "something to read" even as she already had
a book in hand, and many more at hand; to my anthropomorphic
Levant, an affectionate matriarch who in her elegant, reticent wisdom
changed my life, whispering gently, and seldom in words, *Tolle lege!*

To *téta* Mathilde
In memoriam
(1894–1974)

To my very thoughtful, deliciously witty Aarash; keep killing it.

B.C. Feb. 16—'23
Thrs.

Un jour tout sera bien, voilà notre espérance.
Tout est bien aujourd'hui, voilà l'illusion.
—Voltaire (1694–1778)

Contents

Acknowledgments

L ebanese-American philosopher and fellow Bostonian Kahlil
    Gibran once said about his epochal *The Prophet* that it was
    a book that had always lived with and within him; that it had
    been part of his very being, accompanying him in his exile
from the snowcapped highlands of his native Mount Lebanon to the
cold slushy Tremont Street estuaries of his adoptive home in the South
End of Boston. Gibran claimed to have lived, *truly* lived, *The Prophet*
before condensing it in print. I lack the immodesty of those children
of my race who delight in comparing themselves to Gibran, but I must
admit that I still take great pride and pleasure in the fact that I, like him,
am Lebanese by birth and Bostonian by choice.

Yet, I must also admit that like Gibran's *The Prophet,* the present
anthology has in fact been with me for a very long time, tucked away
in the confines of frayed old memories, alongside *other* artifacts from
home, living and breathing and wreathing within me for many decades
now, probably since that sad balmy July morning in 1981 when I bid
a last farewell to the land of my birth, to my beloved Levant. And so,
here I am today, thirty-six years later, letting go again of a sun-drenched
part of my being, a steep towering white-green mountain wading its
feet deeply into the blue Mediterranean below; a living age-old Levantine legend getting ossified—memorialized—in print. And though it is
bittersweet to let go of a part of one's being in this way, I am grateful to

ix

so many who accompanied me on this journey, egging me on, interrogating me, motivating me to question myself, my worldviews, my most intimately held assumptions. In this, I have been assisted by many who deserve recognition for the compilation, research, translation, and writing of this anthology.

A great debt of gratitude goes to my departmental colleagues at Boston College; children of an ecumenical, cosmopolitan, polyglot universe that placed a very high premium on excellence and curiosity and argumentation and diversity of perspectives; who provided the ideal academic home where several years of teaching a survey course in modern Middle Eastern literature contributed to the birth of this volume. My former department chairs Cynthia Simmons, Maxim Shrayer, and Michael Connolly deserve special thanks, first of all, for bringing me to Boston College more than a decade ago, and for their unyielding support and encouragement and trust in subsequent years. Even as I was running out of steam at times, often on the verge of giving up, *they* never gave up.

Michael Connolly's sobriety and composure and wisdom and gravitas—*and* clever, edgy humor—taught me a lesson on judgment and character and tenacity and loyalty, and on, simply put, decency. My faculty mentor Maxim Shrayer is owed special recognition for awakening in me curiosities and ambition and drive, for always challenging me to go beyond my personal finish lines, and to exceed my own expectations. Likewise Margaret Thomas was always generous with advice and backing, teaching me—perhaps without even noticing—how to bring discipline and precision to my language. Lydia Chiang was also a great colleague, always ready with a kind word and sympathetic ears. Cynthia Simmons, a wise thoughtful counsel, will no doubt recognize in the title of this volume an echo of a course that she taught at Boston College: Literature of the *Other* Europe. I pilfered the "other" bit from Cynthia's course title because it was the clever semantic "missing link" that I had been searching for, to depict my own "dissident" Middle East in ways and words that very few in my field dared engage. But I also lifted Cynthia's "other" because, where I come from, *l'imitation est la forme d'admiration la plus sincère*. There is also Atef Ghobrial in my academic department, who is owed special thanks for the interest that he

showed and the support that he always lent; a man who lives by the etymology of his name *without* even noticing. *Atef* means "compassionate"
in Arabic, with Aramaic semantic connotations of "armor," "shield,"
"bulwark," and "protector"; and *Ghobrial* is the Hebrew rendition of
a "Man of God." And so, this compassionate "Man of God" graciously
read various drafts of several of my renditions of Arabic and French
texts, offering a wide range of thoughtful commentaries and constructive suggestions for which I am grateful.

The Boston College Dean's and Provost's offices were crucial resources; I am particularly indebted to Rev. Fr. Gregory Kalscheur, S.J.,
Dean of the Morrissey College of Arts and Sciences, and Vice Provost for
Research Bill Nuñez, for the generous subventions that they allocated
for this volume, allowing me to obtain some of the more onerous copy-
rights permissions in the Middle East, Europe, and the United States.
Likewise, this endeavor was costly in both time and money, and would
have been impossible to conclude without the assistance and support of
the Morrissey College of Arts and Sciences' Service Center. The Center's
director Judith Canty and her staff, in particular grant assistant Moira
Smith, all went far above and beyond the call of duty, and they all deserve my heartfelt thanks. Likewise the staff and administrators of the
Boston College Libraries and the Interlibrary Loans division are owed
special recognition; particularly Anne Kenny, Duane Farabaugh, and
Nina Bogdanovsky.

I would be remiss not to mention the debt of gratitude owed Diana
Pesek at Penn State University Press and the editors of *Bustan: The Middle East Book Review* in Tel Aviv, namely Ambassador Itamar Rabinovich
and Professors Uzi Rabi and Daniel Zisenwine, who published an earlier
version of this anthology's introduction, and who graciously gave their
consent to reproduce large segments of it in this volume, reproduced
with the permission of Penn State University Press and *Bustan: The
Middle East Book Review*. I am likewise indebted to Professor Emmanuel Sivan, former editor of the *Jerusalem Quarterly*, and my editors at
Rowman & Littlefield, in particular Carissa Marcelle and Patricia Zline
at the Lexington Books imprint, for granting me permission to reproduce Charles Corm materials already published by Lexington in *Charles
Corm: An Intellectual Biography of a Twentieth-Century Lebanese "Young*

Phoenician" (Franck Salameh Copyright © 2015) all used by permission of Rowman & Littlefield Publishing Group.

In Beirut, I am grateful for the loyalty, generosity, and complicity of my dear friends (*mes frères de cœur*) David and Hiram Corm of the Éditions de la Revue Phénicienne, who spread their kindness and spared neither resource nor time putting at my disposal a wealth of archives, advice, and personal contacts as I excavated and translated Charles Corm's works. My stay in Beirut was short—and even were it not, it is way too short—but always long-savored and can never be forgotten when Davy and Rami are in it. I should also mention that without their devotion, I would not have been able to identify some of the more elusive copyright owners of a good portion of the works featured in this volume. Chadia Tuéni of Dar al-nahar and Marwan Hamadé of the Fondation Nadia Tuéni deserve heartfelt thanks, as does Omar Nizar Kabbani, heir and representative of the Nizar Qabani Estate, who graciously granted me rights to classics of his father's corpus. Abdo Wazen of *Al-Hayat,* and Michael Young of the Beirut *Daily Star* also deserve special recognition—and more—for all the efforts that they furnished on my behalf with regard to various "orphaned" works with seemingly no copyright owners. I am likewise grateful to Sami Naufal, Emile Tyan, Najla Reaidy, and Pascale Kahwagi of Hachette-Antoine Beirut for the rights to Anis Freyha's work, for the elegance and enthusiasm with which they answered my queries, and for something else that I can only describe as Levantine—and from their purview, *Lebanese*—hospitality.

In Paris, the generous and competent anthropomorphic "Phoenician Island" was an exquisite Phoenician conduit and intermediary, putting me in touch with the Wylie Agency's Sarah Watling and Charles Buchan in the UK in order to secure permissions to the *Identité inachevée* excerpts. So were Adonis himself and his wife, Dr. Khalida Esber, gracious and generous in granting me permissions to other works of the author. The ever gentle and elegant Samuel Hazo graciously granted permission to reuse the *Elegy for the Time at Hand* segment of his *The Blood of Adonis: Transposition of Selected Poems of Adonis.* In fact, I should mention that without Sam's lifelong work, and without his delicate translations of Adonis's Arabic, I would never have been able to approach the impenetrable edifice of Adonis's Arabic language.

Candace Frede of the American Council of Learned Societies in New York, Samir el-Youssef in London, Christine Lee, the permissions supervisor at Simon & Schuster who granted permission to use excerpts of Fawaz Turki's *Exile's Return,* and the authors and editors of *Mongrels or Marvels: The Levantine Writings of Jacqueline Shohet Kahanoff* at Stanford University Press, as well as Jacqueline Kahanoff's niece, the thoughtful Laura d'Amade, all deserve special thanks and recognition for allowing me to reproduce texts, which are foundational to this anthology.

At Yale University Press, wise, skilled, proactive—and most of all, patient—editors made this volume what it is today. Eric Brandt, now assistant director and editor in chief at the University of Virginia Press, took a personal interest in this book project while he was still senior editor at Yale, and while the book was still in its early stages. I am grateful to Eric for having lent his support to this project from its inception, passing it on to the able hands of Laura Davulis, and later to Sarah Miller and Ash Lago, who made it what it is today in its final iteration. I would also like to extend a special thanks to my production editor, Ann-Marie Imbornoni, and my copy editor, Andrew Frisardi, for the thoughtful, meticulous work they expended on this volume. Likewise I should mention with particular appreciation the (sometimes ruthless) anonymous reviewers, who were subjected to various versions of this manuscript over the past four years, and whose cavils and gavels made this final product less imperfect than it might have otherwise remained.

Finally, I would like to pay special tribute to teachers, friends, and family members who were exemplars of inspiration, and whose life-long support made my Levantine eccentricities a lot less discernable, and this volume much more possible. Those owed special recognition include my teachers and mentors Avigdor Levy, Norman Stillman, and Ilan Troen; the inspired poet that I've always wished I were, Roger (Lozé) Makhlouf; the scholar and orator that I long to become, Robert Rabil; and other friends, colleagues, and family members whose support and trust were paramount. Those include Jo-Ann and Tom Deso, Bruce Maddy-Weitzmann, Asher Kaufman, Walid Phares, Nadim Shehadi, Kanan Makiya, Carole Corm, Virginie Corm, Michael Welch, Salim Tamari, Randy Geller, Dana Sajdi, George Ashy, Galil Ashy, and

Georgette Gabriel. Likewise, former and current Boston College students, who were the ideal "testing grounds" for many of the "ideas behind the works" explored herewith, are owed a special debt of gratitude. Among them I ought to mention with particular appreciation and affection, Dorothy Smith Ohl, Christopher Izant, Colleen Daley, Luke Hagberg, George Somi, Jeffrey Skowera, Gabrielle Frawley, Craig Noyes, and Jake Burke.

I would like to conclude with my expression of admiration to the lodestars of my Levantine universe. To my wife, Pascale, and our children Zoé-Charlotte, Chloé-Marie, and Tristan-Julien, who, in living color, bring fragrance and brightness and taste to my liminality; to my *petits levantins franco-libanais* who savor and radiate all the treasures that all the "elsewheres" of their multiple ports of call offer: A jumble of languages and cultures and legacies and palates relished with the alacrity and intimacy of old hands; a melodious chaotic *boucan d'enfer* that has always been my inspiration; a tumultuous Mediterranean conflation always bringing peace and balance and tranquility and *life* into all our lives; a happy delectable "disorder" in a world crippled by too much order.

Note on Translation
and Transliteration

Spellings of non-Western place names and proper nouns were employed in conformance with common usage in various dialectal forms of Arabic, and in keeping with local and phonological peculiarities. This was done even in places where other authors and translators might have adhered to standards of the *International Journal of Middle East Studies* (IJMES). For instance, I use Charles Corm, not Shaarl al-Qurm, and Ashrafiyyé, not Ashrafiyyah, because those are the spelling and phonological norms in Lebanon. Emphases, random punctuations, erratic ellipses, brackets, and other seemingly arbitrary diacritic symbols in Adonis's and Qabbani's works are reproduced as they have occurred in the original Arabic texts (ellipses for where I have left out passages of the authors' texts are in square brackets, while the authors' own ellipses are not). These "visual effects" were some of the many ways in which, Adonis for instance, defied the norms and orthodoxies of his time, plying his Arabic language in both form and content to reflect the fragmentation of Arab culture and the Arab self; textual and linguistic fragmentation, to which he added visual fragmentation emulating the social, cultural, and political mutilation of the Arabs so to speak. Qabbani did likewise at times, albeit not with the same frequency and capriciousness as Adonis. Unless otherwise indicated, all translations from French, Arabic, dialectal languages, and Hebrew originals are my own.

The Other Middle East

Prolegomena

Panoramic Perspectives

I n a modern Middle East consumed by excesses of "uniformity" and "order," diversity and multiple identities are often deemed perverse, inauthentic, divisive. Thus the term *Levant*, traditionally used in reference to lands around the eastern shores of the Mediterranean, often distinguished from strictly or exclusively "Arab" or "Muslim" lands, has come to carry a number of negative stigmas. British historian Albert Hourani famously noted that "being a Levantine" meant living "in two worlds or more at once, without belonging to either; it is to be able to go through all the external forms which indicate the possession of a certain nationality, religion, or culture, without actually possessing any. It is no longer to have one standard of values of one's own; it is to not be able to create but only to imitate; and so not even to imitate correctly, since that also requires a certain level of originality. [In sum, being a Levantine] is to belong to no community and to possess nothing of one's own; it reveals itself in lostness, pretentiousness, cynicism and despair."[1] Yet the children of the Levant seldom viewed things by way of such negative, disdainful biases. To them Hourani's pejorative "not belonging" and "not possessing" things "of one's own" meant exactly the opposite of those terms' degrading intent; it meant being at home with everything, and being at one with everyone, all the time and all at once. Indeed, Levantines—certainly the intellectuals under consideration in this volume—saw themselves as sophisticated, urbane, cosmopolitan, iconoclastic mongrels, intimately acquainted with multiple cultures, skillfully wielding multiple languages, and elegantly straddling multiple traditions, identities, and civilizations. They deemed *their* Near East, both as a physical and metaphorical place of "ascent" and "rising," reflecting the Levant's Semitic and Latin etymologies; a "Levant" as crossroads and meeting place where peoples and times blended without dissolving each other, and where languages, histories, ethnicities, and religions fused without getting confused with one another.[2]

Franco-Lebanese novelist Amin Maalouf (b. 1949), one of the most articulate cantors of this chameleon-like Near East, has described his Levantine exemplar as one that could not be pinned down to narrowness of name, language, ethnicity, or religion. The eponymous narrator of one of his historical novels, *Leo Africanus,* described himself in terms exuding the kind of diversity and cultural humanism that have come to exemplify Levantine intellectuals: cosmopolitan polyglots and cultural intermediaries defined by multiplicity rather than oneness or uniformity; a "dialogue" and a "quest" to use Philip Mansel's description.[3] Presenting credentials bearing a striking resemblance to the lands and peoples of the Eastern Mediterranean, the *carte de visite* of Maalouf's Leo Africanus depicted him as follows: "I, Hassan, the son of Muhammad the scale-master; I, Jean-Léon de Mediçi, circumcised at the hands of a barber and baptized at the hands of a Pope, I am now called the African, but I am not from Africa, nor from Europe, nor from Arabia. . . . I come from no country, from no city, from no tribe. . . . From my mouth you will hear Arabic, Turkish, Castilian, Berber, Hebrew, Latin, and Italian vulgates, because all tongues and all prayers belong to me. But I belong to none."[4] Valorizing multiplicity, diversity, and movement, Maalouf, to whose work this volume refers repeatedly, providing fresher interpretive translations to some of its most precious (and relevant) aphorisms, condenses the fluidity and hybridity highlighted in this selection of Levantine authors. "Others would rather speak to you in terms of 'roots,'" began Maalouf's preface to his self-narrative *Origines,* "but not I," he stresses:

> Roots are not in my nature; they are not part of my lexicon. I dislike the word *roots,* and I dislike the imagery that

it elicits even more. Roots burrow deeply in the soil; they twist and squirm in the mud; they thrive in the darkness . . . they hold the trees above them captive, and nourish them by way of blackmail: "You break free, you die!" they seem to tell the trees. Trees must resign themselves to this blackmail; trees need their roots; humans do not! We humans breathe the light and yearn for the skies, and when we sink into the ground, we do so only to rot and die. The sap of our native soil does not reach our heads by way of our feet. Our feet have but one function; they help us walk and move about. The only things that matter to us humans are roads. It is the road that beckons to us; it is the road that seduces us.[5]

In both the ancient and the modern Levant, the parameters of ethnicity, language, and territory have seldom coincided to the same extent that they may in a modern European context. The familiar European triumvirate model of "Frenchmen" speaking "French" and living in "France"—using terms *all* derived form the same cognate word denoting "Frenchness"—does not obtain in the Levant, whether in modern or ancient times. Language as a framework of ethnic or cultural identity was never a reliable social classifier in the Near East in general, and the Levant in particular. Unlike other human communities that gave birth to great civilizations elsewhere, India and China for instance, the peoples and cultures of the Levant are distinguished by diversity, disjointedness, and discontinuity far removed from India's or China's permanence, cohesiveness, and constancy as recognizable aspects of cultural distinctiveness.

Greeks, Romans, and Arabs, the last three in a succession of conquerors that dominated the Near East over the past two and a half millennia, brought along with them a perceived semblance of universalism and coherence—not a real one. For example, the port cities along the coast of Phoenicia, today's Lebanon, Israel, and western Syria, spoke variants of Canaanite and Aramaic at the height of the Hellenic, Roman, and Muslim periods. But the linguistic and cultural perimeters of their geographic and human space, like the Mediterranean to their west, remained porous, fluid, shifting. Aramaic and Canaanite were thus spoken by many peoples who were not "ethnic" Aramaeans or Canaanites. Moreover, those languages had coexisted alongside other idioms, including Hurrian, Egyptian, Akkadian, Ugaritic, and many others in ancient times, as well as Greek, Latin, Persian, Arabic, and Turkish in more recent periods. This linguistic diversity reflected, not a law of nature, nor a curiosity defying nature, but rather a geographic location at the crossroads of three continents, and the consequent hybrid multifaceted cultural and linguistic accretions of a distinctly Levantine ethos.

Betraying this same polyglossia, endorsing a fluid expansive-identity model during the early decades of the twentieth century, Lebanese intellectual Antun Saadé (1904–49), founder and chief ideologue of the Syrian Social Nationalist Party, depicted the Levantines with the generic term *Syrians,* deeming them a fusion of Canaanite Phoenicians and Hebrews, as well as Akkadians, Chaldaeans, Assyrians, Aramaeans, Hittites, and Metanis.[6] Saadé's omission of the Arabs from his peculiar conception of Levantine identity was deliberate. It was a reflection of animus he had held against exclusivist nationalism and the conception of Near Eastern identities as a function of language—the Arabic language in his case, the dominant idiom in our time. In that sense, Saadé rejected pan-Arabism and was opposed to the labeling of the Levantine peoples as Arabs. To him, such an essentialist label was based on a community of language and religion, which he considered irrelevant to identity formation. Whenever language was used as a criterion of identity, wrote Saadé, the purpose was primarily expansionist and irredentist, as was the case with Nazi Germany.[7] And so, he argued, the notion that the peoples of the Levant—in his case the Syrians—should be defined as Arab is nationalist chauvinism based on political fiction not historical fact. The peoples of the Levant, he cautioned, should relinquish the notion that they are Arab, or that their destiny should somehow be bound to that of the Arabs.[8] On the contrary, insisted Saadé, the peoples of the Levant as he saw them were "the fountainhead of Mediterranean culture and the custodians of the civilization of that Sea, . . . [a Sea] whose roads were traversed by [Levantine] ships, and to whose distant shores [the Levantines] carried [their] culture, inventions, and discoveries."[9] More recently, in an impassioned indictment of the nationalist rigidity and cultural authoritarianism that have plagued the Near East of the past century, Syrian poet Adonis (b. 1930) expressed hope in the restitution, rehabilitation, and valorization of the Levant's millennial multicultural traditions. "I have no doubt in my mind," he writes,

> That the lands that had conceived of and spread mankind's first Alphabet; the lands that had bequeathed and taught the world the very early principles of intellectual intercourse and dialogue with "the other"; the lands that bore witness to processions of the world's loftiest civilizations, from Sumerians to Babylonians, and from Egyptians to Phoenicians and Romans; those lands that spawned monotheism, and humanism, and the belief in a single compassionate deity; those fertile and bountiful lands, I say most confidently, will no doubt shake off . . . nationalist intransigence and immobilism, and will hurtle skyward toward modernity and progress.[10]

The "other" Middle East that is being revealed in this anthology aims to reflect on this hybrid Levantine universe through the literary works of twentieth-century Syrian, Lebanese, Israeli, Palestinian, and Egyptian authors. Writing in a variety of languages—spanning Arabic, French, English and Hebrew—poets, playwrights, and essayists from Adonis and Ali Salem to Charles Corm, and from Nizar Qabbani and Jacqueline Kahanoff to Benyamin Tammuz, seldom fit into the prevalent, often politically soothing, molds of exclusively "Arab" or "Israeli" Middle Easterners. Consequently, their works have often been either unavailable to anglophone readers, or available only in fragments— often selective and static fragments bereft of context.[11]

Striving to reclaim a certain Levantine hybridity as a legitimate parameter of identity, and attempting to restitute *their* Levant as a valid historical, geographic, political, linguistic, and cultural concept, those authors have not benefited from competent treatment or serious in-depth study by Western cultural historians, translators, comparativists, or literary critics. This anthology attempts to fill this lacuna. It does so not only by restituting these Levantine authors and their works to their suitable place in the history of ideas and to the literary corpus that has issued *from* and *about* the Middle East since the early twentieth century; it also gives anglophone audiences and students of the Middle East access to foundational works of Middle Eastern literature, chronicles of ideas as it were, and records of cultural and intellectual history heretofore unavailable—or no longer available—in English.

At times, the selections analyzed here may read like "dissident literature." They are not! Indeed, they are often the works of "traditional," "canonical" authors treating "canonical" themes. But they are also works that somehow "did not make it" into the accepted corpus; works that might have eluded the traditional canon of Middle Eastern literature, arguably because their authors might have deviated from "orthodoxies" willy-nilly assigned to them. In this sense, Nizar Qabbani (1923–98), modern Syria's poet laureate, a beloved cantor of Arab nationalism and a committed feminist, still wrote some of the most devastating poetry of the twentieth century, indicting nationalism—Arabism to be exact— and candidly, even if achingly and perhaps also reluctantly, calling for the dismantlement of "Arab identity" and the putative "Arab nation." Qabbani may be an extreme example, but he is a powerful illustration of a suppressed, concealed, or simply discarded intellectual history. Qabbani is also what Fouad Ajami described as the tale of young Arab nationalists, children of privilege, "who could have chosen acquiescence and security" in their own world—entitlements and assumptions handed them as their birthright—but who "instead, chose to oppose, to dissent, and to lose out."[12]

With eleven authors spanning the canon of modern Middle Eastern literature, and presenting works ranging from poems to prose pieces, and from essays to short stories, this *Anthology of Modern Levantine Literature* treats those whose works do not fit the prevalent assumptions of the media, the academy, or the public discourse on a Middle East presumed culturally, linguistically, and ethnically uniform, unitary, homogenous. Let us consider for instance someone like Samir el-Youssef (b. 1965) a Lebanese-born Sunni Palestinian, or Fawaz Turki (b. 1945) a Haifa-born Sunni Palestinian and product of the same Beirut refugee camp where el-Youssef came of age. Both authors have condensed the nontraditional "spacious identity" models typical to the Levantine mosaic; both have lived through the vagaries, destitution, and violence of the Lebanese wars of 1975–90, and both were raised with memories of exile and dispossession. Yet both rarely have written in Arabic, and neither have interpreted the Palestinian condition from the often compulsory orthodox perspective of rejectionism, rage, and bitterness—brands, as it were, of traditional Palestinian literature of dispossession. In that sense el-Youssef and Turki, like others brought to the fore in this volume, deviate from their cultures' normative themes and traditional social, political, and intellectual exigencies—be they pan-Arabist, Palestinian nationalist, localist, or Islamist. Both el-Youssef and Turki reveal a sober, honest, and brave purview of their culture, producing works that breathe no nostalgia, no lamentations, no self-pity, and no yearnings for olive trees or lemon groves and old house-keys. Neither of them call for revenge, retribution, resentments, compensation, or idealized unattainable returns. Instead, both Turki and el-Youssef advocate for shared humanity (and humanism), for reconciliation, and for a meshing of identities and histories that are always elastic, capacious, fluid, and inclusive. "My soul forever gasped for breath," writes Turki, "in a society whose intolerance for innovation laid waste to our personal meaning. It daily tampered with our individuality and so subverted free utterance that people lost the faculty of communicating anything worthwhile even to themselves, let alone to others."[13]

And so, Turki sets out to escape that universe, where people "were destined to chew their nationalist slogans to the marrow and live out their flat and shoddy political lives in constant conflict."[14] It is for this reason that Turki argues the notion of "a nation" to be immodest and absurd—at least in the context of the humanism that he favors. "I find the idea of unrestrained, militant nationalism to be obscene," he writes: "In the name of territorial integrity and ethnic purity, men have slaughtered one another for centuries. Jewish nationalists who believe that the Jewish nation's boundaries include the territories stretching from the Mediterranean to the River Jordan and beyond, have their counterparts among the Palestinians. I met one of them in Washington soon after the [September 1993] White House ceremony. . . . He assured me that 'in less than thirty years from now the whole of Palestine will be liberated and all the Jews will be gone from our country.'"[15] Turki admits to have always aimed to disassociate himself from that kind of jingoism, from "that kind of venom" to use his words. Even as a child—children, he thinks, are "special guardians of human truth"—Turki claims to have been troubled by the absurdity of nationalism. In the name of untenable nationalist fictions, he writes, Jews and Arabs have been made to turn their backs on each other; then they "moved away from each other, and finally proceeded to murder each other. Who started it? Who cares! History had already poured fire into our blood and ritual reference into our meaning."[16]

Although moved from time to time by scenery instilled in his memory by nature—"the view of the Mediterranean," for instance, *especially* "the view of the Mediterranean"—Turki claims to have felt nothing upon returning to his native Haifa following forty years of exile; the place no longer spoke to him, he writes, and he was even "revolted at the notion of rootedness to a place," and the expectations that he be stirred by a return to a place from which his family had been expelled.[17] Contemplating an alternative, he does not need to "live in Nablus or Jericho or Gaza," he concludes: "I need not die in Haifa, Safad, or Jaffa. Washington will do. Forty-five years of exile are homeland enough. Anywhere where one is free to watch one's favorite movies, reread one's favorite classics, listen to one's favorite music, support one's favorite unpopular causes, and, above all, do one's work without fear of retribution, is homeland enough."[18] Likewise, el-Youssef urges Palestinians of his generation to move on! "We ought to be realistic and accept that no actual return could ever take place," he noted. "People only move on . . . even when going back to their places of birth and early lives, people are only moving on. . . . It is a one-way journey! . . . As for those who claim to return to a place where they never were, they are simply confusing the symbolic and metaphorical with the possible and actual. . . . The Jews who went to Palestine did not 'return' but emigrated."[19] His defiance, even contempt for tradition drives el-Youssef to imagine his dead sister exacting revenge on a stifling traditional misogynistic patriarchal society by marrying a Christian man; "making history" as it were; "a Moslem woman marrying a Christian. Surely there could be nothing more daring for a society [consumed by tradition, and] excessively concerned about who fucked whom."[20]

Incidentally, in one of his Arabic-language essays, *The Language's Head, the Desert's Body,* Adonis, an iconoclast of modern Arabic poetry, speaks of an encounter he had with the late Edward Said (1935–2003) in New York, where even Said himself, an iconic figure in the Palestinian literature of dispossession and dissent, made an eloquent plea against "return" and against "homeland" and nationalist zealotry as such.[21] "The concepts of homeland or fatherland are caricatures and romantic yearnings that do not appeal to me one bit," revealed Said.[22] "Indeed, peregrination and wandering off from one place to the next are what I love most about my own life," he claimed.[23] He called New York "home" precisely "because of its ever-changing, multicolored chameleon-like attributes, allowing one to *belong* to her without issuing from her, and without being enslaved or held captive by her."[24] In that sense, places where Said grew up, he acknowledges—Ramallah for instance—left him utterly unmoved, and could hardly be considered as a homeland; whereas Cairo, like New York, give him a true feeling of "being home."[25] This echoes strongly with Turki's own narrative of dissent, where he stresses "return" to be "illusory" and "tawdry":

> I cannot return ["home" to Haifa], after forty years in exile, with my alternative order of meaning, my comfortable notions about homelessness being my only homeland, and say that I am home. The house is no longer as habitable as when I left it. The toys are no longer in the attic. An awry force in history has changed the place, and my own sense of otherness has changed me. This place could not be lived in by anyone other than its new inhabitants. . . . [As for my true homeland,] I could live anywhere I am with my people—those from any part of the world with whom I share a commonality of values and a certain way of life. Paris, Sydney, or New York will do—especially New York, because New Yorkers are like Palestinians in many ways. They too are born of tragedy. Their ancestors landed at Ellis Island after escaping a czar who claimed to love them, a "brother struggler" who had anointed himself head of the national family, a tyrant

who did not like their ethnic roots, a colonial oppressor who
robbed them and couldn't care less about their famine.[26]

This is the overarching theme of the present anthology; it is a
compendium of Middle Eastern literary figures and public intellectuals attempting to deviate from normative social, cultural, political, and
linguistic models assigned to them, consumed by excesses of uniformity
and order, and obsessed with righting ancient injuries. Instead, the authors under consideration advocate for a return to the essence of the Levant, where diversity, heterogeneity, cosmopolitanism, movement, and
multiple identities were viewed, *not* as perverse, *not* as colonial impos-
tures aimed at rending asunder some presumptive uniform antecedent,
but rather as a space where mobility and motion and transformation are
the natural order of things Middle Eastern.

My intimacy with Arabic, French, and Levantine dialectal literatures of the twentieth century, and my working knowledge of Hebrew
and Syriac, have made accessing, mining, translating, and interpreting
the works of this anthology more faithful to their authors' initial aims
as writers, thinkers, and architects of ideas; authors laying bare snippets of their personal and collective histories, excavating old memories,
and presenting new alternatives to codified versions of Middle Eastern
history which often shun diversity and the region's inherent hybridity
and multiplicity of identities. In this sense, this work is a compilation
with context and framework, not a mere "translating and cataloging"
of Middle Eastern works of literature. It offers an introduction to the
themes, periods, historical settings, and implications of the works and
authors under consideration, before proceeding to the texts and their
annotated translations.

A word of caution may be in order at this point: this volume is
by no means a definitive anthology. Reza Aslan attempted an exhaustive compilation in his commendable *Tablet and Pen.* Yet reading Aslan's
work can be as exhausting as it might have been exhaustive: It provides
no context and no critical commentary to the works placed on display,
producing an otherwise awesome literary "directory," but leaving out
themes and those Middle Eastern authors whose language choices and
cultural accretions do not correlate directly with Islam and Muslim

culture—authors who wrote in Hebrew, Syriac, French, English, and dialectal languages for instance. By the same token, readers may note that some authors who should have figured in this present anthology remain absent—at least in this initial installment. That is so because this is a first step, a prelude and a "first offering" as it were, to whet the appetites and publish those Middle Eastern literati whose works rarely exist (or have become unavailable) in English, and whose realms remain unknown to anglophone audiences: providing snippets of those Syrians who have written strictly in their dialectal languages or in a literary Arabic resembling dialect; those Lebanese who wrote only in French; those Christian and Muslim Israelis who wrote exclusively in Hebrew, and those Jewish Israelis who write only in Arabic.

In sum, this is an attempt at bringing into focus a group of authors—eleven in all, exploring hundreds of pages of text—that do not fit the prevalent assumptions of the media, the academy, or the public discourse on the Middle East. This will therefore reveal broad, diverse, and inclusive conceptual, geographic, sociolinguistic, and cultural settings of the Middle East away from the monolithic images often normalized in the political, academic, and public spheres.

In many ways, this anthology is a corrective to the conventional cultural and intellectual history of the Middle East—especially in times of platitudes and generalizations surrounding the profound transformations that have gripped the region in the early decades of the twenty-first century. Therefore, this anthology attempts to approach traditional assumptions about the Levant from angles heretofore considered anathema, *and* by way of intellectuals and shapers of ideas who have always challenged received wisdom about their region's putative homogeneity and uniformity.

And so, this volume brings to the fore an "other" Middle East, valorizing peoples and stories that may not have made it into accepted narratives and traditional history textbooks. This is done by accessing ideas, intellectual currents, cultural patterns, stories, and literary texts to which the general anglophone public is not typically exposed, with the purpose of elevating and expanding the conversation on and about the Middle East, bringing to it a variety of voices and a diversity of perspectives, and calling to task the traditional confinement of knowledge

about the region to prevalent, fashionable, comforting (and academically sanctioned) models of an exclusively "Arab" or "Muslim" world—
which, albeit not necessarily inaccurate, remain reductive, and in that
sense exclusivist, incomplete, and beholden to a single culture, a single
people, and single narrative.

  With the preceding in mind, this volume presents the Levant and
Levantinism as a form of cosmopolitanism, carrying both positive and
negative connotations. Indeed, being a Levantine denotes a cosmopolitanism straddling multiple worlds, while simultaneously belonging to
or having affective attachment to a well-delineated geographic space.
Amin Maalouf pays tribute to this complexity when he writes:

> This is my Mountain! It is at once attachment to the ancestral
> soil and longing for exile; a sanctuary and a passageway in
> one; a land of milk and honey, and blood; neither Heaven,
> nor Hell; but rather, Purgatory. . . . Many events had come to
> pass; [my] village had witnessed so many upheavals, so many
> destructions, so many bruisings, until one day I resolved to
> surrender to exile. I whispered my regrets to all the ances-
> tors and . . . [I set out to leave.] At my back, the mountain
> stood near. At my feet lay the valley. . . . And over there, in
> the distance, I could see the sea; my cramped plot of sea, nar-
> row and distant, ever flowing forward, ever rising toward the
> horizon, like an endless road.[27]

This imagery of roads, seas, and mountains—perpetuity, rootedness,
and everlasting fluidity and movement—are of paramount importance
to those invested in (and issuing from) the Levant and its Mediterranean bailiwick; "a sea ringed round by mountains," as noted Fernand
Braudel, and "mountains [at once] surrounding, strangling, barricad-
ing and compartmentalizing the long Mediterranean coastline."[28] In the
end, there may be no "happy returns," no "Ulyssean" homecomings,
and only roads and movement and peregrinations and exile; a humanist
dynamism and vitality and universalism.

  The term Levant and its meanings are therefore fluid, shifting, and
spacious, but also well grounded, belonging to both "a group of intel-

lectuals" and to society as a whole—albeit with some fluctuation and variation. One needn't be educated or literate to be a Levantine or to emit Levantine cosmopolitanism—or some other aspect of Levantine attributes. Certainly intellectuals have valorized and idolized Levantine hybridity and cosmopolitanism, and may have raised it to the level of ritual and doctrine. But the plebeians actually *lived* Levantinism— often in a state of banality and unawareness! In other words, the illiterate street porter of Beirut, the unschooled sherbet vendor of Alexandria, and the uncultured prostitute of Smyrna, who could negotiate multiple cultural rituals, who are attuned to multiple worlds and traditions, and who can seamlessly move in and out of multiple variants of Arabic, Armenian, Turkish (and often French, Italian, or English), frequently with the ease and intimacy of a native, are no less Levantines than their learned counterparts. Certainly Amin Maalouf's polyglot Leo Africanus was exquisitely literate and lettered; a man of the world. But Maalouf's illiterate Tanios (the main character of his *Le Rocher de Tanios*) was no less polyglot and "worldly" than Leo, and his Levantine hybridity was no less authentic. The same can be said of Lucine Guiragossian, one of the characters of Rabih Alameddine's *Hakawati;* Lucine is a housemaid and skilled practitioner of linguistic humanism, yet also a woman bereft of formal education. Likewise, the questions being asked—and which this anthology's chosen authors try to answer—relate to the following points.

The Levant and being Levantine are both "inherited" and "invented tradition"; and that which is "invented" may perhaps be "excavated" and "reconstructed," and *does* indeed issue from a template steeped in the region's history. After all, the Aramaeans, the Canaanites, the Egyptian pharaohs, the Assyrians, and others, from whom some of the anthology's Levantine authors claim descent and tradition, are not allogenic productions. The ancients who are deemed to be progenitors of modern Levantines indeed had the very same Levant as birthplace and playground and inspiration. And so their modern heirs *can* be said to stand on solid historical ground laying claim to them and their history—idealized and magnified as that history may be. As Anthony Smith has noted, it matters little that a group's myths and legends and foundational memories are based on historical fact or emotive fiction;

what matters are the bonds that those myths (or this "invented tradition") may create among group members, and between group members and their (real or imagined) progenitors.[29] Ernest Renan's much-
anthologized *Qu'est-ce qu'une nation?* (1882) seems to have confirmed
the preceding, even more than a century prior to Smith: namely that a
group's collective identity is as much the result of "invented tradition"
as it may be the outcome of lived history or "heritage"; that it comes
into being when a collective of peoples come to recognize and celebrate
their possession of certain attributes in common; that it is neither race,
nor religion nor language or history (nor "fact" or "heritage" for that
matter) that bring a people together; rather, it is a collective awareness
of being one (*être un*)—again, falsified or overexaggerated or imagined
as this *être un* may be deemed.

The fact that the population of the Middle East is composed of the
descendants of various peoples is a statement that *does* have relevance to
modern reality. This relevance is by no means comprehensive, and certainly does not apply to all the children of the Levant (or their intellectual representatives) in equal measure. But it is a significant enough aspect of the Levantine mosaic that merits being examined and valorized
and put on par with other contemporaneous parameters of selfhood.

The works included in this anthology *do* describe both "real"
and "imagined" life in the modern Middle East. The daydreamer of
Damietta on the Mediterranean (in Ali Salem's *The Odd Man and the
Sea*), harkening back to ancient pharaohs and the Greek and Phoenician
mariners of classical antiquity, is no less a reality in today's Egypt than
the *mohtasib* keeper of Islamic law may be, or the warden of Arab nationalist oneness. Finally, Amin Maalouf's work, a recurrent influence
on the writers in this anthology, reads like ideas and ideals from the
Levant; perhaps "more ideas and ideals than people" as one critic noted,
but nevertheless "ideas and ideals" *issuing from* people no less real or
compelling than the real thing. Maalouf even brought elements of this,
his supremely Levantine experience, to the acceptance speech that he
delivered during his induction to the Académie Française in June 2012.
Sitting in the Académie's seat number twenty-nine, once occupied by
famed anthropologist Claude Lévy-Strauss, who had himself inherited

it from (among others) Ernest Renan, another admirer of the Levant, Maalouf, "the Levantine guest" intruding on this company of "immortals," pledged to bring to the Académie's legacy all that he had inherited from the lands of his birth; his origins, his languages, his accent, his convictions, his doubts, and more than anything else perhaps, his dreams of harmony, progress, and coexistence among contradictions and opposites.[30] Those dreams are perhaps being corrupted and abused in today's world, admitted Maalouf.

> A wall is being erected on the Mediterranean, tearing asunder the multiple cultural worlds that I have always called my own. I do not intend to climb over that wall in order to move from one of my worlds into the next. This wall of hatred— between Europeans and Africans, between the West and Islam, between Jews and Arabs—I have every intention of subverting it and contributing to its demolition. This has always been my reason for being, my reason for writing. And I shall pursue this humble tradition of mine in your company [that of the Académie Française], in the watchful shadow of our elders, and under the sober gaze of Claude Lévy-Strauss.[31]

But Maalouf is supremely representative in this Levantine exercise, not an outlier. His vision resembles that of Rabih Alameddine's 2008 work *The Hakawati,* another modern exemplar of Levantinism. A rich tapestry of distinctly Levantine metaphor, *The Hakawati* relates the story of the Lebanese Kharrat family, their Urfa-born patriarch Ismail, the illegitimate love child of a British missionary-physician (Simon Twining, "like the tea") and his Armenian housekeeper (Lucine Guiragossian). In sum, *The Hakawati* is the story of Levantine Lebanon, told through the history of a family of "fibsters" and their patriarch, an Armenian-Lebanese Turkish-speaking Anglican Druze named Ismail Twining-Guiragossian *hal kharrat* ("that fibster" or "bullshit artist"). The last few pages of the novel are particularly poignant, and in that sense deliciously Maaloufian *and* Levantine. At one point, clasping the hand of his dying father, the narrator proceeds with an extended, detailed narration of the family's history, as if to ward off death one last time, and buy his father one more night among the living. "Do you hear me?" asked the son:

> Do you hear me? I don't know which stories your father told you and which you believed, but I always wondered whether he ever told you the true story of who he is, [...] Did he? [...] Your grandmother's name was Lucine. It's true. I checked it out. Lucine Guiragossian. Your grandfather was Simon Twining . . . See, you have English, Armenian, and Druze blood. Oh, and Albanian too. You're a man of the world. We always knew that . . . your grandmother died while your father was still a baby. Another Armenian woman raised him, Anahid Kaladjian. . . . She sent him away when he was eleven. He used to say that all he remembered was that she told him to go south, hide in the mountains of Lebanon, stay with the Christians.[32]

Clearly there is much poetic license in such imagery, perhaps yearnings for a bygone era. But still yearnings, this anthology contends, for things that were and can *still be;* not mere fantasy and imaginings and fanciful fairytales. It may be true that one may not always find "Levantinism" in some of the works and among the authors under consideration here. Yet, all the featured selections *do* celebrate some aspect of Levantinism, whether in their chosen themes, or merely in language, in harkening back to non-Arab and non-Muslim ancestors, in celebrating (or merely taking stock of) origins, languages, memories, accents, and convictions that do not conform to the dominant imagery of the Near East (as exclusively or even overwhelmingly Arab or Muslim monolith.)

It may be true that the Levant and being Levantine are "elusive," connoting several meanings, both positive and negative, implying fluidity certainly, but also rootedness—perhaps even rootedness *in* fluidity and versatility. Likewise, seeking the "elusive" is not in itself a vice. For instance, the main character of Amin Maalouf's *Les Désorientés,* a historian named Adam, doesn't know whether to draw solace or consternation from his given name. It is true that being named "Adam" is a "privilege" he noted; "it is true that I carry in my first name a nascent humanity; but alas I also belong to a humanity that may be on the path of extinction. I have always been struck by the fact that, in Rome, the last emperor was a Romulus, like the city's first founder; that in Constantinople the last emperor was a Constantine, also like the city's founder."[33] And so, it may seem as if the Levant—geographically and conceptually speaking—may be coming undone. Yet Maalouf and his Levantine cohorts never despair, never grow weary of clinging to it, to vestiges and memories of it. "I feel as if I were walking down a road that crumbles behind me with each step forward that I take," notes the character Adam in this story.[34] But there is no escaping the Levant, he concedes; even in its madness, even when not living it, even when escaping its frenzies of violence, the Levant still lives in its children, breathing into them the fragrant aromas of pine forests and cedars caressed by breezes bearing the salt spray of the Mediterranean.[35] Amin Maalouf's *Les Désorientés,* not unlike this anthology, may be seen as a "re-orientation," a pilgrimage of sorts; an act of memory and rediscovery dedicated to a vanished past that is still discernable; a historian's quest for memory and memorialization of a bygone era that still echoes. Maalouf's narrator, Adam, says it himself; his return to Lebanon—which he never names explicitly—after a quarter-century absence, was not an act of reconnecting with the land of his youth, but rather a search to recapture his youth.[36] From the looks of things, he wrote,

> I have come back to revive ties with the land of my youth. Yet I am not even looking at the old charms surrounding me; I am only searching in them for traces of my youth. [...] I wish to learn nothing, relearn nothing, discover nothing. My aim is merely to rediscover that which had once been mine, familiar to me. Yes, I am merely after old vestiges, traces, remnants of the things of old. Otherwise, all that is new seems like an unwelcome intrusion, an impingement on my dream, an affront to my memory; in short, an assault. [...] This may be an affliction of mine, a defect perhaps. But this is how I wish to live this homecoming, and that is how I have lived it ever since my arrival. All that had been before and that is familiar

to me, I choose to see it in living colors. The rest, all the rest,
is only ashen grey to my eyes.[37]

It may be true that this is an anthology of "intellectuals" and that the
term Levantine (as I have often used it) refers to "a group of intellectuals and writers"—for the present volume deals with literary works and
literati who were also "myth makers," not commoners who might have
espoused Levantinism. Yet, it is uncertain whether any group other than
literati would have warranted an anthology.

It is important to note here that the term Levantine may be used to
refer exclusively to members of one of the minorities living in Muslim-
or Arab-defined countries, or may be limited to intellectuals and writers,
and never to an entire society. Certainly, not all Middle Eastern societies
can be deemed "Levantine," to the same extent that not all of Middle
Eastern societies can be deemed "Arab," or "Muslim," exclusively. Yet,
there are certain aspects of "being Levantine" that are not singularly
"intellectual," and that cannot (or ought not) relate solely to intellectuals. After all, and as noted earlier, the Levant remains a valid geographic,
historical, and cultural concept that is deemed a positive and legitimate
parameter of selfhood to intellectuals and nonintellectuals alike; it is
both word and content, referring to the Eastern Mediterranean, bereft
of strict (or restrictive) racial, national, religious, or linguistic associations, and which can apply in equal measure to those who dream and
write about the Levant, Levantinism, or the Mediterranean, and those
who simply live those constructs and their geography. After all, the
word echelle (to borrow from Maalouf's Les Echelles du Levant [Ports of
Call]), which is commonly translated into English as "ladder," derives
from the Turkish word skele, which refers to a "jetty" or "pier"—again,
a place of "departure," or even a "launching pad," connoting the fluidity
and movement associated with the Mediterranean and the people who
called its basin and port cities home.

It is not entirely true that only certain ethno-religious minority
groups (Maronites, Jews, Armenians, Copts, etc.) can be deemed Levantines writing on Levantine life and their condition as minorities.
Certainly non-Muslim and non-Arab minorities were (and continue to
be) perhaps overwhelmingly attracted to Levantinism and its ancillar-

ies, most probably because of Levantinism's capacious conceptualization of identity and its repudiation of the exclusivity of nationalism—compulsory Arab nationalism in particular. But membership in this Levantine "club" is hardly limited to minorities. Ali Salem for instance, who appears in this anthology, is a Sunni Muslim, hardly a minority in a largely Sunni universe. His forerunners were also Sunni, from Taha Husayn, to Tawfiq al-Hakim, to Tawfiq Awan and Ahmad Lutfi al-Sayyed, among others not particularly enthralled with normative Arabism or Islamism. Likewise, Adonis is an Alawite (Muslim), and both Fawaz Turki and Samir el-Youssef are Sunnis, members of the dominant "ethnos" as it were.

Although they are deemed Arabs and Muslims by prevalent academic conceits about the Middle East and its peoples—often portrayed as monochromatic, homogenous, and immutable, as if reflecting a law of nature—the above-mentioned figures see themselves and their universe as constructs defined by diversity, variety, divergence, heterogeneity and even fragmentation. The Levant and Levantinism, regardless of how one opts to define them, do provide a model for diversity; *not* a "utopia," a mere model, a historical template. One exemplar of this is perhaps best expressed by Palestinian novelist Samir el-Youssef, who, in defense of this multifaceted Levant, has weighed in on the place of his birth—the Rashidiyyé refugee camp in southern Lebanon. Rashidiyyé was and still is a bad place, he writes;

> as bad as a refugee camp could be. A mere fifteen minutes walk from the camp stood the ancient Phoenician port-city of Tyre; a harbour town housing the awesome vestiges of one of the greatest, most pacifist, most benevolent builders of civilization. The refugee camp (in its indigence), and the ancient city (in all its glory), standing side by side, are a stark example of the Levant[. . . . In] the old school of my boyhood, back in Rashidiyyé [. . .] teachers then talked up a storm about politics, the conflict, the hopelessness and indigence of our situation. Yet I don't remember any of them suggesting a school tour to the nearby Phoenician port-city of Tyre, a living testament as it were, to the ancient Levant; a

place where we could, even for a fleeting moment, forget the
misery of our present days and learn something new, something different, something hopeful; learn how when looking
at what lay outside the "prison walls," and when considering
that which challenges prevalent assumptions, one might be
able to see above the clouds of past traumas, and beyond the
paranoia of present days.[38]

This is ultimately what the authors in this anthology are proposing:
again, not a "utopia," but a summons in favor of accepting and valorizing the diversity of the Levant, rather than dismissing it, or obscuring
it, or submitting it to the whims of a single, rigid, unitary conception
of selfhood.

Some may contend that Phoenicianism, Pharaonism, Canaanism,
and other contemporaneous currents valorized by some of the authors
in this volume and folded into some normative "Levantinism," may
not in fact be "Levantine." The Maronite authors from Lebanon, for
instance, may have "invented" a Phoenicianist ideology to distinguish
themselves from Muslim Lebanon and from pan-Arabism. That may
not be an altogether flawed assessment. Yet it is an oversimplified judgment of the late nineteenth- and early twentieth-century Levant, where
intellectuals and commoners alike were still trying out new ideas and
still wrestling between new and old parameters of identity. Indeed, one
may correctly argue that Phoenicianism, or Canaanism, or Pharaonism
were "invented" identity constructs. But so could "Arabism" likewise
be deemed an invention of the twentieth century. Indeed, there had
never been a united "Arab world" or a cohesive "Arab nation" antecedent to the modern twentieth-century Middle Eastern state system that
the British willed into being after the collapse of the Ottoman Empire.
Even T. E. Lawrence, Lawrence of Arabia, one of our times' most committed advocates of Arabism, scoffed at the notion of an "Arab nation"
and a putative cohesive "Arab people" as such, calling it a "manufac-
tured" nation.[39] "Arab unity," upon which the current Middle Eastern
state system was erected, was described as an illusion by Lawrence; a
fairytale akin to "English-speaking unity [. . .]; a madman's notion—
for [the twentieth] century and the next."[40] Lawrence even conceded

the Arabic language itself—the supposed cement of Arabness—to have gained primacy in the Middle East *only* recently, and *only* by sheer "accident and time," maintaining its ostensible dominance to "not mean that Syria—any more than Egypt—[was] an Arabian country," and further noting that on the Mediterranean "sea coast there [was] little, if any, Arabic feeling or tradition."[41]

Even as pertains to the Arabic language itself and the role that it might have played in coloring modern perceptions of the Middle East (as an exclusively Arab space) linguists are in agreement as to the puzzle that is Arabic, and the ambivalence that users of the Arabic language may feel when defining their parameters of selfhood, or when speaking about (or naming) their spoken idioms. And whereas this "ambivalence" may be unintelligible to English-speaking audiences who may be unanimous as to what constitutes "good spoken English"—that is to say, English that adheres closely to the "written language"—users of Arabic don't have an equivalent to "good spoken Arabic," and mean only one thing when they utter the phrase "Arabic language."[42] To them Arabic is *only* the "classical" or "Qur'anic" idiom brought forth by Islam, and its more recent nineteenth-century descendant—Modern Standard Arabic. Simply put, Arabic is *not* any of the region's spoken languages, which Arabs often dismiss as "vernaculars," or "colloquial," or simply "vulgar accents." Yet many of those so-called "accents" may in fact be languages in their own right from a sociolinguistic point of view, differing from each other, and from Arabic *tout court*, as French may be different from English, and as both French and English are different from Latin.[43] As early twentieth-century Egyptian writer Tawfiq Awan notes: "Egypt has an Egyptian language; Lebanon has a Lebanese language; the Hijaz has a Hijazi language; and so forth—and all of these languages are by no means Arabic languages. Each of our countries has a language, which is its own possession; so, why do we not write [our native language] as we converse in it? For the language in which the people speak is the language in which they also write."[44] But as Bernard Lewis has remarked, were this reality to come to pass, and were "the Egyptians, the Syrians, the Iraqis, and the rest" to heed Awan's advice and "develop their vernaculars into national languages, as the Spaniards, the Italians, and the rest had done in Europe, then all hope of a greater Arab unity would be lost."[45] Yet the engine of history seems to be heading in that direction. And rather than Phoenicianism, Canaanism, Syrianism, Pharaonism, and the rest being an aberration, it seems that Arabism would also belong in that lot—that of ideas and parameters of identity that are equally "constructed," "invented," "imagined," and ultimately illusory and elusive in a Middle East of millennial history, where identity cannot be reduced to a single component without oversimplifying and misleading. And although it may be true that Phoenicianism and the rest may not fit snugly into a larger "Levantine" construct, they *do* remain supremely Levantine creations, and they *do* share many attributes of Levantinism; namely in their espousal of spaciousness, fluidity, adaptability, and diversity, and in their valorization of "other" models of Middle Eastern identities, away from the narrow parameters of nationalist dogmas.

One might argue that the "city-state" of classical antiquity, often forming larger confederacies and local alliances, or falling prey to regional and international empires, still has its analogs in the modern Middle East. With many scholars speaking of the unraveling of Sykes-Picot in our times, a State of Latakia or Aleppo, or a Sanjak of Jerusalem or Mount Lebanon—resembling formations from the late nineteenth and early twentieth centuries—does not seem like an anomaly anymore; indeed, it may be a more honest way of heeding history's reckoning. This anthology recognizes this eventuality as a Levantine axiom; *not* as a way of anticipating or predicting the unraveling of the Middle East's current system, but as a way of taking stock of the region's past, which, reflecting the spirit of the works under consideration, is a Middle East of "divisions" based on ethnicity and religion, and (often brittle) "nation-states" deriving from ethnic, religious, and cultural fragmentations.

Again, it is important to stress that this is an anthology of Levantines (and *some* Levantines at that, *not* all of them). In that sense, there are editorial and space constraints that may inhibit and trump my desire to make the present work a more exhaustive and comprehensive survey. Therefore, the anthology's presentation of authors may seem somewhat selective, passing over, quite often, the substance of the ideologies or agendas that underlay some of the authors' claims of hybridity. At the risk of being repetitive, I must reiterate that the purpose of this anthology is certainly not to be exhaustive, but rather to be "Levantine," and in that sense perhaps "selective" and "divergent," and therefore intro-ductory—note that the volume's subtitle is after all "An *Anthology*" not "The *Anthology of Levantine Literature.*" This is all in order to throw light on some representative selections summarizing the Levant and the notion of Levantinism and Levantine identities—*not* other ideologies and intellectual currents dominating the field, namely Arab nationalism and Zionism.

Once again, the purpose and premise here are intended as a chal-lenge to common assumptions about the Middle East; an invitation to take to task accepted norms and orthodoxies shaping our knowledge of the region; an attempt to enrich public and academic discourse sur-rounding the Middle East and its peoples, bringing to the fore an "other" Middle East often overshadowed by traditional scholarship. The aim is therefore not to showcase Arabism or Zionism (both of which are already very well represented in the field of Middle East studies), but rather to elevate and expand the conversation on and about the region, bringing to it a variety of voices and a diversity of perspectives, and call-ing to task the traditional confinement of knowledge about the Middle East to prevalent fashionable comforting (and often academically sanc-tioned) models of an "Arab-Israeli conflict," or an exclusively "Arab" or "Muslim" world against the rest—which, albeit not necessarily ill-suited, remain reductive models, and in that sense exclusivist, incom-plete, and beholden to a single culture and a single narrative.

With regard to some of the chosen authors' possible animus vis-à-vis Arabism or Zionism, which some readers may detect, it should be reiterated that the present anthology is after all one of "Levantine" literature, not of Arab nationalist or Zionist literatures, both of which are, again, richly, even disproportionately, represented in the field. I sus-pect that bringing Arab nationalist or Zionist voices into this conversa-tion would have defeated the Levantine premise of the volume—which, again, remains an invitation to cast an eye on the region's heterogeneity through a variety of authors and themes that were not particularly en-thralled with orthodoxy, be it Arab nationalist, Zionist, or Islamist.

For example, Lebanese thinkers Michel Chiha and Antun Saadé, whose works are referred to throughout this volume, rejected the conceptions of their world as one strictly "Arab." But their approaches, or rather their repudiations of Arabism were different from one another's. Saadé's bent perhaps was doctrinaire, whereas Chiha's remained humane and humanistic, and in that sense supremely Levantine. And whereas Saadé may be fairly depicted as "anti-Arab," Chiha was not anti-*anything;* he was indeed prodiversity, multiplicity, and hybridity, celebrating Lebanon's distinctness rather than a mandated adherence to a single identity.

Yet in fairness to both Chiha and Saadé, their alleged "separatism" and "narrowness" ought to be considered in their historical context, and in the context of Arab nationalism's own aggressive irredentism during the first half of the twentieth century. Indeed, the Syrianism of Antun Saadé and the Phoenicianist Mediterraneanism of Michel Chiha—both of which are interpreted in this volume as emanations of Levantine hybridity—were anterior to Arab nationalism and the Arabist conception of the Middle East, which views the region as an essentially Arab monolith somehow fragmented (or carved out) by Western intrusions and colonialist rapacity. That assumption, today a truism of Middle East studies, flies in the face of historical realities alluded to earlier. And so, rather than being an aberration, the ostensible "separatist" tendencies attributed to Chiha and Saadé may be looked upon as an honest reading of the Middle East's past—that is to say a past defined by hybridity and multiplicity of identities, languages, and cultural accretions.

Moreover, it is worth noting that in our times' fragmented Syria and Iraq, there had never been a uniquely Syrian or Iraqi territorial identity as such—perhaps less so a cohesive unitary Syrian or Iraqi political will to live in a single unitary state, let alone in a larger Arab-defined polity. In fact, what became the Kingdom of Iraq under British Mandate in 1920, had previously constituted three distinct Ottoman administrative units—that is to say three *vilayet*s, or states in today's parlance, each as discrete and divergent from the other as, say, a Prague, a Vienna, or a Budapest would have been disparate in an Austro-Hungarian Empire. And so, the Ottoman *vilayet* of Mosul in the north, today the capital of Iraq's Nineveh Governorate, which in 2014 fell to the Islamic State of Iraq and Syria, had historically-speaking consisted of a majority mix population of Kurds, Turkmens, Assyrians, Armenians, and others, often with more kinships—as well as historical, cultural, and geographic ties—to Aleppans in present-day Syria, and even Anatolian Turks and Iranians in the north, than to populations further south in what became Iraq proper. Likewise, the *vilayet* of Baghdad, with even the etymology of its name recalling Persian rather than Arab origins, shares equally in the heritage of ancient Akkadians, Babylonians as well as Persians and Arabs, and until the middle of the twentieth century, still boasted a majority Jewish population. The same hybridity and multiplicity of identities and cultural accretions apply to the southern Iraqi province of Basra; another district with a storied past, corralling Sumerians and Elamites in ancient times, Aramaeans, Arabs, and Persian in more recent history. Today, with its majority Shi'ite population, the province of Basra is deemed—perhaps inaccurately, but not unfairly or without reason—to be more Persian than it may be Arab.

This Mesopotamian ethno-religious conundrum has a parallel that is equally puzzling in neighboring Syria. In fact, just as historically speaking there had never been a distinct political or cultural identity defined in exclusively "Iraqi" terms before the British contrived one in 1920, so has there never been a Syrian identity as such before the French willed one into being during the 1930s. Indeed, what the French named "Syria" in 1936—a state *not* "carved out," but cobbled together out of the distinct Ottoman *vilayet*s of Beirut, Aleppo, and Damascus—displayed great difficulty transitioning from discrete multi-ethnic Ottoman administrative units to a cohesive modern territorial state defined by a single identity and common bonds of national kinship. Isabel Burton, wife of famed British explorer Sir Richard Francis Burton, summed up the ethnic enigma of the Damascus *vilayet* of the 1870s as one of various groups living "together more or less, and [practicing] their conflicting worships in close proximity. . . . [But] in their hearts [the inhabitants of the State of Damascus] hate one another. The Sunnites excommunicate the Shias, and both hate the Druse; all detest the Ansariyyehs [Alawites]; the Maronites do not love anybody but themselves, and are duly abhorred by all; the Greek Orthodox abominate the Greek Catholics and the Latins; all despise the Jews.[46]

Writing in a similar vein a mere thirty years later, another British traveler, Gertrude Bell, noted Syria to be "merely a geographical term corresponding to no national sentiment."[47] This observation was further confirmed by many Levantine contemporaries of Bell (Chiha, Khairallah, Tyan, Noujaim, and others) who claimed there never to have been a distinct Syrian entity; that what Europeans referred to as Syria was but a bevy of disparate groups and loose geographic entities brought together by conquest and ruled forcibly through terror and tyranny.[48] "The tale of Syria was not ended in this count of odd races and religions," observed T. E. Lawrence in the early decades of the twentieth century. Albeit known by a single name, a European bequest, Syria is not one but multiple entities, he noted, "each with its character, direction, and opinion," often "like twins disliking one another."[49] Yet the terms "Syria" and "Syrian" were alien to those upon whom they were foisted, stressed Lawrence; "for in Arabic there was no such name, nor any name for all the country," thus indicating not only a lack of unity, but a lack of historical precedence and political coherence as well.[50] In history, concluded Lawrence, "Syria had been a corridor between sea and desert, joining Africa to Asia, Arabia to Europe. It had been a prizering, a vassal, of Anatolia, of Greece, of Rome, of Egypt, of Arabia, of Persia, of Mesopotamia. When given a momentary independence by the weakness of neighbors it had fiercely resolved into discordant northern, southern, eastern and western 'kingdoms' with the area at best of Yorkshire, at worst of Rutland; for if Syria was by nature a vassal country it was also by habit a country of tireless agitation and incessant revolt."[51] Heralding the disintegration of a Syria still under construction, at a time when the current (Sykes-Picot) map was still on the drawing board, Lawrence warned that an Arab government in any future Syrian entity "would be as much 'imposed' as the [Ottoman] Turkish Government, or a foreign protectorate, or the historic [Muslim] Caliphate."[52] For, in his view, Syria then, not unlike Syria in modern times, "remained a vividly coloured racial and religious mosaic," and any attempt at forming a unitary state where none had existed or was warranted "would make a patched and parceled thing, ungrateful to a people whose instincts ever returned towards parochial home rule."[53]

From the preceding, one may deduce that the alleged "separatism" of Chiha and the Levantines might not only have been a way of heeding history, but was perhaps also a more just and humane manner in which to view and manage the ethno-religious diversity, not only of Syria and Lebanon, but indeed of the entire Levantine Near East. For the main cause of the strife gripping the region today, reduced to its most simple particle, pertains to "ethnic" or "ethno-religious" conceptions of identity pitted against the liberal "civic" parameters of selfhood that Sykes-Picot might have envisioned. Though this identity dichotomy may be a flawed and outmoded model from a postethnic and postreligious Western perspective, it is one that still has its adherents in the Middle East, where an organic, atavistic, often compulsory conception of identity, poses a challenge to—and indeed spurns—the civic liberal patriotism that is the hallmark of the modern Western state.

To put things in even simpler terms, the Middle East—and for our purposes today's Levant—is a bevy of peoples and ethno-religious groups who, for centuries, had defined themselves (and were defined by others) invariably as Assyrians or Alawites, Maronites or Jews, Druze or Shi'ites, Kurds or Armenians, Greek-Orthodox, and others. Yet inhibiting this diversity, unitary "national" notions spawned by Sykes-Picot demanded those people forget whom they thought they might have been, and begin referring to themselves as "Syrians" and "Palestinians," "Iraqis" and "Transjordanians," "Arabs," and such; names (etymologically speaking) and conceptions of identity that were primarily a Western innovation and a reflection of Western typologies and Western ways of looking at the lands of the Eastern Mediterranean. So by all means, and with profound sympathies to those who may still have a soft-spot for the notion of a coherent "Arab world" or a cohesive "Arab people," one must recognize that the current ailing Arab-defined Middle Eastern state system does not reflect a law of nature; indeed, it may prove to be an aberration in the *longue durée* of the region's millennial history.

Well-intentioned Western scholars may prefer not to deal with questions of identity and diversity in the Middle East. They may also prefer not to take seriously those Near Easterners who *do* deal with such questions (or dismiss them as "separatists"). This is the case because at least some of the conceivable answers may upset the comforting cliché that all human beings (and perhaps their ideas and ideologies) *can* relate to on some level, whatever the cultural differences. The purpose of this volume is to face the unsettling reality of a society and reveal it as it is lain bare by some its own children, bereft of the cosmetics of traditional normative Middle East scholarship.

To this point, Taha Husayn's *The Future of Culture in Egypt* (1938) was a "manifesto" of rejection of any conception of Egypt as an Arab nation. And it was *this,* Husayn's very public, very strong, and very open rejection of Arabism that provoked Sati' al-Husri's sharpest critique— resulting in a duel analyzed with minute detail in Bassam Tibi's *Arab Nationalism: Between Islam and the Nation-State* (expanded edition, 1997). In a nutshell, Husri, the guiding spirit behind linguistic Arab nationalism, could not abide Husayn's commitment to a Pharaonic Egypt and his strong disputation of Egypt's putative Arab character. This drove Husri to accuse Husayn of "of having embezzled 'at least thirteen centuries of Arab history from Egypt,'"[54] concluding that the latter had no choice in the matter of Egypt's identity, and that the Egyptians were still Arab simply because Husri himself had deemed things so—that is to say, that one "is an Arab whether he wishes to be so or not."[55]

Of course, a more nuanced and sensitive treatment of Arab nationalism may be in order, as it is true that Arab nationalism, like the Middle East itself, is not a monolith. Yet, the paragons of Arab nationalism today, and those still making the case for a "single Arab nation with an eternal vocation [*umma 'Arabiyya waahida, thaat risaala khaalida*]," to use Michel Aflaq's dictum, or one that extends "from the Ocean to the Gulf," remain disciples of Sati' al-Husri's and Michel Aflaq's conceptions of Arabness and Arab nationalism as a coercive "organic" immutable construct, not some liberal innocuous notions of an *identité élective* as proposed by many of those who opposed Arabism, advocates of Levantinism among them. The "Arab nationalism" of Saddam Hussein's Halabja and Al-Anfal extermination campaigns perpetrated against the Kurds in northern Iraq; the "Arab nationalism" of today's unraveling Syria; the "Arab nationalism" of Yassir Arafat and his pledge in the mid-1970s that "the road to Palestine go through [the northern Lebanese Christian towns of] Jounié and Tarshish," and that the "Arabization of Lebanon" become part and parcel of the "struggle for Palestine"; the "Arab nationalism" of Jamal Abdel-Nasser's failed union with Syria and his Yemen civil war adventure—all remain the main accomplishments and the only recognizable facets of "Arab nationalism." And again, rather than being an oddity, the preceding may indeed be in line with what the "elders" (from Husri, to Aflaq, to Farrukh and others) had preached. It is this very same "Arab nationalism" that Adonis and Hazem Saghieh and Nizar Qabbani (and others still) indict and call to task in this volume.

Again, this anthology's purpose is not to make the case for Arab nationalism—nor to bring a case against it for that matter. Indeed, its purpose is to bring to light those intellectuals who have proposed capacious parameters of identity in the Levant, often at odds with nationalism in general, but especially at odds with Arabism's—or let us say at odds with the dominant strain of Arabism's—coercive and negationist tendencies. Indeed, the anthology's representation of Nizar Qabbani for instance, a committed Arab nationalist during the early stages of his intellectual journey, shows him to espouse an innocuous Arabism, arguing for a "people made out of jasmine," not "daggers," and in that sense a humanistic conception of the "Arab world" more in tune with the geographic and conceptual space proposed by the Levantines. Likewise, Adonis in this volume shows himself to be a former Syrian nationalist, a later convert to Arab nationalism, and even at times (albeit briefly) an advocate of Islamism, finally acquiescing in the complexity of his world and settling for diversity, fluidity, and spaciousness in the choice of parameters of selfhood. It is worth noting that in his darkest of hours, even as he criticized Arabs, Arabism, and Arab nationalism, calling for their repudiation and dismantlement in favor of other identity models, and even as he mounted a relentless assault against the Arabic language itself (one of the most sacred and most powerful symbols of Arabism) Adonis never relinquished the Arabic language, which he still argued to be his *only* homeland. Again, it needs to be emphasized that this volume brings to bear a decent amount of nuance in its treatment of Arab nationalism, even though its aim is not Arabism per se, but rather the works and authors that "did not make it" into traditional scholarship on the Middle East—precisely because of issues they raised with Arabism.

As pertains to semantics and taxonomy, the anthology's "Arab nationalism" may at times shade into "Arabness," "pan-Arabism," and perhaps even "Muslimness." This tendency may be attributable to the fact that no clear distinction between Arabness, pan-Arabness, and Arab nationalism exists in Arabic literature in general, but neither is to be found in Arabic texts and the Arabic language itself. *Uruba* in Arabic is the term used in reference to Arabism, Arab nationalism, pan-Arabism, and Arabness all at once. On this point Adeed Dawisha has noted that, "As a concept, 'Arab nationalism' has tended to be used in the literature of Middle Eastern politics and history interchangeably with other terms such as Arabism, Pan-Arabism, and even sometimes Arab radicalism, thus blending the sentiment of cultural proximity with the desire for political action."[56] That perhaps should not always be the case. Indeed, an expression of fealty to an Arab "cultural heritage" ought to be distinguished from, say, the "Arabness" of literature (as is that of Adonis for instance, and as there may be a literary "francophonie" distinct from "Frenchness"). Likewise identifying with an Arab "cultural heritage" should not have to correspond with one's desire for political unity among users of the Arabic language, or call for political action against those who may impugn *uruba*. Unfortunately, those distinctions and nuances are not expressed (at least not without ambiguity) in the canon of the Arab nationalists themselves. A "French" example may perhaps be especially relevant in this case: In French, when one speaks of a *littérature française* and a *littérature francophone,* one means two different things: "French literature" *tout court* "written by Frenchmen" on one hand, and "literature expressed in the French language, but written by non-Frenchmen," on the other hand. No such distinction exists in Arabic, where *adab 'arabiyy* means both "Arabic literature" and "literature expressed in the Arabic language," with producers of both "literatures" being perforce Arab—or folded into an Arab mold. In that sense a Persian Abu-Nuwwaas (756–814) would morph into an Arab poet without raising an eyebrow.

With regard to the anthology's "Arabness" seeming to identify with "Muslimness," this too is an issue that Arabs, Arab nationalists, and Muslims have been wrestling with since the early stirrings of Arab nationalism, during the first decades of the twentieth century, and is a topic treated in some detail in the introduction.

It bears repeating that this anthology does not intend to bring *only* "unknowns" of Levantine literature to anglophone audiences. Indeed, some of the authors in this volume may already be well represented in

English translations—Adonis, Taha Husayn, Nizar Qabbani, and Kahlil Gibran for instance. But the purpose of this anthology is to provide new interpretations and new annotated cultural critical translations. For example, only a single facet of Gibran's work is available to anglophone audiences—*The Prophet* and whatever ancillaries it instigated. Yet most of Gibran's social criticism that is not cloaked in poetry and short stories remains unknown (hence the choice of an Arabic text in the anthology, which isn't known even to arabophone audiences, and which besides bringing it to light in English, provides another previously unknown facet of its author). Likewise both Husayn and Adonis are represented superficially and monochromatically in available English translations.

With the preceding in mind, the anthology's reconsideration of the named authors provides a fresher reinterpretation and (in some cases a more accurate annotated critical) translation of their works than has been available. Similarly, only Husayn the Arab nationalist and the "dean of modern Arabic literature" is known to anglophone audiences. Things are likewise with Adonis; only the Adonis of the early 1970s is available to anglophone readers, whereas the Adonis of the late twentieth and early twenty-first centuries remains a relative unknown, except perhaps for the snippets brought forth in Fouad Ajami's own work on the intellectual and social history of the modern Middle East.

Some specialized readers may deem the annotated texts of the anthology a bit "cumbersome," providing too much information where only "hints" might have sufficed. But for a volume intended for specialists and nonspecialists alike, including students of the Middle East and a general audience, I deemed the abundance of detail not necessarily disadvantageous. Indeed, this may be the single most important special feature setting this anthology apart from comparable endeavors, which remain merely "reproduction" of texts.

Finally, a few words on the anthology's translations and transliteration of foreign expressions: All translations from Arabic, dialect variants, and French are my own, unless otherwise indicated. Also, transliterations not conforming to prevalent standards set by the *International Journal of Middle East Studies* (IJMES) take into consideration the wide variances in Arabic dialects and the different phonologies and spelling conventions (in roman renditions) of a variety of Arabophone countries.

In this regard, scholars *have* traditionally been given some leeway in rendering non-English names and proper nouns in a transliterated form of their own choosing—and not necessarily conforming to IJMES or any such standards. In the case of this anthology, I have attempted to keep transliterated proper names and nouns in conformity with the way they are spelled by their owners, and/or the "simplified" way in which they occur in most of the literature consulted; e.g., "Jounié" not "Djouni-yah," and "Beirut" not "Bayroot." By the same token "Sa'id 'Aql" would be rendered "Saïd Akl" because the poet himself used that spelling (even though Arabists may disapprove.) Likewise "Antun Sa'adah" is rendered "Antun Saadé" because that is how the name occurs in literature issuing from Lebanon; and "Taha Hussein" is likewise "Taha Husayn" as is "Adunis" "Adonis" because that is the standard form in which those names have occurred in the majority of the works consulted.

In sum, this anthology may be deemed dissident historiography; it may question the field's orthodoxies; it may be delving into topics and contexts not ordinarily valorized by the doyens of Middle Eastern studies, excavating peoples, intellectual currents, stories, and ideas that might not have "made it" into traditional history books. All that may be true! But, at the risk of redundancy, this is precisely what academic investigation must do: Teach and learn how to follow evidence. Question and investigate and scrutinize *even* prevalent dominant fashionable paradigms, lest we end up in a guild of likeminded automatons; a sanctuary for old and soothing ideas, rather than a laboratory for new ones and fresher perspectives on established norms.

The book is divided into four sections representing four countries of the Eastern Mediterranean: Syria, Lebanon, Israel-Palestine, and Egypt. Each country or section features a brief historical introduction, biographies of the headlined authors, and a sampling of each of the authors' works rendered in an annotated English translation. This is a scholarly work with the general reader in mind, aiming to serve as an introduction to the modern Middle East's intellectual history—or at least one facet of the region's intellectual history that is not always given its due. But this is also a work that can be used as a textbook for introductory college courses such as Modern Middle Eastern Literature, Memory and Identity in the Levant, and History and Nationalism in the

Modern Middle East. For this, the choice of authors and topics in this volume have answered to a number of criteria:

1. Although some were prominent intellectuals and well-known literary figures, most of the authors are virtually unknown to anglophone audiences.
2. The authors did not write, as expected, *in* (or exclusively in) Arabic.
3. Some of the authors were Jews who wrote in Arabic and French (Jacqueline Kahanoff), Muslims who wrote in Hebrew and English (Samir el-Youssef and Fawaz Turki), others who valorized nontraditional and nonofficial speech forms, or Christians who straddled all of the region's linguistic mediums.
4. The authors often deviated from the cultural and linguistic norms of their respective societies—they were not Zionists, or Arab nationalists, or religious fundamentalists.
5. The authors (or most of them) initially proceeded from ultranationalist beginnings or nationalist assumptions (whether Arabist, Zionist, Islamist, or localist) but ultimately relinquished doctrinaire rigidity to excavate, restitute, and espouse the region's fluidity.
6. Finally, the authors under consideration wrote in languages (French, Arabic, Hebrew, dialect speech forms, and Syriac) that my own training and background allowed me to render in English as close to the original as possible—in semantics, prosody, connotations, symbolism, and historical relevance.

Introduction

Levant as Crossroads of Civilization and Culture

The specificity of the Levant, both geographically and emblematically speaking, dwells largely in the imagery that it elicits as a melting pot, a meeting ground, a crucible, and a passageway for peoples, conquerors, ideas, and cultures. From Assyrians to Persians and Macedonians, and from Romans to Muslim Arabs and Turks, every other culture and civilization from classical antiquity into modern times has coveted this sliver of Eastern Mediterranean shores, conquering it, possessing it, and staking claims to its resources, its peoples, its cultures, and its storied heritage.

Many were the nations foisting their histories, their languages, and their cultural peculiarities and accretions on the peoples of the Levant. Some did so peacefully, others with bloodstained steel and firestorms and engines of war. The placid Levantines, whether ancient Hebrews and Phoenicians or their modern descendants, generally quite unskilled in the arts and sciences of warfare, often had but words for self-defense, simple words drenched in the aromas of their soil, drunk in checkered histories and stirring emotions; words seared on the vault of heaven, streaking like a "rising sun"—the etymological origin of the lands of the *Levant*—shining brightly from East to West.

And so, out of the remarkable early human societies of the Levantine region would issue mankind's first prototypes of architecture, ethics, religion, literature, and the art of recording those human endeavors in written form—alphabetic writing. Human language and words in the forms of prayers, hymns, myths, tales, proverbs, and fables—the very foundations of our modern literatures and systems of social ethics —were forms and concepts antedating the Homeric epics and even the Hebrew scriptures by close to a millennium, and they all arguably emerged *in* the Levant and *within* ancient Levantine societies before any other place on earth.[1]

Moreover, and in order to make their words resound more clearly and fan out more broadly to the four corners of the earth, the children of the Levant resolved to adopt the foreign idioms of other nations, refining their inflections, rendering them their own, molding them into sublime universal tools of cross-cultural intercourse. And so, the Levantines became polyglot multicultural intermediaries, long before the terms had yet come into being. And not unlike their ancient progenitors, who wielded the languages of Tutankhamen, Hammurabi, King Solomon, Cyrus the Great, Cadmus, Jesus, and Ptolemy, the modern children of the Levant also reveal themselves to our own times as gifted and committed polyglots, plying (among others) the languages of Florence, Paris, London, and Castile, partaking of them with the intimacy and affection of natives.[2]

All those languages are ultimately part and parcel of the aged venerable cultural and literary heritage of the Levant. As stressed by early twentieth-century Lebanese poet Charles Corm (1894–1963), those languages, deemed by some to be foreign to the true essence of the Near East, are nevertheless still native to us:

> For, it seems that our hearts
> Can still recall remembrances
> Of having fashioned them
> And styled their graceful sounds!
>
> Indeed, it is they
> Who disowned their lineage;
> Uprooted from us,
> Torn from our embrace,

Embellished by exile,
They now disown their race
Like beloved ingrates.[3]

Still, maintained Charles Corm,

For, even as I write
In someone else's language,
And even when I speak
In someone else's tongue,
It is still you in my voice,
My sainted mother's voice
Mingling with my own,
Snug like a lover's warmth!

For, Man here below,
In spite of having learned
His brute oppressor's tongue,
Has kept the looks, the tone,
Has kept the pitch, the pulse,
Of his forefathers' inflections,
Of his ancestors' voice![4]

In this sense, today's Modern Standard Arabic, the language most
closely associated with the modern Middle East and its Levantine neighborhood, can be argued to be no more authentic (and no more indigenous) to the region than may be Hebrew, Syriac, and even French and
English—the latter, if not sui generis Levantine competencies, then at
least paramount literary and intellectual mediums intimately associated
with the Levant and Levantine history. It should be noted that the major
milestones in the region's millennial history were all embodiments and
imbrications of many successive waves of ethnic and linguistic groups,
all of which left their distinct enduring ripples on the eastern shores of
the Mediterranean and on the linguistic habits of the region's children.[5]
On this point, the Brill *Encyclopedia of Arabic Language and Linguis-*

tics maintained that the area now commonly referred to as the "Arab world,"

> had hosted many other cultures, including . . . Sumerians, Babylonians, Assyrians, Phoenicians, Ancient Egyptians, Persians, Greeks, and Romans. . . . The legacies of these [pre-Arab] pre-Islamic peoples did not all simply disappear with the advent of the Muslim Arabs. [. . .] Some peoples of the region resisted the forces of Arabicization, Islamicization, or both; even among those who underwent both these processes, this was not always accompanied by a total abandonment of their earlier culture. Thus, there are still pockets across the [Arab-defined Middle East] using languages other than Arabic and practicing religions other than Islam, and there are still groups convinced that their ancestors belonged to a people different from [the Arabs dominating the region's cultural and linguistic landscapes of today].[6]

And so, the Levant's endogenous and congenital multilingualism in our own times may simply be a way of life; most importantly perhaps, it may be a way of heeding history.[7] For, even at the height of the Arab Muslim conquests of the Near East (ca. 636 A.D.), which brought along with them the religious and legal exigencies of a new language, the region's linguistic habits and cultural and ethnic accretions did not undergo notably profound changes—at least not immediately.[8] Christians would continue to constitute the bulk of the populations of the Eastern Mediterranean's newly Islamized dominions long into the Crusader era, and variants of Greek and Aramaic would remain daily spoken idioms to sizeable communities in what are today Syria and Lebanon through the eighteenth century. Indeed, it is within this distinctly "Phoenician crucible," argued Sélim Abou, which has since time immemorial been a passageway to motley conquerors and their languages, that the Levant ought to be considered. Relative to this, Raymond Weill noted that the Levant "had never submitted, in any substantial measure, to being incorporated into the cultural or linguistic habits of [newly arrived] imperial organizations."[9] Elaborating on this remark, Étienne de Vaumas comes to the conclusion that "the modern [Levantine] mentality is the child of the highly sophisticated Phoenician mentality, given both their permanent contact with the 'Great Powers' of their times."[10] And so, in addition to anthropological and ethnic filiations between Phoenicians, Lebanese, and Levantines, one may add linguistic filiations—that is to say linguistic "habits" rather than "language-use" as such. It is worth keeping in mind that, given its geographic location, at the edge of three continents, there has always been cultural, ethnic, and linguistic contact and "mélange" and "métissage" in the Levant, which means that polyglossia may in fact be a historical as well as an anthropological reality—and a reality to be reckoned with, and recognized, and valorized, rather than brushed aside.

Polyglot middlemen and cultural intermediaries to the core and by their very temperament, strewn about at the crossroads of Europe, Africa, and Asia, the peoples of the Levant would therefore go on speaking a variety of idioms, and heeding a rich linguistic ecosystem many centuries into the Muslim era.[11] Even as they began internalizing the idiom of their new Arab rulers, the linguistic communities of the Levant would remain firmly ensconced astride multiple languages, often taking on additional ones; namely the languages of the Crusaders, which would begin trickling into and coexisting with their Latin, Greek, and Semitic antecedent in the early twelfth century.[12]

That is the overarching rationale behind the present anthology's spanning the spectrum of languages and idioms spawning the literary tradition of the modern Middle East. Yet their polyglot nature notwithstanding, the literatures under consideration here are also just as thematically diverse as they may be linguistically varied. Not unlike elsewhere within literate societies, Levantine literary production can be viewed to be a form of "dissent"; the tool, as it were, of those suffering—or those convinced of being victims of—defeat, suppression, or exclusion. Levantine literature may thus be seen as a form of protest, a medium of rebellion against orthodoxy, against occupation, against irredentist or negationist nationalist ideology, against social norms and cultural autarky that, in and of themselves, spoke eloquently of the region's endogenous diversity.

From the preceding would evolve a century or more of literary trajectories, often in the form of individual tracks—rather than well-delineated "schools of thought" or "literary currents"—generally driven by individual (even if at times *also* communal) thematic tendencies motivated by transformative historical events: From the collapse of the Ottoman Empire (1918), to the emergence of the modern state system and the onset of the Arab-Israeli conflict (1918–48), to the birth of Arab nationalism and the latter's countercurrents of Islamism and motley "localisms" and state patriotism throughout the first half of the twentieth century; all of those are themes brought to the fore in this anthology.

Mapping Out the Levant

More than a century after its genesis, Arab national identity as an overarching parameter of selfhood remains a vexing question for many Middle Eastern writers and intellectuals. In its early twentieth-century heyday, Arab nationalism frequently overshadowed any other identity frameworks, its vocal proponents dismissing all alternatives to Arabism as sole legitimate social identifier, placing Arabist ideological convictions over any other competing force.

Writing in the second half of the twentieth century, Lebanese Arab nationalist ideologue Omar Farrukh (1906–87) argued that it is irrelevant should Iraqis deem themselves a hybrid of Aramaeans, Persians, Kurds, Turks, Indians, and others: "they still are Arabs, in spite of their racial diversity," even in spite of themselves, "because the overriding factor in their identity formation is the Arabic language."[13] Likewise, Farrukh stressed, the inhabitants of today's Morocco, Algeria, Libya, and elsewhere in Northern Africa, may very well be a mix of Berbers, black Africans, Spaniards, and Franks; "but by dint of the Arab nation's realities [*sic*], they all remain Arabs shorn from the same cloth as the Arabs of the Hejaz, Najd, and Yemen."[14]

Behind these ideological positions undoubtedly were more practical concerns; fears, perhaps, of undermining a political cause intended to unite all users of the Arabic language under a single political banner. Such high-pitched rhetoric also had a damaging effect on the new "nation-states" established after the Ottoman Empire's demise at the

end of World War I. To the Arab nationalists, these new state formations, "artificial creations" as they were defined, entities serving the interests of foreign powers or their local cronies, were a pale substitute for
the more appealing dream of a united Arab state. And so Arab national
identity and its ideological trappings reigned supreme. But despite
this ringing endorsement of Arab nationalism, mostly by arabophone
Middle Eastern intellectuals, allegiance to the cause of Arab nationalism
was not always given or evident. At times, even leading proponents and
promoters of Arab nationalist ideology went through various stages,
during which they explored—and frequently endorsed—alternative
creeds, before formally accepting the tenets of Arab nationalism, only to
subsequently abscond Arabness altogether and consent in a congenital
Levantine hybridity and a Mediterranean cultural fluidity.

Syrian poet Adonis is perhaps the most notable among those
modern voices. His personal intellectual and ideological journey took
him from siding with the Syrian social nationalism of Antun Saadé—
which vociferously challenged the conceit and purported legitimacy of
Arabism—to embracing an all-encompassing Arab national identity,
to committing, more recently, to fostering pluralism across the region.
Adonis embodied these nuanced positions, serving as a leading individual who emphasized differing ideological positions at various points
of his life. This *Anthology of Levantine Literature* highlights Adonis's
transitions (and the transitions of others of his generation) along with
the peoples and ideas that paved the way for these changes. The volume
explores the lives, thought, and works of some twelve Levantine literati,
while assessing the possibility of valorizing a greater degree of pluralism in Middle Eastern public life, even as the modern Middle East as
we have come to know it through the twentieth century seems to have
"collapsed" in the aftermath of the 2010 events formerly known as the
"Arab Spring."

Such pluralism may be found in a number of salient features of
Levantine society, among them Levantinism, Mediterraneanism, Pharaonism, Phoenicianism, and Syrianism. Indeed, the authors under consideration in this volume have dramatically shifted their opinions and
orientations over the years, often in meteoric bouts and at breakneck
speed. Adonis for instance had started out his intellectual journey by

making the case for a composite Syrian identity as imagined by Antun Saadé in the early decades of the twentieth century. He even dabbled briefly with Arab nationalism and a pan-Arab outlook. He later turned on Arabism, and his critique of it was as devastating as his despair of Arab nationalist intransigence was disheartening. "In its brutal exercise of power," wrote Adonis of Syria's Arab Nationalist Baath Party,

> Arabism has molested and desecrated the cultural identity of the Syrians. It submitted the richness of Syrian selfhood to a single linguistic, cultural, "racial" and "religious" Arabism, laying down the foundations of a uniform, monolithic, one-dimensional culture. In sum, the Baath Party presented us with a narrow, regurgitant, exclusivist culture, constructed solely on negating, apostatizing, marginalizing, and obviating "the other," in addition to accusing "the other" of treason; in other words, it brought us an Arabist replacement of theology and the religious creed [. . .] therefore dismantling a diverse pluralistic Syria, and foisting upon it a closed, brutal culture of "oneness." Thus, Syrian culture was rendered one of Arabist proselytism, publicity, and propaganda linked to a brutal security apparatus. And so, Syrian culture was entrapped between two closed cultic mentalities: one arguing in the name of religion, heritage, the past, and Salafism; the other, a Baathist creed, making the case for an oppressive Arab identity, in total contravention of freedom and basic human rights, rejecting cultural pluralism, the very essence of Syria's distinct personality.[15]

But Adonis also clung to some hope in the waning and decline of Arab exclusivism. The creed of the Arab nationalist, he wrote, is one that rejects the existence of the "other" as such; it promotes a culture that devalues human existence: "But I have no doubt in my mind that the lands that conceived of and spread man's first Alphabet the lands that bequeathed and taught the principles of intellectual intercourse and dialogue with the 'other,' since the very early discovery of Alphabetic writing; these lands that bore witness to processions of the world's loftiest

civilizations, from Sumerians to Babylonians, and from Egyptians to
Hebrews, Phoenicians and Romans; these lands that spawned monotheism, humanism, and belief in a compassionate deity, etc."[16] There is a
clear celebration of cosmopolitan humanism and multiple identities in
these words. There is also an invitation to cast aside the narrow resentful chauvinism espoused by Arab nationalists of Adonis's generation.
In their brutal exercise of power, claims Adonis, Arab nationalists have
abused and etiolated the hybrid cultural identities of the Middle East.
They have reduced the region's human richness to a "single linguistic,
racial, and religious totalitarianism"; a monolithic Arab culture, as it
were, "obsessed and consumed by a need for 'oneness' in thought, opinions, language, and belief."[17] In sum, from Adonis's viewpoint, Arab nationalism and the Arab identity that it foisted presented the Middle East
with a faulty essentialist cultural prism, built solely on negating "the
other," and accusing that non-Arab "other" of treachery and subversion
should he dare stand up to the only sanctioned dominant "one-culture"
jingoism.[18]

But the walls of resignation and fear had begun tumbling down
by 2011. Meeting in Antalya, Turkey, in May–June of that year, and as
the event formerly known as the "Arab Spring" was beginning to gather
steam, a group of Syrian expatriates and dissidents attempted to suggest a "non-Arab" model for an impending "post-Assad Syria." In addition to demanding the ouster of the Baathist regime — one of the Middle East's last remaining avatars of Arabism — the fourth clause of the
Antalya Final Declaration read as follows: "We, participants in the Syria
Conference for Change, affirm that the Syrian people are a composite of
many ethnicities, including Arabs, Kurds, Chaldaeo-Assyrian, Circas-
sians, Armenians, and others. The conference recognizes and asserts the
legitimate and equal rights of all of these constitutive elements of Syrian
identity, and demands their protection under a new Syrian constitution
to be founded upon the principles of civil state, pluralistic parliamentary
democracy, and national unity."[19] The early twentieth-century conception of Syria — and its "Levantine" backyard — as a cultural and ethnic
mosaic, had come full circle by the early twenty-first century. The heaving Middle East of 2011 and beyond may perhaps be putting an end to
a tragic chapter of the region's history. Arab nationalists, on the retreat,

can no longer hide the hybridity of their universe. They have suppressed the Middle East's diversity for far too long, but they could not desiccate its multi-ethnic personality to suit their monistic impulses. The Middle East, in spite of its current intersectarian dissentions, may be at a crossroads in the early decades of the twenty-first century, perhaps veering away from confessional identities and one-language nationalism toward a more encompassing diversity—blemished and brutalized as this diversity may become as it gets past its growing pains.

This is not, however, the way things began. A century ago, the idea of a dominant Arab national identity gained traction across the region. By the middle of the twentieth century, Arab nationalism, as noted earlier, was the leading ideological force in the Middle Eastern marketplace of ideas. It was Sati' al-Husri (1880–1967), Arab nationalism's chief theorist, who popularized the notion that all users of the Arabic language were perforce Arab, regardless of their own wishes.[20] Husri, a Turkish-speaking Syrian-born writer who would become the spiritual father of linguistic Arabism, lectured throughout the 1950s and 1960s about how one is an Arab simply because *he,* Husri himself, had so decreed. In a widely anthologized political snippet, Husri harangued enraptured audiences about how:

> Every person who speaks Arabic is an Arab. Every individual associated with an Arabic-speaker or with an Arabic-speaking people is an Arab. If he does not recognize [his Arabness] . . . we must look for the reasons that have made him take this stand. . . . But under no circumstances should we say "as long as he does not wish to be an Arab, and as long as he is disdainful of his Arabness, then he is not an Arab." He is an Arab regardless of his own wishes, whether ignorant, indifferent, recalcitrant, or disloyal; he is an Arab, but an Arab without consciousness or feelings, and perhaps even without a conscience.[21]

Husri was aware, indeed he was proud, of the fascistic impulses of his brand of Arab nationalism. In fact, he bragged about the Arabism that he yearned for as one that had to exude totalitarian rigidity and partisan regimentation in order for it to triumph: "We can say that the system to which we should direct our hopes and aspirations is a Fascist system," he famously wrote.[22] But if Husri had been intimidating in his advocacy for a compulsory Arabism, his disciple Michel Aflaq (1910–89), cofounder of the Baath Party, promoted outright violence and called for the extermination of those users of the Arabic language who refused to conform to his prescribed Arab identity. Arab nationalists must be ruthless against those members of the Arab nation who have gone astray from their ascribed Arabness, wrote Aflaq; "they must be imbued with a hatred unto death, toward any individuals who embody an idea contrary to Arab nationalism. [. . .] An idea that is opposed to [Arab nationalism] does not emerge out of nothing! It is the incarnation of individuals who must be exterminated, so that their idea might in turn be also exterminated."[23] This is in a nutshell one of the foundational tenets of Arab nationalism, and a dominant theme in the Arabist narrative of Middle Eastern history as preached by its avatars: hostility, rejection, negation, and brazen calls for the extermination of the non-Arab "other." And there has been in a way a "conspiracy of silence" vis-à-vis the pre-Arab and non-Arab bits of Middle Eastern history and memory in the normative literature on the region. If not a "conspiracy of silence," then at least a veil of scholarly contempt has shrouded memory and identity narratives valorizing those who do not fit the prevalent Muslim-Arab mold; a strong "antiminority" thrust to the study and analysis of Middle Eastern history and memory; an "antiminority" thrust that deems a celebration of pre-Arab narratives an affront to Arabism—and by association an affront to Islam. This is as if the seventh century Muslim conquest of the Middle East—and its aftermath—had taken place in a vacuum. In an American context, such a stance would be tantamount to suggesting the study and valorization of "Native-American" history may be subversive to the unity of America and the virtues of America's "European" foundations; or that the early American colonies somehow issued in a vacuum, on deserted uninhabited territories, bereft of precursor peoples, traditions, languages, and monuments to memory.

Yet, the pre-Arab and pre-Muslim peoples of the Near East—and their remaining memories and monuments and cultural and literary artifacts—are indeed the "Native Americans" of the region, the Middle

East's "first nations" as it were. Admitting and normalizing this reality ought not be an affront to any one or anyone's particular culture! Not doing so may in fact be tantamount to cultural suppression and destruction of historical memory by other means; indeed by better means. It is intellectual iconoclasm tidier than the actual destruction and plunder and looting of memory being perpetrated by the Islamic State group (ISIS) in today's Syria and Iraq. And this tidy intellectual "iconoclasm" of the keepers of orthodoxy in normative Middle East studies circles—practiced by Arab nationalism in the twentieth century, by ISIS and its clones in more recent times—is a long-standing process, fourteen centuries in the making, and may in fact have its origins in certain, distinctly Muslim, precursors.

Islam, we ought to remember, is fundamental to Middle Eastern politics and the politics of "identity" in the Middle East. Islam may challenge, at any time, any given secular political order. The Islamic Empire, both actual and fancied, is viewed by many, Muslims and Arab nationalists alike, as the zenith, the pinnacle of human existence. Islam is superior to any other human order. Whatever came before Islam is not worth remembering, let alone is it worth preserving; it belongs to the age of darkness and ignorance, *Jahiliyya* in Arabic. Likewise, whatever may come after Islam can never measure up.

In that sense, the destruction and devastation that ISIS is visiting on venerable remnants of pre-Islamic Near Eastern civilizations is not mindless unjustifiable malicious vandalism; it is not only "looting for profit," nor is it "collateral damage" or a natural outcome of war. Indeed, the Islamic State's deeds are willful deliberate actions; grounded in orthodoxy. And so, ISIS may be said to be iconoclastic in a deliciously accurate and learned and authentically Muslim way. Indeed the Prophet Muhammad himself may be described as the first iconoclast of the Arabian Peninsula, the Calvinist of his day, zealously dismantling vestiges deemed unsuitable to the worshipers of the one true God, providing a template to those who would later come to claim his mantle.

In today's Syria, the ancient stones of Palmyra, having braved the centuries, are now turning to silence and dust, consumed by the Islamic State's vandals. In the summer of 2015, it was the temple of Baal Shamin, the Lord of the Heavens, one of the chief deities of the Phoenicians, venerated by other Semitic peoples, arguably influencing both Judaism and Christianity—*and* our own *modern* systems of social ethics, and by association even Islam—*that* temple too was demolished in the name of Allah. Before Baal Shamin, it was the ancient city of Hatra, in Iraq's Nineveh Province, that was visited by the wrath of those righteous zealots. And the assault on history and memory persists; an ongoing cultural erasure dress-rehearsed in the destruction meted out by Arab nationalists, a century prior, against the pre-Arab and pre-Muslim cultural assets of the Middle East. And if those dismissed as crazed disciples of Allah are trigger-happy in matters of ancient sculptures and statues and temples and cultural effects in our time, it is because they are indeed fighting on behalf of an ultra-orthodox, conservative—and in their view legitimate—doctrine that calls for the rehabilitation and return to the pristine purist practices of early Islam; a rigorous monotheism that the majority of modern Muslims might have long since abandoned. But to those Salafists, remnants of ancient pre-Islamic civilizations—whether living physical monuments or human progenies of times past—are abominations, evils committed by Man against Allah. And so they see themselves in the role of destroyers as noble enforcers of a "neglected duty." Theirs is the burden of the righteous to set things right, to root out "evil" from the world.

But this aversion to what preceded Islam is not an innovation; it is not heresy either; it draws on principles rooted in orthodoxy; a learned interpretation, not a perversion. It bears repeating that Islam is the pinnacle of human existence; what came before it is Jahiliyya, ignorance, and therefore ought to be rejected; not because it is defective, but because it is false. And that falsehood ought not be merely corrected, but supplanted. That is at least *some* of the thrust behind the actions of the Islamic State group in the early decades of the twenty-first century. And a great deal of overlap—perhaps even an osmosis—exists between the Islam of ISIS and the Arabism of their nationalist (secular) predecessors. The destruction of memory that ISIS may be perpetrating in the second decade of the twenty-first century did have twentieth-century Arab nationalist precursors, as briefly outlined earlier. Indeed Arab nationalism itself has claimed its emotive and communal foundations in Islam. Michel Aflaq was a committed secularist by all account, even though he might have remained a Christian secularist. But Michel Aflaq could not escape the centrality of Islam to the secular Arab nationalism that he promoted. He conceded that being an "Arab" and being a "Muslim" were complementary if not synonymous.[24] From the time of the Prophet Muhammad during the seventh century, to the time of the prophets of Arab nationalism in the early twentieth century, little has changed in the sense that identity and self-awareness had always been religious in the Middle East, rooted in Islam. So, in a sense, not only is there no opposition between Islam and "secular Arab nationalism" of the modern Middle Eastern state system; indeed there may be a great deal of conflation and harmony and cooperation and synonymity. Aflaq himself held that the Prophet Muhammad was also ipso facto the founder of the Arab nation, and was to be venerated as such by every Arab nationalist, whether Muslim or not.[25] Indeed Aflaq practiced what he had preached, and is believed to have converted to Islam so as to better live his Arabness.[26] There are many vignettes and adages in the literature of Arab nationalism that confirm the fact that "secularism" as a source of legitimacy in the Middle East is at best a pipe dream that defies the region's "laws of nature," which remain overwhelmingly defined by Islam. "Islam *is* Arab nationalism," according to Aflaq, and Arab nationalists ought not "distinguish between nationalism and religion"— that is to say between Arabness and Islam.[27] A leading Iraqi-Arab nationalist writer, Abdurrahman al-Bazzaaz, chimed in noting that Islam is the religion of the Arabs and by the Arabs par excellence; "there could in no way be a contradiction between Islam and Arabism," he stressed.[28] This axiom is perhaps no more exquisitely manifest than in the official seal of the Arab League, which is emblazoned with a fragment of a verse from the Qur'anic *Surat al-'Imran* (Qur'an 110), which reads "You are the finest nation [Islamic *umma*] brought forth to Mankind."

Reconsidering the Arabist Narrative

Still, and notwithstanding the dominance of Arabism as a cultural and political construction, the Middle East's intellectual history of the past

hundred years has been heedful of the region's diversity, taking stock of
its non-Arab and pre-Arab heritage, and laboring to valorize historical
memories, parameters of identity, and geographic concepts—namely
in the Levant region—as crossroads of varied cultures, languages, and
civilizations, Arab and otherwise. Indeed, as noted earlier in the prolegomena, in today's Arab-defined Middle East, there are still peoples
using languages other than Arabic, cherishing memories predating the
Arabs, and practicing religions and cultural rituals besides and predating those of Islam. Indeed, there are also millions of Middle Easterners
today who remain convinced that their ancestors (and *they*) belong to a
people different and distinct from the Arab and Muslim people.[29] The
distinction, or dichotomy, is between those who endorse "Arabism,"
and Arabic speakers who may not link their language to wider cultural
and political goals. In recent times, as the Arab nationalist edifice appears to be coming undone, and as the legitimacy of states previously
defined by the "Arab order" is being shaken, suppressed non-Arab and
pre-Arab identities are being restituted, forgotten narratives are being
dusted, and dormant intellectual traditions (and nontraditional notions
of selfhood) are getting a new lease on life.

Yet, this is hardly a novel phenomenon. It has been years in the
making and is a truth evident to many Middle Easterners. But the Western world's infatuation with terse, neatly essentialist labels—like the generic "Arab" or "Muslim" worlds—and their long brilliant academic
and journalistic careers, have tended to blunt the realities of a diverse,
multiform Middle East.

Long before the creation of the Syrian Republic in 1936 (the precursor of today's unraveling "Syrian Arab Republic"), indeed long before the establishment of any of the modern Arab-defined states in the
Middle East, Lebanese intellectual and activist Antun Saadé, founder
of the Syrian Social Nationalist Party (ca. 1932), advanced a unique
conception of Syrian identity as an Aramaic crucible and synthesis of
many cultures, civilizations, ethnic, and linguistic communities; a rich
tapestry of Levantine peoples—Canaanite Phoenicians and Hebrews,
Aramaeans and others—who could not be defined as "Arabs" without
oversimplifying and misleading. Saadé urged his Syrians to "completely
do away with the myth that they are [Arabs], and that their destiny is

somehow linked to the destiny of the [Arab] peoples. We, the Syrians, are not [Arabs]. On the contrary, we are the fountainhead of Mediterranean culture and the custodians of the civilization of that sea which we have transformed into a Syrian sea, whose roads were traversed by our ships, and to whose distant shores we carried our culture, our inventions, and our discoveries."[30] Saadé categorically rejected any claims made by Arabs or Arab nationalists over his geographic and conceptual notion of "Syria" and the "Syrian people." Drawing on his belief in the interaction between biology and geography in molding the spirit and body of the Syrian people, Saadé recognized the diverse racial origins of his *Homo Syriacus;* Syrian identity, he claimed, was a function of the racial fusion of multiple ancient civilizations; "Canaanites, Akkadians, Chaldaeans, Assyrians, Aramaeans, Hittites, and Metannis."[31] But this hybrid Syrian crucible, in Saadé's view, had at best a negligible "Arab" component; one that did not warrant mention, let alone did it deserve the dominant place it occupies today.

Adonis is perhaps the most notable Middle Eastern intellectual who has made the case for a composite Syrian identity as imagined by Saadé some eighty years prior. Known primarily by his *nom de plume,* Adonis was born Ali Ahmad Said Ispir in the Alawite village of Qassabin. A secluded hamlet wedged between the Syrian port city of Latakia—the ancient Greco-Roman Laodicea—and the Assad family's fiefdom of Qardaha in the Alawite Mountains, Qassabin rests on the lower northern confines of the geological fold known as "Mount Lebanon" further south. Not unlike his Alawite birthplace teetering above an ancient Phoenician promontory wading deep into the Mediterranean Sea, Adonis is the outcome of a conflation of geographic, cultural, ethnic, and linguistic elements. Even his given name and surname reflect the crossbreed of traditions and historical memories that arguably define him and the land of his birth: "Ali" betrays Alawite, possibly Shi'ite ancestry, and "Ispir," of mixed Greek and Turkish etymology, is a likely reference to an eastern Anatolian town by the same name in Erzurum Province.[32] Interestingly, although the Turkish name of a Turkish region, Erzurum's etymology issues from the Arabic cognate *Ard el-Rum,* literally meaning "the land of the Romans," which is to say "the land of the Christians," which Arab, and later Turkic Muslims would come to conquer. Given this checkered background, Adonis's intellectual trajectory, eluding Arabism and bending barriers of language culture and geography, was perhaps not too difficult to forecast.

To begin with, the Qassabin into which Adonis was born in 1930 had not yet become Syrian, and so, neither had young Ali himself. Indeed, Syria as we know it today, a state established by the French in 1936 and granted independence in 1944, had its beginnings as four autonomous entities carved out of the Ottoman *vilayet*s (or states) of Beirut and Damascus, reflecting to some extent an Ottoman administrative precedent. Those early "Syrian" states—or rather, what became Syria in 1944—were the État de Damas, État d'Alep, État Djébel Alaouite, and État Djébel Druze. What is more, the Alawites of the first half of the twentieth century, and most notably among them Suleiman al-Assad, grandfather of the current president of the Syrian Arab Republic, had passionately lobbied French Mandatory authorities and legislators against attaching their autonomous state to a projected Syrian Federation. A November 1923 open letter addressed to French Deputy Maurice Barrès revealed the Alawites' *desiderata* and bespoke their apprehensions of an impending united "Syrian" entity. "It is with immense gratitude," wrote Bachar al-Assad's grandfather, "that we applaud [Barrès's] unfailing defense and advocacy on behalf of our nascent Alawite State; a young State which some seek, unjustly, to attach to a future Syrian Federation, oblivious to the will of the overwhelming majority of our people. [. . .] We urge you [Maurice Barrès] and the French National Assembly to take all measures necessary to safeguard our continued and complete autonomy, under the auspices of French protection, and we ask that you kindly accept our heartfelt appreciation and our warmest thanks [for your efforts on our behalf]."[33] The Syrians were too ethnically fragmented to merit a single unitary state, argued the Alawites of the early twentieth century, and they warned the French repeatedly that the abolition of the Mandate regime would leave the Alawites prey to annihilation by Muslim mobs.[34] "The Alawite people [. . .] appeal to the French government," wrote an impassioned Suleiman al-Assad in June 1936 "to guarantee [. . .] their freedom and independence within their small [Alawite] territory."[35]

And so, not unlike the land of his birth, stitched together in a patchwork of varied geographical and cultural fabrics, Adonis is "a child of the catacombs";[36] a hybrid and a conflation of cultural legacies, ethnic accretions, and geological deposits seldom compatible with prevalent paradigms. He was an Alawite, turned Arab, then Syrian, then a post-Arab and post-Syrian shoring up new identities, unhindered by the barriers of his time's ideological, conceptual, and spatial orthodoxies. Indeed, Ali Ahmad Said Ispir's chosen name, Adonis, a Hellenized form of the Canaanite-Phoenician Tammuz—the shepherd-hunter god of fertility and eternal youth and renewal—carried with it a set of beliefs reflecting an iconoclastic, nontraditional approach to identity, memory, language, and history; an approach informed to a large extent by Adonis's own surroundings and his people's ancient legacies, but one also influenced by Antun Saadé's Syrian Social Nationalist Party (SSNP), of which Adonis would remain a card-carrying member until 1960.

Some have even claimed the very name Adonis was bestowed upon the poet by Antun Saadé himself. In an anecdote related by Sadiq Jalal al-Azm, Saadé is said to have made a stopover at Qassabin during a 1947 "pastoral visit" to the Syrian coast—the Mediterranean lungs of his proposed Syrian nation.[37] Adonis, then still a young Ali, alongside a group of local SSNP partisans, formed the welcoming company sent to acclaim the visiting "Zaim" (Ar. "Leader"). Saadé, a gifted and charismatic orator in his own right, was reportedly smitten by the poetic tribute that young Ali had delivered in his honor. But upon learning that the name of his budding bard from Qassabin was Ali, Saadé was said to have exclaimed that "Ali ought not be your name; you are a testament to our nation's authenticity and genius and ancient pedigree; your name ought to reflect that; it ought to be Adonis, not Ali; a symbol of our vigor, our rebirth, and our eternal renewal."[38]

It matters little whether this story of Adonis's "coronation" is true or not. What matters is that the poet's intellectual trajectory lived up to the reputation of his Greco-Canaanite namesake and patron-god. Unlike most Arabic-language poets of his generation, and certainly unlike contemporary "Muslim" poets, Adonis was personally, artistically, and emotionally invested in the symbolisms and humanism of Christianity,

Canaanite mythology, and ancient Levantine pagan cycles of life, death, and renewal. His mood, often evoking funereal lamentations, was simply a prelude to an ever impending rebirth; a foundation of Christianity's triumvirate—not to say Canaanite paganism's trinity—of suffering, death, salvation, and resurrection. "What concerns me is that my [work] be visionary," wrote Adonis, "that it engages in spawning a new society, a new culture, a new civilization, and a new language. [. . .] If poetry is not in a constant state of renewal, it is dead poetry, written in a dead language that is no longer capable of communing with the word, with the language of life and motion."[39]

Producing a new language, a new society, and a new culture that recognized the region's textured identities is a fundamental necessity for the dignity of man in the Middle East, argued Adonis. Arabism, he claimed, a mere extension of religious fundamentalism's ethos of insularity and intolerance, and an obsessive preoccupation with issues of "roots," "authenticity," and "the evil that the 'others' do," devalues human existence.[40] Arabs have an obligation to recognize their shortcomings, and recognize the history and narratives of the "other" among them, just as they may deem their own history and their own narratives legitimate and worthy of recognition; they must recognize their region's diversity as a fountainhead of vitality rather than rendering it a continuous source of conflict.[41]

In the end, claimed Adonis, it is the Arabic language itself, its rules of conduct, its prosody, and its obsolete assumptions that confine man to a cloistered existence.[42] "Bury the ignoble face of Arab history, and lay to rest its dull heritage and traditions," he urged, already during the 1950s and 1960s.[43] This ruthless assault on the sacred icons of a culture was Adonis's way of challenging Arab nationalist pieties; a way of slaying all elements of a previous existence and engaging new, dynamic, regenerated non-Arab and pre-Arab referents. "The magic of Arab culture has ended [. . . and] I am puzzled, my country," he wrote:

> For, each time I see you, you will have donned a different form,
>
> . . .
>
> Are you a graveyard or a rose?
> I see you as children, dragging their entrails behind them,
>   resigned,

Bowing obediently before their shackles,
Wearing for each crack of the whip a corresponding skin [. . .]

. . .

You have killed me, my country,
You have killed my songs.
Are you a bloodbath or a revolution?

. . .

And I chant my own calamity.
And I can no longer see myself,
Save as a man on the fringes of history, teetering on a razor's
    edge.
I should hope to begin a new beginning.
But where?
From where?
How shall I describe myself and in which of my languages I ought
    to speak?
For, this [Arabic] language that suckles me, also cheats and
    betrays me.
I shall embalm and purify her,
And resurrect myself on the edge of a time that has passed,
Walk on the edge of a time that is yet to come.[44]

Apocalyptic, harsh fighting words, issuing from one of the most celebrated and most widely read Arabic-language poets of modern times;
a devastating indictment that also condenses the Canaanite myth of
Tammuz-Adonis, a myth of rebirth and regeneration. It is arguably an
invitation to relinquish an outmoded cultural ethos, destructive identity frameworks, and crippling national neuroses, so as to "resurrect"
once more a scintillating Levantine mosaic.

Levantine Hybridity: The Retreat
from Sectarian Nationalism

The shift from Arab nationalism and its narrow outlook on society toward a more diverse paradigm that recognizes multiple poles of identity
is identifiable in the history of several key countries across the region.

This includes Egypt and Lebanon, both of which went through a phase of dominant Arab national and cultural identity, only to be bitterly disappointed with the ideology of Arab nationalism, which did not live up to its promises. The move away from Arab nationalism may yield a more sincere and clear-throated recognition of the region's pluralist setting, which may in turn leave room for alternative frameworks no longer beholden to a dominant narrative. Such a setting invokes the concept of the Levant.

Stemming from the Latin verb *levare* (to rise) and by way of its French cognate noun *levant* (an abbreviation of *soleil levant*, "rising sun"), Levant is the term used traditionally in reference to Mediterranean lands east of Italy and Southern France. And although geographically part of the Middle East, and of crucial importance to the expansion of the Arab-Muslim civilization during the seventh century, it may be simplistic and misleading to view the Levant as the exclusive preserve of Arabs and Muslims alone.[45]

The Levant, wrote Fernand Braudel, the intellectual father of Mediterraneanism, is a great cultural and civilizational "turntable": it is a place where peoples get "caught up in a general tide of creative progress," where "civilization [...] spreads regardless of frontiers," where "a certain unity [gets] created among [...] countries and seas," and where, beyond the violence and bloodshed there, emerges "a story of more benign contacts: commercial, diplomatic, and above all cultural."[46] And so, culturally and sociologically speaking, Levant and Levantinism came to mean a cosmopolitanism blurring (or rather straddling and bridging) various ethnic, linguistic, and religious barriers, where "all kinds of exchanges were possible [in] artifacts, techniques, fashions, taste, and of course people."[47] There were many geographic and cultural conditions that had made this legendary Levantine cosmopolitanism a possibility—indeed even a necessity—claimed Braudel. But most importantly, he wrote, there was a dauntless "spirit of curiosity, [...] verging on an obsession with everything that was foreign," that animated the Levantine type and begat what can be called a uniquely Levantine topos.[48]

Perhaps the most definitive depiction of the Levant was that of one of its unlikeliest proponents, Kamal Jumblat, Lebanon's preeminent socialist and champion of Arab causes. Yet, going against his Arabist grain,

Jumblat still portrays the Levant in terms reminiscent of Braudel's, as "the birthplace of the first City-State, the first national idea, the first maritime empire, and the first representative democratic system [. . .] at a time when early humanity was still stumbling clumsily through its very first footsteps. Very near to this Mediterranean Sea, which radiated in the grandeur and reason of Sidon, Byblos, Tyre, Carthage, Alexandria, Athens, Rome, Constantinople, Beirut, and Cordoba [. . .]; here on this very unique spot in the world, where the Mountain and the Sea meet, frolic, and embrace, [one finds] the homeland of humanism; receptive and open to all of the world's intellectual currents."[49] In its modern incarnation, Jumblat's Levant had the added task of transmitting to the West the faintest pulsations of the East, as had been its immemorial calling to interpret "the life ripples of the Mediterranean, of Europe, and of the universe [. . .] to the [Eastern] realms of sands and mosques and sun."[50] "Such is an element of 'Eternal Truth,'" claims Jumblat.[51]

In Lebanon, this Levantine conception of identity was generically referred to as "Phoenicianism" during the early twentieth century, and as "Lebanonism" more recently, beginning in the early 1950s. Exponents of both schools of thought were largely young Francophone poets, playwrights, businessmen, and diplomats, who ascribed to their loose association the sobriquet of "Jeunes Phéniciens" ("Young Phoenicians").[52] Those latter-day Phoenicians viewed the modern Lebanese as a singular, unique, complete nation, descendants of the Canaanite seafarers of antiquity, unrelated to the more recently arrived Arab conquerors. They are described most exquisitely by one of their youngest cantors, the doyen of French-language Lebanese literature, Charles Corm. "From the remotest antiquity, when they were still known as Canaanites, and later as Phoenicians," writes Corm, "the Lebanese people have created, preserved, defended, affirmed, and advanced an expansive and liberal civilization with universal impulses and predilections so accessible to other peoples, to the point that some of those, even the loftiest and brightest among them, had come to assimilate these attributes of Lebanese civilization as if they were their own, adopting and identifying them with their own national genius."[53] Like their ancient forefathers, Corm's Young Phoenicians were skilled mariners, industrious traders, intrepid explorers, gifted teachers, inspired inventors, shrewd bankers,

and subtle intermediaries who valued linguistic humanism and practiced cultural fluidity with striking finesse and competence. The *Revue
Phénicienne,* a cultural and literary journal founded by Corm in 1919,
became the Young Phoenicians' mouthpiece and their main political
clarion. Its pages featured the works and worldviews of two future Lebanese presidents and a number of distinguished literati, diplomats, and
businessmen—all of whom would become "distinguished" subsequent
to their association with Corm and his journal.[54]

An eminent "graduate" of the *Revue Phénicienne* was none other
than Michel Chiha (1891–1954). A banker, poet, political thinker, con-
stitutional scholar, and diplomat, Chiha was also the coauthor of Lebanon's 1926 constitution, which consecrated and codified the country's
hybrid, cosmopolitan identity and its liberal cultural fluidity. Like his
younger mentor Charles Corm, Chiha was an exquisite exponent of
multiple identities, advocating for an expansive, syncretistic, humanist
approach to selfhood, rather than one defined by "oneness" and cultural
dogmatism. He wrote that a mere thirteen centuries of Arab domination
in the Middle East were not nearly enough to make the Lebanese oblivious to, or dismissive of, the fifty centuries that preceded the Arabs.[55]
"Even if relying purely on conjecture," argued Chiha, "the blood, the
civilization, and the language of today's Lebanese cannot possibly be
anything if not the legacy and synthesis of fifty centuries of progenitors
and ancestors" preceding and superseding the Arabs.[56]

For Chiha, Corm, and the Young Phoenicians, Lebanon and the
entire Levantine littoral were a diverse, multiform, polyglot, bastardized
cocktail of cultures and languages; a conception of identity that valued
composite, complex patchworks of ethnicities and historical memories;
a millennial universe of varied civilizations, where peoples and times
blended without dissolving each other, and where languages and histories fused without getting confused with one another. Lebanon and the
Levant, wrote Chiha, "are the meeting-place into which peoples flock
and assimilate regardless of their origins. [They are] the crossroads
where varied civilizations drop in on one another, and where bevies of
beliefs, languages, and cultural rituals salute each other in solemn veneration. Lebanon [and the Levant are] above all Mediterranean constructs, but like the Mediterranean itself, [they remain] discerning and

sensitive to the stirring music of universal poetry."[57] The importance of the Young Phoenicians lay, not simply in their advocacy of hybrid, multilayered identities, but also in their remarkable humanistic, flexible conception of identity, which while opposed to essentialist Arabism, did not disown the Arabs or their rich cultural, linguistic, and literary patrimony. Indeed, Chiha was passionate about the preservation of the Arabic language in the pantheon of Lebanese, Levantine, and Mediterranean polyglossia—from his perspective, a splendid addition to Lebanon's vaunted cosmopolitanism. What Chiha and other Phoenicianists repudiated, however, was linguistic dogmatism, national rigidity, and cultural parochialism. Arabic is a wonderful language, affirmed Chiha;

> it is the language of millions of men. We wouldn't be who we are today if we, the Lebanese of the twentieth century, were to forgo the prospects of becoming Arabic's most accomplished masters to the same extent that we had been its masters some one hundred years ago. . . . [How] can one not heed the reality that a country such as ours would be literally decapitated if prevented from being bilingual (or even trilingual if possible)? . . . [We must] retain this lesson if we are intent on protecting ourselves from spiteful [monolingual] nationalism, and its inherent self-inflicted deafness [to other languages], an affliction that leads to assured cultural mutism.[58]

This is one of the most exquisite celebrations of cosmopolitanism and forceful rejections of nationalist jingoism that one might find. What's more, the Young Phoenicians' intellectual heirs abound in modern Lebanon, despite a prevalent image of the country as a bastion of authoritarianism dominated by Hezbollah and the like. Francophone Lebanese novelist Amin Maalouf, mentioned earlier, in the prolegomena, is chief among the modern representatives of Levantine-Phoenicianist thought, where the overarching leitmotif remains multiplicity and hybridity.

Speaking of Leo Africanus, a fifteenth-century character in his eponymous novel, Maalouf described his hero's anthropomorphic Levant—and by association his tiny Lebanon, which he held to be a microcosm of the larger Middle East—as an elegant cosmopolitan mongrel, and a splendid cultural protean. His *carte de visite,* which bears repeating from the prolegomena, presented him as follows:

> I, Hassan, the son of Muhammad the scale-master; I, Jean-Léon de Médiçi, circumcised at the hands of a barber and baptized at the hands of a Pope, I am now called the African, but I am not from Africa, nor from Europe, nor from Arabia. [. . .] I come from no country, from no city, from no tribe. I am the son of the road; a wayfarer. My homeland is the caravan; my life the most spectacular of pathways, the most riveting of travels. [. . .] From my mouth you will hear Arabic, Turkish, Castilian, Berber, Hebrew, Latin, and Italian vulgates, because all tongues and all prayers belong to me. But I belong to none.[59]

Not unlike his Lebanese-Christian author, the presumably Muslim Arab-Moorish European Catholic named Hassan was neither Arab, nor African, nor even European; he was a composite cosmopolitan polyglot, who was intimately at home with the cultures and ways of Europeans, Africans, and Arabs alike, and who wielded all of their languages and cultural rituals with the ease and affection of a native. Like his author, Leo could not be reduced to a single, politically soothing national label. He was, as Maalouf would subsequently describe himself in his 2004 self-narrative, *Origines,* a man of illusive ancestry,

> the child of a tribe of eternal vagabonds, wandering off endlessly in a limitless desert, wide as the universe is infinite; a native of oases perpetually abandoned, always in search of greener pastures and faraway harbors; [. . .] a holder of varied nationalities that are only a function of random dates in time, or another steamship setting off on a new voyage; sharing only one common denominator [with members of my own family]; a common denominator beyond the generations, beyond the open seas, and beyond the Babel of languages that are mine and my people's appanage. [. . .] Akin

to the Ancient Greeks, my identity is grounded in mythology that I know to be false, but a mythology that I revere regardless, as if it were the only true bearer of my only truth.[60]

"I was born on a planet, *not* in the strict confines of this or that country," noted one of Maalouf's characters in *Les Désorientés*.[61] Of course, he admitted, he *had* to be born in a country as well, in a city, a communal group, and a family. But being "born" in Maalouf's telling is "coming into being," as it were; it is *venir au monde* or "coming into the world," as he aptly put it, not *venir dans un pays* or "coming into a country."[62] Maalouf admits that it is Lebanon—and its Levantine bailiwick and vantage point—that imbued him with this sort of universalism and capacious notion of identity. In his mind's eye, even in the bustle of his adoptive Parisian sanctuary, Maalouf still imagined himself lulled by the Levant, dangling between the rounded summits of the Lebanese mountains and the boundless maritime stretches of their Mediterranean conflations.[63] Even in the thick of war, in the heat and urgency of escaping the Levant, Maalouf still surrendered to its pull and its universalism.

But Lebanon and the Lebanese were not alone in brandishing and celebrating this form of Levantine cosmopolitanism. Early twentieth-century Egyptians trotted out similar themes; namely a "Pharaonic" identity model championed most notably by Taha Husayn (1889–1973), but by others as well. Considered by many the doyen of modern Arabic *belles lettres*, Husayn still claimed Egypt to the millennial tradition of the ancient Mediterranean Levant—even a European Levant—*not* a more recent Arab ancestor. Not only was Egypt a contributor to this ebullient Mediterranean cultural blend, argued Husayn, it was indeed the crucible, progenitor, and cradle of Western civilization.[64] Egypt is not the outcome of some Eastern sand maiden, he wrote in his magnum opus, *The Future of Culture in Egypt;* the Egyptians have had "regular, peaceful, and mutually beneficial relations only with the Near East and Greece"—that is to say with the Syro-Phoenician and classical worlds of the Levant—*not* with the Arab-Muslim world further east.[65]

This is a theme adopted more recently by Egyptian playwright Ali Salem (1936–2015), who, like his mentor Husayn, was wary of confining his country's age-old identity to a narrow, exclusivist Arabism. "Egypt is the child of the Mediterranean," professed one of Salem's characters when challenged by an Arab nationalist opponent decreeing Arab oneness and uniformity.[66] "One day," claimed Salem's Pharaonic protagonist, "thousands of years ago, this [Mediterranean] sea was just a lake, crossed by [Egyptian] ships loaded with thoughts and art toward Greece, carrying the product of minds and souls, returning from there, loaded with other products of minds and souls."[67] Egyptians cannot be expected to privilege their recent Arab ancestors and disown their Pharaohs, their distant original forefathers, argued Salem.[68] "The Arabs are my fathers," he wrote in response to an Arabists' exhortation that he embrace a domineering Arab identity, "but the [ancient] Egyptians are my forefathers; do you advise me to inherit from my fathers and ignore the treasures left to me by my forefathers?"[69] The answer from Salem's Arab interlocutor came discharging an ominous decree, one as if taken straight out of Sati' al-Husri's playbook: "I don't advise you," said he, "I order you!"[70]

Despite being savaged by unreformed proponents of Arabism, Salem's remains a remarkably relevant model of identity; not only because it aims to rehabilitate and commune with an ancient, neglected, culturally flexible ancestor, but more importantly because it seeks to subvert an overbearing, compulsory, often aggressive nationalist discourse as advocated by Arabism. And there is the rub: this innocuous, humanistic conception of selfhood has a charming parallel in modern-day Israel; an Israel which, ironically, in Arab nationalist discourse is often depicted as uniform, aggressive, colonialist, domineering, irredentist.

Israeli Levantinism

As a 2009 study by Alexandra Nocke makes clear, the "place of the Mediterranean" as a space of Levantine hybridity and fluid identities has been a conspicuous theme in modern Israeli literary productions and conceptions of selfhood.[71] Even in pre-state years, when few in the *Yishuv* ("Settlements") would readily have challenged the Zionist enterprise, a "Canaanite movement" consistent with Adonis's approach to identity, and boasting convictions akin to those of the Young Phoenicians of Lebanon and the Young Pharaohs of Egypt, attempted to advance a "cultural nationalist" narrative of a multilayered Israeli identity integrating the disparate populations of the Fertile Crescent: Jews, Arabs, Christians, and others.

To be sure, Canaanism sought to replace the Jewish attributes of Israel with a Levantine crossbreed identity meaningful to the Jews of the Yishuv, but also inclusive of local Druzes, Christians, and even Arab-Muslims. The children of the Levant—or the Land of Kedem as the "Young Hebrews" called it—were ultimately Canaanite Hebrews. They were Arabized, Christianized, some even Judaized over the millennia; but in the end they all belonged to the same Canaanite-Hebrew nation, a nation now rent asunder by the relatively recent impieties of Judaism, Christianity, and Islam. In sum, what Canaanism advocated was a commingling of Levantine identities, and their fusion into a single native Canaanite essence.

One of the most eloquent exemplars of this spacious conception of Israeli identity came in a 1972 novella, *The Orchard*, by Benyamin Tammuz (1919–89.) In this fictional narrative, Tammuz told the story of two brothers, Daniel and Obadiah (later Arabized into Abdallah), one Jewish, the other Muslim, both battling over an orchard in the land of Israel during the period spanning the downfall of the Ottoman Empire and the Israeli-Egyptian war of 1956. *The Orchard* was also the tale of two brothers fighting for the favors of a mystical woman, Luna, also symbolizing the land. Luna is depicted as a radiant halo, ageless, haunting, mysterious; born to Jewish parents but raised in the household of a Turkish Muslim landowner from pre-Mandate "Palestine." *The Orchard*'s story is one of love, violence, and loss; but it is also the story of brotherhood and hope, and the triumph of history and memory over forgetfulness.

Uncertainties abound in *The Orchard*. The reader is constantly pressed into questioning the protagonists' origins and motives. Is Luna Jewish? we are prompted to ask. Is she a Muslim? Was her son the offspring of Daniel or Obadiah/Abdallah? Was Obadiah truly a Muslim? A half-Muslim? A half-Jew? Does it matter? In the end, the narrator tells us that all these questions are for naught; that it doesn't really matter who

is what; that all of *The Orchard*'s protagonists were the offspring of the
Land of Canaan, children of the same Levantine cultural enigma:

> Whether [Luna] was a child of a Jew or a Muslim, for her I
> was both; for I was of the first [new Jewish] settlers and spoke
> the language of the Arabs like one of them. With the passage
> of time, my face had grown tanned and my skin sunburned,
> and I looked like one of the Arab fellaheen, who are perhaps
> the surviving traces of those primitive Jews who never went
> into exile and gradually became assimilated with the coun-
> try's Muslim inhabitants. Perhaps Luna thought that I was
> the ancient link connecting Obadiah's race to Daniel's; for, if
> truth be told, she, in her deafness and dumbness, faithfully
> served both together, sharing her favors between them—if
> not equally, then according to the degree of the demands and
> firmness of each, according to their changing temperaments
> during the changing days.[72]

This pleasing definition of the Levant and Levantine complexity is ri-
valed perhaps only by Amin Maalouf's description of Leo Africanus,
mentioned earlier. Regardless, this is an identity theme that continues
to preoccupy Israelis of the twenty-first century as well.

In a recently published collection of papers and short stories by
(relatively unknown) Egyptian-French-Israeli essayist Jacqueline Kahanoff (1917–79),[73] Deborah Starr and Sasson Somekh suggest that Levantine fluidity and hybridity have had their champion in the State of Israel.
Kahanoff, write Starr and Somekh, in the early 1950s had already begun
envisioning a solution to the Arab-Israeli conflict; a solution culled
from the confines of her native Egypt, where Jews, Muslims, Christians,
Greeks, Syrians, Arabs, and others had lived together for centuries in
peace and harmony, celebrating their multi-ethnic heterogeneity and
partaking of each other's languages and cultural rituals without even
being conscious of their differences. As a child in Egypt, wrote Kahanoff, "I believed that it was only natural for people to understand each
other even though they spoke different languages, for them to have different names—Greek, Muslim, Syrian, Jewish, Christian, Arab, Italian,

Tunisian, Armenian—and at the same time be similar to each other."[74] Like the Israel of her old age, the Egypt of Kahanoff's youth was a symbiosis of religions, national origins, languages, and histories that were all uniquely Levantine.[75] It was nationalism, and in the case of once cosmopolitan Egypt, it was Arab nationalism of the 1950s that brought an end to Levantine diversity: under Nasser, "the idea of a liberal, pluralistic Egyptian nationalism which included the non-Moslems and was accepted by them had died," lamented Kahanoff in 1973.[76] And she was not lamenting a utopia, but indeed a smothered reality. After all, the liquidation of Middle Eastern cosmopolitan societies had been a generational feature of an Arab nationalism dedicated to cultural homogeneity. In Egypt, this meant the destruction of old venerable Italian, Greek, French, and Syro-Lebanese Christian expatriate communities— in addition to a millennial Jewish society—which had once constituted the core of Egyptian culture and its urbane Levantine ecumenical way of life.

From Kahanoff's perspective the Middle East will know peace *only* by recovering the halcyon times of capacious ecumenical Levantine identities, where Arabs, Jews, and others lived together in friendship, and where hybridity and pluralism were celebrated elements of unity and overriding parameters of selfhood.[77] Likewise, Kahanoff intimated that Israel itself may never find peace unless Zionism—in her telling, a natural companion of Arabism—came to terms with its own Middle Eastern essence and in turn integrated Levantine hybridity.[78]

The guiding spirit behind Kahanoff's intellectual journey had seen Israel as "an integral part of the Mediterranean or Levantine world, a vision that was very much an intimate part of her life."[79] She incarnated most exquisitely the hybridity and cultural flexibility of a model intellectualized by Fernand Braudel, the architect of the idea of a Mediterranean "continent" as "cultural stew; [. . .] a sea ringed round by mountains [. . .] the flesh and bones of a shared Mediterranean identity."[80] However, to claim, as do Starr and Somekh, that Kahanoff might have singlehandedly developed the social model of "Levantinism" may be a bit of a stretch; especially when the Levant of her time—namely the Levant of her native Egypt, and later her adoptive Israel—had already been brimming with syncretistic notions of Pharaonic, Phoenician,

Canaanite, and Mediterranean identities, long before she had set out on her own Levantine experiment.

Born in Egypt to an Iraqi-Jewish father and a Tunisian-Jewish mother, Jacqueline Kahanoff was raised in the port city of Alexandria, and grew up proud of her hybrid Mediterranean pedigree. Like many Christian and Jewish minorities of her generation, issuing from Ottoman coastal centers like Izmir, Alexandria, or Beirut, Kahanoff was intimately acquainted with her own city's maritime conflations, touched by its fluidity, a gifted polyglot at home in several of its languages— possessing a native knowledge of a number of Arabic vernaculars, and also knowing some French, Hebrew, Italian, Turkish, and English— and she straddled multiple cultures and multiple religious traditions. So, Kahanoff's intimation that Israel "become part of the Middle East" was a reflection of her background, the outcome of her upbringing and the human space in which she came of age. Most importantly, this attitude represented the cosmopolitan ethos of Kahanoff's times, already expounded by Lebanese, Syrian, and Egyptian precursors from the 1920s on. Like some of her Mediterraneanist elders, the language of Kahanoff's literary output avoided Arabic and Hebrew, languages that she knew well but which she might have deliberately by-passed due to their political implications and their exclusivist association with Arabist and Zionist political ethos.

Kahanoff's relevance was not that she dared live and utter anti-nationalist—and according to some, even nihilist—precepts. Her relevance, as this anthology will demonstrate, was that the intellectual current she embraced in her work is excavated, rehabilitated, and valorized in modern-day Israel. Israel as "an integral part of the Mediterranean or Levantine world" is not an unorthodox notion. Israel is, after all, *of* and *from* the Middle East, despite its detractors' claims to the contrary, and even if the Zionist ideology that was behind Israel's creation was the outcome of European—rather than Middle Eastern—political tradition. Arabism, the region's prime opponent of Zionism, was also, by the way, equally an outcome of European thought. Still, the rehabilitation of Kahanoff's vision is not an idiosyncrasy—nor, for that matter, is it a repudiation of Zionism and an espousal of an Arab "Middle East." Being Middle Eastern and being Arab are not synonymous. The Middle

East is much more complex than to be relegated to the narrow interpretations of overarching Arab, Muslim, or for that matter Jewish, nationalism. And so, the rehabilitation of Kahanoff can be deemed a "sign of the Times!" It is also a "sign of the Space and Place"; an honest way of heeding history and geography; a recognition of the Middle East's—and the Levant's—cultural and ethnic diversity, beyond the assumptions of twentieth-century nationalism, and past our times' fashionable exuberance in the face of inchoate "Arab Springs" and miscarried "Arab Revolutions."

Reviving Kahanoff and rehabilitating suppressed Levantine identities might be naïf nostalgic yearning for a golden age of hybrid Middle Eastern identities; an era preceding resentful nationalisms, where multiplicity—rather than uniformity—was the dominant social classifier and identifier. But reviving Kahanoff is also a way of communing with the true spirit of the Middle East, and coming to terms with its true essence: an intertwined, multilayered, pantheistic crucible of identities, rather than the prevalent image of a uniform universe of Arabs alone (or for that matter Jews alone) to which advocates of exclusivist identities all too often still cling.

Conclusions: Toward a Pluralist Middle East

As mentioned earlier, there remain a number of stigmas attached to being Levantine; stigmas often plotted by advocates of homogenous identities who deem cultural hybridity incongruous, spurious, nihilistic. Chief among such antagonists was the eminent British-Lebanese historian Albert Hourani—arguably himself a delicious product of the very Levantine cultural amalgam that he might have wished suppressed. Yet, "Being a Levantine," he wrote during the Phoenicianist and Pharaonic heyday, "is to live in two worlds or more at once, without belonging to either; it is to be able to go through all the external forms which indicate the possession of a certain nationality, religion, or culture, without actually possessing any. It is no longer to have one standard of values of one's own; it is to not be able to create but only to imitate; and so not even to imitate correctly, since that also requires a certain level of originality. [Being a Levantine] is to belong to no community and to possess nothing of one's own. [Being a Levantine] reveals itself in lostness, pretentiousness, cynicism and despair."[81] Carping and contemptuous as this characterization might seem, nothing could have depicted the Levantines and their bastardized identities more accurately, and nothing could have flattered them more. The very cosmopolitanism, polyglossia, and urbane sophistication that Hourani derided were elements of pride that intellectuals like Kahanoff, Adonis, Corm, Tuéni, Salem, and others featured in this volume flaunted like a badge of honor.

In 1999, long before the fitful rise and fall of the 2011 "Arab Spring," former Arab-nationalist author and public intellectual Hazem Saghieh published a scathing critique of what he considered outmoded Arab dogmas and delusions. His book *The Swansong of Arabism* is a work of painful introspection, in which he calls for casting aside the jingles of "Arab unity" and discarding the assumptions of "Arab identity." Saghieh urges his former comrades-in-arms to bid farewell to the corpse of the Arab nation.[82] "Arabism is dead," he writes, and Arab nationalists would do well in bringing a healthy dose of realism to their world's changing realities: "They need relinquish their phantasmagoric delusions about 'the Arab world' [. . . and let go of their] damning and outmoded nomenclatures of unity and uniformity [. . . in favor of] liberal concepts such as associational and consociational identities."[83]

To return to Adonis, the now former Arab nationalist wrote an "Open Letter" in 2011 to Syria's embattled dictator, in which he notes that a culture that accepts and privileges Arab identity at the expense of others is a culture doomed to extinction: "A nation consumed by a need for 'oneness' in thought, opinions, language, and belief, is a culture of Tyranny, not singularity; it is a collectivity stunting personal and intellectual enlightenment. [. . .] History beckons to the Arabs to put an end to their culture of deceit; for, [the] states of the Levant are much greater, much richer, and much grander than to be reduced to slavery for the benefit of Arabism [. . .] and no amount of cruelty and violence emanating from Arab nationalists will change the reality that the Middle East is not the preserve of Arabs alone."[84] The 2011 upheavals that rippled through the Middle East, the tenuous realities of the modern Middle East's crumbling patrimonial (Arab) dynasties, the region's striking cultural diversity, and its remarkable intellectual and historical accretions, might very well be the charter of a newly resurrected emergent Levant—a new Middle Eastern state order in the making, but one already dreamed up (and dreamed about) close to a century ago by Israeli, Lebanese, Syrian, and Egyptian Levantines. The hybrid Levantine Middle East, at peace with its diversity and multiplicity, might not materialize for some time. But there is no doubt that it is coming, just as there is no doubt that its suppressor may be breathing its last. "Bring along your axes and follow me," wrote Adonis already in 1972: "Pack up your <Allah> like a dying Arab Sheikh, open a pathway to the Sun away from Minarets, open a book to a child besides the books of musty pieties, [and] cast the dreamer's eye away from Medina and Kufa. Come along with me! *I am not the only one . . .*"[85] In *A Lull between Ashes and Roses* (1972), *The Language's Head, the Desert's Body* (2008), and *Identité inachevée* (Unifinished Identity; 2004), Adonis provides additional indictments of the idea of a "united Arab nation" as "an obscenity and a profoundly flawed and unattainable abstraction."

Interestingly, in *The Language's Head* Adonis relates an encounter with Edward Said in New York, during which Said revealed something to the effect that "the concepts of homeland or fatherland were caricatures and romantic yearnings that did not appeal to me one bit. . . . Indeed, peregrination and wandering off from one place to the next are what I love most about my life," argued Said.[86] Said further called New York "home" precisely "because of its ever-changing, multicolored chameleon-like attributes, allowing one to *belong* to her without issuing from her, and without being enslaved or held captive to her."[87] In that sense (and this is still Said speaking), places where he grew up, Ramallah for instance, left him utterly unmoved, and can hardly be considered a "homeland" to him; whereas Cairo, like New York, gave him a true feeling of "being at home."[88] "Not only is it possible for a man to partake of multiple identities," said Said to Adonis, but "multiplicity, hybridity, and composite identities should be man's very mission and ambition."[89]

Answering to the preceding, Adonis explains why he remains critical of (and even loathes) Arab nationalism, which he calls a "conceited, narcissistic self-love pathology, represented by the Baath Party, which elevated Arabness to the level of a metaphysical postulate bordering on an alternate theology second only to Islam; a theology whereby the non-Arab "other" would amount to nothing more than depravity and evil."[90] Adonis recalled one of his elementary-school history teachers, a Baathist "petty demagogue" named Abdelhamid Darkal, "a hack enthralled with the sound of his own voice, haranguing his charges about Arabism and the authenticity of Arab nationalism, the Arab fatherland, the Arab nation, and its everlasting mission. [. . .] His rants were like earworms, still looping in my head, warning us about "the despicable insects rejecting Arabism, advocating for [so-called] Sumerian, Babylonian, Assyrian, Pharaonic, and Phoenician identities; human vermin that needed be crushed under noble Arab heels."[91] Adonis claims that this sort of cultural and ideological narrowness was among the chief things that drove him into the ranks of the Syrian Social Nationalist Party, for in the late 1940s the SSNP was perceived to incarnate a distinction from the rigidity of the Arab model of nationalism. What made the SSNP attractive to a minoritarian like Adonis was its rigorous secularism, its rejection of racial, ethnic, and linguistic purity as advocated by Arabism, and its celebration of diversity and hybridity. And it was in the context of the SSNP that Adonis would relinquish his given name (Ali) and integrate a pagan—and a no less Greco-Canaanite pagan— moniker; an assault, as it were, on the assumptions and smugness and linguistic postulates of Arabism, and a call for new, expansive, resurrected, multifaceted, and enlightened identities.

Arabism, wrote Adonis, is incompatible with Levantine identities; it is a negationist ethos obsessed with rejecting the "other," denying the legitimacy of the "other," and refusing to reflect on the "other" in language, temperament, and social habits.[92] It is precisely for these reasons that one can no longer write, think, or create in today's Middle East, revealed Adonis. Many of his peers, he claimed, still invested in old Arabist (and of late Islamist) assumptions, "are harkening back to a closed, blinkered, repetitive kind of culture, where there is nary the opening to the outside, where the only 'other' is Evil, Hell, Satan. The prevalent logic is the following: 'You are either like me, or you are nothing.' Distinctness and plurality are not viable options."[93] This is "cultural pollution" par excellence, claims Adonis, whereby Arab thinkers submit to and perpetuate an "intellectual obscurantism" institutionalized by way of symbiotically linked linguistic and religious traditionalism. Adonis's critique of the Syrian regime's brutality, and in equal measure his denunciation of the religious impulses of those rebelling against the regime, were dismissed by some of his opponents as the rantings of someone "disconnected from reality; an elitist bourgeois poet obsessed with removing Islam from the lives of Muslims."[94] Ahmad al-Shuraiqi wrote recently that it is morally reprehensible that Adonis somehow equates and loathes both the brutality of the Syrian regime and the religious zeal that drives some of the insurgents—whom Adonis mockingly has called "the mosque revolutionaries."[95]

Indeed, although Adonis has come out very strongly against the Assad regime, even in early 2011 when the Islamist element was hardly a factor in the Syrian rebellion, he still expressed deep apprehensions toward an impending Islamist takeover, and the possibility of an Islamist theology replacing "secular" Arabist dogma.[96] Adonis's lifelong advocacy on behalf of Levantine hybridity has always presupposed relinquishing all manners of orthodoxy and chauvinism, religious and nationalist alike. He has been unyielding in his defense of change and his opposition to political and religious cultures that "devalue individual freedoms and reject the 'other,' either by casting him off, by blasting him alternately as 'infidel' or 'traitor,' or by simply killing him."[97] The bedrock of Arab and Muslim identities, writes Adonis, is "text and scripture"; religious texts and nationalist scriptures; "it is based on those scriptures that Man in Arab culture is lent legitimacy or is banished; indeed, it is for the sake of those scriptures, and often for the sake of a certain interpretation of those scriptures, that Man is killed—both intellectually and physically."[98]

So, Adonis's apprehensions of an Islamist takeover remain in line with his humanist convictions and his lifelong struggles to rid Middle Eastern societies of orthodoxy. The infatuation of the "loud few" with the "divine unitarianism of nation and culture," he writes, and their fear of a looming, ever-present "humanist earthly [. . .] Levantine essence, is a fated, congenital, enduring essence."[99]

It took Adonis's vision a good forty years to begin materializing, but salvation is perhaps at hand. Pitfalls notwithstanding, *this* vision of Adonis's is the authentic Levantine Middle East that many of its decent children—Arabs and non-Arabs alike—have been dreaming and yearning for. *This* is ultimately the future of the region as imagined by the Levantine thinkers of the early twentieth century. And *this* is what the *Anthology of Modern Levantine Literature* hopes to bring to English readers and students of the Middle East: a rich mosaic of varied cultures, languages, and ethnicities; a "new order" looming on the horizon of "the other" Middle East; a preserve of Arabs and *non*-Arabs alike, who would be ill-served by not heeding their congenital diversity and multiplicity of identities.

Syria

The establishment of a new European-inspired state system in the early twentieth-century Levant brought with it confusion and loss of identity. Citizens of new entities such as Syria, which had no prior experience in self-rule—let alone a historical memory of a distinct "Syrian" political identity—had great difficulty adjusting to new parameters of selfhood and political personality. Peoples in this newly formed entity knew no longer who they were or how to define themselves. The Ottoman millet system, which had governed the empire's disparate ethno-religious communities through administrative units based on religious identities, allocating responsibilities and obligations according to distinct religious and geographic affiliations, no longer obtained with the collapse of the Ottoman order. With this, came the disruption of religiously defined identities and the transition to the concept of a "territorial state" and its modern, largely European, parameters of selfhood. This spawned political and social confusion in an area where the basic social classifier had for centuries been predicated primarily on ethno-religious affiliations.

In Syria more so than in Lebanon or Egypt, this difficulty in accepting, or even attempting to integrate, the transition to a territorial state was most salient. At play was the "artificiality" of an ethnically diverse place like Syria, and the challenges that this artificiality might have posed in devising territorial-historical legitimacy to be shared by all components of the newly formed state. Like the rest of the modern states of the Levant, "contrived points on a map" in Fouad Ajami's telling, joining together disparate peoples, fractious ethno-religious groups, apprehensive confessional communities, and distinct autonomous provinces into uneasy, compulsory, and ultimately unhappy matrimony, was bound to be challenging.

As noted earlier, historically speaking, in what is today the modern Syrian Arab Republic, there has never been a uniquely Syrian territorial identity nor a distinct Syrian entity as such. Indeed, in the newly established state in 1936—cobbled together out of the distinct Ottoman *vilayet*s (or states) of Aleppo, Beirut, and Damascus—there was great difficulty accommodating the transition from autonomous administrative units grounded in Ottoman imperial tradition to a cohesive territorial personality. Moreover, prior to Syrian independence in 1946, there had been very little in terms of national history, territorial attachment, Syrian identity, and a distinct "Syrian" ethos associated with the new Syrian republic. In fact, up until 1946, no such Syrian entity existed in literature, historiography, or even popular expression.

There had, of course, always been the name *Syria*, from classical antiquity until Ottoman times. But this was at best a purely topographic concept and an amorphous one at that, confined to European geographic usage and European obsession with the Eastern Mediterranean. In fact, the name Syria is widely believed to be of Greek, not Syrian or Arab, provenance. Syria is arguably, at least in classical Greek usage, a reference to the place name of those "speakers of Syrian"—or in modern times "Syriac," a dialect of Middle Aramaic prevalent throughout Syria, Lebanon, and Israel of classical antiquity, and widely spoken until at least the eighth century of our era.

Arabs and the Arab nationalists who have ruled the new Syrian entity since independence were themselves newcomers to this name, and could only lay claim to it through semantic trickery and verbal embellishment. *Shaam* is otherwise the name that Arabs bestowed upon "Syria," beginning in the seventh century—that is to say *Shaam* or "North" in southern Arabian usage, as a geographic reference to the "northern territory," and later its capital city, Damascus. Thus, today the

Arabized form of "Syria" (*Suriyya*), used as the official country name, is a toponym imported from Western languages and Western geographic and historical norms.

Likewise Syrian identity, or a sense of "Syrianness" as such, had been alien to the Arabs of Syria, at least until the early twentieth century. Conversely, there had been a strong bent toward Syrianness among Levantine Christian expatriates in the New World, fleeing the vagaries and injustices of the late Ottoman period. But the Syria that emerges from the writings of those émigrés was distinctly Christian, separate from the inchoate Arab nationalist concepts being sputtered in the early twentieth century. Indeed, the term Syria that those Levantine Christians might have used in their literary works, correspondence, and political writings, issued from the language and intellectual heritage of their premodern national churches, which were essentially "Syrian Churches" whose languages were Syriac. "Syria is no more Arab than it is Ottoman," writes Lebanese intellectual Jacques Tabet in 1920. "Syria is Syrian, and Phoenician," he claims, and both "its history and geography attest to that undeniable reality. Today, its aspiration is to become itself again, and to live its own independence and specificity."[1]

Arabs, Turks, and other conquerors can certainly impose their language on the vanquished populations of their newly acquired territories, but Tabet argues they can never impose their own ethnic markers:

> It is well established that the Syrian race maintains to this day a remarkable degree of ethnographic unity. This fact is so true that it is well nigh impossible for an outsider— it is indeed impossible for the Syrians themselves—to note any differences in appearance between the Syrians and the Phoenicians. The Syrians are no less the true descendants of the Phoenicians than the French are descendants of the ancient Gauls. Let their current customs and languages cast no doubt on their true origins! Where is it written that modern nations, Romans, Greeks, Persians, and Egyptians, still wear the clothes and still speak the languages of those from whom they have inherited their lands and their names? Only a difference in manners distinguishes them from their earlier

ancestors, and there is indeed no evidence suggesting that, had the Phoenicians maintained their independence to this day, they would not appear identical to the Syrians today.[2]

It should be noted that, in line with his contemporaries who wrote in both Arabic and French, Tabet spoke of the Phoenicians, the Lebanese, and the Syrians as a single people, using the three ethnonyms interchangeably to mean the same thing.

As this distinct Syrianness began evolving and expanding politically in the early twentieth century, some of its exponents went to great lengths to distinguish it and the concept of "being Syrian" from the nascent contemporaneous idea of "being Arab." One such advocate of Syrian identity, Antun Saadé, wrote that "the Syrians have done away with the myth that they are Easterners [read: Arabs], and that their destiny is somehow linked to the destiny of the [Arab] peoples. We the Syrians are not [Arabs . . . , rather, we] are the fountainhead of Mediterranean culture and the custodians of the civilization of that sea, which we have transformed into a Syrian sea, whose roads were traversed by our ships, and to whose distant shores we carried our culture, our inventions, and our discoveries."[3] This laid down the foundations of the conceptual, geographic, and cultural notion of "Syria" and the "Syrian people" as a crucible of cultures that cannot be folded into a larger "Arab" ethnos without oversimplifying and misleading. And so, when the current Syrian state came into being, and when it later became independent, it was already a profoundly divided entity, beset by deep-seated ethnic apprehensions, religious differences, sectarian animosities, chronic instability, and failed interpretations of the territorial state. In a sense, Syria was bound to disintegrate, and its contrived tenuous unity—predicated on a putative Arab essence—was predestined to come undone. The intransigence of the Arab nationalist Baath Party, and the cruelty of the Assad family who has ruled under its auspices—tenuous as their own Arabist credentials might have been—simply prolonged the afflictions of this unsettled mosaic. Therefore, the dissolution of the Syrian entity had always been a matter of when, *not* why or how.

Like the rest of the Levant, Syria is a mosaic of languages, premodern national churches, sects, and tribes all in a rule-or-die struggle for survival. Already in 1936, cautioning French Mandatory authorities against contemplating the notion of folding an autonomous State of the Alawites—established by the French in 1918—into an envisioned "Syrian Union," Suleiman al-Assad, grandfather of the embattled president of early twenty-first century Syria, wrote to then French Prime Minister Léon Blum, urging him to protect the rights of Alawites and other minorities in the Levant, pleading with him to forestall their inclusion into a projected Syrian federation. "We assure you that treaties have no value in relation to the Islamic mentality,"[4] noted the elder Assad. The Anglo-Iraqi treaty of 1930, he reminded Blum, did not prevent the slaughter of the Assyrians. Suleiman al-Assad wondered "if French leaders want[ed] the Muslims to have control over the Alawi people . . . to throw them into misery? The Alawis refuse to be annexed to Muslim Syria, because, in Syria, the official religion of the state is Islam, [and this] will only mean the enslavement of the Alawite people and the exposure of the minorities to the dangers of death and annihilation. [. . .] The Alawi people appeal to the French government [. . .] and request [. . .] a guarantee of their freedom and independence within their small territory."[5] Certainly one may detect parochial apprehensions in such historical texts. But those apprehensions are scarcely unwarranted or unexplained by historical precedent. As noted earlier in the prolegomena, Isabel Burton summed up the ethnic conundrum of "Syria" as "various religions and sects [living] together more or less, and [practicing] their conflicting worships in close proximity."[6] Burton noted that "outwardly, you do not see much, but in their hearts [the inhabitants of the Vilayet of Damascus] hate one another. The Sunnites excommunicate the Shiahs, and both hate the Druse; all detest the Ansariyyehs [Alawites]; the Maronites do not love anybody but themselves, and are duly abhorred by all; the Greek Orthodox abominate the Greek Catholics and the Latins; all despise the Jews."[7] Writing along those same lines in 1907, another British traveler, Gertrude Bell, noted that Syria was "merely a geographical term corresponding to no national sentiment."[8] This view was echoed by many Levantine contemporaries of Bell, most of whom maintained that, historically speaking, there had never been a distinct Syrian society; that what Europeans referred to as Syria had always been a bevy of disparate groups and loose geographic entities brought together by conquest and ruled forcibly through terror and tyranny; in sum, "a society based on a despotism of brutal force modeled on that of the ruler."[9]

Historians are at their best when they avoid forecasting future events: "I never make predictions," said eminent Oxford historian Charles Issawi, "especially about the future!" Not unwise cautionary words for those untrained to excavate the past and draw lessons for their times. But poets and artists have often been given to poetic license, and Syria's own literati have been producing work alluding to the nebulous nature of their modern state, and perhaps foretelling its unmaking; not because multi-ethnic nation-states are by their very nature doomed to failure, but because inherently multi-ethnic states preening themselves to be unitary, monocultural, and monolingual, must sooner or later come to terms with their diversity, and must find ways to valorize and celebrate that diversity. The authors featured in this section on Syria attempt to do their part in acknowledging textured identities.

∾

NIZAR QABBANI (1923–98)

Recognized as the Arabs' leading feminist, an advocate of women's rights who at times also dabbled with Arab nationalist themes, Nizar Qabbani's post-1967 poetry morphed into anti-Arab "vitriol" as it were; a violent response to the Arabs' defeat in the 1967 Arab-Israeli war, and a virulent indictment of Arab politics, Arab conceits, and Arab phobias.

Qabbani was actually one of very few Arab intellectuals to have referred to this 1967 event as a "defeat," avoiding the traditional escapisms and euphemistic depictions of that trauma as "tragedy," "setback," or "mishap"—that is to say something "written," "fated," and "beyond the Arabs' control." It is worth noting that there exists a tendency, generally among Middle Easterners as a whole, but certainly among Arabs, to avoid calling unseemly events or grim circumstances by their names, as if to exorcise them, ward them off, or wish them away. By way of this sort of semantic witchcraft, verbal talismans of sorts, ominous concerns or negative facts of life are occulted, averted—even if only perceptually and psychologically speaking. Cancer, for instance, is never referred to by name in Arabic, but always by way of circumlocutions and verbal amulets along the lines of "that unnamed illness," or "that which Allah may keep far and away from us."

Physical intimacy and sexuality, at the forefront of the Arabs' taboo topics, are likewise referred to euphemistically. By the same token, the State of Israel is almost never referred to directly by name, but rather through euphemisms and attributes, often derogatory designations such as "the entity" (*al-kayaan*) or "the scourge" (*al-'udwaan*)—again, by way of "protective" amulets as if to exorcise Israel, ward it off, and wish it away.

Qabbani would come to shatter all such manners of taboo, thematically, linguistically, and conceptually speaking. In that sense, he would remain, until his death in 1998, true to his reputation as an engaged feminist and a pungent critic of misogyny and the Arabs' hyper-virile mentality. Yet, his post-1967 works were primarily a frontal assault on most *other* features of modern Arab life, whether in their political, social, linguistic, religious, familial, or intellectual facets. In that sense, Qabbani's work was controversial, rambunctious, combustive. Yet he was also at times part and parcel of the very "establishment" that he sought to dismantle. His stint as a diplomat and an official representative of the Syrian Arab Republic in Spain, Britain, and China perhaps provided him with some immunity to mount his offensive without risking stigma, marginalization, or worse, in a society that did not often take kindly to honest, open criticism.

Qabbani's popularity stemmed not only from his themes, but probably more so from the language that he used. His Arabic paid no heed to the formalisms and grandiloquence that defined the poetry of peers wishing to make for themselves glowing names in the pantheon of Arabic literature. As one observer put it, Arabic *belles lettres* were "not so much a means of expression but an end in itself: A great writer was not measured by the worth of what he said but by his mastery of the language. The language—its nuances, its rhythm—was an instrument of entertainment rather than a medium for transmitting thought and information. Unless liberated from the spell of the language, the Arab would remain a captive of a sterile system of thought."[10] This was not

Nizar Qabbani's poetry. His language was pellucid, accessible, intelligible to both those trained in the rudiments of classical Arabic and those who were not, rendering his work available to literates and illiterates alike. Even as an older seasoned poet, he remained youthful, rebellious, irreverent, brave, iconoclastic, spontaneous, unvarnished, and unconcerned with authority, tradition, *and* the Arabs' hallowed cultural, linguistic, and moral inheritance. That is why he may at times come across as somewhat jarring, sometimes even bordering on lunacy—especially among those beholden to orthodoxy, tradition, and religious and cultural pieties. But Qabbani was a committed and principled poet, who asked difficult questions, shattered idols, and commanded attention and respect without ever pausing to take stock of whether or not the intensity of his work or the vigor of his commitments made others squirm. His poetry was known and appreciated by millions, many of whom often recited it from memory. His books frequently went into ten, twenty, even thirty printings—a phenomenon unheard of in the history of Arabic literature, and one no other Arabic language poet could even dream of competing with. And so, Qabbani must have known that he needed not pause to take stock of whether or not the intensity or pungency of his work (and words) offended, or battered, or bruised orthodoxy and its wardens.

The present selections only scratch the surface of Qabbani's work. But they are supremely representative of his thematic and linguistic choices, spanning some fifty years of frenzied cultural production, and shedding light on a man's complexity by way of a literary medium that was an exemplar of simplicity, transparency, honesty, and depth.

Bread, Hashish, and Moonlight (1954)

When the new moon rises in the Orient,
The white rooftops slumber
Beneath heaps of flowers . . .
And so, people leave their places of employment
And walk out in processions
Toward their date with the moon . . .
They carry off with them their bread rations, their transistor radios,

And their drug paraphernalia . . .
Then they set out to sell and buy fantasies
And imageries,
And they pass out as they swoon
The minute they get a glimpse of the moon.

What does this orb of light
Do to my land?
To the land of the Prophets
And the dimwits,
The land of tobacco chewers
And drug dealers and pushers?

What is it that the moon does to us,
Making us shed our pride,
Making us live for the sole purpose
Of beseeching the heavens?
What have the heavens got for us,
A bunch of idle weaklings
Who pass out
The minute the moon rises,
Weaklings who solicit the graves of Saints
Imploring them
For rice, and children . . .

Then they spread out their elegant soft rugs
And entertain themselves with an opium
Named "fate"
And "destiny,"
In my land . . .
In the land of the dimwits.

What weakness and decay
Take hold of us
The minute the moonlight gushes out . . .
When the rugs, and the thousands of baskets
And tea cups and children
March onto the hilltops,

In my land.
Where the gullible weep,
And live one more day under a light
That they see not,
In my land . . .

Where people live bereft of eyes,
Where the gullible weep,
And pray,
And fornicate,
And live, dependent, submissive, subservient
Ever since they came into being, as a people,
They live dependent, submissive, subservient.

And they go on beseeching the crescent moon:
"O crescent-moon . . .
O spring gushing with diamonds
And hashish and slumbers . . .
O hanging marble divinity,
O object of wonderment,
May you remain ours, the pride of the Orient,
A cluster of diamonds,
For us millions of pinheads.

During those Eastern nights,
When the full moon reaches its apex,
The whole of the Orient sheds its pride,
And gives up the fight . . .

For, those millions, running barefoot . . .
Those millions, advocates of polygamy and four wives,
And believers in the Day of Judgment,
Those millions who know not the bread crumb,
Save in their fantasies,
Those millions who, come night fall,
Dwell in homes made out of coughing . . .
Those millions who know no remedy for their ills,

And render themselves corpses
Under the moonlight.

In my land,
Where the gullible weep,
And die weeping,
Every time they see the face of the crescent moon,
And then they weep and weep some more,
Every time the sound of a contemptible lute moves them,
And the strain and refrain of a *ya leili ya leil,*[11]
That curse, which we, in the Orient,
Describe as "singing" and *ya leil,*
In my land,
In the land of the dimwits . . .

In this land, where we regurgitate
Long drawn-out *tawashih* refrains and recitations,[12]
This plague that lacerates and disables the Orient,
Those long drawn-out refrains and recitations,
That Orient of ours, that is continuously regurgitating old stuff.

Regurgitating History . . .
And idle dreams
And hollow fantasies,
This Orient of ours,
In constant search
For heroics,
In the empty bravado
And bombast
And poetic sabre rattling
Of (Abu Zaid al-Hilaali).[13]

MARGINALIA ON THE NOTEBOOK OF DEFEAT (1967)

My Friends,
I bring you news of the death of our old language,
The death of our old books;

I bring you news of the death of our hollow vocabulary,
And our abusive word-lists of debauchery, defamation, and insult.
I bring you news of the death of the ideas that have led us to defeat.[14]

The taste of poetry is bitter on our tongues,
Bitter are women's tresses as well,
And bitter are our nights, our curtains, and our benches,
Bitter are all things before us.

O, sorrowful fatherland,
You have turned me in an instant,
From a bard of love and yearning,
To a poet carving out verse with a knife.[15]

Because the fears gripping us are larger than the papers that we
    write on,
We must feel ashamed by the futility of our rhymes.

We mustn't be surprised by failures on the battlefield,
For we wage our wars armed with the Oriental's knack for oration and
    verbiage,
Empty bravado, sabre rattling, and boastings,
Which never hurt a fly;
We wage our wars with bombast and the logic of trumpets and drums.

The core of our tragedy is that
Our cries are louder than our voices,
And our swords are taller than our stunted statures . . .

This is the summary of our history:
We have donned the veneer of culture
While our very souls have remained primitive . . .

You can't win a war
Armed with trumpets and drums.

Our obsession with virility and manly spontaneity
Has cost us fifty thousand new tents.[16]

Do not curse out the heavens
For having forsaken you . . .

Do not curse out circumstance.[17]
For Allah gives victory to those who desire it . . .
And you haven't even one blacksmith
Chiseling your swords for you.

It pains me to listen to your news in the morning!
It pains me to hear your bombast and barking!

The Jews did not breach our borders.
Rather, they crept in like ants
Through the cracks of our flaws.

Five thousand years, and we're still languishing in the dungeon,
With overgrown beards, curious and unknown currencies,
And vacant eyes that have become harbors for maggots and flies . . .

My friends,
Do try to break down the doors!
Do try to cleanse your thoughts and wash your clothes!
My friends, do try to read a book!
Better yet, for once, do try to write a book!
Do try sowing letters and pomegranates and grapes!
Do try sailing to the lands of fog and snow . . .
People beyond your dungeons don't know who you are . . .
People beyond your walls think you're some curious breed of beast . . .

Our skins have become numb to pain;
Desensitized.
Our souls are bankrupt.
Our days are spent idly, beholden to stale rituals and witchcraft,
Chess games, or slumbers.
Are we truly
"The Finest Nation Raised Up for Mankind?"[18]

Our oil, gushing out of desert sands,
Could have been rendered a flaming burning dagger
Instead.
Oh, shame of the nobles of Quraysh!
Oh, shame of the houses of Aws and Nizar,[19]

It is being squandered
At the feet of bedmates and concubines . . .

We run up and down the streets, aimlessly,
Sporting ropes under our arms. .
We memorize and regurgitate verses mindlessly.
We shatter windows and smash down doors. .
We praise like frogs,
We curse like frogs. .
We preen our thugs like heroes,
And we dismiss our righteous as crooks and villains . . .
We improvise valor like fools. .
We mill around our mosques,
Torpid, shiftless, indolent . . .
We compose pointless poetry,
We contrive corny proverbs . . .
And we beg Allah to hand us victory and withhold it from our enemy . . .

If someone were to grant me immunity,
If I were allowed to meet with the Sultan,
I would tell him: O my Sultan,
Your wild dogs have torn my cloak,
And your informers are relentlessly after me,
Hounding me
With their eyes hounding me,
With their noses hounding me,
With their feet hounding me,
Like inescapable destiny,
Like fate hounding me,
Interrogating my wife,
Keeping tabs on me,
Drawing a ledger,
With my friends' names on it.

O my Sultan,
Because I dared approach your cruel and deaf high walls,
Because I dared speak my sorrows
And my hardships and afflictions,

I was beaten with a shoe.[20]
Your soldiers made me eat my own shoe,

O lord,
O, my master, Sultan,
Twice you were defeated in war
Because half of our people have no tongue.
What value has the people who have no tongue?[21]
Because half of our people
Are besieged like rats and ants,
Inside the walls.

If someone were to grant me immunity
And keep the Sultan's soldiers away from me,
I would tell him: twice you were defeated in war
Because you abandoned the cause of man.

Had we not buried "unity" in the sand,
Had we not torn her young flesh with our spears,
Had we kept her protected inside our eyelids,
The dogs would not have dared sack us and ravish our flesh [making it
    Halal].

We demand a raging young generation.
We demand a generation capable of plowing the horizons,
Digging up History from its core,
And drilling for new ideas, from the roots up.
We demand a forward-looking generation,
Different-looking, with different features.
Merciless, unforgiving.
Firm, unbending.
A generation bereft of hypocrisy and duplicity.
We demand a
Pioneering generation
Of giants.

Hear ye, O children, "from the Gulf to the Ocean,"[22]
You are the seedlings of hope,
You are the generation that will break our shackles,

And wipe us clean of the opium infusing our heads.
You are the generation that will slay our delusions.

O you children, you are—still—untarnished,
Chaste and pure, like snow and morning dew.
Do not read about our defeated generation,
For we are a failure and a letdown.
We are irrelevant and trivial, like the skins of watermelons.
And we are decayed, like worn-out shoes.

Do not read about us!
Do not seek out our traces!
Do not accept our ideas!
We are the generation of nausea, syphilis, and tuberculosis.
We are the generation of deception and fraud.
O children,
O spring showers,
O seedlings of hope,
You are the embryos of fertility in our barren lives,
And you are the generation that shall conquer our fears
And defeat our defeats . . .

WHEN WILL SOMEONE FINALLY ANNOUNCE
THE DEATH OF THE ARABS? (1994)

I've been trying since my very early beginnings
To sketch out a land I could figuratively call the "Arab World."
{ A homeland that would forgive me
{ Were I to shatter its moon,[23]
(And one that would thank me
(For writing poetry of love,
A land that would allow me to make love
Freely, like birds up on the trees . . .

I've been trying to sketch out a land
That would allow me to always be
Worthy of love and passion,

A homeland that would let me spread out
My lover's cloak before you, in the summertime;
A homeland that would let me dry up your dress after the rains.

I've been trying to sketch out a land
With a parliament redolent with jasmine,
And a tender cultured people, also redolent with jasmine.
I've been trying to sketch out a land
Where doves could slumber over my head, in peace,
A land whose minarets could cry out in my eyes, for peace.

I've been trying to sketch out a land
That could be my poetry's muse,
A land that would not breathe down my neck,
Whose soldiers would not trample my head . . .
I've been trying to sketch out a land
That would reward my poetry,
And would absolve me of my sins
And forgive me my folly . . .

I've been trying to sketch out a land,
A metropolis of love . . .
Free of phobias and inhibitions,
A city on a hill, that would not slay women and womanhood . . .
A city that would not suppress and subdue their bodies . . .

So I moved southward
And I moved north
But I did so all for naught.
For the coffees of all the Arabs' coffee shops
Had the same distinctive blandness . . .
And all of the Arabs' womenfolk,
Should they dare shed their cloak,
All had the same distinctive smell,
And all of my homeland's tribesmen
Turned out to be all the same;
Men who barely chewed their food,
Males who devoured their mates,

In an instant,
The second they laid eyes on them . . .

I've been trying, since my very early beginnings,
To be different from you all,
To shun your stilted pre-packaged language,
To shun your idol worship . . .

I've been trying to set your Texts on fire,
To set ablaze this accursed language that I was made to don,
For some of our poetry is graveyard,
And some of our language funerary shroud.

And so, I set out to go out on a date
With this land's last remaining female,
But alas, I went to our meeting place
Long after time had passed,
Long after she had lapsed.

I've been trying to set myself free from your stifling semantics,
Free from the accursed "Subject and Predicate" . . .[24]
I've been trying to scrub the dust of your dead language off of my skin,
Cleanse my face with rainwater . . .
And free myself form the tyranny of your scorching sands . . .

So long Quraysh,[25]
So long Kulayb,[26]
So long Mudar. . . .[27]

I've been trying to sketch out a land
I could figuratively call the "Arab World."
A place where I could have a permanent pillow under my head,
A permanent bed;
A place where I could hang my hat,
And learn the difference between peregrinations
And homeland . . .

But alas, they took away my paintbrush and sketchbook,
And they prevented me from drawing
The features of this fatherland . . .

I've been trying, since my very early childhood,
To spawn a space filled with jasmine.
So I set up a "lovers' sanctuary,"
The first of its kind in the history of the Arabs,
A place intended to be welcoming of lovers,
And I erased all the ancient wars
Between women and men,
Between doves and those who slay doves,
And between the marble and those who lacerate the whiteness of
     marble . . .
But alas, they shuttered my "lovers' sanctuary,"
They told me that passion was unbecoming of the Arabs and their
     history,
Unbecoming of the Arabs and their chastity,
Unbecoming of the Arabs and their patrimony;[28]
Amazing those Arabs, aren't they!!

I've been trying to imagine
The exact shape of my homeland's features!
I've been trying to reclaim my space
In my mother's womb,
Trying to swim against the tides of Time . . .
Trying to furtively pick figs
And peaches
And almonds off of trees,
And soar up high, free as a bird taking flight,
Racing with ships over the waves.

I've been trying to imagine
The Garden of Eden,
And how I would spend Eternity there,
In the Garden of Eden,
Frolicking in rivers of ruby,
Bathing in rivers of milk . . .[29]

But then I awoke
To discover the silliness of my dream . . .
For, there is no moon in the sky of Ariha,[30]

And there is no fish in the waters of Furat,[31]
And no coffee in Aden . . .

Through poetry, I've been trying to
Grapple with the impossible . . .
I've been trying to plant date-palms,
But people in my land
Uproot the date-palms . . .

I've been trying to make our horses' neighs
Resound louder, higher,
But our city dwellers abhor horses and disdain their noble cries . . .

I've been trying to love you my beloved,
To love you clear of all rituals,
Past all Texts,
And outside all Shari'as and systems of law . . .
I've been trying to love you my beloved . . .
Even in my exile, I've been trying to love you,
So that, as I pressed your body against my own,
I might have felt like being in the embrace of my native soil.

I've been trying ever since my early childhood
To read anything I could get my hands on, telling the stories
Of Arab Prophets . . .
Arab Sages . . .
And Arab Poets . . .
But I found no poetry
Save the empty flatteries and hollow panegyrics of the Caliph's
    bootlicks,
So-called poets, obsequious men, demeaning themselves and their
    craft
For a pathetic handful of rice . . .
For a miserly fistful of pennies.[32]
Amazing those Arabs, aren't they!

Still, I saw nothing by tribes
That could barely tell the difference

Between a woman's tender flesh
And the flesh of a date-fruit,
And I saw no newspapers,
Save for those eagerly shedding their undergarments
Before the first President that is bestowed upon us,
The first petty colonel trampling us,[33]
And the first usurer coming to fleece us . . .
Truly amazing those Arabs, aren't they!

I've been watching the sorry state of the Arabs
For the past fifty years, and for fifty years
I have been listening to them thundering without raining,
I've been watching them rushing into wars
With nary the plan to walk out of them,
Chewing on the husks of "eloquence"
Mindlessly,
But saying nary a word of substance . . .

For the past fifty years
I've been trying to sketch out a land
I could figuratively call the "Arab world" . . .
At times I've sketched this land in the colors of my veins,
And at times in the colors of rage . . .

But when I was done sketching,
I asked myself:
"Were someone to, one day, announce the death of the Arabs,
In what cemetery would they be lain to rest?
And who would want to be caught weeping at their graveside?
For they have no begotten daughters,
And they have no begotten sons,
And they have begotten precious little of substance,
Nor have they earned anything worthy of being mourned . . ."

I've been trying, since my early dabbling with poetry,
To measure the distance between myself
And my Arab ancestors.
And I saw armies

Like no armies,
And I saw conquests
Like no conquests . . .
And I've watched all of our wars,
Very closely,
On our television screens . . .
For there were casualties
On our television screens,
And there were victories
Descending upon us from Allah,
All courtesy of our television screens . . .

Ay, my beloved homeland,
They have rendered you a freak show,
A soap opera gluing us to our television sets at night.
Pray tell me then, how are we to see the conclusion of this horror show
Should someone shut off the power?

For the past fifty years,
I've been writing down my impressions . . .
And all I could see was a people
Persuaded that the secret police is Allah's will,
Decreed my Him, Almighty,
Just like migraines,
Just like the Flu,
Just like Leprosy
And Scabies . . .[34]

Fifty years have passed,
And all I can see is Arabism
Still on display,
Being auctioned off at an old furniture store . . .
Yet no buyers are in sight,
And, alas, no Arabs are in sight . . .

I Reject You, All of You! (1997)[35]

I reject you, all of you,
This is the end of dialogue.
My language has despaired of you,
And I have nothing left to tell you!
I have set fire to my lexicons,
I have set fire to my clothes . . .
I have absconded Amru Bnu Kulthum,[36]
And tedious Farazdaq.[37]
I want out of my voice,
I want out of my writings,
I want out of my place of birth,
Out of the your metropolises of salt
And your hollow poetry of clay.

I have carried to your deserts my trees,
But out of despair
My trees chose suicide.
I have carried my rains to your parched lives,
But soon my rains ran dry . . .
I planted poetry in your barren wombs,
But you smothered my rhymes . . .

O womb . . .
Heavy with thorns and dust,
I did try to uproot you
From the sludge of history . . .[38]
From your calendars of fate
From your tedious classical poetry,[39]
And from your idolatry,
I tried to breach
The siege of Troy,
But I ended up besieged
By your siege . . .

I reject you,
I reject you,

You who concocted your God
Out of a date stone,
You who built a dome
To each of your village idiots,
And a shrine
To your petty charlatans . . .

I did try to save you
From the moving sands of the hourglass
Swallowing you
By day and by night,
And from the veils hiding your breasts,
And from the recitations
Spilled out over your graves . . .
I did try to save you
From your circles of males,
From your culture of soothsayers and sorcerers . . .
I did try to save you
From your duplicity and rope jumping,
I did try driving nails
Through your dead thick skins,
But I despaired of your skins,
And I despaired of my nails,
And I despaired of the thickness of your walls . . .

∾

ADONIS (b. 1930)

What concerns me is that my poetry be visionary [. . .]; that it engages in spawning a new society, a new culture, a new civilization.
[. . .] If poetry is not in a constant state of renewal, it is dead poetry,
written in a dead language that is no longer capable of communing with the word, with the language of life and motion. Creating
poetry in a language that spawns a new society, a new culture, and a
new set of relations among members of that society or that culture
is a fundamental—an urgent—necessity in Arab societies.

ADONIS[40]

The Syro-Lebanese writer Ali Ahmad Said Ispir—known primarily by his *nom de plume*, Adonis—was born in 1930, in the Alawite village of Qassabin; a remote, secluded hamlet nestled between the Syrian coastal town of Latakia—the ancient Greco-Roman Laodicea—and the highest point of the Alawite Mountains—a natural extension of Mount Lebanon. But like his Alawite village, perched on the tail end of a Lebanese promontory wading deep into the Mediterranean Sea, Adonis was the outcome of a conflation of geographic, cultural, and linguistic references, teeming with varied traditions and historical memories.

For one, the Syria of Adonis's birth had not yet become the Syrian Arab Republic of today, a state established much later by the French, inaugurated in September 1936, and granted independence in 1946. Indeed, and for the sake of avoiding anachronistic toponymies, one must acknowledge that Adonis was actually born in the State of the Alawite Mountain (État Alaouite), one of four states that the French inherited from the Ottomans in 1918—the remaining three being the State of Aleppo, the State of Damascus, and the State of Jabal al-Druze (the Druze Mountain).[41] And so, in a sense, like the land of his birth, stitched together in a patchwork of varied geographical and cultural fabrics, Adonis was "a child of the catacombs,"[42] a hybrid and a conflation of mixed legacies, ethnic accretions, and topographic features. But Adonis was also the outcome of Alawite tradition; arguably Shi'ite tradition. And Shi'ites, if one is to perceive them through their own conceptual frameworks and by way of their own lore and historical memory, are the offspring of tragedy, ever teetering on the edge of an abyss, ever awaiting impending redemption, ever missing out on salvation unfulfilled, ever slighted and eluded by an awaited "messiah" who is a notorious historical no-show.[43]

But Adonis, grim and distressed as his poetics might seem to the uninitiated—a mirror of the condition of his people as it were—is much more than a melancholy "Shi'ite," and much more than a lachrymose elegist of the Shi'ite condition. Adonis is an erstwhile Arab shoring up a new identity and advocating for new parameters of self-perception in a Middle East mirroring his own hybridity and stifling it at once. Like his native Alawite Mountain—and in later years his adoptive Lebanon—Adonis is a complex, composite personality, unhindered by the reductive personal and spatial barriers of Arabists and Arab nationalists of his generation. Indeed, Ali Ahmad Said's chosen name, Adonis, a Hellenized form of the Canaanite Tammuz—the pagan shepherd-hunter-god of fertility, youth, and renewal—was the epitome of compassion, optimism, eternal metamorphosis, revival, and vitality. But the name Adonis was also a powerful symbol of joy in the rebirth and rediscovery of an ever-permutating, ever-evolving, refreshed, invigorated self.

If Adonis's seemingly stormy and somber poetics are any indication, his are lamentations over an "extinct" imperious culture—arguably an Arabic culture—still persuaded of its vitality, still convinced to have supplanted and transcended precursor cultures, even as it wallowed in abandon and lostness.[44] "I am puzzled, my country," begins a poem of his:

> For each time I see you, you will have donned a different form.
> At times I hoist you upon my forehead, teetering between my
>   blood and my death:
> Are you a graveyard or a rose?
> I see you as children, dragging their entrails behind them,
>   resigned,
> Bowing obediently before their shackles,
> Wearing for each crack of the whip a corresponding skin . . .
> Are you a graveyard or a rose?
> You have killed me, my country,
> You have killed my songs.
> Are you a bloodbath or a revolution?
> I am puzzled, my country,
> For, each time I see you, you will have donned a different form.
>   . . .
> And I chant my own calamity.
> And I can no longer see myself,
> Save as a man on the fringes of history, teetering on a razor's
>   edge.
> I should hope to begin a new beginning.
> But where?

From where?

How shall I describe myself and in which of my languages must I
   speak?

For, this [Arabic] language that suckles me, also cheats and
   betrays me.

I shall embalm and purify her,

And resurrect myself on the edge of a time that has passed,

Walk on the edge of a time that is yet to come

And yet I am not the only one.[45]

Arab civilization, Arabic culture, and its linguistic conveyor are no
more, maintains Adonis. Like credulous zombie-children, in a scene
straight out of a gothic nightmare, dragging their soiled shorn tripes
behind them, the Arabs are still unconvinced of their death, Adonis
claims, still clinging to putrefied entrails that have long since abandoned their decaying bodies. But Adonis's message, like that of his
theophoric Canaanite namesake,[46] was also, always, one of unbounded
hopefulness, innovation, vigor, and renewal; a belief that a new identity will no doubt emerge out of the vestiges of the defunct Arab one;
a new receptive identity, open and sympathetic to its precursor—and
arguably its progenitor—Levantine civilizations. Whence and how
shall this new identity begin anew, asks Adonis? The answers he provides posit a number of options requiring a cleansed revitalized language culled from the Babel of "languages at [his] disposal," and new
inclusive ecumenical categories of self-perception, complemented by
the millennial diverse traditions, ethos, and cultural accretions of the
Levant.

   Culture and identity transcend tradition and fixed monistic definitions, argues Adonis, as one of his more recent works, *Identité inachevée*, argues.[47] Although often rejecting Arabism in seemingly violent
imagery, and indicting Arab nationalism's jingoistic impulses in mor-
bid fatalistic metaphors, boundless compassion, humanism, energy,
optimism, and joy are what drive Adonis's poetic themes. Sometimes
his imagery is frightening, nightmarish in its realism and finality, but it
remains joyful and hopeful for a new beginning, regardless.

Because the earth survives beneath my feet,
the pale god of my despair rejoices.
A new voice speaks my words.
My poems bloom naked as roses. . . .
Silence rises on the sand.
There are hearts to touch.
Some ink. . . .
Some paper. . . .
Where is your home?
What camp without a name?
My homeland is abandoned.
My soul has left me.
I have no home.[48]

This is a most exquisite example of Adonis's funereal gloom. Yet, in the midst of the dread and despair, "a new voice" is resurrected in Adonis's language, a new heart is beating and bursting with life as "silence" unfolds on the barren sands of Araby.[49] To use an analogy attributed to Michelangelo, in every unsightly block of stone dwells a beautiful statue; one need only remove the dreadful, the crass outer layer, to reveal the life lurking, pulsating within. This is Adonis. "Perhaps it's time for a new beginning," his work and name seem to say: death is part of the cycle of life and the only way for complete renewal and everlasting existence—it is so, at least in the Canaanite-Phoenician cultic calendar, whose symbols and allegories play an important role in shaping Adonis's life and belief systems, and charting his poetic and philosophical trajectory.

Unlike any Arabic-language poet of his generation, and certainly unlike any other contemporary "Muslim" poet, Adonis is personally, intellectually, emotionally, and historically invested in the symbolisms and humanism of Christianity, Canaanite mythology, and ancient Levantine pagan rituals of death and renewal. His mood, often resembling funerary lamentations, is simply a prelude to a looming, impending rebirth, that is the foundation of Christianity's triumvirate—not to say Canaanite paganism's trinity—of suffering, death, salvation, and renewal.

Syrian Social Nationalist Roots

Adonis's early beginnings drew on a stint in the ranks of the Syrian Social Nationalist Party—the SSNP (also known by its French initials PPS, for Parti Populaire Syrien). Curiously, and unlike most former members of the SSNP—e.g., Lebanese nationalist thinkers Salah Labaki and Saïd Akl—Adonis does not attempt to obscure his association with that group. Nevertheless, the SSNP involvement remains a period in Adonis's political and intellectual journey that is not given the relevance and attention it deserves in profiles and biographies of the poet.

The SSNP deeply influenced Adonis's worldview and philosophical frames of reference. Some have claimed that even his pen name, Adonis, was bestowed upon him by Antun Saadé, the founder and until July 1949 the supreme leader of the SSNP. In an anecdote related by Sadiq Jalal al-Azm, Adonis claimed that in 1947, after returning to the Levant from a nine-year exile, Saadé was visiting the Syrian coast—the Mediterranean lungs of his proposed Syrian nation—and made a stop-over at Qassabin. Adonis, then still Ali Ahmad Said, along with throngs of Syrian Nationalists, were reported to have sent a welcoming party into the village square to greet Saadé. Adonis recited a poem he had prepared for the occasion. The "Zaim" ("Leader")—the title by which Saadé was known at the time—clearly smitten by the young poet's tribute and oratory skills, asked what his name was, and upon hearing it, reportedly exclaimed, "Your name ought to be Adonis," a symbol of the Syrian nation's rebirth.[50]

Of course, Adonis's chroniclers and biographers tell a different story, the most prevalent being his inability to publish under his real name—arguably because Ali is a recognizably Alawite and Shi'ite name—motivating him to settle on the openly un-Arab, pre-Arab—not to say anti-Arab, pagan—Adonis. And the rest is history. What matters is that the sobriquet Adonis stuck. What matters more is that *Adonis* carries with it a set of beliefs and cultural accretions that reflect an iconoclastic, nontraditional approach to Middle Eastern history and an assent to the region's varied cultural traditions. Whether Adonis chose the name himself or accepted someone else bestowing it on him, by embracing it he was clearly endorsing the beliefs, ideology, and historical memory as advocated by the SSNP. But what was the SSNP, and where does it fit in Adonis's activities, poetics, and philosophical convictions?

The SSNP is one of the oldest and most curious political organizations in the Levant—more precisely in modern Lebanon. Indeed, in spite of the political and ideological imagery that a name like the Syrian Social Nationalist Party might invoke, the SSNP was in reality a Lebanese—not a Syrian—party. Strangely enough, it was also a Lebanese nationalist party; not in the sense that it advocated for a Lebanese cause per se, but rather due to its strong opposition to Arabism and Arab nationalism—and certainly due to its rejection of the idea depicting Syria as part of some Arab national and cultural space.

Founded in the early 1930s by Antun Saadé, the SSNP sought to propound the notion of a "Syrian nation" as an entity distinct and separate for the "Arab nation"; one composed of Levantine ethnic and cultural groups with histories predating Judaism, Christianity, Islam, and the cultures that they spawned on the eastern shores of the Mediterranean. With its unique conception of the Syrian nation as a crucible and synthesis of many cultural, ethno-religious, and linguistic groupings, the SSNP's definition of Syrian identity came to mean a total repudiation of the neighborhood's Arabs, a rejection of pan-Arabist irredentism, and a complete divorce from all things religious—especially the symbiotic relationship between Arabness and Islam.

The SSNP was virulently opposed to religious identities, which for centuries constituted the traditionally accepted bases of loyalty and ethnic identification, not only in the Middle East, but also throughout the Islamic world. Saadé's secularism was a function of his dedication to modernism and his adherence to the antitranscendental ideas of French positivist thinkers—like Ernest Renan and August Comte— with whose writings he and other Arabic-speaking Levantine Christian secularists of his time were evidently familiar.[51] Therefore, Antun Saadé viewed national identity in organic geographical terms, not by way of religious or linguistic criteria. He saw the "Syrian nation"—whose diversity, timelessness, and perpetuity Adonis would begin writing about in the 1940s and 1950s—as a unique synthesis of Phoenician, Canaanite, Jewish, Christian, Druze, and other groups living in present-day Syria,

Lebanon, Jordan, Israel, and Cyprus, and who in Saadé's view had to be united under the banner of an egalitarian, secular, socialist, uniquely Syrian national identity.[52] In sum, Saadé's aim appeared to have been the restitution of a Levantine secular polity, where Middle Eastern minorities, who had fallen under the sway of the allogenic Arab-Muslims of the seventh century, would reclaim their millennial pre-Arab heritage, and reintegrate a humanist, multifaceted, polyglot, cosmopolitan identity, separate and distinct from strictly Arab-defined identities.

As a minoritarian—and indeed as the child of a traditionally detested and suppressed "heretical" sect—the young Adonis was naturally seduced by Saadé's fluid, inclusive, and multilayered framework of identity. From an SSNP perspective, Adonis could be a user of the Arabic language—the language of the politically dominant culture of his neighborhood—and still vaunt non-Arab cultural accretions without running the risk of the harassments and vexations often associated with being an Alawite. Indeed, Syrianism as Adonis had espoused it, and as it had been elaborated by Saadé, was an identity defined, not by its purity of race, but indeed by its very taintedness, hybridity, and bastardized nature. The Syrians, argued Saadé, were an old people, the outcome of a *longue durée*, nourished and infused by layers of civilizations, cultures, languages, and traditions, all of which, over time, got fused into a specific, uniquely "Syrian" whole. Saadé was violently opposed to labeling the Syrians Arabs; to him, such a label was based on a presumed community of language and religion; two components conspicuously absent from the SSNP's definition of the nation. Indeed, Saadé regarded language simply as a means of communication, not a relevant criterion of identity. "Whenever language is used as a basis of nationhood," he wrote, "the purpose is primarily the aggrandizement and expansion of that nation as is presently the case in [Nazi] Germany. German thinkers have sometimes harked back to the unity of race and sometimes to the unity of language in order to justify their expansionist aims and their desire to bring all the German-Speaking peoples into one state."[53]

In this, Saadé was not merely divorcing his definition of the nation from assumed linguistic trappings; he was expressly separating Syrianism from Arabism and in a sense assaulting pan-Arabism's domineering proclivities—impulses, which in the view of Arab nationalists of the times, were justified by what they described as "the mystique" of the Arabic language. Saadé was essentially saying that Arabs could adduce neither historical nor geographical criteria justifying their claimed kinship to, or dominance over the Syrians. His consciousness of being Syrian was very similar to the consciousness of being French, as expounded in Ernest Renan's articulation of an *identité elective*. In tune with Saadé's Syrian "nationhood," Renan deemed the nation to be

> a soul, a spiritual principle [. . .] the possession, in common, of a rich legacy of memories [and] a desire to live together. [. . .] The nation, like the individual, is the result of a long past rife with struggles, sacrifices, and devotion to duty. The worship of ancestors is, more than anything else, most legitimate; our ancestors have made us who we are. A heroic past, great men, glory, that is the stuff of the social capital upon which rests the national idea. Having common glories in the past, a common will in the present; having accomplished great feats together, wanting to accomplish some more: those are the conditions essential to becoming a people.[54]

This is obviously a broader, much more liberal and inclusive framing of identity, which clearly had a great appeal to Saadé and Adonis. Indeed, in his *Syrian Social Nationalism's Book of Teachings,* Saadé seemed to have duplicated Renan's definition of the nation as defined in *Qu'est-ce qu'une nation?* In this work, Saadé asserts that his aim in reviving the Syrian nation is not to establish the common stock of the Syrian people, but to give them reason to exult in their glorious common ancestry and timeless identity; an identity, which was the outcome of a long history and an imbrication of civilizations comprised of Chaldaeans, Canaanites, Hebrews, Phoenicians, Aramaeans, Assyrians, and Akkadians; all of whom were, over the centuries, molded into a unique "Syrian" nation.[55] Saadé defined the Syrians as "a group of people who share a common life (i.e., have common interests, a common destiny, and common psycho-physical characteristics) within a well-defined territory which, through its interaction with them in the process of evolution, imparts to them certain special traits and characteristics that distinguish them from other groups."[56] As was the case with Renan, language and religion were conspicuously absent from Saadé's definition of the nation; for, had he included language and had he at least alluded to a commonality of language (even a literary one) between Syrians and neighboring Arabs, he would have implicitly acquiesced in the existence of an Arabic component to his Syrian nation. Yet, like Adonis himself, Saadé had no reservations about the written, literary, Modern Standard Arabic language (MSA). Indeed, he admitted MSA as a possible unifying factor—a *langue savante*—transcending all other primordial loyalties that characterized the diverse ethnic components of his composite Syrian nation. In Saadé's view, MSA possessed a unifying attribute to be sure, but it remained a mere written literary vehicle, a *lingua franca* as it were, akin to the Latin of medieval Europe; in other words, not a valid vehicle for a national program. The Syrians, he argued, had too rich a tradition, and too deep and layered a cultural heritage to be reduced to frail linguistic definitions.[57] And so, although "Arab" in its written expression, Saadé's brand of Syrian nationalism stressed the pre-Arabic and pre-Islamic progenitors of Syrian culture. He utterly disregarded fourteen centuries of Arab and Muslim presence in Syria and stressed the notion of Syrians as a distinct, millennial, non-Arab nation.[58]

True to form, and in clear devotion to his Syrian Social Nationalist formation, Adonis also repudiated the reductive linguistic parameters of identity as advocated by the Arabists of his generation, and labored to pilfer his inclusive, Levantine-Syrianist impulses into poetry, political writings, and literary criticism.

This Is My Name

Khalida Saleh, a Sorbonne-educated Arabic literary critic, and the wife of Adonis since 1956, has described her husband's 1970 poem *This Is My Name* as "the canon of change" in Arabic literary and linguistic tradition. She has seen the poem as a "ferocious forward movement," undoing fixed Arabic linguistic assumptions and subverting classical Arabic orthodoxies as mandated and condensed in traditional Arabic poetry.[59] Indeed, the patina of ostensible Arab unity and Arabic cultural continuity and harmony, as conveyed in the postulates of a common

Arabic language and a shared historical memory, flaked and peeled under Adonis's pen. *This Is My Name* was the beginning of a lifelong Ado-
nisian assault on the Arabic language and its monistic, narrow cultural
premises. It was the beginning of a controversial intellectual journey in
which Adonis mercilessly confronted Arab heritage and questioned its
validity as the sole referent and basis of Levantine Middle Eastern culture. Through this work, Adonis called for the destruction of the function of the old language and demanded that it be drained of its prevailing, traditional meanings. Through this decree, the poet also advocated
for an exploitation of positive aspects of Arabness, and for the excava-
tion and restitution of the pre-Arab heritage of the Levant. Language is
not a sacred static essence, argued Adonis; it is a transient, changeable
tool. *This Is My Name* asserts just that, with no less authority and no less
finality than God telling Moses these very same verities in Exodus 3:15:
"This is My name forever, and this is my memorial to all generations";
an invitation to the integration of all the pre-Arab civilizations of the
Near East into an inclusive, ecumenical identity, without preconcep-
tions or prejudice.

The opening passage of Adonis's *This Is My Name* recurs several
times throughout the poem, in a kind of formulaic incantation, as if
proclaiming a new birth, adopting a new identity, embracing a new historical memory, and spawning a new civilization:

> This is my name
> Erasing every wisdom
> This is my fire
> No verse has remained—my blood is the verse
> This is my genesis.[60]

Thus, erasure, fire, and flame become the harbinger of a new beginning
for Adonis; a new genesis as it were, expunging the old history, the old
textbooks and scriptures, the old assumptions, the old identities, the
old religions and their old rituals and "verses"—presumably, perhaps,
Qur'anic verses.[61] In order to regenerate itself, the old culture must be
charred and re-created from the flames, embers, and ashes of its past
incarnations. Like the legendary phoenix bursting into flame and com-

ing back to life out of its blazing ashes, so must the old civilization of the Arabs be set aflame and be made into a new self.[62]

Thus, "No verse has remained—my blood is the verse/This is my genesis" would become, in Adonis's telling, the new "blood" of a new covenant, a new beginning, a new creed, a new "verse," and a new gospel of eternal renewal. Indeed, Adonis's very definition of poetry challenges the traditional Arab view of this distinctly "Arabic" literary medium. Thus he views poetic expression not as the Arabic art form par excellence—the Arab poet being traditionally his tribe's advocate, chronicler, and panegyrist—but rather as a feat of creation, an act of spawning new life.[63] The syncretistic symbolism of the imagery used by Adonis, wading into pagan, Christian, and biblical traditions, is an iconoclastic—even heretical—onslaught on aspects of Arab life that excluded elements of Levantine cultural antecedents.

Throughout his career, Adonis has often harkened back to his name choice. Again, whether a sobriquet he picked of his own volition, or whether one bestowed upon him by an ideological mentor, Adonis admits to the liberating qualities of his *nom de plume*. It was a name that allowed him to break out of an identity that had not been his first choice; an identity defined above all by one religion, sullying his pantheistic horizons, shutting him out from the rest of the world, impeding his communion with humanity at large.[64] In that sense "Adonis" delivered the poet from Ali, and Ali from himself, rescuing him from closed social kinships twined to a restrictive identity defined by religion.[65] Through his new, unfettered identity, Adonis had chosen a humanistic persona; a pure, unlimited, free "self" that laid him bare and flung him into the embrace of "other" human beings, untainted by the prescribed customs imposed by the Arab society of his birth.[66]

But there was still more to Adonis's chosen name. Lebanese cultural historian Fouad Ajami notes that through "the pen name he chose for himself, Adonis picked a [distinct] political and cultural identity," electing to define himself as a son of the Mediterranean and of the Levant's syncretistic millennial heritage; heir to multilayered cultures and civilizations.[67] Pan-Arabists and Arab nationalists, to whom both Syria and Lebanon were deemed subordinate entities, addenda as it were to a wider "Arab space," had cultural referents harking back to the Arabian

Peninsula. They had not developed a palate for the Levant's pre-Islamic history and pagan cultural lore.[68] Islam and the culture it spawned was all that mattered to the Arabs; whatever preceded Islam was not worth remembering—let alone was it worth celebrating in poetry and in literary pseudonyms. Whatever came after Islam could never quite measure up. And so, pan-Arabists and Arab nationalists never have taken a liking to Adonis and never have trusted his jarring philosophical and political excursions. From being a Syrianist and a card-holding member of the anti-Arab Parti Populaire Syrien, to being active sometimes as a committed Arab nationalist and songster of Palestinianism, to flirting briefly with Islamic revivalism, to advocating a national agnostic, humanistic, syncretistic Mediterranean identity, Adonis has done it all. Yet Arab nationalists have resented him and taken his intellectual fickleness (and his Phoenician *nom de plume*) as proof of his atavistic affections for the Phoenician and Greco-Roman heritage of Syria and Lebanon. Never mind that one—as he does—could argue that his own critiques of the Arabs emanated from affection. Yet Adonis has never claimed to shore up one identity to the detriment of another, nor does he advocate on behalf of, say, Phoenicianism or Syrianism to cast out the Arabs. Adonis simply has been an avid practitioner of cultural and linguistic hybridity, recognizing the Middle East's inherent diversity, heterogeneity, and multiplicity of cultures, bereft of dogmatism, exclusivism, and ideological rigidity.

In 1942, Lebanese thinker Michel Chiha described the cultural and ethnic hybridity of the Lebanese people as an imbrication of traditions, languages, and historical narratives that could not be reduced to a single, monochromatic, and politically soothing identity. He argued that "the past fifteen centuries [of Lebanon's history] should not make us oblivious or disrespectful of the fifty centuries that preceded them! Even if relying entirely on conjecture, the blood, the civilization, and the language of today's Lebanese cannot possibly be anything but the legacy of fifty centuries of progenitors and ancestors."[69] In 1939, around the same period Chiha was shoring up his gospels of Lebanese-Mediterranean conflations and cultural fluidity, Antun Saadé was advancing similar claims with regard to the Syrian people's diversity, and the complexity

of their ethnic and cultural composition. Like Chiha's, Saadé's invocation of the Eastern Mediterranean's millennial history as a component of
Syrian identity was clearly an amulet with which to ward off the specter
of a rising Arab nationalism.[70] The francophone Lebanese poet Charles
Corm had already began elaborating similar themes during the early
1920s, positing that the modern Lebanese were descendants of classical antiquity's Phoenician seafarers, not the offspring of some modern Arab ancestor. In that sense, Corm suggested the Lebanese were
relatives and cultural kinsmen to the variety of peoples strewn around
the Mediterranean Basin. Since the remotest antiquity, wrote Charles
Corm, "when they were still known as Canaanites, and later as Phoenicians, the Lebanese people have created, preserved, defended, affirmed,
and advanced an expansive and liberal civilization with universal impulses and predilections so accessible to other peoples, to the point that
some of those, even the loftiest and brightest among them, had come to
assimilate these attributes of Lebanese civilization as if they were their
own, adopting and identifying them with their own national genius."[71]
It is against this backdrop that Adonis began advocating a revamping
and a rediscovery of new, inclusive, pantheistic identities for the varie-
gated peoples of the Middle East. And it is against this background that
one must frame Adonis's combustive critiques of Arabist orthodoxies
and the Arabs' fear of diversity. All is in need of transformation and
rehabilitation in Arab society he claimed:

> My peers and I live in a society that must be reconstituted,
> from A to Z, on every single plane and from every facet. One
> must take a completely new look at [Arab] society [. . .] To
> better understand my poetry, one must read it from this
> perspective; one must realize that I am the product of a so-
> ciety that is in dire need of rebuilding, from the foundations
> up; a society whose culture and politics must be reexamined
> with a fresh new set of eyes; a society in which I find noth-
> ing worth defending, nothing worth safeguarding, nothing
> worth adopting or learning from. I come from a society
> that is still living in a primordial political and social state;

a society still stuck at ground-zero; ground-zero in the sense
that everything about that society needs to be redefined, reviewed, reinvented, and remade. It is this distressing situation
that constitutes the background of my poetry, that drives my
poetry, and that illuminated my poetic vision—which is not
only purely literary, and not only purely linguistic.[72]

In short, "the Arabs are ailing," according to Adonis, "and the roots of
their ailment are embedded in their language"; an ornamentally beautiful language, and the depository and repository of a rich cultural heritage, but an opulent, affected language that continues to be propped up
at the expense of accuracy and functionality. "Arabic is abundantly rich
in expressing old ideas," claimed nineteenth-century Lebanese linguist
Butrus al-Bustani, but it is "in dire need of terms that suit modern needs
and concepts" where it remains handicapped, burdensome, afflicted,
and broken.[73] It is this language that Adonis sought to dismantle; a language that in his view was no longer capable of communing with the
spoken word, with the feelings, the concerns, the labors, and the conflicts of everyday life.[74]

This Is My Language

Adonis's assault on Arabism and Arab nationalism has been mounted
on multiple fronts; he has attacked in equal measure the Arabs' cultural,
historical, social, and literary ethos. But his most pungent critique is the
one he has directed at the Arabic language. The Arabs have collapsed,
he claims; they are being extinguished as a meaningful culture because
their language is no longer a vital tool of communication capable of
coexisting with and contributing to modernity.[75] The only way for the
Arabs to resurrect, argues Adonis, is to discard the social, literary, and
cultural orthodoxies hanging around their language's neck like an alba-
tross, keeping it shackled to obsolete values and belief systems.[76]

Here, let the gazelle of history lay my entrails open/ . . . A
river of slaves thunders ∧ [No prophet that hasn't been de-

meaned remained, no god remains / we come to discover
what has already been discovered; bread /] We discovered a
light that leads to earth, we discovered a sun emanating from
a clenched fist. Bring along your axes and follow me. Pack
up your <Allah> like a dying Arab Sheikh, open a path to
the sun away from Minarets, open a book to a child besides
the books of musty pieties, [and] cast the dreamer's eye away
from Medina and Kufa / Bring along your axes and follow
me! *I am not the only one.*[77]

It is only through destruction of the idols and gods of old—by spurning
Allah, his letters, his hallowed language, his texts, and his monuments—
that the new Middle East shall emerge. Only by spawning a new, toler-
ant, open, uncluttered language can a new society and a new, humanistic, liberal Middle Eastern identity evolve; an identity unhindered and
unashamed by its variety and its multiple faces. Adonis began creating
this new identity as he began honing his poetry. It was in the midst of his
poetic production that he became conscious of the creative dimensions
of his chosen name; the name of a begetter, a creator, a life giver.[78] This
consciousness has goaded Adonis to embark on a tireless odyssey and
a continuous process of creating, re-creating, and regenerating his own
identity. Adonis came to realize that just as language is a transient tool
with fleeting associations, so is identity a continuous work-in-progress,
one that can go on living, long after death, simply because it is an antithesis of preordained, "authentic," ossified identities. Adonis's aim was to
create a new foundation for an open, new Middle Eastern culture and a
new Middle Eastern identity receptive to the liberal Renanian concept
of "elective identities."[79]

Everything of value in Adonis's "preordained" native society was
intimately wedded to religion, and religion to Adonis's society was at
once culture, identity, ethics, law, *and* language.[80] That is why, in attempting to liberate himself from the stifling embrace of his culture,
Adonis first had to liberate the Arabic language itself, rendering it, like
the hybrid identities of his Levantine backyard, a tongue that communicates in many tongues.[81]

In doing so he was going against deeply rooted traditions, ensconced in a highly ordered, hallowed language. Taking this ethos and
its linguistic medium to task has not been an easy enterprise. Indeed,
challenging the Arabic language can be a foolhardy and perilous activity
in a society beholden to tradition. Language is the condensation of all
that is "tradition" for the Arabs, and tradition as such is a set of laws,
edicts, and interdictions that emanate from immutable divine sources.
Challenging these carries heavy penalties, often paid in blood tributes.
Adonis was well aware of the hazards he was incurring, yet he threw
down his gauntlet and took on this challenge to Arab tradition and to
Islam.[82] He made the claim that in his (Arab) society things that are out
of the ordinary are not merely dismissed, but are seen as defects "arising
from some type of madness . . . they are looked upon with curiosity and
astonishment."[83] "The culture of the Arabs," Adonis has claimed, "is
part of the culture of their forefathers [the "Salaf"]; their life is a continuation of their forefathers' lives."[84] In sum, the proper way of doing
things in such a society, in order to be accepted, "is not to innovate, but
to imitate," not to create but to rearrange and embroider what has been
inherited and claimed to be immutable. That is why Adonis's critique,
bold and searing as it has been, still has employed a heavy measure of
dissimulation, *taqiyya*, a practice that is not uncommon among minoritarian Levantines—Druze, Alawites, and others—whereby one keeps
his or her own beliefs and ethos to himself or herself, and outwardly
spouts—even at times defends—those of others, especially domineering others. *Taqiyya* is in a sense a "self-preservation" tactic.

Today, an octogenarian, Adonis lives between Paris and Beirut, in
the security and the comfort of a middle-class literature professor's life.[85]
But since the late 1960s he has been the victim of several *fatwas*. One
must not think for a moment that Adonis takes these *fatwas* lightly. If his
body language and the tone of his voice are any indication—even the
very semantics he uses in televised interviews where he touches upon taboo topics—Adonis is infinitely cautious and concerned for his safety.

In an interview with Dubai TV, Adonis was, true to form, criti-
cizing Arabic social, cultural, religious, and linguistic traditions. Very
cautiously, however, he prefaced his talk by noting that "words [in the

Arab world] today, are treated as if they were a criminal offense." This sentence is very important, as Adonis the atheist, humanist agnostic felt obligated to issue the traditional formulaic incantations usually uttered by God-fearing practicing Muslims when mentioning the name of God. As Adonis states in the interview, "Even Allah, may His glory forever reign, in the Holy Qur'an Itself, even He Listened to Satan, His sworn enemy."[86] Then Adonis bursts out into a short spate of forced, anxious, apprehensive laughter. His laughter, as he was leveling his critique of Arab intolerance, was clearly not the laughter of someone amused by the topic at hand (or the comments he had just made). Rather, it was the laughter of someone fully aware of the terrible repercussions of his words.

Monotheism—and in its most rigorous incarnation, Islam—is a set of divine prohibitions, restrictions, and taboos, argues Adonis.[87] As such, Islam epitomizes violence—not only in the tangible physical sense, but rather in the perceptual psychological sense, given that behavioral prohibitions and restrictions on human freedoms are, by definition, a form of cruelty and an assault on human dignity and sovereignty.[88] These indictments are all related to language, in Adonis's estimation; the Arabs are not an audacious and intellectually daring lot, simply because their revered language does not promote or encourage those instincts. There are rules of utterance, perception, and response that are essential to the Arabic language itself; a linguistic straitjacket, as it were, which nourishes negative traditions of paternalism, voluntary servitude, and fear of authority. Nevertheless, Adonis has remained an avid practitioner of Arabic even though his work relentlessly drives home its lack of directness, spontaneity, and intensity of feeling—which are ordinarily the stamps of living language. Adonis claims that Arabic blunts and stultifies the spontaneity and directness of the human spirit, dictating formality and dissimulation. Still, his work has chosen to continue dissimulating (and disseminating) his critiques in ambiguous, profoundly abstruse Arabic.

Adonis seems to be in tune with Fawaz Turki's extreme claims that the Arabic language standardizes conformity, submissiveness, and repression. Indeed, Turki (explored in the chapter on Palestine and Israel) argues that the Arabs' adversarial, critical, creative, and informative instincts are actually repressed by language—which, in his view, is the creator of culture. In this sense, it is language that demeans—and for that matter, when allowed to do so, ennobles—the value of human existence.

Like Qabbani, Adonis has spoken of the death of Arab civilization. There comes a time, he has said, when people can no longer give. In Beirut's chaos and clash of ideas (and later during its wars of the 1970s and 1980s), Adonis had seen all the grand ideas emanating from Arabism and local nationalisms end up in bloodshed and wars of extermination. In the mid-1980s Adonis no longer recognized the city that had once been receptive—even protective—of his unorthodox ideas. But Adonis's work in the 1960s and 1970s had predicted an apocalyptic end resembling Beirut. He even viewed a self-immolating Beirut as a harbinger of things to come elsewhere in the Middle East—Syria for instance, in the second decade of the twenty-first century, as a result of an "Arab Spring" turned deadly. In his *Elegies for the Times at Hand*, one of his most haunting poems, written in the late 1960s, Adonis writes of tyranny, silence, destruction, and exile as a rendition of the Arabs' nightmares—past, present, and future—which needed be exorcized if they are to be vanquished and upended.

ELEGY FOR THE TIME AT HAND (1961)[89]

1.

Chanting of banishment,
Exhaling flame,
The carriages of exile breach the walls.

Or are these carriages
The battering sighs of my verses?

Cyclones have crushed us.
Sprawled in the ashes of our days,
We glimpse our souls
Passing
On the sword's glint
Or at the peaks of helmets.

An autumn of salt spray
Settles on our wounds.
No tree can bud,
No spring . . .[90]

. . . Whatever will come it will be old

So take with you anything other than this
Madness—get ready
To stay a stranger . . .[91]

They found people in sacks:
One without a head
One without a tongue or hands
One squashed
The rest without names.
Have you gone mad?
Please,
Do not write about these things.[92]

Darkness.
The earth's trees have become tears on
heaven's cheeks.
An eclipse in this place.
Death snapped the city's branch and the
friends departed.[93]

The flower that tempted the wind to carry its
perfume
Died yesterday.

The sun no longer rises
It covers its feet with straw
And slips away . . .

Now in the final act,
Disaster tows our history
Toward us on its face.
What is our past

But memories pieced like deserts
Prickled like cactus?[94]

What streams can wash it?
It reeks with the musk
Of spinsters and widows
Back from pilgrimage.
The sweat of dervishes
Begrimes it as they twirl
Their blurring trousers
Into miracles.[95]

Now
Blooms the spring
Of locusts
Over the dead nightingales.
The night itself
Weighs and weighs.
The day inches to birth
While the shut and bolted door
Of the sea rejects us.[96]

We scream.
We dream of weeping,
But tears refuse our eyes.
We twist our necks
In zero hurricanes.[97]

O my land,
I see you as a woman in heat,
A bridge of lust.[98]

The pharaohs take you
When they choose,
And the very sand
Applauds them.
Through the clay of my eyeshells,
I see what any man can see:

Libations
At the graves of children,
Incense
For holy men,
Tombstones
Of black marble,
Fields scattered
With skeletons,
Vultures, mushy corpses
With the names of heroes.[99]

Thus we advance,
Chests to the sea,
Grieving for yesterday.
Our words inherit nothing,
Beget nothing.
We are islands.[100]

From the abyss
We smell ravens.
Our ships
Send out their pleas
To nothing but the crescent moon[101]
Of despair that broods
A devil's spawn.
At riverfall,
At the dead sea,
Midnight dreams its festivals,
But sand and foam
And locusts
Are the only brides.[102]

Thus we advance,
Harvesting our caravans
In filth and tears,
Bleeding the earth
With our own blood

Until the green dam of the sea
Alone
Stops us.[103]

2.

What god shall resurrect us
In his flesh?
After all,
The iron cage is shrinking.
The hangman
Will not wait
Though we wail
From birth
In the name of these
Happy ruins.[104]

What narrow yesterdays
What stale and shriveled years . . .
Even storms come
Begging
When the sky matches the gray
Of the sand,
Leaving us stalled between seasons,
Barricaded by what we see,
Marching under clouds
That move
Like mules and cannon.
The dust of graveyards
Blinds us
Until our eyes
Rhyme with ash.
No lashes fringe the sun.
No brows can shade the day,
And life comes
Moment by moment
As it comes to the poor only.

Shadowed by ice and sand,
We live.

And so live all men.

All men . . .
Mere scraps from everywhere,
Fresh baits of arsenic.
Under their sky
What green can sprout?[105]

All men . . .
Choked by ashes,
Crushed
By the rocks of silence,
Mounted
By empire builders,
Paraded in arenas
For their sport,
So many footstools,
So many banners. . . .
No one whispers
In Barada or the Euphrates.
Nothing breeds or stirs.
O my barren
My dry and silent land,
Who left you
Like a fossil?
On the map
You're virile,
Rich with wheat,
Oil, ports,
Counter-colored by migrations.
Shall a new race grow
In the poppy fields?
Shall fresh winds
Rearrange the sand?

Let the rain come.
Let rain wash us
In our ruins,
Wash the corpses,
Wash our history.
Let the poems
Strangled on our lips
Be swept away
Like rocks in the street.
Let us attend to cows,
Doves, flowers, gods.
Let sounds return
To this land
Of starving frogs.
Let bread be brought
By locusts
And the banished ants. . . .

My words
Become a spear in flight.
Unopposable as truth,
My spear returns
To strike me
Dead.

3.

Braid your hair,
My boys,
With greener leaves.
We still have verse
Among us.
We have the sea.
We have our dreams.
"To the steppes of China
We bequeath our neighing horses,
And to Georgia, our spears.

We'll build a house of gold
From here
To the Himalayas.
We'll sail our flags
In Samarkand.
We'll tread the treasured
Mosses of the earth.
We'll bless our blood with roses.
We'll wash the day of stains
And walk on stones
As we would walk on silk."

"This is the only way.
For this we'll lie
With lightening
And anoint the mildewed earth
Until the cries of birth
Resound, resound, resound."

"Nothing can stop us.
Remember,
We are greener than the sea,
Younger than time.
The sun and the day are dice
Between our fingers."

Under the exile's moon
Tremble the first wings.
Boats begin to drift
On a dead sea,
And siroccos
Rustle the gates
Of the city.
Tomorrow
The gates shall open.
We'll burn the locusts
In the desert,

Span the abyss
And stand
On the porch
Of a world to be."

"Darkness,
Darkness of the sea,
Be filled
With the leopard's joy.
Help us to sacrifice,
Name us anew.
The eagle
Of the future waits,
And there are
Answers in its eyes."

"Darkness,
Darkness of the sea,
Ignore
This feast of corpses.
Bring the earth to blossom
With your winds.
Banish plague
And teach the very rocks
To dance and love."

"The goddess of the sand
Prostrates herself.
Under brichthorn
The spring rises
Like colocynth from the lips
Or life from the sea.
We leave the captive city
Where every lantern is a church
And every bee
More sacred than a nun."

4.

"Where is your home?
Which country?
Which camp without a name?"

"My country is abandoned.
My soul has left me.
I have no home."

When pharaohs ruled
And men were cannibals,
The words of poets died.
While pharaohs rule,
I take my books and go,
Living in the shade of my heart,
Weaving from my verse's silk
A new heaven.

The sea
Cleanses our wounds
And makes of wounds
The salt's kin. . . .
The white sea,
The daily Euphrates,
The Orontes in its cradle,
The Barada—
I have tasted them all,
And none could slake me.
Yet I learned their love,
And my despair
Deserved such waters.

Though desperate,
I still hate death.
Though lost,
I seek my way
Through all the lies

And doubts
That are the crust
And quicksand
Of the earth.

Give me
The exile's sail,
The pilgrim's face.
I turn my back on jails
And holocausts.
I leave the dead
To death.

And I go,
Keeping my endless sorrows,
My distance from the stars,
My pilgrimage,
My girl
And my verses.
I go with the sweat
Of exile on my forehead
And with a lost poem
Sleeping in my eyes.
I go,
Dreaming of those buried
In orchards and vineyards,
And I remember
Those I love,
Those few.
When the sea
Rages my blood
And the wind kisses
My love's hair,
I remember my mother,
And I weave
In memory
For her

A mat of straw
Where she can sit and weep.

Amen to the age of flies.

Because the earth
Survives beneath my feet,
The pale god of my despair
Rejoices.
A new voice speaks my words.
My poems bloom
Naked as roses.

Find me some paper,
Some ink.
Despair is still my star,
And evil
Is always being born.
Silence rises on the sand.
There are hearts to touch.
Some ink. . . .
Some paper. . . .

"Where is your home?
What camp without a name?"

"My country is abandoned.
My soul has left me.
I have no home."

A Lull between Ashes and Roses (1972)

O curdling blood, flowing like deserts of idle talk,
O blood weaving tragedy and twilight,
Perish, wither away!

The magic of Arab history has ended.
Come along with me, let us bury its ignoble face,
And lay to rest its dull heritage,

And pardon us, forgive us
O gazelle horns, o antelope eyes . . .[106]

I am confused, my country,
For, each time I see you, you will have donned a different form.
At times I hoist you upon my forehead,
Teetering between my blood and my death:
Are you a graveyard or a rose?
I see you as children, dragging their entrails behind them,
Resigned,
Bowing obediently before their shackles,
Wearing for each crack of the whip a corresponding skin . . .
Are you a graveyard or a rose?

You have killed me, my country,
You have killed my songs.
Are you a bloodbath or a revolution?
I am puzzled, my country,
For, each time I see you, you will have donned a different form . . .

                                                        . . .

. . . And I chant my own calamity.
And I can no longer see myself
Save as a man on the fringes of history
Teetering on a razor's edge /
I should hope to begin a new beginning,
But where? From where?
How shall I describe myself
And in which of my languages must I speak?
For, this [Arabic] language that suckles me, also cheats and betrays me /
I shall embalm and purify her,[107]
And resurrect myself on the edge of a time that has passed,
Walk on the edge of a time that is yet to come

And yet, I am not the only one

. . . And here is the gazelle of history laying my guts bare /
The river of slaves roars ^
[Nary a prophet remains among us

Who has not rendered himself a tramp
Nary a god remains /
And we think we have discovered bread /]
We discovered a light that leads to Earth
We discovered a sun emanating from a clenched fist
Bring along your axes and follow me,
Pack up your <Allah> like a dying Arab sheikh,
[Open a pathway to the sun away from Minarets,
Open a book to a child besides the books of musty pieties,
And cast the dreamer's eye away from Medina and Kufa /
Bring along your axes and follow me

I am not the only one . . .[108]

UNFINISHED IDENTITY (2004)

Adonis, the Committed Poet

CHAPTER 1: GOD

My mysticism is clear and drained of any religious content. God, in strictly religious terms, has fallen silent. That which is concealed has been revealed once and for all. However, in my own variety and manner of mysticism, that which is concealed is constantly and everlastingly speaking, and in this sense all inspired creative beings are prophets in their own right—constantly and everlastingly. Consequently, in my own conception of mysticism, there is no difference between us humans and that which we refer to as God. From this premise, Man can attain a level of ecstasy, which connects him to the quintessence of this universe, beyond masks, veils, or any other sort of physical impediment.

What is spirituality, then, in the third millennium? It is perhaps the mission of literature, perhaps especially poetry, to define what could be termed the New Spirituality, a spiritual revival of sorts, which could resurrect and reinvigorate our old planet . . .

Arab mystics used to say, "We cannot come to know God through reason. We can come to know God only by way of our hearts, because reason itself is confined and bounded, and what is finite and fixed cannot possibly comprehend and explain that which is limitless. In order to comprehend the limitless, one needs thought that is itself limitless."

The prevalent religious reading of the monotheistic revelations gives us an impression of God as one unconscious to, or unaware of, the Eternal concealed within man and in the confines of the Universe.

Read the revelations in the books! They do not reveal God. The revealed books are not God. They are not the spiritual God. God is above and beyond the books that feign to reveal Him [. . .] There is a certain religious reading of God which restricts and confines Him to a trivial discourse, where he is transformed into a simple exercise, whereas God—as knowledge—supersedes all kinds of discourses and systems. He is the Unbounded Eternal, perpetually open toward a deeper sense of the infinite and the eternal. That is at least what mystics advance vis-à-vis the discourses that seek to formulate God.

Balqis, the Queen of Sheba, in Yemen, met the King once. The Prophet Solomon went to meet her, to ask her in marriage. They ended up being dragged into a heated discussion. One of the questions that the Queen asked Solomon was, "What color is God?" Solomon could not answer! He didn't know. I think she—the Queen of Sheba—mocked him. This is an anecdote that dates back to the times of Solomon! . . .

[. . .] A mystic said once, in order to reach that which is concealed —the invisible, that is to say God—we must pass through the human body; the female human body. The world that does not become feminine [le monde qui ne se féminise pas] is worthless.

When God becomes exclusive to one or some of us, one can say that the entire universe turns into the privileged domain of those with the restricted beliefs—claiming to be recipients of an exclusive revelation. This is how wars break out! This perhaps explains the logic behind religious wars, wars, which have in effect never ended, wars that continue to rage under different forms and names, but remain raging religious wars nonetheless. God is a big deal: each of the great religions claims to be a recipient of the greater truth, the greater God, and each one of them wages war to ostensibly defend Him—in spite of the fact that God, I suppose, would be quite capable of defending Himself on His own, without human mediation. He hardly needs soldiers, tanks, suicide bombers, or kamikazes to vindicate or advocate for Him and intercede on His behalf. Nevertheless, violence is intimately related to Man's prevalent conception of the Divine. This violence is well nigh sacred, from the perspective of monotheists. How can violence—the very antithesis of sacredness—be possibly sacred? Yet violence is omnipresent in the practice of monotheism; it is exemplified and expressed in the treatment of men, and especially women. We become violent the minute God's name is summoned; we are not supposed to act a certain way, speak a certain way, think a certain way, and so on . . . *all* in the name of God. This is the essence of violence, from which emerges social and political violence. If we are incapable or unwilling to rethink the roots of violence—from this premise—if we are unable to realize how rooted it is in religion, then we shall never be able to do away with war and violence.

The whole notion of—divine—prohibition, restriction, and taboo, epitomizes violence. Certainly, the levels and degrees of violence vary from one society to the next. But those are variances and differences in degree, not in kind. And it remains that the only—divine—prohibition, or commandment, that would have stamped out violence—the one that says, "Thou shalt not kill"—has never been observed.

CHAPTER 2: ARABIC NUANCES

Allow me to criticize the Arabs, to criticize myself! Criticism is warranted and legitimate, so long as it is fair and just. And when one speaks of Arabs, a clear differentiation ought to be made between Arabs as individuals and human beings, and Arabs as an institution, as establishments, as regimes, and so on . . . , (and this, incidentally, applies to all peoples against whom criticism must be leveled).

One of my overriding ambitions as a person and a poet is to wipe out paternalism where paternalism is no more than a social manifestation of the Divine, where it plays a negative, debilitating, emasculating, castrating role in society. If my aim is to do away with the concept of God's singularity—or uniqueness—this aim applies all the more legitimately to the concept of the singularity—or uniqueness—of the father, of paternity, and paternalism. For, uniqueness of the father in our Middle Eastern societies has also contributed to the marginalization, nay the eradication, of motherhood, maternity, womanhood, and femininity. In our Middle Eastern societies womanhood in the shadow of our social paternalism has become well nigh nonextant. Were paternalism an upright and virtuous concept, one needn't call it paternalism. For, in that case, that upright and virtuous paternalism, that paternity, would have been widespread and prevalent throughout life and friendships; it would have been human and humane, unlike the paternalistic absolutist "fatherhood" pervading our Middle Eastern societies.

Iraq, for instance, was the outcome of the father, the blunder of the father, the father incarnated in the person of the leader. And in that case, the omnipotent, omniscient father had at one point become so full of himself, so blinded to everything around him but himself. He thus proceeded to anoint himself in the image of the absolute, the supreme father. He so loved his so-called children, that he was no longer able to see them; that he ended up annihilating them. Unfortunately, Iraq was but the tip of the iceberg. All political leaders throughout the Arab world are fathers; absolute demiurges, tyrannical, abominable fathers. Therein dwells one of the foundational constitutive elements of Arab civilization. Therein dwells the major ill of Arab societies: an omnipresent totalitarian paternalism that must be eradicated by any means possible.

Paternalism exists elsewhere. In America it takes the form of a hegemonic paternalism defined by raw concrete—physical, military, economic—power. American paternalism is often expressed by a need to police and reorder the world. It's a paternalism akin to authoritarianism. However, the United States do not suffer of the kind of paternalism afflicting the Arabs, the primitive retrograde arbitrary male-chauvinistic "fatherly" kind of paternalism. Other patterns of relationships do exist within American society. There are no "President in the image of the Father" patterns of relationships in America—the way these patterns pervade Arab societies. There are no President-demiurges in America. Indeed, in America, the country itself, in its entirety, is a demiurge vis-à-vis other nations. And this stems from a form of innocuous patriotism spouted by most Americans. Conversely, in the Arab world, the man in power is at once a President, a Prince, a King, *and* a Father. This cultural flaw stems from the totalitarianism pervading Arab societies; a deep-seated, almost congenital despotic proclivity.

In the Arab world, the children, the country itself, the army, the present, the future, all the constitutive elements of the nation, revolve around the person of the Father-President. If the people are defeated, it is the Father himself who suffers defeat and bears the burdens of defeat. The people are but mere accoutrements, incidentals, paraphernalia; they abide by and admit victory and defeat. But it is the Father-President himself who, in reality, clinches victories and suffers defeats. Indeed, there can be no victories without him, and defeats are not necessarily his fault or his responsibility. That is the basic structure of Arab societies. That is precisely why such societies have never, throughout their history, known democracy. The Arab world is the essence of patriarchy. Citizens gain—or lose—relevance depending on their relationships with, and their "obedience" to, their leader, their "Father." [...] And this, actually, has plenty to do with the Arabs' religious concept of "submission." [...]

Yes, all is in need of revamping and changing in my society. My peers and I live in a society that *must* be reconstituted, from A to Z, on every single plane and from every facet. One must take a completely new look at that society, for which I, incidentally, feel the utmost friendship and love. The fact remains, however, that there is an extraordinary job to be undertaken there, where the individual must be free to see things from his or her own perspective, and to react to society and the world according to his or her own means of expression and stemming from his or her own concerns.

In order to better understand my poetry, one must read it from this perspective; one must realize that I am the product of a society that is in dire need of rebuilding, from the foundations up; a society whose culture and politics must be re-examined with a fresh new set of eyes; a society in which I find nothing worth defending, nothing worth safeguarding, nothing worth adopting or learning from. I come from a society that is still living in a primordial political and social state; a society still stuck at ground-zero;[109] ground-zero in the sense that everything about that society needs to be redefined, reviewed, reinvented, and remade. It is this distressing situation that constitutes the background of my poetry, that drives my poetry, and that illuminates my poetic vision—which is not only purely literary, and not only purely linguistic. What concerns me is that my poetry be visionary, innovative, inspired; that it contribute to spawning a new society, a new culture, a new civilization, and a new language. A poet is an artist whose craft is a feat; an act of creation, an act of bequeathing life. There is no living poetry except that spawned through a new poem. If poetry is not in a constant state of renewal, it is dead poetry, written in a dead language that is no longer capable of communing with the word, with the language of life and motion. Creating poetry in a language that spawns a new society, a new culture, and a new set of relations among members of that society or that culture is a fundamental—an urgent—necessity in Arab societies; a necessity that inspires and possesses me during my moments of creativity. And, naturally, my aim is always to create friendships, love, and a new aesthetic, in constant renewal.

On an international global level, it is shameful to watch innocent children die of hunger. Similarly, on an Arab level, it is shameful to have let a hoodlum like Saddam stay at the helms of government in Iraq. It is ignominy and humiliation for the Arabs to have produced leaders of Saddam's stripe. Saddam has mass-murdered numerous rebels, and he never stopped. He went so far as to order the mass-murder of those merely suspected of rebellion, summarily, without due process. [. . .] Iraq was hell on earth. [. . .] If anyone dared bring this situation, this reality to light, they were summarily executed, exterminated! For instance, if anyone dared take any measure deemed noxious to the reality of [Iraq's] dictatorship, not only would they have been executed, but their entire families, their brothers and children were done away with. In the warped vision of the tyrant, society must be purified, cleansed of those who defy or criticize it; the people must be cleansed, the impure must be purified—liquidated—for merely saying "no" to the ruthless Father. [. . .] Ever since its infancy, Islamic society and the Islamic religion have reinforced this sort of absolutism and this sort of opposition to change. Islam actually reinforced and institutionalized these pre-Islamic patterns of relationships, these primordial structures of pre-Islamic Arabian societies. But instead of obedience and submission to the "tribe," Islam postulated obedience and submission to the "Umma."[110]

[. . .]

The Arabs have, historically speaking, constructed a society consumed by continuous disputes and warfare. Never, in the span of almost sixteen centuries, has the war among Arabs or among Muslims abated. To this day this continuous war rages on; not only pitting Arabs against foreigners, but also Arabs against each other. One could say that for the past sixteen centuries the strength and the energies of the Arabs were being squandered in fratricidal conflicts. What are the reasons for this? Perverse and harmful paternalism! "I refuse to recognize the other. He who is not like me, he who does not share my views is to be cast off. The entire world must 'repeat after me,' the entire world must acquiesce to my whims and abide by my worldview; otherwise it is banishment or imprisonment, and worse still." Throughout our history, brutal gangs have always monopolized political power. Never through our long history has there been an experiment or a tradition in universal suffrage or democratic elections; we've always been stuck in absolutism and authoritarianism. Why? Because in our part of the world religion is intimately linked to politics. As long as a separation between the religious and the temporal is not instated, there will never be democracy in Arab societies.

CHAPTER 5: THE ARABS AND THE WEST

One must never generalize and fall prey to jaded bromides such as "the Arabs are ignorant, despotic, anti-Western, terrorists, and so on . . ." To the contrary, most Arabs are extraordinary, wise, kind, and reasoned individuals! One must never identify Muslims with Muslim fundamentalists, or a people with their regime. Falling into that trap is an exercise in restrictive ideology; it serves a political objective. Being a Muslim is an issue of faith, not politics. People deserve that their creeds be respected. Personally, in my capacity as an artist and a poet, I am against institutionalized religion although I am for religious rights and the freedom of religious practice. I am against religion as an institution imposed on the whole of society. I am not against the individual who possesses a religious conviction; I have tremendous respect for the human being, and therefore for that human being's faith, so long as this faith is not transformed into a general set of laws. Society must be civil, secular, benefiting from civil laws that respect diversity, particularism, and pluralism.

Faith is a private intimate matter, and individuals should be free in their choice and their expression of their religious beliefs. Being an atheist is an expression of a certain belief! One can believe in the invisible without necessarily being a mystic. [. . .] I for one, am a pagan mystic. Mysticism, to my sense, is founded on the following elements: First, reality is comprehensive, unrestricted; it is both that which is revealed and visible to us, and that which is invisible and concealed. Second, that which is visible and revealed to us is not necessarily a faithful expression of truth; it is perhaps an expression of a superficial, transitory, ephemeral aspect of truth. To be able to truthfully express reality, one must also seek to see what is concealed. Third, truth is not ready-made, prefabricated. [. . .] We don't learn the truth from books! Truth is to be sought, dug up, discovered. Consequently, the world is unfinished business. It is in constant flashes of revelation, creation, construction, and renewal of imageries, relationships, languages, words, and things. Identity itself is in a state of constant creation; a work-in-progress as it were. Therefore, depicting or "writing" the world is not tantamount to expressing it as it is. Depicting the world or existence is like creating new rapports and harmonies with words and things. [. . .] For instance, what I write does not express me. What I write completes me as a human being; makes me into a better, more perfect individual . . . What I write does not express me, precisely because a word is never capable of expressing a thing, an inanimate object; how can it then express a complex human being? Words express aspects, and only aspects; forms without essence. My writings are a continuation of my existence; they are my other self. [. . .] In this sense, the world is one, single. The West and the East are not separable. This is the kind of mysticism to which I belong. This is how I see myself as a mystic. The being is one. Knowledge, science, philosophy are an inseparable unit.

The East is a source of enlightenment. With the advent of monotheism, in practice, the East became a source of twilight and violence.

In this sense, the Judeo-Christian West is but one form of the East, nicely concealed, camouflaged, made up with a great literature of tolerance. Those Westerners who continued to see the East as a source of enlightenment, and a luminous creative East, those like Hölderlin, Novalis, Gœthe, Rimbaud, and Nerval, do not represent the West. Their vision of the poet, the great Western poet, has not been accepted in its essence. The political West has prosaically advanced economic and strategic aims.

One must remember that it was through Ottoman imperialism, which was in reality obscurantist, that the West sought to respond to the Muslims' discourse. The Ottomans used to say: Westerners are backward. After the downfall of the Ottoman Empire, Westerners took the place of the Ottomans, repeating the same clichés: Muslims are backward barbarians, and we the Westerners are civilized; we're more human! Thus the East became the "other," the retrograde; and if the East possesses anything worthy, it must necessarily be a Western borrowing! The West therefore became the master of the East, which had initially been the master of the West. It's a mere role change. With Europe's industrial revolution, the West took its turn at the helm of imperialism, and the East became the occupied, the colonized, whereas it had previously been the occupier and the colonizer.

One wonders if Rimbaud is an Easterner or a Westerner? Great human accomplishments and creations, the Sumerian and Babylonian Gilgamesh, the Egyptian civilization, the Greek civilization, the great masters of antiquity, and so on . . . all represent human history. They are neither Easterners nor Westerners. They are universal. They are the great earthlings; products of our inspired Earth; a great human voice that hems in continents and oceans. Of course, geographically and politically speaking, one can appreciate the fact that an East and a West do indeed exist. But if we are on a quest to interpret the human condition, if we aim to depict Man in a more human image, to elevate him to a cosmic dimension, these sorts of divisions would no longer be extant.

[. . .]

Writing is a kind of creation. Reading is also a kind of creation. A great creator necessitates a great reader. A reader is a creator in his own right. In our new mediatized Western culture, creativity and poetry are not longer extant because readers are no longer part of the process. The urgency of the future is, therefore, to reinvent the future, in modern literature, and in the perspective of an authentic culture of the third millennium answering to both the West and the East.

In the Arab World, one can no longer write. People and intellectuals are harkening back to a closed, blinkered, repetitive kind of culture,
where there is nary an opening to the outside, where the only other is
Evil, Hell, Satan. The prevalent logic is the following: you are either like
me, or you're nothing. Distinctness and plurality are not celebrated, they
are not even accepted. Arabs during the ninth and tenth centuries used
to say: I am the alterity, I am the distinctness, the distinction. Instead of
saying, "Je est un Autre" ("I is someone else, an 'other'"),[111] in the manner of Rimbaud, the Arabs used to say, "The other is me." Today, there is
a return, among Arabs, to a negationist "I" which refuses the other if the
other is not in the image of the self. This is a sort of "cultural pollution"
whereby a kind of "cultural obscurantism" is actuated by institutionalized religion.

CHAPTER 8: POETRY

If I were to define my own work, I would say that it is poetry that tran-
scends detail in order to attain more complex aggregate elements; it reveals that which is seen and that which is not seen at once. In looking at
a small detail, it is imperative for me to see that detail in the context of a
whole, in relationship to all the components of that whole. It is not suf-
ficient for a poet to have an intimate relationship with his readers, but
also with the things and objects of his work; the world around him. This
is all the more true when we realize that every little detail in our universe
is interconnected to a host of other little details; nothing can exist on its
own, independent of the world surrounding it. So that we may better see
a bough one needs to look at the tree in its entirety. Isolating the branch
destroys or risks destroying the entire vision. And what is important is
not only what one does see; it is also what one does not see. A tree does
not have only one side or one perspective; it is open, accessible, and
exposed from all its sides, from all perspectives. Moreover, a tree is not
only horizontal; it is vertical as well. I love describing a great poem or a
great story as a great tree! It is just like the human body! A literary work
that lacks verticality and openness to the horizon has no shell, no skin;
it is an extremely poor work of art.

[. . .]

A woman in my poetic vision possesses a virile aspect, a masculine side in her being and in her life. The same applies to men; a man bereft of a feminine aspect is a lacking being, ontologically speaking. Was man not both masculine and feminine "in the beginning"? Of course he was. But was subsequently separated from his feminine substance, and ever since that separation, man has embarked on an interminable quest for his lost component, gone astray within him; it is love in the true Platonic sense. I believe it was Plato who first told this story. A true man, in order to be true to himself, must find his missing part. This is the true meaning of love; and love is Man's ultimate perfection. The mare which the prophet Muhammad took from Mecca to Jerusalem was androgynous; a female's face with a male's body [. . .]

The verbal root of the Arabic word for *reason* is *'aql,* which, ironically, has the semantic connotations of "confinement," "bondage," "restraint," and "shackles." This means that "reason" in Arabic, at least etymologically speaking, is a prison; a hindrance and a limitation of sorts. The same sort of etymological origins do not apply for the word reason in European languages. Over time, the word reason in Arabic came to take on meanings similar to those connoted in the European variants of the word. Nevertheless, the word itself, in our [Arabic] tradition, hinders, diminishes, and dwarfs us; it is an impregnable obstacle stunting imagination, fantasy, and all that which is instinctive, abstract, and fancied. That is why, I have attempted throughout my intellectual journey to transform reason into a wandering gazelle, and to pour a "wine of the heart" into "reason," so that reason may become as intoxicated and intoxicating as the heart. The aim of my poetry is to entwine body and soul, so that reason may become a second heart.

Thankfully, one can never translate the body of the beloved into words. Thankfully! Because when we get to know or grasp the meaning of something, we often feel as if we possess or own that something; and "owning" contradicts "loving." Indeed, it is well nigh impossible to completely and definitively know and understand something; less so when considering the remarkable and extraordinary, such as the human body for instance. The human body is a mystery that remains always open for new discoveries, perceptions, and revelations; like love, it is dynamism and movement. The human body cannot be constrained in writing. For one to be able to express himself or herself in Arabic, one needs a prodigious amount of words, especially when one needs to express a single element or concept—because, in Arabic, one rather expresses an image of that which is being described, rather than the object itself. Therefore, language cannot really express reality, regardless of that language's poetic depth; the human body cannot be delineated and defined by language. The human body is infinite, and the language used to describe it is often a finite tool. In this sense, I would say that expressions of intimacy, sex, are unique. Sex is something inexplicable, indescribable. We live it, but do not express it. We can talk about that which is lived through the human body, that which is perceptible, pulsations, and so on . . . but the human body is an ocean, it is in constant movement, it precedes and follows us. How can we, then, delineate and define this extraordinary sort of movement when no wave is similar to the next one? That is why I say that the human body is something inexplicable, indescribable. Every wave within the human body is unique. And if one deigns or imagines being able to express or describe the human body, chances are we are dealing with an inanimate corpse at that point; this sort of description can be said to kill. At that point the human body would no longer be a body; it would no longer be itself. Only religion dares describe things in definitive, absolutist terms, and it is through this sort of arrogance that religion proves itself to be limited.

[. . .]

CHAPTER 9: MY ORIGINS

I was born and lived in a cultural milieu where the person was bereft of individuality. The individual in my society was diluted, watered-down and hidden in an overwhelming whole; this whole was the family, and we all somehow originated in that big "whole." The concept of the *Umma* is a concept specific to Islam. The word itself, *al-Umma,* is the feminine form of Mother, *Umm* in Arabic. Therefore, my relationship with my own mother, in addition to my relationship with my father, was as if we were in the midst of a sea or an ocean. We were all integral parts of that ocean, that sea, that "mother," *Umma.* . . . As a child, I never had a special or a distinguishing relationship or bond with my mother. During adolescence, when I began reading books, I discovered that there was indeed a special, personal rapport, or bond, between a mother and her child. I read all the works of Freud. The things that Freud wrote about belong in a universe that is widely distant from and diametrically opposed to mine. In the universe into which I was born, there wasn't the slightest aspect of anything that Freud had written about; none of the neuroses that consume my life and work today. I grew up in a world where only the group mattered, and where the individual was but a small branch in this huge tree that was the collective.

I did not have a childhood in the modern, Western sense. By the time I took my first steps, I was already entering the routine daily life of my village; the life of trees, fields, toils, seasons, rivers, harvests, crops, tilling, and agriculture. Thus, ever since my early childhood, I had become a laborer, and I never developed any sense of having been a child, let alone my own parents' child—at least none of the parent-child consciousness or bonds in their Western sense. My mother couldn't read; she was illiterate. However, I feel that she was cultured, polished by life, by the hardships of life, the toils of life, and by memory. I suspect that "memory" plays an extraordinary role in the lives of people who are illiterate. [. . .]

To my sense, my mother was a tree, a speaking tree. She was also a river, but a river that toiled and labored. My mother, the way I perceived her, was part of nature; she was a living nature; and in that sense she had tremendous influence on me—even though we hardly spoke. Conversely, my father was cultured and educated; he taught me, tutored me, and initiated me in the rudiments of Jahiliyya (pre-Islamic) poetry, mysticism, post-Islamic poetry, and so on. . . . But most importantly, he taught me mystic poetry. It was he who laid before me the path to poetry. He even wrote traditional poetry himself, and it is to him that I owe my early education and general culture. I was thirteen years old and I had not yet gone to school. I had frequented my village's soil and her fields until the age of thirteen, but until then I hadn't even known or seen what a school looked like, let alone what electricity, a radio set, or a car looked like. I was an integral part of nature; like a cloud, or a tree—that's why I say that I never had a childhood in the modern Western conception of the term. It is now, in my old age, that I try to imagine and discover my childhood. It is of great importance for me now to try to remember, for instance, how I had spent the first thirteen years of my live. I try to picture myself when I was a year, two years, or three years old for instance. It is not easy. I sometimes ask my mother, but at her age [ninety-eight years old], she has completely lost her memories of those days. Some of my old friends from the village do jog my memory sometimes, but only with events dating back to when I was perhaps six; definitely not before then. I think that I am pretty much cut off from my childhood. That is perhaps what stimulates and drives me artistically: this search for a lost childhood. Sometimes, even now in my old age, I feel as if I am inventing an atmosphere of childhood; as if wanting a sort of continuity or prolongation of my own childhood.

One of my childhood friends related to me how we used to learn the alphabet in the village, in the shadow of a large old tree. He told me that I hated being there, that I always found excuses to elude the teacher and slip out of "class." Sometimes, to dissuade me from running away, the teacher would place his long flogging-cane at my feet. But I still tried to skip class. According to my friend, I was unable to sit still for two hours reading and writing; I didn't like doing that. I must have always cherished being alone, independent, free, unbound.

I used to model sexual organs in the dirt; I would play with them, open them, and almost feel the intensity of an orgasm. The power of sexuality is amazing. Never in my life have I had any hang-ups or problems with sex. To me, the human body is like air or water. If someone is free and uninhibited in their heads, they should ordinarily feel the same with regards to their bodies. Purity is antireligious, because Religion-Law is unnatural and antihuman. If freedom cannot be—or cannot translate into—physical freedom, then it would be no more than an abstraction. I lived my entire life doing whatever pleased me and whatever seemed to me as good to do. To me, the foundation of ethics or ethical behavior is to never hurt another . . .

I spent my childhood in nature. My first sexual encounters took place in nature, in the open air, in a river behind our village, where a girl slightly older that me used to take me. I must have been twelve or thirteen years old back then. It was like making love to nature, to the grass and the trees, to Spring. Love was beautiful in the Spring. I used to go into this verdure every day during the Spring. To me, nature, with its green pastures and its clods of earth is very much like the female body; a sensual female body, inspiring love and physical intimacy.

[. . .]

I have chosen my name, Adonis, to liberate myself from a religious identity that was not of my own choosing. My chosen name opened new horizons before me; unexpected horizons in our society. This name, Adonis, delivered me from my own given name, Ali. It delivered me from a closed social allegiance intimately linked to the constraints and restrictions of religion. Through my new, unattached identity, I laid myself open to other human beings. With Adonis, I have chosen an identity in the absolute; a pure, unlimited, free identity, rather than the restricted preordained one imposed upon me by society.

I began creating this new identity when I began creating and honing my art. It is then that I became conscious of the creative dimensions of my chosen name; the name of a begetter, a creator, a generator of life. The result of this journey is that I'm still in the process of creating, re-creating, and regenerating my own identity. This experience has taught me that identity is a never-ending work in progress, a work in progress that defies death and goes on even after death. [. . .] I see myself at this point as an antithesis of my preordained "original" identity. And I am constantly attempting to transpose this freedom, this choice of identity, so that it may create new foundations for Arab culture, to create a new Arab culture and a new Arab identity; one open to the concept of a free elective identity.

Given that everything of value in my society is religious, that all aspects of life are dominated by religion, and that this religion of the Muslims is not only rituals and faith—but most importantly perhaps, language—religion is at once culture, identity, and a set of values. That is why my own liberation was actuated by my attempts to liberate the Arabic language. And as soon as I felt liberated, I began realizing that "me," "the self," would be unable to understand or comprehend itself if it did not attempt to understand "the other." By the same token, I could not understand the East without attempting to understand the West—just as the West itself remains untrue to itself without attempting to understand the East. Cultural identity is like love; it is a continuous dialogue, an alliance between the "self" and the "other." For, the "other" is not only an expression of a need for dialogue; rather, the "other" is a fundamental component of the "self." A tongue that communicates in many tongues.

SEWING THEIR LIPS SHUT IN THREADS SPUN IN THEIR OWN HANDS' WEAVING (2012)[112]

Prophecies from the vantage point of reality

People on the Left Bank of this world's River are entitled to inalienable rights; an axiom we are all expected to defend. On the Left Bank of this River, people are bereft of inalienable rights; an axiom we are all expected to accept. But sometimes the opposite is equally true.

Policies enforced by a global policeman, in the name of Peace, and Freedom, and Human Rights.

In vain a magician attempts to transform the world into a space packed with pipes spewing war fumes.

In vain does he try to force people to sew their lips in threads spun in their own hands' weaving.

In vain does he try to pour falsehoods into their heads: suggesting hens give birth to elephants, and elephants chirp like birds.

Springtime harvests rain like dust between my footsteps, yet I see not a single star to carry me in pursuit of the fleeting steed of time.

There are letters that somehow get written improperly. Behold those letters erasing me by the powers of falsehood invested in them.

He reads: he fades away. He writes: nothingness.

A body teetering on the edge of the word. The word an iron nail inside a furnace / in which a hen's egg can turn into a wing, among many other wings, belonging to birds and other fowl, and a bevy of other animals.

A computer being switched between the fingers of the horizon. Each finger a different rumor.

The lung of daybreak is filled with the air of carnage. The air extends its arms to receive the dust.

In the heart of the language dwells an algebraic formula—a tower of cement letters overpowering public squares and preparing for the conquest of space.

No writing endures in the world of finance, lest its ink itself is money.

A stone whose mere invocation renders the insect a cow, and the cow a tree. And the older the stone gets, the more youthful it becomes.[113]

Arabic words today,
Indict Semantics.
Semantics today,
Indict the Arabic language.

A mystery rendering yesterday's poison today's antidote:
Must you change the view or change the onlooker? Or is the ailment in the eye?

The act of killing no longer requires an overarching noble objective. Indeed the act of killing has itself become the objective. Today's chivalry is to kill, not forgive.

Whatever became of a century-long of talk about freedom of thought and freedom of opinion, and how is it that bullets have replaced words?[114]

Strange how quickly maps and scales and measures shift; strange how quickly fortresses of words crumble![115]

The difference between the elephant and the mosquito in the culture of this new reality is that the mosquito is larger than the elephant simply because it is composed of more letters.[116] Likewise, the raven in this culture is white, and the whale is more agile than a gazelle. Only money is money.

Go ahead and place your lips behind your ears if you wish to make it into the lexicon of this culture.

As expected, the sun arose. Yet it was unable to burn off the fog filling
the skies.

Prophecies emanating from the vantage point of life
Who invented dance?

Who plotted the first dance step?

I am sure, whoever he may be, he was smitten by love.

Behold the lovers dancing,
Gliding in open spaces of wings.

Man no longer exists, save in words that have died, or in bags tossed
out of the window.[117]

What a shame! Azure blue engraved on the neck of Earth. Is this
another history, belonging to another space?

Is this how the West fancies you, O Arab, or is this you:
An extinguished lamp hanging from the neck of a history nearing
extinction?

Death skates faintly, quietly, on the roofs of things. Chilliness in the
soul, and pragmatism is glacial. No warmth except in the act of
refusing to belong to a Time that devours its idols.

A culture of ingrown blisters. Mites of lineages and ancestries
consuming the forests of life. Unbearable those trumpets filling the
mouths of angels. Spare me your gestures and invitations to join
whatever caravan. However, there is another way; a corner at the
end of a road near the last border of the final province. Those of you
sitting will never understand what I am saying. A crowd of women
concealed in black shrouds, and the stars dumping the bowels of the
twilight over their bodies.[118]

I could use a cave where I am able read Plato's Allegories. I could use
prophecies capable of piercing ashen walls, so as to sketch out the
outlines of another time to come.
No, O poet, do not hesitate! Go ahead and hurl your words into the
belly of the tempest, in honor of exhaustion and error. The tempest

herself is susceptible to exhaustion and error. Otherwise, how does one explain her cradling soot and embers?

The lung weeps to the sound of the *Shahada*,[119] whereas the nails submit to the very holes they pierced themselves.[120] One final commentary written by the final embers.

No longer are there fairies among us initiating us to the pleasures of the flesh. And there is the moon, broken, dangling from the cross of desire.[121]

Death is the last of our improvised paper-cutters, upon which we shall place and amputate our dreams.

An Arab age boasting of its grime.

How can you be an enigmatic dream in a clear-eyed view? How can you deem yourself human when you are in the image of a savage issuing out of mysterious jungles.

Life practicing its absence.
Woe to goodness harboring but evil.

Empty words taking the place of things; becoming themselves those things.

Perhaps there is no more room in our world for the winds of Araby; save, perhaps, should it per chance rise in the West. And behold Arabism: a body scraping its own skin, laying it down on a bed of horrors.

As if the station of the Arabs has been rendered merely a safe harbor and passageway for pirates, wading deep into Arab blood.

Lebanon

Modern Lebanon is arguably the Middle East's only mountainous haven for minority populations where—until very late in the twentieth century—Arab-Muslims were themselves numerically inferior and culturally less dominant than the country's Christians. Geographically and demographically speaking, Lebanon is strikingly different from its neighboring countries: Syria, Israel, and Egypt for instance. Traditionally, aside from its Sunni population, Lebanon's minority communities have never been particularly enthralled with the idea of Arab nationalism, or the notion that the Lebanese people were organically tied to their neighbors by bonds of Arabness, Arab culture, and Arab history.

Lebanon's distinction in the past hundred years of its modern political history has been that it viewed itself—and was recognized by others—as a mosaic of ethno-religious groups; a "federation of minorities" as it were, where the native Maronite Catholics, with a long and strong association with Europe, namely and traditionally with Catholic France (*la fille aînée de l'Église*, or the elder daughter of the Catholic Church), benefited since the times of the Crusades from official French protection. And so it had been precisely this strong association with France that differentiated Lebanon's Christians from the rest of their co-religionists in other parts of the Middle East—and within the Ottoman

Empire in earlier times, before the emergence of the modern state system in 1918. Even postrevolutionary anticlerical secular France remained
committed to Lebanon's Catholics, devoted to their autonomist bent.
But Lebanon's uniqueness was evident in many other respects as well.

Various *emirs* (mountain princes) from Lebanon, beginning with
the Maanid Dynasty of the early sixteenth century and throughout the
country's four-hundred-year history as an Ottoman province, strove to
maintain autonomous control over Mount Lebanon and its surroundings, often extending their dominions all the way into Palestine in the
south and to the gates of Damascus in modern-day Syria to the east.
The Egyptian invasions of the Levant by Muhammad Ali's son Ibrahim
Pasha during the 1830s constituted a turning point for Mount Lebanon's
population, and for the Maronites among them in particular. During
those times, the Egyptian viceroy, with autonomist impulses of his own,
attempted to create buffer states between his dominions south of the
Sinai, and Istanbul in the north—the seat of Ottoman authority—so as
to buttress his sovereignty and independence, and shield Egypt from the
influence and control of the Ottomans. As an upshot of their invasion of
the *vilayet*s of Damascus and Beirut, the Egyptians disarmed the Druze
inhabitants of Mount Lebanon and empowered their Maronite rivals.
This emboldened the Maronites and encouraged them to begin expanding their areas of influence (which traditionally were largely confined to
the central and northern portions of Mount Lebanon) southward into
the Druze heartland.

When Ibrahim Pasha's troops withdrew in 1842, a struggle for
power and control ensued between France on the one hand and the Ottomans and their British sponsors on the other, in an attempt to fill the
vacuum left by the departing Egyptian legions. This resulted in a protracted Maronite-Druze "civil war," reaching its pinnacle in 1860, and
ending with the systematic butchering of more than fourteen thousand
Maronites in Mount Lebanon and surrounding areas. Those events of
1860, referred to colloquially by the Christians of the Levant as *mdéébih
el-sittiin* (the massacres of 1860), bolstered the Maronites resolve to establish an independent and exclusively Maronite state in what they now
controlled of Mount Lebanon. During that time, the French landed an
expeditionary force in the Beirut Harbor to lend moral and military

support to their Lebanese-Catholic protégés, and sought to help them establish an autonomous province in their area of influence, with a Maronite "governor" at the helms of its government. The Ottomans with the support of Britain, France's traditional rival in the Levant, objected to the projected exclusively Maronite canton, and a special "power-sharing" regime instead was instated for Mount Lebanon, the Règlement Organique, which bestowed on the province an autonomous status ("Mutasarrifiyya," or "provincial sovereignty"), investing it with self-rule by a Christian (albeit a non-Maronite) Ottoman subject, who by tradition was an Armenian.[1]

This arrangement met the Maronites and the French stipulations for a semblance of autonomy, without instigating the concerns of Mount Lebanon's Muslim neighbors, nor raising the misgivings Ottoman suzerains and their British allies. In 1861, the Mutasarrifiyya came to represent Lebanon's ethno-religious communities proportionately, and became a forerunner of sorts to the modern Republic of Lebanon. In the Mutasarrifiyya, the Christians—not to say the Maronites—constituted an overwhelming majority of the population, thus giving rise to an era of self-assurance, which ushered in a relatively lengthy period of prosperity and stability and freedom for the mountain's people, justifying a popular adage of the time boasting that "happy is he who owns a mere shed large enough for a single goat on Mount Lebanon."[2]

But this autonomous province was abolished in 1915 by the Ottoman authorities who set out to exact revenge on the inhabitants of Mount Lebanon, namely the Maronites among them, in retaliation for their open cooperation with the French who were now the Ottomans' Great War archrivals. This triggered widespread Maronite migrations, further compounded by the Ottomans' mobilization of Mount Lebanon's resources for the war efforts, instigating pervasive deforestation, draughts, loss of arable land, and ensuing famines, which contributed to the destruction and liquidation of one-third of the mountain's population—three hundred thousand people—by the end of the war in 1918.

This traumatic experience would remain seared in the memory of early twentieth-century members of the Maronite political elites who were now lobbying the French for the establishment of a "Greater Leba-non." The new entity they were now claiming had to be one unconfined to a land-locked mountain region—easy prey as the Mutasarrifiyya had been to blockades and ultimately starvation. Hence a new Leba-non would emerge on the debris of the Ottoman Empire; an enlarged Mutasarrifiyya as it were, endowed with coastal cities and western sea-ports—Beirut, Tripoli, and Tyre—open to Mediterranean trade and an uninterrupted intercourse of goods, peoples, and ideas. The new "Greater Lebanon" was likewise endowed with an eastern fertile plain in the ancient Bekaa Valley, the "Granary of Rome" in classical antiq-uity, which would now become the country's breadbasket come what may, and reflect the Maanid principality "in its natural and historical frontiers." No longer would Lebanon be starved to death vowed the Ma-ronites of 1918, and "Greater Lebanon" would be inaugurated in 1920 with that objective in mind.

The choice of Lebanese authors featured in this chapter spans the period of the "pioneers" of modern Lebanese literature. The intellectu-als in question were all "engaged authors," some of whom lived during the Ottoman era, and most used theater, poetry, short stories, and jour-nalistic writing to illustrate a certain conception of an emerging or re-vived "Lebanese" national identity. Kahlil Gibran, Nadia Tuéni, Charles Corm, and Anis Freyha, whose works spanned the first century of Leb-anon's modern history, wrote tirelessly, extolling the glory of ancient Lebanon, recalling the "golden age" of its Phoenician ancestors and the era spanning "classical antiquity," expressing both hope and concern for the future of a nascent political entity gushing out of a region torn by conflict, irredentism, and resentful nationalisms.

With both sincerity and conviction, sometimes rhetorical, often lyrical, the authors featured in this chapter wrote with spontaneity, in-nocence, optimism, and determination, infusing their literary produc-tion—which *always* upheld lofty universal ideals—with a distinct sense of national and cultural commitment. Writing in French, Charles Corm set the tone for those who would follow, rendering themes inspired by his own worldviews and conceptions of Lebanese history, in languages spanning French, English, Arabic, and dialectal Lebanese. In all, the literary production of this period was one infused with passion and enthusiasm, inspiring faith in a bright destiny and a confident future—for Lebanon in particular, but also for generally for the entire Middle East.

In these works we touch upon elements and profiles of Lebanese life, Lebanese history, and Lebanese landscapes unfolding with both precision and symbolism. We witness Lebanon's intermingling of mountains and seas; we walk along the shores of port cities like Byblos, Tyre, Sidon, and Berytus; we climb to snow-covered mountain hamlets— the "spiritual source" as it were of Lebanese history—we explore the "traditional" Lebanese home and hermit's hut, and we pass in review relevant stages of Lebanon's millennial history. But still more is revealed in this selection: political, linguistic, and educational themes bearing local relevance, to be sure, but also possessing universal civilizational and spiritual dimensions pertinent to places, peoples, times, and events far removed from the specificity of Lebanon.

∾

KAHLIL GIBRAN (1883–1931)

Kahlil Gibran was born in 1883, in Bsharri, a Maronite village of northern Mount Lebanon perched at a five-thousand-foot altitude astride the edge of the famed biblical cedar forests and the mouth of the Maronites' celebrated Valley of the Sainted, Wadi Qodishè. Gibran grew up poor, but rich in the love of his parents and siblings, swaddled in the mystical beauty of his rugged surroundings perched at the edge of an abyss, teetering between heavens and valleys. Gibran often marveled at the spirituality of these magical settings, noting how, often on clear starry nights, one might find it difficult to make out the lines separating Mount Lebanon from the heavens overhead.

This was the kind of awe-inspiring atmosphere that fed Gibran's imagination and nourished his pride of place as he came of age. And it was against this heavenly backdrop, a uniquely Lebanese one, Aramean-Maronite in its spirituality and Phoenician in its legends, mythologies, and yearnings, that Gibran was to set his literary narratives in the years to come.

Gibran received his early education in the shadow of the majestic cedars, racing with singing brooks and running among the terraced orchards of Bsharri by summer. And by winter, seeking physical shelter from the bitter cold, and spiritual solace from the isolation of winter, Gibran often hid in Bsharri's secluded churches and monasteries, many of which were carved out of Mount Lebanon's impregnable rock. Until the age of twelve, Gibran was also instructed in the rudiments of Syriac, French, and Arabic, by local priests, in the same churches and monasteries that were his retreats and sanctuaries during long snowy winters.

In 1895, due to a family dispute—and partly because of his own father's run-in with the Ottoman authorities—Gibran, his mother, and his siblings, like many Maronites of their time, had to flee the tenuous safety of Mount Lebanon and settle in the anonymity and isolation of Boston, in the New World. But Boston and the United States in general were not as unkind to the young immigrant as one might have imagined. It was in America, separated from the splendor and his native Bsharri, that Gibran's national consciousness began blossoming. His stay in Boston—his encounters with the Boston public school system, and the long hours he spent in the reading rooms of the Boston Public Library—was a period of contemplation and gestation for the "national" themes that were to later emerge in Gibran's literary work. The bucolic Maronite surroundings that had fed his youthful imagination back in Bsharri, and the Phoenician legends and symbolism that were introduced to him by his teachers of Syriac and Arabic back in the old country, as well as motifs whispered to him by Bsharri's majestic surroundings—from towering mountains and cedars, to hermits' huts and ancient temples, tombs, and churches—were finally being refined into a coherent "Lebanese national" narrative fed by distance, nostalgia, and longing for the ancestral homeland.

Charles Corm and a cohort of intellectuals who gravitated around his journal, *La Revue Phénicienne,* were for all intents and purposes the pioneers advancing the distinct "Phoenicianist" conception of Lebanese identity, which deemed Lebanon a progeny of Phoenician, not Arab cultural and historical accretions. This notion became more articulate and assertive in Lebanon proper under Corm's leadership during the 1920s and 1930s, and its intellectual language was almost exclusively French. Yet Phoenicianism had an "overseas" iteration in the person of Kahlil Gibran, who advanced motifs and narratives similar to Corm's, in literary expression produced in both English and Arabic, and emitted from the New World. Mention of Phoenician deities, Phoenician temples, Phoenician belief systems, and the Phoenicians' humanistic impulses, woven into the distinct landscape of Mount Lebanon and the Mediterranean, populated Gibran's literary themes.

Even Gibran's best-known English work, *The Prophet,* a book of wisdom and a collection of reflections on life and the human condition, managed to weave into its narrative allusions to the Phoenician origins of its central character, the prophet Almustafa. Arguably a depiction of Kahlil Gibran himself, the prophet's story recalled its author's own personal peregrinations and his exile to the New World, culminating in his ultimate return to Mount Lebanon. After longing for the land of his birth during twelve long years of exodus, dwelling in the embrace of his adoptive city, Orphalese, Almustafa readied himself for a return and a long-awaited homecoming—to the "land of [his] memories and the dwelling place of [his] greater desires."³ But like the archetypal Phoenician mariner, whose only homeland had been "riding the tides" and spawning new homelands wherever he made land, Almustafa had grown fond of Orphalese and its people, and had resolved to depart from them only with an aching in his heart and a wound in his spirit.⁴ Yet the lure of the land of his "ancient mother" was too strong to repel, and "the sea that calls all things unto her" likewise called out to him. And so he had to set sail.⁵ And when he gazed toward the sea, "and he saw his ship approaching the harbor, and upon her prow the mariners, the men of his own land, [. . .] his soul cried out to them, and he said: Sons of my ancient mother, you riders of the tides, How often have you sailed in my dreams. And now you come in my awakening, which is my deeper dream. Ready am I to go, and my eagerness with sails full set awaits the wind. [. . .] And then I shall stand among you, a seafarer among seafarers."⁶ The preceding not only extolled the Phoenicians as forefathers and countrymen of Gibran, but it did so in imagery, language, and style which recalled the biblical prophets Isaiah's and Ezekiel's poetic visions of Tyre, Sidon, and their children.⁷ But Gibran normalized the vector

of continuity between the ancient Phoenicians and the modern inhabitants of Lebanon throughout his literary production, not only in *The
Prophet.* In a chapter titled "Between Christ and Ishtar," for instance, in
the 1912 Arabic collection *The Broken Wings,* one of the book's heroines
is compared to the Phoenician goddess Ishtar (Ashtaroth, the consort
of Adonis, who is himself an emanation of the chief Phoenician deity
El), suggesting a Phoenician dimension to the Christian component of
modern Lebanon—where the story itself was staged. In another chapter of *The Broken Wings,* the main protagonist, a likeness of Ashtaroth,
is seen entering an abandoned Phoenician shrine accompanied by her
beloved. Inside the temple, before a painting of a Byzantine Jesus and
the Phoenician Ashtaroth, the two lovers are abandoned for hours on
end, entranced in reveries before sarabands of Phoenician lovers from
the distant past, walking past them in processions, offering themselves
in oblation to the goddess of love and fertility.

But a representative sample of Gibran's work was chosen for this
anthology for reasons at first glance not necessarily pertinent to strictly
speaking Levantine or Phoenicianist themes.. Given his importance in
the corpus of modern Lebanese and Arabic literatures, as one of the
pioneers of modern Arabic *belles lettres* and the Arabic literary *nahda*
(renaissance movement), it would not only have been natural to include
Gibran in an anthology of modern Levantine literature, but indeed righteous. However, the Gibran selection chosen for this volume does not
fall within his strictly "literary" production, and certainly not within
the strictly "Levantine" (or "Lebanese patriotic") themes otherwise residing in his work. Rather this is a text written in Arabic that deals with
issues of Arabic linguistics and questions pertaining to the future of the
Arabic language. Aptly titled "The Future of the Arabic Language," the
text was published in interview format in the Egyptian literary maga-
zine *Al-Hilaal* in 1922. In it, Gibran predicts the future of the Arabic
language—likening it to Latin—and defends the Middle East's dialectal
speech forms, placing them and their themes on a par with the "one-
language" tyranny of Arabic and Arabic purists who deem *only* "classical" or "Modern Standard" Arabic worthy of recognition.

It should be noted in this regard that although he was an innova-
tor and rejuvenator of "classical Arabic," and wrote some of his most

beautiful and groundbreaking work in Modern Standard Arabic, Gibran remained a realist and could not help but foresee that the future of Arabic would resemble the past of Latin and other cultic ceremonial languages. Like Taha Husayn during the 1930s, another titan of modern Arabic *belles lettres,* Gibran considered classical Arabic, the Arabic of literary and official expression, foreign to the true nature of the children of the Middle East, whether or not they deemed themselves Arabs and Arab nationalists. Gibran was like many modern Middle Eastern academicians and literati who promoted the valorization of spoken languages and called for the acquisition of knowledge—and the basics of reading, writing, and the sciences—in native spoken languages (and through mother tongue–based approaches to education).

For Middle Easterners to acquire knowledge in Modern Standard Arabic, suggested Gibran in 1922, was analogous to their acquiring knowledge in a foreign language.[8] Subtle as it was, his advocacy on behalf spoken languages did have its opponents during his days. And the topic still garners hostility in our own times. Despite research demonstrating that literacy and educational attainment are enhanced when learners are taught in their native languages, purists and Arab nationalists today deem the valorization of native spoken languages—that is to say Middle Eastern vernacular speech forms that do not integrate Modern Standard Arabic—divisive and detrimental to religious (that is to say Islamic) conformity and regional (that is to say Arab) unity.

As will be gleaned from his text, Gibran appealed for broader perspectives, making the case for a Middle East as a crossroads of civilizations and languages, a home to several distinct cultural, religious, and linguistic traditions, and a language area where Arabic can be revived and can survive—and indeed must be made to survive—but *alongside* other languages, not *instead* of them.

THE FUTURE OF THE ARABIC LANGUAGE (1922)

1. What is the future of the Arabic language?

Language is a manifestation of a nation's innovative capacities, or rather an incarnation of the nation's very specificity as a nation. Should this innovative capacity drift away, so would the nation's linguistic evolution come to a halt. And with this halt often comes stagnation, and from stagnation emanate death and extinction.

Therefore, the future of the Arabic language is wholly dependent upon the future of living—and departed—creative minds issuing from the various nations that speak this language.[9] Where creativity is extant, the future of the language itself will no doubt come to be as glorious as its past. But where creativity is extinct, as may be the case with Arabic today, so does the future of the Arabic language come to resemble the present of its two sister languages, Syriac and Hebrew.[10]

And what are those elements which one may call a given language's "innovative capacities?" National creative or innovative capacities consist primarily of a nation's determination to move ever forward on the path of progress. Innovative capacities are therefore a constant hunger, an insatiable thirst, and a steady longing to uncover the unknown; they are a series of dreams that a nation seeks to make into reality; dreams that no sooner were realized than new ones were spawned and began to be pursued. So, in a sense, a nation's innovative capacities lie in the genius of its individual members and in their collective enthusiasm as a single people. And the genius of individuals lies in their ability to channel the latent desires of the collective into concrete visible form.

And so, during Jahiliyya (pre-Islamic) times, the poets of the Arabs were circumspect because the Arabs themselves were in a state of circumspection. But Arabic-language poets also grew and expanded their horizons later during the early Islamic period, and they broached new themes in later times, when non-Arab Muslims began employing Arabic as a literary medium—mainly because the Islamic *umma* itself had become ethnically and linguistically more diversified.[11] This allowed the Arabic-language poet to evolve and grow and transform over time, appearing in the garb of a philosopher at times, a physician at other times, or even an astronomer in other given circumstances. And this would remain the case until lethargy set in and beset the innovative capacities of the Arabic language, throwing it into torpor and deep slumber. Consequently, the Arabic language's poets were rendered versifiers and dilettantes, its philosophers turned into wordsmiths, its physicians became charlatans, and its astronomers morphed into fortune tellers.[12]

If the above is correct, then the future of the Arabic language will become a function of the innovative capacities of the various nations that speak this language.[13] And should each of those nations benefit from their own national specificity and their own collective consciousness, and should each of their own specific innovative capacities awaken from deep slumber, so will the future of the Arabic language itself become as glorious as its past. Absent that, no such rebirth can ever be expected and none will take place.[14]

2. *What role might modernization, urbanization and Europeanization play in the future of the Arabic language?*

The effects of these factors constitute nourishment of sorts; a kind of food intake that the language receives from its surroundings, chewing it and swallowing it, and rendering what is useful of it a part of its own being, in the same manner in which a tree may turn the elements of light and air and soil around it into buds, then flowers, and ultimately fruits. However, should the language seeking nourishment lack the requisite teeth for biting, or the stomach for digesting, then all the food along its path shall go to waste, and indeed may turn into deadly poison. And many are the trees that swindle life and pretend to be vibrant and alive when protected in the shade, yet shrivel and wither and die the minute they are brought into the sunlight. In the end, "whoever has, to him more shall be given, and he will have an abundance; but whoever does not have, even what he has shall be taken away from him."[15]

And so, the "spirit of the West" is simply one of the aspects of mankind's collective journey; one phase among others in our lifetime. And the life of mankind is one awesome procession, moving ever forward, stirring a wondrous cloud of golden dust on its path. It is out of this golden dust that mankind's languages and governments and schools of thought are spawned. The nations that lead this human procession are the innovators among us—and innovators by definition are influential. Conversely, those nations among us that walk on the tail end of the procession are the imitators—and imitators by definition are often followers and subordinates. And so, when Easterners were once the pioneers of this awesome human procession, and the Westerners its followers, our Eastern civilization exerted the greatest influence on the ways and languages of the West.[16] Today, however, the West is at the forefront

of human achievement, and we [in the East] have fallen far behind. Subsequently, and by virtue of its preeminence, it is now the civilization of
the West that is leaving its markings on our language, our intellect, and
our value systems.

   3. *What influence does the evolution of the current political situation
in the Arab regions have on the language?*

   Authors and intellectuals, whether in the East or in the West, are
in consensus that Arab regions are currently in a dire state of political,
administrative, and psychological confusion. Most also agree that this
sort of confusion and disarray is an assured path to the decay and ruin of
Arab societies. But my question is the following: can what we are dealing with today be truly deemed confusion, or is it apathy? If it is apathy,
then apathy is truly the death knell of nations and the demise of peoples:
apathy is the agony of death in the form of stupor; it is death pure and
simple, taken for slumber.

   If on the other hand what is gripping the Arab regions today is
mere confusion,[17] then, to my sense, confusion is always beneficial, because it often has the function of revealing that which had previously
been concealed in the spirit of the nation, replacing a nation's stupor
with alertness, and awakening it from its torpor. This, to the same extent that a tempest may vigorously shake the trees in its path to their
foundation; not so much to uproot them, but rather to purge them
of their dead branches and scatter their yellow leaves away. Therefore,
should confusion emanate from a nation that may still possess some of
its essence, this confusion may prove to be the clearest indication that
the innovative instincts of the nation are still alive at the individual level,
and that alacrity is still extant in its collective. After all, wasn't chaos the
first, rather than the last, word in the Book of Life?[18] And isn't chaos but
life in a state of confusion?

   Therefore, the impact of political evolution in the Arab regions
may at some point transform that which is disarray and confusion into
structure, and that which is ambiguity and dubiousness into harmony
and order. Yet, political evolution could never transform those regions'
apathy into passion, nor morph their tediousness into enthusiasm. For
the potter may well be able to make a jar for wine or vinegar out of clay,
but out of sand and gravel he would not make anything.

4. Will the teaching of Arabic prevail in elementary and secondary schools, and will Arabic ever be used for the teaching of the sciences?

The teaching of Arabic will not become the norm in secondary and elementary education until schools truly become national institutions with a national character all their own. Likewise, the sciences will never be taught in Arabic before schools have passed from the hands of charities, confessional committees, and monastic missions, to the hands of local governments.

Take Syria for instance,[19] whose educational system has been largely a Western bequest and the outcome of Western philanthropy.[20] And so we, the children of this land, have devoured this bread of charity voraciously because we are and remain famished for knowledge. Yet this bread, which has been given us by others, has in turn revitalized us and killed us. It revitalized us because it awakened our senses and made our minds somewhat alert. But it killed us as well because it rent our world asunder, it weakened our unity, it ripped the ties that bound us together, and it separated our communities to the point where our lands have become a collection of tiny colonies of different tastes and stripes, each promoting the interests of a different Western nation, each raising a foreign nation's banner, each upholding values and singing glories different from our own. Therefore, those of us who have savored knowledge at an American institute became American agents, and those who sipped knowledge at the fountain of Jesuit schools became French ambassadors, and those who cloaked themselves in fabric shorn from Russian colleges became Russian representatives. . . . The strongest evidence of this can be noted in the wide differences of opinion and the competing allegiances that are being disputed in our day over the political future of Syria.[21] Therefore, those who have acquired knowledge by way of the English language seek to place their countries under American or British guardianship. Likewise those whose acquired language today is French, insist on French protection. Conversely, those of us who have studied neither French nor English reject both and stick to policies limited to their own narrow worldviews and their own particular brand of knowledge.[22]

It may be that our biases in favor of those nations that fund our education are attributable to Easterners' innate sense of propriety and gratitude. But what kind of "propriety" and "gratitude" is it that erects a stone on one side and demolishes a wall on the other? What is this "innate" ethos that plants and nurtures a flower on the one hand, only to uproot a forest on the other? What kind of an emotion is this that brings us back from the dead one day, only to smother us for an eternity a day later?

Our true Western benefactors and the true magnanimous souls that have bequeathed knowledge to us certainly did not slip thorns and thistles into the bread that they fed us. Their noble intention no doubt has been to benefit not to harm us. Yet I wonder where the thorns sprang from, and what the origin is of those thistles? But this is another question altogether, the answer to which I shall leave for another day.[23]

Yes, Arabic will prevail in elementary and secondary education, and the sciences will be taught in Arabic so that our political tendencies will merge and our national affections will clarify. For, schools are the places where one's impulses get consolidated, and where one's frame of mind gets refined. Yet this will never become the case before we are able to educate our charges out of our own national funds. A single Arabic language will never become the sole language of instruction unless we ourselves become the children of a single nation, instead of two nations each of which negate the other. And the latter shall not take place before we switch from receiving the bread of charity to kneading our own bread in our own home. For, the needy beggar can hardly afford to make demands of his benefactor, and he who puts himself in the position of a beneficiary can never protest the benefactor—as the beneficiary is forever the sheep, and the benefactor is the eternal shepherd.

5. And will Modern Standard Arabic ever overcome and defeat the various spoken languages of the Middle East and unite them into a single idiom?

Spoken idioms will evolve and change, and the coarse among them will become refined. However, spoken idioms will never be overcome by Modern Standard Arabic—nor should we wish them to be overcome. They are, after all, the foundation of that which we deem eloquent and elegant among languages.[24]

Indeed, like all beings and organisms, language is subject to the laws of evolution and the survival of the fittest. And among the spoken languages of the Middle East there exists a plethora of speech forms deemed to be the "fittest"; speech forms that will remain and will evolve, because they are the closest constitutive elements of the concept of a nation and its very specificity as a nation. I said it before, and I shall repeat it for as long as necessary: the so-called dialects shall bind themselves to the corpus of languages and shall become bona fide languages in their own right.

After all, all of Europe's great languages have at one time or another in their history benefited from vernacular variants, all of which have in time produced lofty literary and artistic elements all their own. [. . .] Likewise, in the Middle East today, one can find in the *mawwal, zajal, 'ataaba,* and other popular forms of poetry elements that transcend and outstrip the very best and the most eloquent of what has been produced in pure literary Arabic. Indeed, should we dare juxtapose our popular literature, as produced in "vulgar" vernacular languages, to the "eloquent" Arabic that crowds our newspapers and magazines, the so-called "vulgar" languages would loom like fragrant bunches of basil atop bundles of dry firewood, or like a flock of beautiful dancing singing maidens before a heap of mummified corpses.[25]

Indeed what we call "the Italian language" today had its early beginnings as a vernacular, often referred to as a "vulgar language" during the Middle Ages. Yet, it was precisely *this* "vulgar" that became the language of Dante, Petrarch, and St. Francis of Assisi, all of whom ultimately wrote their timeless masterpieces in an "inferior" idiom that in time became Italy's "eloquent" standard language and its national literary medium.

And so, Latin was subsequently relegated to the status of an ambling temple, a casket as it were, hoisted on the shoulders of reactionaries. Today, the vernacular languages of, say, Egypt, Syria, and Iraq are no less worthy of the idiom of Ma'arri and Mutanabbi,[26] than are the "vulgates" of Italy vis-à-vis the language of Ovid or Virgil.

And so, should an exceptional writer arise in the Near East some day, publishing a great work of note in one of the region's vernacular languages, it is not inconceivable that this language could become another regional "standard" replacing the Modern Standard Arabic of today. However, I see the likelihood of this coming about in the Arab regions far removed from our present time. Easterners remain far more attached to their past than they could ever become concerned with their present or their future. They are hopelessly conservative, and the talented among them practice their literary craft by emulating their forebears rather than charting a new innovative course for themselves. Yet the ways of the ancients are nothing if not the shortest distance between creativity's cradle and its grave.

6. And what are the best means to revive the Arabic language?

The best and indeed the only way to revive a language dwells in the heart of the poet, on his lips, and at his fingertips. Poets are the mediators between the creative and innovative capacities of their nations and the rest of humanity. They are the live wires that carry what emerges in the realm of feelings, transmitting it into the realm of science. They are likewise the conduits of that which is spawned in the intellectual sphere, transferring it to the sphere of memory and codification. Indeed, a poet is nothing if not the father and mother of his language, moving her along wherever he may go, and causing her to lie in hiding whenever he lies in hiding. And should the poet pass on, his language would usually sit at his graveside in sobs and lamentations, until another poet passes by and takes her by the hand. And to the same extent that the poet should be deemed the father and mother of his language, so is the imitator a gravedigger and a weaver of the language's funerary.[27]

And by poet I mean every inventor, be he big or small, every explorer, be he weak or strong, every creative mind, be he glorious or contemptible, every lover of life, be he aristocrat or tramp, and every person who stands alert and sparkling with vigor, by day and by night, be he philosopher or vineyard watchman. An imitator, on the other hand, is one who uncovers nary a thing in the course of his life and begets nothing of value. Rather, the imitator pilfers the elements of his spiritual life from his contemporaries, and weaves his moral cloaks out of rags lifted from the mantles of those who came before him.[28]

By poet I mean the sower of seeds who furrows and turns his field with a plow that differs, even if slightly, from the plow that he might have inherited from his father, so that those succeeding him may call that new plow with a brand new name; by poet I mean the gardener cultivating flowers of yellow and of red, and then new flowers of orange, so that those succeeding him may call his new flowers with new names; by poet I mean the tailor spawning from his loom a new kind of fabric woven with threads and fibers differing from textiles woven by neighboring tailors, so that those succeeding him may call his new fabric with new names; by poet I mean the sailor who hoists a third sail on a two-masted vessel, or the builder who raises a house with two doors and two windows among homes built with single doors and windows, or the dyer who fuses colors that no one had dared meld together before him, yielding a brand new color, so that those succeeding the sailor, the builder, and the dyer may call the fruits of their labor with brand new names, adding a new sail to the ship that is the language, and a new window to the house that is the language, and a new color to the mantle that is the language.

The imitator, on the other hand, is one who ambles blindly on the beaten path of a thousand and one caravans preceding him, never deviating from the trails left behind for fear of getting lost; he is one mimicking others in the way he lives, dresses, drinks, and earns his daily bread, the ways of a thousand and one generations preceding him, rendering his own life a mere echo of what has come before, freezing his very being into a faint shadow of a distant truth about which he knows very little and cares even less.

But the poet is a votary entering the temple of his own being, falling to his knees, weeping, jubilant, mournful, rejoicing, listening intently and communing. Then, when he exits the temple, his lips and tongue radiate new nouns and verbs and letters and word patterns set to new forms of devotion, in permanent daily renewal and transformation, thus adding through the poet's labors a new silver string to the lute of his language and a new fragrant timber to its hearth. Conversely, the imitator is he who regurgitates other worshipers' prayers and other supplicants' pleas, mindlessly, bereft of emotion, leaving the language where he found it, forlorn, parched, bereft of prosody, rhetoric, or a distinct personality of its own.

A poet is he who, when in love with a woman, feels his soul isolating itself and averting the ways of humans so as to better adorn his dreams with emanations from the splendors of daytime, the awe of nighttime, the howling of tempests, and the stillness of valleys, all to mold out of those experiences a crown to grace the head of the language, and spawn from his soul's contentment a locket to the neck of the language. But the imitator remains an imitator even in his love and in his poetry of yearning to his beloved. And so, should that imitator allude to the face or neck of his beloved, he would compare them to the "full moon" and the "gazelle."[29] And should he ache for his beloved's hair, for her gaze, or for the shape of her body, he would recall "the night," a "drawn arrow," or a supple "arched twig." And should he lament the distance separating him from his beloved, he would speak of a "sleepless eyelid," a "faraway dawn," and a "nearby reprimand." And should he be inspired to feign a rhetorical wonder in honor of his beloved, he would utter gems to the effect that "my beloved beseeches the pearl of tears to sprinkle like rain from her narcissus eyes, and dampen her rosy cheeks, as she nibbles her jujube[30] fingers, with her hailstone teeth."[31] And so would our imitator-friend carry on infatuating himself, regurgitating obsolete imageries and outdated songs, oblivious to the fact that his intellectual inertia is poison to the language, and his silliness scorn for her nobility and her honor.

I have already spoken about the benefits of that which is "innova-tive," and the harm of that which is "barren." But I have not yet men-tioned those who spend the precious hours of their lives putting to-gether dictionaries, composing long-winded sermons, and establishing linguistic societies. I did not mention them because I consider them like a seashore, subject to the ebbs and flows of language, whose sole func-tion is acting as a sieve. To be sure, sifting is an honorable job. However, what is a sifter to sift when the nation's innovative capacities in language sow only husks, harvest but straw, and heap but thorn and thistle on the nation's threshing floors?

Let it be said again (because it bears repeating) that the life, uni-fication, and propagation of language, and all that which pertains to language, was and shall forever remain a function of the toils and re-sourcefulness of poets. But, have we any poets in the East?

I reckon that we do, and every child of the East has the capacity of becoming a poet in his own right; a poet in his field, in his garden, before his loom, inside his temple, atop his pulpit, and at his desk. Every child of the East is indeed capable of freeing himself from the prison of imitation, orthodoxy, and tradition, and surging forth into the sunlight, and joining in the procession of life. Every child of the East is capable of submitting to the power of innovation lurking within his soul—that eternal never-ending power capable of transforming stones into Children of God.

As for those who have devoted their lives and talents to poetry and verse, to them I say: Let your inclinations for specificity and originality prevail over the instincts of emulating the elders. For, you would render yourselves and the Arabic language a far greater service building a modest hut out of your humble selves than erecting a towering edifice by mimicking and borrowing from others. Let your dignity inhibit your tendency to compose panegyrics, elegies, and poetry of praise.[32] For, it is far better for you and the Arabic language to die neglected and despised than to consume your hearts and souls like burning incense before idols and tombstones. Let your national zeal move you to depict Eastern life in all its oddities and miracles and joys. For, it is far better for you and the Arabic language to treat of the most humble and mundane of events surrounding you, and outfit them with fabrics of your own lives and imaginations, than to translate into Arabic the loftiest and the most beautiful of that which has been written by Westerners.[33]

༄

NADIA TUÉNI (1935–83)

Born to a French mother and a Lebanese father issuing from the notable Druze Hamadé dynasty of Mount Lebanon, Nadia Hamadé-Tuéni, in the image of the conflation of identities that was the land of her birth, was the product of an exquisite cultural hybridity. Nadia Tuéni came into the world in Baaklin, in the Shoof Mountains of Lebanon, on July 8, 1935. She completed her elementary and secondary schooling at both parochial and secular francophone institutions—the École des Soeurs de Besançon and the Mission Laïque Française in Beirut. She was later to earn her *baccalauréat* from the Institut Français of Athens, where her father, Ali Hamadé, a diplomat and author in his own right, headed Lebanon's diplomatic mission. Upon returning to Beirut in the mid-1950s, Nadia Hamadé was admitted into the Jesuit Université Saint-Joseph law school. Soon thereafter, she met—and eventually married—Ghassan Tuéni; a Harvard-educated journalist and publisher of Lebanon's Arabic-language newspaper of record, *Al-Nahar*. Ghassan Tuéni would eventually become a deputy to the Lebanese parliament, and later a minister, a diplomat, and ultimately one of Lebanon's most respected and beloved elder statesmen. Nadia Tuéni's work brims with allusions to Lebanon's diversity and multiplicity of identities, a reflection of her own personal hybridity in a region often buckling under multiple forms of extremism always mandating uniformity and orthodoxy. She saw her role as a poet as one not all that different from the personality of her countrymen; children of a land well endowed with cultural diversity, where multiple religious and ethnic traditions meet, and where the West and East meet and dialogue more often than they may battle and compete with one another. And so, Tuéni wore her skin (and her role) well as cultural conduit and mediator reconciling cultures often viewed in our times as clashing with and negating each other. Long before the concept of "dialogue of civilizations" became the fashionable endeavor of scholars and prelates of multiculturalism in the West, Nadia Tuéni and many other children of her generation foretold and practiced what one might call a native Lebanese twining of culture. In her *Juin et les mécréantes,* a feminine voice, possibly Tuéni's own, pays homage to hybridity and multiplicity of identities, perhaps her own, as an essential element of the dialogue and syncretism that she valorized:

> O you, my four beloveds,
> My four kinships . . .
> Four different women, hailing from the same hinterland . . .
> Tidimir the Christian
> Sabba the Muslim
> Dahoun the Jew
> Sioun the Druze.[34]

Nadia Tuéni's poetry can be argued to have been a celebration of Lebanon itself rather than a celebration of diversity and multiplicity in general. After all, the diversity that she treasured and memorialized was one

that she savored as a child, a diversity strewn about between Lebanon's
mountains and Mediterranean shores. Reveling in diversity was not a
learned value for Tuéni; it was an innate, natural instinct, part of the
microclimate of her Lebanon, as revealed in the poems produced here:
Blonde Stanzas (1963); as well as *Promenade* and *Beirut*, two of the poems of in her 1979 collection, *Lebanon: 20 Poems for a Beloved*, dedicated
to her young daughter Nayla.[35]

Blonde Stanzas (1963)

In the shadow of an old olive tree, a fragrant jasmine surges,
And soon my childhood flows before me,
Sweet scents of basil, and dried thyme flowers,
Mingling with the cicadas' lullabies in the velvety pines,
Like a hymn to the sun,
A grateful "thank you" for being part of existence,
In the presence

Of the red-tiled roofs
On the side of the valley,
Of moving distant seas
In a piercing azure blue.

And of you, the Bedouin maiden,
With your eyes of Arabia,
Transformed long ago
By my westerly winds!

Prurient arcade
Rusty Arabesque
Cloister of silence
Punctuated by fig trees,
My love has been deemed
under a white veil
A swarthy summer fling
Of an odalisk . . .

PROMENADE (1979)

Mountain, O magnificent beast,
Our roots deep in your mane,
Four exquisitely algebraic seasons,
A blue cedar to add to the inventory.
Smooth and regal, the sea is ageless,
The wind is gentle, like a sacrament,
And God has ceded his cabin-crews
In return for a home on the peaks of Lebanon.

Mountains, O mountains,
Let me love you
Like those who are unsure about their real age;
Let me love you
Like we pick off the beads of a rosary of legends and of whispers.
Let me love you,
On my knees, like the farmer and his land.
Let me love you,
Softly, like the moon on the evening of your hair.
Let me rock you to sleep
In the tendons of the warm air.
Into limitless peace
Fluid like a scherzo.

BEIRUT (1968)

Be she concubine, scholar, or zealot,
Peninsula of noise, of gold and colors,
A pink merchant city, like a fleet of ships,
Adrift,
Scouting the horizons for the warmth of a seaport,
She's a thousand times dead, and a thousand times still living.

O Beirut of the hundred palaces, O Béryte of old stones,
Where people throng from everywhere
Jostling to hoist idols and statues,

That make men bow in prayer,
That make wars shriek and howl.
O Beirut, your women, with eyes like beaches, sparkling in the night,
And your paupers, straggling, like ancient oracles.

Here in Beirut, in every house dwells a different idea.
Here in Beirut, every word is pomp and pageantry.
Here in Beirut, people unload thoughts and caravans,
Merchants of the heart, priestesses and sultans.

Be she pious nun, or be she sorcerer,
Be she both, or be she the swivel
To the portal of the sea or the Levant's entryway,
Be she adored, or be she accursed,
Be she bloodthirsty, or be she holy water,
Be she innocent, or be she deadly,
Just the mere fact of her being, Phoenician, Arab, or plebian,
Just the mere fact of her being, this Levantine of varied vertigoes,
Like those quaint delicate flowers, brittle on their stems,
Beirut is in this Orient the very last shrine,
Where mankind can still adorn its kind with a mantle of light.

∾

CHARLES CORM (1894–1963)

Charles Corm was an early twentieth-century Lebanese poet, entrepreneur, painter, philosopher, publisher, socialite, philanthropist, and patron of the arts. His intellectual trajectories, political activities, literary contributions, and commercial ventures were so broad and richly varied that one may safely brand him *the* consummate overachiever and polymath. Ambitious, precocious, restive, visionary, constantly seeking knowledge, and always eager to succeed and avail himself to the service of his country, Charles Corm burned through the stages of his own life—and the life of a new nation that he helped found and that he so cherished—like a fleeting meteor.

In addition to his poetry, fiction, short stories, and plays, Corm also produced a wealth of political essays and aphorisms on art, music, history, and current events. Yet in Middle East studies circles he is remembered best — often remembered exclusively — as the intellectual spark and *spiritus rector* behind the Young Phoenicians movement of early twentieth-century Lebanon, a national and cultural current that advocated for a millennial hybrid Lebanese identity and an independent Lebanon, distinct from the motley unitary political entities taking shape on the rubble of the defunct Ottoman Empire beginning in 1918. But Charles Corm was much more than a notable man of letters — even though that alone would have guaranteed him immortality in the pantheon of modern Lebanese cultural history.

Born on March 4, 1894, to painter and doyen of modern Lebanese religious art Daoud Corm and his wife, Virginie Naaman, Charles Corm received a traditional Catholic education in Beirut, at one of the Levant's most illustrious Jesuit institutions. Among his friends and classmates one could count eminent Lebanese literati and national figures such as Joseph el-Saouda, Michel Chiha, Hektor Klat, and more importantly perhaps Riad el-Solh (a future prime minister), and Émile Eddé (a future president of the nascent Republic of Lebanon). Although his earliest and best-known publications date back to 1919 (inaugurated namely with the launching of the short-lived but legendary *La Revue Phénicienne,* Charles Corm did not become a full-time writer until 1934, on the day of his fortieth birthday, when he decided to liquidate all his business assets, abscond all commercial activities, and cease being Lebanon's "Mr. Ford." By then, explains Asher Kaufman, Corm had become a very wealthy man, and was no longer concerned with earning a living; his aim was now mainly to work in the service of his country, vaunting its grandeur, excavating its history, and trotting out its bequests to mankind.[36]

Driven at a young age by his love of painting — perhaps goaded to follow in the footsteps of his own father — Charles Corm resolved soon after his 1911 high school graduation to dedicate himself full-time to artistic endeavors. Yet, he was uneasy at the thought of having to rely on parental largesse to subsidize his creative passions. He therefore set out to jump into the business fray before indulging his artistic affections.

This took him to Paris where he spent a few fleeting months soaking in the city's charms and rubbing shoulders with the bohemians of its *belle époque*. Pre–World War I Paris left a lasting impression on an adolescent Charles Corm, and it was the city's symbolist, expressionist, modernist, and art nouveau artworks that grabbed hold of his affections, dominated his emotions, and made him decide on the life that he had fancied for himself. But Charles Corm the artist was overruled by Charles Corm the pragmatist in those days, even if only briefly, and even if for purely practical reasons. So he elected to trade in his fancies of Henri Matisse for the ways of Henry Ford; industry and wealth production as it were, before artistic creation. Thus, in mid-July 1912, reluctantly perhaps, but driven by vernal ambition and boundless ardor, Charles Corm boarded the Royal Mail Steamer *Olympic* from the Port of Southampton heading to New York, where he would live and would operate a successful import-export business on Broadway, until the outbreak of the Great War.

It was during his American sojourn that a vernal baby-faced eighteen-year-old Charles Corm—who in 1912 looked more like a high school sophomore than a serious entrepreneur—would secure a meeting with the founder of the Ford Motor Company, from whom he would obtain a pledge of exclusivity for the assembly, marketing, sales, and distribution of Ford automobiles and agricultural machinery throughout the Levant.

At its height, what would become Charles Corm's Société Générale could boast dozens of Ford automobile showrooms, and a number of Firestone, John Deer, and McCormick-International Harvester branches, assembly shops, and distribution centers sprawling from Turkey to Transjordan and Palestine, and from Damascus to Baghdad and Teheran. In all, Corm's enterprises employed upward of a thousand Turks, Lebanese, Syrians, Iraqis, Transjordanians, and Palestinians—Jews, Christians, and Muslims alike—became synonymous with the livelihood of thousands of families, and contributed to developing the infrastructure and networks of roads, railways, and bridges in countries that had not yet come into being at that time.

But commerce and wealth creation were not Corm's only achievements in modern Levantine social life. In 1921, at the tender age of twenty-seven, in the bustle of his commercial ventures—and while he was still serving as commissioner of the Lebanon postwar relief organizations—he would contribute to the founding of Lebanon's first modern public library, the National Library of Beirut, to whose collections his friend Prince Albert I of Monaco (an amateur oceanographer and lover of the Mediterranean) would contribute some fifty thousand volumes. Charles Corm was also a founding member, along with Albert of Monaco, of the Mediterranean Academy, a learned society that encouraged and produced scholarship on Mediterranean civilizations. Still engaged in the demands of his postwar relief project—a program that brought moral, material, and financial assistance to Lebanese victims of World War I—Corm headed the Committee of the Friends of the Beirut Museum; a commission of private donors, intellectuals, and cultural figures who drew up the blueprints of what would become the Beirut National Museum. In 1934, Corm inaugurated and began hosting, in his Beirut home and the former Ford Motor Company headquarters (at a stone's throw from the museum that he brought into being), the iconic Amitiés Libanaises cultural salons. Before long, this intellectual society would become a trendy and much-coveted weekly "gathering of the minds," to which flocked a number of eminent local and international political, cultural, and intellectual figures—among them Pierre Benoît, Paul Valéry, Charles Plisnier, and F. Scott Fitzgerald; figures whom an adolescent Charles Corm had no doubt encountered a quarter of a century earlier during his brief stay in Paris. The Amitiés Libanaises forum was also home to a number of Lebanese literati, politicos, and aspiring authors, who, hard as they might have tried, seldom escaped the spell of their host's charm and infectious energy.

Even Israeli scholars (or at least members of the pre-state Yishuv community) had also partaken of the cultural and intellectual activities issuing from Corm's salons.[37] Of course, this was at a period in time where the (barbed) borders of an emerging Middle Eastern state system had not yet been finalized, and when the brewing animosities between Muslims and Jews had not yet reached their pinnacle. Nevertheless, Charles Corm would always remain outside the petty disputes of the region's competing nationalisms, and as mentioned earlier, his business emporium, cultural exchanges, and cordial collaborations reached across borders and bypassed ethnic, religious, and political barriers.

And so, that his Amitiés Libanaises brought together Muslims, Christians, Jews and others was a natural order of things for him; a reflection of his own humanism and his ecumenical temperament—in literary, artistic, commercial, and human endeavors alike.

In addition, Eliahu Epstein—a representative of the Jewish Agency who had somewhat of a "second home" in Beirut—was a friend of Corm's and a bit of a fixture at the Amitiés Libanaises. In a series of correspondence between Corm and Epstein during the late 1930s, there figure a number of invitations that Charles Corm had extended to Jewish archeologist Nahum Sloucshz, and sculptor (and friend of Marc Chagall) Chana Orloff, proposing they present their work at the Amitiés Libanaises and a number of other Beirut venues. Naturally, Corm was particularly interested in Slouschz's work on the Phoenicians, and in Orloff's personal ties to a number of French and European artists whom Corm admired greatly, whom he had encountered earlier in his youth, and who were often hosted at his gatherings.[38]

Yearning for those interrupted weekly gatherings, Lebanese author Rushdy Maalouf (1914–80), father of francophone novelist and member of the Académie Française Amine Maalouf (b. 1949), noted in his 1963 elegy of Charles Corm that although the meetings of the Amitiés Libanaises had become sparse during Corm's final days, the legacy that they and he left behind, "like the Cedars of Lebanon, never ceased to lavish glory and grandeur on the altar of Humanism that is his Lebanon."[39] Charles Corm was "our first teacher," wrote Maalouf; he was Lebanon's "national school," its "national museum," its "national torch and beacon," and the "fountainhead and spring eternal of its humanism."[40] Charles Corm, asserted Maalouf, "was the first one to show us *how* to love Lebanon; *how* to chant and rhapsodize Lebanon, *how* to vaunt and defend Lebanon, and how to become master builders of this Lebanon of his yearnings; Humanists, Cosmopolitans, Ecumenical friends and allies to mankind, yet steadfast in our love and affection for our homeland."[41] Maalouf further noted that it was not unusual for artists, intellectuals, and cultural and political figures visiting Lebanon for the first time to have Charles Corm, and his "Maison Blanche,"[42] on their itinerary of peoples and places to see: "They visited Lebanon seeking out Charles Corm the way some of us may visit France to see Da Vinci's *Mona Lisa*,

or the way we may visit Athens to see the Acropolis."[43] This is the veneration that many, Lebanese and foreigners alike, held for Charles Corm,
and it is still this mystique of Charles Corm's that haunts the walls and
halls of his now-muted Maison Blanche de Beyrouth.

In the samples of Corm's work produced in this anthology, the
reader can survey the span of the author's work in poetry, short stories,
and aphorisms. Although the themes of the poetry culled form Corm's
The Hallowed Mountain (1933), may seem at first glance patriotic in
nature, specific to Lebanon and early twentieth-century Lebanese history, the work's scope and outlook, namely its focus on humanism,
syncretism, and an intercourse of ideas and peoples, is universalist in
its breadth and its capacity to reach those molded by different experiences and affected by different circumstances. Likewise, the short story
An Easter Story (1915–18), written by a twenty-one-year-old Corm, in
the thick of the famine that devastated Ottoman Mount Lebanon during the Great War, may have resonance and find meaning among those
touched by the horrors, the destitution, and the dispossession wrought
by war—as much during the early decades of last century as during the
early decades of our own.

Those readers socialized in the West and who may be familiar
with the horrors of World War II and the inhuman conditions of ghetto
life—as intrinsic riggings to the machinery of the Nazis' systematic destruction of European Jewry—will no doubt recognize some striking
similarities in *An Easter Story*. "Who, after all, speaks today of the annihilation of the Armenians,"[44] is a sentence attributed to Adolph Hitler,
alluding to war crimes committed by the Ottomans in the early decades
of the twentieth century; crimes that had fallen from consciousness and
historical memory by the time Hitler himself had embarked on his own
extermination campaigns. Charles Corm's *Easter Story* is a summons
to memory. It provides gripping, devastating testimonials on both
"perpetrators" and "spectators" of "ghetto life" in Ottoman Lebanon a
good quarter-century before Hitler's "Final Solution." As Corm's narrative suggests, although unprecedented in its "irrational rationality"
and the horrors that it perpetrated, the Holocaust was not unique in its
intent and finality; it had precedents and early exemplars, and it is not
farfetched that the recalcitrant Levantine Ottoman dominions during

World War I might have provided Hitler's Germany with a suitable template.

Yet, one discerns no grudges, no acrimony, and no calls for revenge or retribution in Corm's *Easter Story;* only dignity and grace and charming humanity, and most of all perhaps uplifting resilience and will to survive. Indeed, these qualities seem to populate Corm's work as a whole, where he is always able to derive hope and light from the darkest, direst of times. That, to him, was the precondition and condensation of "being human": a way of "bursting out of one's own twilights, repelling the darkness [. . .] defying death, and propagating and procreating far beyond the grave."[45] Rancor and resentment drain the human spirit, insisted Corm,

> and love quenches the soul;
> For, the more loving Man is, the more joyous he is;
> For, loving one's enemy, is even more thrilling,
> Than a beloved's embrace, to a tender dazzled heart!
>
> . . .
>
> And loving one's enemies, wicked as they may be,
> Is a way of thwarting evil,
> A way of gleaning light,
> From the shadows of night.[46]

Besides its lyrical value as a saga of survival and an exalted ode to humanism, Corm's *Easter Story* provides a vital historical framework, and arguably a rationale, for the establishment of Greater Lebanon in 1920: a state far exceeding the dimensions that the Maronites of Corm's generation might have been entitled to, but one then deemed necessary for the security and survival of a hunted-down and traumatized community, barely reemerging from the throes of death.

Finally, the selection from *Erotic Tales* (1912), a collection of short poems, aphorisms, reminiscences, written by a seventeen-year-old Charles Corm, invoke "lived memories," often sublimated youthful yearnings that Corm might have held for women he encountered in Lebanon, and during his first trips to Paris, London, and New York between 1911 and 1914.

In all, Charles Corm's corpus reflects the profound impact that World War I (and World War II) had on him personally and his world-view. Wars and the devastation that they wrought taught Charles Corm the value of tolerance and humanitarianism, put him in touch with the absurdity of violence and the futility of resentful nationalism, and made him realize that only a spacious, humanist, hybrid, universalist "patrio-tism," bereft of all manners of orthodoxy and chauvinism—religious, linguistic, and national alike—could offer a panacea to the Levant's volatile interidentity quarrels, and give the Lebanon that he dreamed of respite from its endemic ethnic dissentions.

In a sense, Charles Corm's lifelong literary, intellectual, commer-cial, and humanitarian work was intended as an act of defiance and con-frontation directed at orthodoxy—*all* orthodoxy, whether in politics, art, architecture, historiography, or literature. But his work was also a summons to the inherently pacifist impulses of the peoples of the Le-vant as he saw them, and namely Lebanon's much disputed and debated Phoenician forefathers.

THE HALLOWED MOUNTAIN (1933)

THE SAGA OF ANTICIPATION[47]

The heart spoke:
A famed maimed old man has come
To unshackle my mutilated nation

The arm spoke:
With his one remaining arm[48]
He has brought back to my embrace
My dismembered cities!

The brain spoke:
Beirut shall, again,
Be the capital of my thoughts and yearnings![49]

The eyes spoke:
I can make out, in the distant light,
My ancient Phoenician coastline!

The ears spoke:
We shall again hear,
Without shame or fear,
The old motherland's name!

The mouth spoke:
I shall eat, again,
The native bread of my forefathers' plains[50]

The lungs spoke:
Our harbors can finally breathe
The boundless air of the open seas![51]

The feet spoke:
Again and with firm steps
We shall march toward the future,
With heads held up high!

The bones spoke:
Again will we rest
In the reclaimed peace
Of our ancient graveyards!

The blood spoke:
I am surging out of my veins
And coursing to the summit of my soul!

The soul spoke:
I was once immortal,
He brought me back to life![52]

And so, old Lebanon,
Like an ancient cathedral
Whose old statues
Had fallen silent
Since the Middle Ages,
Has suddenly surged back to life!

And so, the graceful outlines
The modest sculptures

And the candid paintings
Of its glowing stained-glass windows,

Once more set ablaze the golden hues
Of once obscure contours,
Along the edges of moldings
And the threshold of frames,

Suddenly coming alive
In their alcoves
And along the ledges
And entablatures,

And within the cusps of stones
Shaking off their dust
And their past quietude,

From the outer sanctuaries
To the sanctums of chapels,
And from the high altar to the flying turrets,
They all told me, with a blushing glow,

This simple and solemn plea
Between a smile and a tear:

The poet spoke:
The muse has come back!

The gardener spoke:
The laurels are green once more!

The shepherd boy spoke:
I shall have more than just one lamb!

The poacher spoke:
Never again will I steal!

The lumberjack spoke:
I shall plant Cedar trees.[53]

The woodworker spoke:
I shall raise new altars!

The carpenter spoke:
I shall arm battleships!

The emigrant spoke:
We are finally coming home!

The sailor spoke:
The sea has no more wrinkles!

The street porter spoke:
There are no more burdens to bear!

The blacksmith spoke:
We will forge new cannons!

The shoemaker spoke:
Our old hiking boots
No longer befit our lofty routes!

The architect spoke:
The path on which we walk
Has never been clearer!

The tailor spoke:
I sized him up
To the glory of his battlefields!

The smuggler spoke:
There are no more boundaries!

The merchant spoke:
Business is great!

The indigent spoke:
It matters little to go hungry!

The doctor spoke:
Only too much happiness
Is now the cause of death!

The lawyer spoke:
All plaintiffs are reconciled!

The peasant spoke:
A liberated homeland
Is newfound paradise!

The maidservant spoke:
I am now a princess!

The princess spoke:
I am now a servant
To all my countrymen!

The convict spoke:
I shall sin no more!

The nun spoke:
We are no longer needed!

The little girl spoke:
In my dream I saw him sleeping,
And I was kissing him![54]

The young maiden spoke:
I shall be married soon!

The old lady spoke:
Freedom is a fount of youth!

The old man spoke:
I shall die without regrets!

The atheist spoke:
I believe in God;
May he protect us all!

The songster spoke:
The hymns of Lebanon,
Which had been sobs and tears,
Are joyful again!

The musician spoke:
The spirits of Lebanon
Are true symphony!

The painter spoke:
When I try to paint him,
My brushes quiver
And the colors run pale![55]

The goldsmith spoke:
I shall emboss with gold
The iron of our swords!

The sculptor spoke:
Venus of Milo!
Nike of Samothrace!
General Gouraud![56]

THE SAGA OF MEMORIES

We Have Stirred up This Planet

If I dare remind my countrymen
Of our Phoenician forefathers,
It is because, back in their heyday,
Long before we ever became
Mere Muslims and Christians,
We were a single nation
At the forefront of History,
United in a single glorious past.

Today, having grown
Into what we have become,
And by virtue of all our modern creeds
—which are all praiseworthy—
We owe it to ourselves
To love one another
The way we did when we were still
Splendid humanist pagans.

[. . .]

We have stirred up this planet,
Labored it to its core,

Plowed its continent,
Molded their laws and lore;
Yet our language has fallen,
In the stillness of night,
And we've remained alive!

Never have we buckled
Under the weight of fate,
Never have we bowed
From calamity's weight
Without feeling a rush
Of blood coursing in our veins,
Heralding redemption,
Proclaiming the return
Of the ancient spirit
That propelled our forbears.

Many were the nations that charged our land,
This tiny plot of land,
Which quelled them in the end!
We have witnessed the passing
Of peoples and of Ages,
Yet withstood and endured,
In the glistening horizon,
Steadfast on our peaks,
Peaceful, sober, wise,
Since the early dawn of time!

Many were the magi,
Poets, and princes;
Many were the gods,
Pompous kings and tyrants,
Who walked in procession
At the foot of our mountain!
O Ramsis, Asarhaddon,
O Barkuk, Caracalla,
Transcending all your crimes,

Outlasting all your horrors,
The mouth of Nahr-el-Kalb[57]
Has kept but broken shards
Of your gory passage,
On its quiet peaceful shores.

There has never been a nation,
Anywhere on this earth,
Equally small as ours,
With proud destinies like ours,
With fortunes such as ours,
Destined for even more
Glories and good fortunes.

Our apanage as a people
Is our restraint and poise,
Our weapons and coat-of-arms
Have been, for six millennia,
To think! and to love!!
To always bear in mind,
That all else comes to naught!!

For rancor drains the spirit,
And love quenches the soul;
And the more loving Man is,
The more joyous he is;
That, loving one's enemy,
Is even more thrilling
Than a woman's embrace
To a tender dazzled heart!

· · ·

Loving one's enemies,
Hurtful as they may be,
Is a way of thwarting evil,
A way of gleaning light
From the shadows of night.

Grief, Good Grief!

Grief, good grief!
O unspeakable grief! . . .
Once upon a time, our grandparents spoke
Syriac at Ghazir,
Syriac, where the Phoenicians' flair,
Their vigor and finesse
Are still extant today;

Alas, no one in our times,
Can fancy finding shades
Of our grandparents' footsteps,
In the shadow of old vines;
The bygone language of yore,
Is choked for evermore,
In our gagged skinny throats.

And now our Mountain,
Ever kind to her sons,
Beholds its splintering skies
Riven by the sounds,
Of foreign Western tongues;
It is a bitter clash
That ails and torments her
With quarrels and heartaches.

For, languages like Italian,
English and Greek,
Turkish and Armenian
Clutter and jam her voice,
While she willingly yields
To the sweet tyranny
Of the language of the French.

Yet, I know that in London,
In Paris and in Rome,
Our writers can never hold

The station they deserve,
That everywhere they go,
Despite their humanity,
They shall always remain
Outside the human race.

For, a people is orphaned
When it hasn't a tongue;
And the languages of others
Are borrowed outer cloaks,
In which one seems dubious,
Shameful, lifeless, frail,
Obnoxious and strange!

For, a man without his language
Is like an intruder barging in,
On someone else's feast,
Even when turning up
With the best of intentions,
Loaded with gifts and zeal;

Yet, these foreign-sounding words,
Which are taught to our children,
To us are not that strange;
For, it seems that our hearts
Can still recall remembrances
Of having fashioned them
And styled their graceful sounds!

Indeed, it is they
Who disowned their lineage;
Uprooted from us,
Torn from our embrace,
Embellished by exile,
They now disown their race
Like beloved ingrates.[58]

O *Spirit of My Land*

O spirit of my land,
I miss you, ancient glories,
Your treasures and your feats,
You inspiring stories,
I miss your high deeds . . .
I miss your golden years,
Your benevolent prestige!

O spirit of my land,
I miss your boundless wealth,
Whence mankind once drew out
Oceans of abundance;
I miss the high seas
That once carried your ships,
Your benevolent missions,
And your children's ambitions!

No, no, my mother tongue,
You aren't a fallen corpse
In the abyss of time!
I still can feel your verve,
Swelling up in my veins,
Rising like springtide,
Surging up like a wave!

And I still can hear
Your sparkling silver springs
Churning up from the past,
Whispering to my soul.

. . .

And I still can feel your blazing breath
shimmering over these Eastern shores!

In all of nature's shudders,
Which molded the spirit
Of my distant forefathers,

It is still your warm voice,
And it is still your whispers,
That move about the Eastern skies!

Your soft and graceful inflexions
Still slip their ancient drawl
In all the modern languages
Swarming on our shores;
Your sparse and scattered caresses,
Still flow in my veins
And cuddle with my soul!

And I still can feel your faithful fingers,
Gently knock on memory's door,
Awakening my heart,
With flashbacks of ancient glories,
Filling my soul with joy!

For, even as I write
In someone else's language,
And even when I speak
In someone else's tongue,
It is still you in my voice,
My sainted mother's voice,
Snug like a lover's warmth!

For, Man here below,
In spite of having learned
His brute oppressor's tongue,
Has kept the looks, the tone,
Has kept the pitch, the pulse,
Of his forefathers' inflections,
Of his old ancestors' voice!

Exiles and vagabonds,
Through all their ports of call,
Still bring along their language,
Still cling to their old brogue,

Still pilfer its perfumes,
Still tinge it with the hues,
Of their first mother's voice!

From one universe to the next,
In spite of time and space,
The languages of mankind
Still seek each other out . . .
So, let their sounds embrace,
Let their melodies mingle,
Let their clamors entwine!

For, even these sweet words,
Stolen from France's lips,
With impassioned affection
Quivering in my heart,
Still taste on my lips,
Where my smiling sorrow sits,
Still taste of a Lebanese kiss.

MIRACLES OF OUR LADY OF THE SEVEN SORROWS (1949)

AN EASTER STORY (1919)[59]

Some of the events of this story take place in the high mountains of Batroun,[60] in one of the poorest villages of northern Lebanon. Like a bundle of dry wood bearing down on the hunched back of an elderly woman, the village consists of twenty or so flat-roofed homes piled up on the spine of a solitary peak, mingling with the gaunt limestone of surrounding mountains.

Proceeding from the Beirut-Tripoli coastal road, the village cannot be reached except by taking the only rocky exit leading up to it; an exit that wiggles its flaky snakelike skin in between the green coastal hills above the port city of Byblos.[61] From there, one needs upward of a nine-hour ascent through the tangled bushy circuitous foothills of Batroun, which would then begin an abrupt climb through receding goat trails that often get lost in the crumbling rubble of majestic peaks towering overhead.

Before reaching the village, there whispers a silent brook, hidden timidly under the gravel of a pine grove buried in a canyon dropping to the foot of the village. A half-hour later, we are at Elché.

Well before reaching the meager vineyards surrounding the village, the visitor is often greeted by a swarm of children, sturdy and carefree, besieging strangers in their midst with their large sunny eyes, bickering like some warriors from Homer,[62] trying to outdo one another offering visitors the hospitality of their neat and modest little hovels.

It was there, in this little lost corner of the world, that in 1902, Morcos Hanna Morcos, who had just returned from a long exile in Mozambique, rich but still proud of his native village, would set out to construct a castle of sorts; an inordinately fantastic structure in its dimensions; a place where he had intended to spend the remaining years of his adventurous life, quietly tending to his weary days and the needs of his beloved countrymen.

Morcos wore a thick black mustache that went all the way back to his ears, forming two giant hooks almost snaring his bushy eyebrows. He took great pleasure proudly stroking and smoothing them with his big hairy hand, whose pinky finger, in addition to motley rings, was adorned with an impressive diamond. On his broad chest, swelled up with confidence and effusive optimism, hung two huge gold-watch chains, each holding a timepiece the one fancier than the other, each bedecking one pocket of his lavish coral-buttoned vest. A number of multicolored pens, which he could never use given that he could neither read nor write, graced the little breast pocket of his jacket. Finally, a pair of big flashy spectacles, for which his sharp eyes had no need at all, rested like a proud conqueror astride his prominent nose.

As the fruit of his thirty years of hard labor in the African jungles, he had brought back with him a thick well-padded purse, overflowing with banknotes. And in order to prove that what he had stashed in that purse was real currency, real Pounds Sterling, and that he had plenty of them to spare, he took great pleasure lending parts of his hard-earned fortune, free of interest, to the notables of Byblos—among whom he had dwelled for some time, and with some ostentation, as he awaited the completion of the work on his dream mountain-castle.

But before Morcos was able to finish installing his roof trusses and sheathing, and cover them with the prized Marseille red tiles, and long before he could complete the monumental internal staircase that was to lead up to the mansion's first floor, most of his debtors, now less willing to pay him back his monies than to ply him with nebulous promises, no longer had qualms openly declaring themselves bankrupt.

And so good old Morcos would now begin cursing the day he had returned to the homeland, complaining and railing loudly about everything and everyone around him; pulling his hair in despair at the mere thought of having to waste what had remained of his fortune on costly liens and endless lawsuits—that may or may not retrieve even a portion of what he had already lost. But like any and all the brave folk of this impregnable mountain, Morcos could not imagine himself resigned to his misfortune. Looking at the bright side, he kept consoling himself with the notion that his castle was almost half-finished, and that it was already the talk of the town, from Jounié to Tannourine.[63] And so, all he had left to do now was to count his blessings, cut his losses, and go ahead and complete that castle once and for all. Gathering up all the courage he could muster, and entrusting the liens owed him to lawyers as devious as his deadbeat borrowers were deceitful, Morcos decided to go back to South Africa, vowing to amass another fortune that would allow him to return once more to Elché and finish the construction he had pledged to complete. This time around, he convinced himself, he would not lend his money to anyone, and he would spend his hard-earned bread solely to cover the costs of completing his sumptuous pink Ehden-marble staircase, and finishing his Marseille red tiled roof—both feats that would compel the admiration of the entire mountain, spanning a radius of some twenty leagues or more.

Morcos was so certain that he could soon return to the country with a new fortune in tow, that he left sweet Martha, his young bride, behind in Byblos, along with their newborn, Farid. But time had passed so quickly, and the money that he had left behind for Martha to provide for herself and their little boy was depleted in a few years' time. Tired of waiting much longer, and anguished by the lack of news coming from Morcos, Emm-Farid set out gradually to sell off her jewelry and home furnishings,[64] so as to afford raising her young boy on her own, bereft of the support of a husband and father.

Behind the towering powerful and colorful trait of character that was Morcos Hanna's had lain the modest figure of sweet Martha—that is at least until her husband had vanished. Martha was diffident, quiet, her character drawn out in a faint, discrete watermark. But ever since she found herself alone, raising her young boy on her own, fighting all the adversities of life with great love and determination for his sake and her own, the faint watercolors that had defined her self-effacing personality soon began revealing themselves in glowing bolder vigor, displaying hidden virtues that would come to leave a profound imprint on her own destiny, and on the drama that was being played out in the life of her household.

She ended up selling off, for next to nothing, the mahogany piano that glitzy Morcos had bought her on their wedding day; a beautiful instrument that no one knew how to play anyway. Then she sold off the buffet, which had been stocked up with cumbersome and unnecessary serving dishes. Then it was the turn of the lush green and gold armchairs that once graced the living room, soon to be followed by her lingerie and Morcos's brand new wedding suit, which he had worn only once. Finally, getting to the end of her rope, Martha picked up the barest of necessities, carried her little one on her back, and headed out on foot, up to Elché, where she reluctantly resigned herself to living in the cellar of her husband's unfinished castle—that structure's only room that could provide a roof over her son's and her own head. And as a memento from the days of her fleeting opulence, she had kept but a few security vouchers and written pledges from deadbeat borrowers, along with a promissory note valued at five hundred pounds gold signed by a reluctant village mukhtar.[65] And by the time she found out from Lebanese natives of Tartej returning home from Transvaal that Morcos had died half mad and in most abject poverty,[66] the war of 1914 had already broken out.

During normal times, and save the obligatory—albeit few—vines and fig trees strewn, here and there, around the modest properties of the Lebanese countryside, the people of Elché, like most of the mountaineers of the Batroun district, had made their living from the tobacco industry. A rare few fistfuls of arable land, often torn with great effort from the nooks and crannies of the rocky terrain, and preciously maintained with much skill and sweat and patience on superimposed terraced fields, over time became the ideal setting for tobacco farming, somehow insuring the always frugal, often austere, livelihood of those hardworking brave villagers.

Even Martha would end up planting and caring for hundreds of tobacco plants, grown in the flowerbeds that Morcos had reserved for the Capetown carnations that he had intended for the entrance of his dream castle. A little patch of potatoes, with a little bed of lentils, mint, and parsley, formed the basis of the vegetable garden to which Martha would tend devoutly.

Wheat, barley, and corn grew only with much difficulty in the bitterly cold high altitudes of Mount Lebanon, and so the villagers got in the time-honored habit of buying their grains and wheat stocks from faraway Jounié, which in turn imported those staples from Syria or Egypt. Martha herself often went down to Jounié, and brought back—lugged on her back—her seasonal wheat supplies, which she would stop over to grind on her way back to the village, at a mill near the River Adonis. But the events that were about to grip Europe, a thousand leagues from Lebanon, were going to have their tragic effect on the poor people of the mountain, making life for Martha more difficult and more perilous by the day.

Ever since Turkey entered the war on the side of the Triple Alliance, its main fixation had become the repudiation of Lebanon's independence and the punishment of its people, long-time friends of the Western powers.[67] Unable to massacre the Lebanese en masse, the Turks set out to instate so-called war effort measures and wartime austerity laws whose sole mission, it seems, had been to starve out the people of Lebanon and annihilate them.

Busy with its own war effort and the hostilities that it was enduring on its own territory, France was unable to lend effective support to her Lebanese friends,[68] who found themselves squeezed in between a Syrian interior blockaded by the Turks, and a Mediterranean coast sealed off from all contacts or exchanges with the outside world. Meanwhile, Allied warships patrolling the high seas beyond the Lebanese coastline had the limited aim of establishing a modest intelligence service, more or less clandestine, and were therefore reluctant to land either troops or supplies to come to the aid of the besieged populations of Lebanon. In turn, the Ottomans took advantage of the situation by expelling the country's main religious and political leaderships, summarily executing sizeable batches of vocal patriots, and exterminating the rest of the population by way of a systematic, well orchestrated, drawn-out government-induced famine.

All grain harvests and foodstuffs were thus confiscated by local agents of the Turkish government, who would overnight become the administrators of Turkish "high deeds" on Mount Lebanon. Only a tiny minority of Turkophiles was maintained and pampered and replenished, and indeed fattened during those times. And it was this very same minority, in connivance with the tyrants, who set up the "black market," thus reaping benefits on the corpses of our martyrs.[69]

Based on statistics collected by the Austro-Germans, nearly three hundred thousand Lebanese perished from hunger between 1915 and 1918—that is to say about one-third of the country's population. No other country on earth has ever had to pay such high and ignominious a blood tribute to the war effort.

Going back to Elché, the inhabitants of this little hamlet, not unlike the other villagers of Batroun and Byblos, were forced by the famine to sell off all that they could dispose of: Entire buildings and their furnishings were sold off to petty shopkeepers in Tripoli and Beirut;[70] upstarts who got promoted overnight to the rank of major businessmen. For a rotten crumb of bread, Lebanon's proud farmers were despoiled and depleted of their dearest possessions. Restaurant owners in the bazaars of Tripoli, most of whom at the beginning of the war had run vile decrepit little taverns selling chickpeas and beans to street porters and dock workers, were suddenly buying entire villages with vineyards and orchards spanning towering hillsides on the Lebanese mountains. In some villages, they even went so far as to purchase cemeteries wholesale. Fleeced of their resources, and half-dead, the peasants of Mount Lebanon would now begin flocking to Beirut, the "big city" of their day, hoping to feed themselves from the leftovers of its municipal garbage dumps. City sidewalks, private doorsteps, and church courtyards down to the last and least accessible of public spaces were all literally littered with the dead and dying—some of whom often spending upward of two entire months in the hunger throes of unimaginable suffering before finally breathing their last.

The Beirut municipality, under the close watch of the Turkish Vali and the executioners of the occupying Ottoman army,[71] soon began heaping dead bodies onto municipal carts, dumping them into the sea. At times, the waves having vomited one too many cadavers onto the shore and all the way into the Beirut harbor, the Ottoman authorities resigned themselves to changing practice, beginning to dump the corpses directly on the coastal sands south of the city. And Beirut, having of all times had this curious specialty of populating its blue skies with flocks of white doves, often raised by mellow peaceful local lunatics, would soon witness its horizons obscured by clouds of crows, noisily flocking to the spoils.

Jamal Pasha,[72] who often came to spend some time in the wonderful world of the capital city, partaking of its sumptuous orgies, was reportedly outraged one morning at the sight of dark clouds of black birds croaking furiously over his head. He therefore rebuked the Beirut municipal services, which later resolved to dig out new ditches in the cemeteries of Beirut's outskirts, and prepare fresh mass graves to receive new heaps of the freshly dead.

The old Maronite cemetery of the Medawar quarter was at the time deemed too small and overcrowded to contain all the villagers expiring on the city streets. The new cemetery of Ras el-Nabeh was therefore chosen instead; it was still relatively empty at the time, given that it had only recently been donated to the community by Archbishop Chebly of Beirut, who later died in exile in Adana.[73]

"I'm hungry! . . . I'm hungry! . . . I'm hungry! . . ." Shrunken and shriveled skeletons, belly-up atop heaps of city garbage dumps, unable to move even to beg for a scrap of food, could still be heard beseeching passersby for help, for a crumb of bread. Utterly reduced to an abominable skeletal state, passed out as if entranced by the stench of the vermin emanating from their own decomposing bodies, excreting this god-awful hideous hallucinating smell that seems to imbibe this city by day and by night. Some, having already succumbed to their bodies' and their souls' devastation, seemed to have (beforehand) spat up their entrails, dragging them behind them in the filth and the dust of the city streets before collapsing atop the municipal garbage dump; their last hope for a scrap of food.

Bellies swelled up by putrid gazes, sheared shriveled and perforated skins, monstrous gory human waste, feculent and turbid wounds, tortured and gnarled by famine, expired souls, ambulant cadavers, wholesale mass despair. That, in brief, is what has become of the best, the healthiest, the purest, the strongest, the most gentle, the most beautiful, benign, noble, and brave from among the peoples of this assassinated mountain . . .[74]

Haven't we seen all too many of those scenes back in those days? Haven't we encountered such dreadful sights as if they were the most normal and banal in the world? Innocent babies, rendered to the status of hideous fetuses by famine, still suckling their dead mothers' worm-eaten breasts, until the dreaded municipal dumpster carts came to sweep them all helter-skelter, and ditch them into ghastly mass graves? . . .

Of course, poor Martha had done her best to spare her son that bitter cup and dodge the general calamity gripping the country. Farid was already twelve years of age when the war had broken out. And Martha would manage things, through a series of ingenious ploys, until 1917, saving her son from guaranteed starvation. Having remained alone with him in Elché, even after many waves of villagers had already abandoned their homes in search of livelihood, Martha was finally constrained to follow suit. She ended up abandoning the cellar and selling the iron of its reinforced concrete to Miniyé profiteers who had come to retrieve the metal when the unfinished castle had finally been demolished.[75]

Martha moved down to the coastal town of Fidar,[76] where she got temporary employment with a group of woodcutters.[77] And when all the forests had been felled and were depleted to the benefit of fueling the Ottoman railroads, Martha landed herself a housekeeper's position at a nearby inn by the River Adonis.[78] Farid, who was pushing fifteen years of age by that time, did his best to help his mother with her work, but the inn soon closed its doors, and both mother and child found themselves on the streets again, destitute, without employment, clutching the mukhtar's five-hundred-pound promissory note—which Martha had kept hidden, attached around her neck alongside her scapular.

The mukhtar had become a millionaire by that time, managing the Ottoman government's food warehouses. And Martha, by dint of insistence and supplication, managed to snatch from him the payment of the debt owed to her. But the mukhtar, now a wily profiteer, agreed to pay her only after having made a few readjustments of his own to the original bill. And so, instead of giving Martha her five hundred pounds gold in full, he gave her paper banknotes, and attached to this payment a new onerous ransom: He demanded that she use the money he had just given her to purchase from his own stockpile a qantar of wheat,[79] at black-market prices. This came up to five pounds per rotol.[80] She agreed, and set out with Farid, dragging the qantar of wheat to the Nahr el-Kalb mill.[81] But the mukhtar's wheat had already been adulterated with sand and gravel, to the point that even after having sifted it, Martha's qantar yielded a mere thirty-five rotols of wheat—instead of the one hundred she had paid for. In other words, Martha was defrauded by the very same mukhtar who was supposed to protect her, and she ended up paying upward of fifteen pounds per rotol instead of five—once more depleting whatever little money she had left in her possession.

At any other time, five hundred pounds gold would have bought an entire farm and a dozen small orchards in Lebanon; yet they yielded Martha less than a hundred kilos of bad wheat. And such meager pittance is hardly long lasting. Soon, Martha and Farid found themselves scrambling again for ways to keep the specter of death away from them. Martha no longer dared looking her son in the face, as Farid became more emaciated by the hour, gnawed as he had been by hunger, helplessness, and the terror of death drawing ever nearer by the day.

"Go to Baabda,"[82] said Martha to her son one morning, "go see our friend Nessib Bey. I hear he is so well off these days that I doubt there would be a thing he wouldn't do to lend us a hand. Remind him of the times he'd spent at our house in Byblos; how he'd pass the hours smoking hookah with your father, designing all these grand business schemes together. Show him all of our ration vouchers, and ask him if he would at least give us one quarter of our allowed quota. Awaiting your return, I will try to go work in the onion fields of the Deir el-Jose monks; this should allow us to pay our friend Nessib Bey for whatever amount of wheat he will have given you."

And so Farid would set out for Baabda. But it wasn't until after long and humiliating supplications at Nessib Bey's doorsteps that he would be granted an audience with his father's "friend."

"Oh, your dear father! . . . Oh, your dear mother! . . . Dear friends of mine! . . . Of course I will help! . . ." pretended Nessib Bey, with much histrionics. [. . .] "Of course I shall help! However, at present, all I have in my silos is the lousy grubby kind of stale wheat, which is unworthy of your dear mother, and which has moreover been allocated for the troops. Come see me next week. I want to make sure you are treated like the dear friend that you are, and I insist on giving you only the best wheat in my possession; the one I reserve for my own family. Come back to see me next week!"

Farid waited a week, then two, three, and four, only to find himself eventually booted out of the property by Nessib Bey's orderlies; Nessib Bey who suddenly no longer had time to spare for the son of a friend to whom he had owed much.

The little odd jobs that unfortunate little Farid had managed to cobble together here and there in Baabda no longer squelched his searing hunger. In desperation, he decided to head down to Beirut, to try to seek out employment there, any employment there. But Farid was so worn out and bone-weary by fatigue and hunger that he fell flat on his face several times along the way. He resolved to remain in place, motionless, just for a short while to gather up some strength, and he began begging passersby for anything they might hand him. But he ended up collapsing from exhaustion and starvation on a sidewalk near the Café des Glaces,[83] at the corner of the Place des Canons.[84]

The utter slaughter to which waves of cattle succumb daily, with utmost deliberation and brutality, in the slaughterhouses of Chicago, offer a privileged spectacle of death by comparison to the wicked savagery of the mass killings by hunger meted out on the inhabitants of Mount Lebanon cramming the streets of Beirut.

Death by starvation is not dying only once and for all; it is dying horribly; it is dying a tortured, ulcerated death, tearing at one's throat and chest and heart and loins; it is dying endlessly, all the time, multiple times, every minute of every day, and every week for several months.

Farid was now, no doubt, facing this terrible end.

Seeing her son having tarried much longer in Baabda than she had expected, Martha set out to go look for him. But he was nowhere to be found. And so she began running frantically from one village to the next, from Hadath, to Wadi Chahrour, to Chiaaah and Bourg el-Brajneh, where someone finally mentioned to her having perhaps glimpsed a small street vendor fitting Farid's description. Unkempt, disheveled, panting, and with her mouth frothing with dust and foam, Martha desperately clung to people on the streets, begging passersby, invoking all the saints, and screaming her little boy's name out loud, through the countryside, lest he would hear her. The insatiable voracious hunger already strangling her could no longer cause her pain, now that both her heart and her eyes—whose sole nourishment had been the sheer presence of her beloved little Farid—were more famished than ever for a mere glimpse of him.

By dint of drinking water, and drinking water some more, thus dosing the fires searing her charred heart, and no longer being able to eat anything besides the unhealthy wild grasses torn along the roadsides as she was roaming the streets aimlessly, her belly began swelling up and weighing her down as if it had been carrying lead, and her loins were rendered burning embers, embedded like red-hot irons inside her back . . .

But the most horrible of all her encounters, as she ran desperately across the deserted countryside that was in this new season beginning to anoint itself with new scents of orange blossoms, was her constantly stumbling against the carrion stench, leaping out at her from the shadow of some green bush, scratching her in the face like a heart-wrenching reminder of the probable fate awaiting her own beloved child . . .

Then one day, as she had collapsed and lain exhausted before a small spring in the town of Choueifat, she felt as if surrounded and overtaken by those cruel smells of death. Soon enough, she realized that she had been in front of the remains of a beautiful young woman, already in a state of decomposition, and whose one-year-old baby was ceaselessly kissing her head swarming with flies . . .

Ya waladi! Ya waladi! Ya Farid! Yaaa Farid!"[85] she cried out staggering away in horror. Words emanated from her as if torn from her chest, crumbling in her parched throat, falling in fragments, carrying with them into the void little pieces of her heart.

She finally dragged herself all the way down to Beirut. But when she saw the scenes of the doom and damnation of an entire people filling the streets with their moans, and when she came upon heaps of the dead and half-living piled up together, being readied to be ditched outside the city walls, she fell straight down in the direction of Caracol el-Abd, and kept on crawling on her stomach, perhaps for days on end, in the direction of the sands south of the city, then in the direction of the Karantina, north of the Beirut harbor, in order to scratch and dredge around the mass graves, looking for some vestige of her lost child.

But all in vain; it was all in vain. And all the heroic efforts of a poor soul in agony would do nothing except drain and exhaust Martha's heart further, and deplete her completely of what had remained of her energy, until she blanked out and got ever closer to the looming eternal twilight beckoning to her. As for Farid, he too had also bit the dust, for many, many weeks now, hardly able to get back up on his feet again.

Meanwhile a banana peel, the skins of a few peanuts, and empty bean pods thrown out the window of the Café des Glaces sustained Farid for another week. Then one day, around noon, a caravan of some five camels laden with Sidon oranges made their way through the Place des Canons—which, at that time, had not yet been paved. A springtime shower of sleet and rain had turned the streets into a quagmire of soft frozen mud. One of the camels slipped into this tide, fell over, and dropped its load of oranges onto the mud, causing torrents of fruits to roll from all sides all over the square, and toward the curb where Farid lay. For Farid this was like a God-sent celestial manna. He braced himself unto the pavement, and gathering all the strength that his drained body could muster, he crawled onto his chest until he got ahold of a single solitary orange. Grasping it while it dripped with mud and dung, he brought it closer to his chattering teeth. But suddenly, the Bedouin leading the caravan pounced upon Farid, snatching the orange from his hand and kicking him toward the wall of the café where the boy would fall again, unconscious.

That same evening, paralyzed, lifeless, cataleptic, Farid was carried away with piles of corpses, hauled over onto the municipal truck and driven off to the nearest mass grave.

It was the evening of Good Friday. The terrified and tongue-tied city of Beirut seemed to be slumbering under heavy darkened skies. Yet the smothered hearts of its people were hardly dreaming; rather they were ruminating sinister nightmares.

At the very same moment that Farid was being thrown into the common grave of Ras el-Nabeh, Martha was awoken and shaken to the depths of her soul by a sudden commotion. Unconcerned by any of her surroundings, she began rowing with both her arms and legs in the filth that the city had become, in the direction of the Jesuit college chapel, to beseech the Madonna of the Seven Sorrows to return her disappeared child to her.

It took her an entire day before she finally made it to her destination. But the church was bolted shut, guarded by a Turkish sentry. Determined to somehow enter the sanctuary, Martha leaned back against one of the church's outer walls, and recalling in her mind's eye the altar where the Blessed Virgin had her compassionate arms stretched out to the faithful, revealing her pierced mother's heart, she cried out to her: ""Mary! Mary! Save my child! Give my son back to me! . . . Have mercy on him! Have mercy on my Farid, Mary, in the name of your own Son! . . ."

Then Martha felt an inexplicable jolt running down against her back as she leaned on the edge of the church door. It was as if all of the university buildings had suddenly begun convulsing in response to the call of her heart; as if telling her that the Blessed Virgin had heard her plea.

What happened next was so outrageous, so implausible, that the reader is urged to check the facts for himself before reaching a conclusion.

The custodian of the Maronite cemetery of Ras el-Nabeh, Salim Feghalé, who is still living, and who is now married and raising a beautiful family residing in the very lodge of this very same cemetery, where anyone can go visit him today, relates lying down for the evening in the alcove to the left of the cemetery's entrance gate. It was a balmy, muggy evening, with nary a breath of air, nary a noise, and nary a movement disturbing the stillness of the night. The cemetery's common grave, though covered as it was with a film of sand, overwhelmed the entire neighborhood with its offensive stench, and prevented Salim Feghalé from sleeping a wink that night. Suddenly, shattering the first-light of that quiet Easter Sunday, Feghalé reported having heard a scream rising from the back of the cemetery, from behind the young olive trees, the area marking the common grave. He ran to the window to look in the direction of the scream, and felt as if his eyes and ears were being torn from his face and hung onto the howl that had pierced the darkness of early dawn.

Then, there was a voice that would have sounded almost human had it not emitted a timber of a wild monstrous sound, like the throttling of an inverted bark, like a cry from beyond the grave. Then Salim saw something moving at the edge of the pit, something rolling in the sand, then collapsing, then standing up halfway, staggering, then bolting through the front gate and out of the cemetery, running up toward the hills of Ashrafiyyé, panting a disgusted breath, shaking off long bony arms as if revolted by something it might have brushed against.

It was Farid.

Salim never found out whether the resurrected boy was ever reunited with his mother—whom Salim himself never had the pleasure of meeting. But Salim nevertheless did run into Farid, on multiple occasions after the war, and he realized that this ghost of the dark days of yesteryear was now leading a normal existence, without anyone even fathoming what living hell he had actually returned from.

Salim even remembers one day coming upon a person with an uncanny resemblance to Farid, at a hardware and building supplies store. The ghost was inquiring about the price of Marseilles red tiles, and the cost of their transport from Beirut to Elché.

The last time that Farid and Salim would meet again was following a procession of the Congregation of the Children of Mary, at the Jesuit chapel, gathered before the bleeding (and always generous) heart of Our Lady of the Seven Sorrows.

Erotic Stories (1912)[86]

Preface

Let him the first among men who has never experienced the ecstasy of
    carnal love, Let him cast the first stone.
Here are the little white pebbles
That I have tossed along the way,
A little Tom Thumbling of Love,
In the thicket of forests of big cities.
I would not venture to say
That the ogress of Pleasure
Has eaten me whole yet,
However, I will say the following:
I am no longer able
To find my way
To the footprints that may lead me back
To the home of Childhood.

dedication

An immodest and respectful tribute
To the one who will be my wife.
To Pierre Louÿs,
Whom I love very dearly, and who does not know me.

phoenicia: an opening prayer (1912)[87]

She stands erect and bare before my ecstatic eyes. The sun coats her with
caresses. Her perfectly harmonious outlines stand out against the dark
background of old Phoenician curtains. Her feet tread an ancient carpet
of Asia; a red carpet; red with the blood of souls poured out in tribute
to her.[88]

On a tripod next to her, an old inlaid silver incense burner quietly
    consumes itself. Spirals of fragrant smoking incense curl up lovingly
    around her youth.

Like the ascending outlines of burning incense enshrouding her, the
    outlines of my imagination enfold her as well, in sly searing words:

imperfect exaggerated words, like the outlines of the burning
incense . . .

Her hair is a sea whose copper-colored waves come crashing on the
sunny beach of her shoulders.[89]

Her forehead is a mirror reflecting light; her forehead is a cultic cry!

Her eyebrows are two black comets, two curved swords, and two
triumphal arches.

Her eyes are two vistas. Her eyes, between the streams of eyelashes, are
two lakes of damp shade reflecting an internal moonlight.

Her pupils are two large black grapes.

Her cheeks are two downy peaches, with hints of rose petals.

Her aquiline nose is a miniature hallowed hill.[90]

Her thin translucent nostrils, quivering and delicate, are two wings of a
butterfly.

Her tiny plump ears are seashells that carry the mysteries of a voice;[91]
they are homes peopled with melodies; they are temples where my
prayer goes to kneel.

Her lips are Cupid's drawn bow, whence a word is on the verge of
being discharged, to strike me in the heart. Her lips are triumphal
banners, blood-soaked and happy. Her lips are smiles.

Her teeth are white Carrara marble surrounding the pool that is her
mouth.

In the pool that is her mouth, wiggles the little goldfish that is her
sweet tongue. Her tongue is a bountiful bit of jam.

Her chin is sexed up with a dimple that seems to be a nest for a kiss.

Her tender neck is round like the collar of a fresh alcarazas.[92]

Her throat is bathed in milk and ticklish amber.

Her armpits are retreats for blonde foam and fragrant shade.

Her arms are a stirring gesture. Her arms are a soaring ascent. Her arms are wings!

Her folded elbow is like a living handle for the vase that is her body.

In the crease of her elbow a blue dipping beckons the red lips.

Her hands are the rare flowers of an outlandish hothouse.

Her slender fingers awaken like the rays of a star.

The fingernails of her hands are like delicate mica.

At the root of her fingernails, I was surprised to find a silver crescent.

The fine grain of her skin is the celestial manna.

Her delicate and firm breasts are twin siblings. Her white, soft, and round breasts, like two full moons, never make like quarter-moons.

Her breasts are quilts to lull the sleep of heroes and of gods.

The tips of her breasts are blooming buds, buttons of ruby, crimson candy.

Her smooth belly is a shield of shivering pearl.

And the navel is in the middle, like a mouth made for silence, like a lock for the mystery below.

Her pubis is a gentle slope . . .

And her secret, in the foam, is a source of intoxication and perfume. Her pink secret is rebounded like an apple. Her beautiful secret is a ripe fruit in a divine orchard.

Her dear secret fills my caressing hand, and its frizzy hairs exhaust the eager energy of my fingers.

In the middle of the secret, two small vertical lips emerge, even and crimsoned. They open and they close, as if silently whispering troubling and mysterious invocations. More so than the lips of the mouth, the lips of the secret are beautiful indeed!

More so than the mouth of the face, the lips of the secret have a tongue erect and mischievous, although it only leaves the temple when beckoned by the supplications of love.

Her hips curve up, like pure amphora. Her hips drip with freshness, like the falling snow. Her hips are slippery, like the glaze of fortresses.

Her slender legs are the pillars of heaven. Her elegant legs are like leaping gazelles.

Her knees are little sachets of benzoin soap; little honey cakes.

Her calves are molded in a nervous alabaster; subtly, they go thinner as they drop to the neck of her foot.

The neck of her foot, veined with emeralds, deserves the most beautiful necklaces of the most beautiful necks.

Her arched foot is the most precious ornament in the world. Her little delicate impressionable foot, is worthy of musk, nard, and myrrh, and Magdalena's humiliated hair.[93]

Her toes are carved in coral and carmine, in nougat and fondant.

Her tiny toenails are glistening droplets of holy water.

And the soles of her feet are made to walk all over the life of humans.

Proceeding to the back of her "legs," her hamstrings are a resting place for the bewildered eyes.

Past the globes that home in on the earthly pleasures, one happens upon a narrow valley, where another mouth smiles like a grenadine flower falling onto a bed of violets, or like a golden ring in a fold of velvet.

Then the valley widens, revealing her loins, rising again, safely, between the plains of her majestic back, and along her spine, like a beautiful path leading up to the horizon.

And on the left and right sides of her back, her light shoulder blades unfold upon her torso, like exquisite fans.

The back of her neck . . .

And I'm back, safe and sound, thank God, to her hair, whose braided
strands are like the heavy clusters of an immortal vine.

It is there, under the Lebanon skies, which flood you in a shower of
lights; it is there, on the holy land, which holds you piously before
the enchanting Mediterranean sea cradling your dreams; it is there,
in the breath and in the skies of an ancient East, nostalgic and
outdated, that I recall, trembling, the eternal landscape of your
beloved body. And it is in memory of our beautiful love that I drew
these helpless arabesques.

May you forgive me their unworthiness, if only in memory of our
beautiful love, O child of my race, O daughter of Lebanon, O
Phoenicia.

ANIS ELIAS FREYHA (1903–93)

Linguist, novelist, journalist, philologist, folklorist, and college professor, Anis Freyha's research and publications focused a great deal on language, dialectology, proverbs, epics, and legends and mythologies. He
taught Semitic languages and classical Near Eastern civilizations at the
American University of Beirut and at the Lebanese University's College
of Information. In the tradition of the classically trained historians and
philologists of his generation, Freyha mastered a dozen or more Semitic
and European languages, including Biblical Hebrew, Aramaic, Phoenician, Ugaritic, German, and English, in addition to the obligatory Latin
and Greek. Freyha took great interest in many aspects of Lebanese history and folklore, and much of his canon of novels and short stories
treated topics of Lebanese proverbs, popular culture, and traditional
country life, mainly related to Mount Lebanon. His published philolog-
ical work in Arabic treated topics of Lebanese toponymy (*Dictionary of
Place Names of Lebanese Towns and Villages*) and the origins of spoken
Lebanese (*A Lexicon of Popular Lebanese Expressions* and *A Dictionary of
Lebanese Proverbs*). Freyha was also a committed advocate on behalf of
dialectal languages, and wrote extensively on methods and approaches

to codification and the formal teaching of dialects. His most famous work of literature was arguably *Listen Up, Rida!* (1956), a series of short stories, life lessons, and "teaching moments" from Lebanese country life, addressed to his real-life son Rida. The book is written in a simple unpretentious Modern Standard Arabic style, peppered with spoken Lebanese colloquialisms, arguably to make an otherwise impenetrable literary Arabic intelligible to a ten-year-old still untrained in the rudiments of the learned language. It is from *Listen Up, Rida!* that the following selection is excerpted. *Dinner on the Roof-Deck* is a picturesque tableau of Lebanese country life, offering a glimpse into traditions, rituals, landscapes, linguistic and social habits, and all the rhythms of life— which may be specific to Lebanon, but which are also shared in varying degrees throughout the Levant, often seeping into places further north and west, around the basin of the Mediterranean.

Dinner on the Roof-Deck (1956)[94]

Listen up, Rida!

Tonight I shall tell you the story of the roof-deck of my own father's house, and lull you into slumber the way I used to fall asleep in my mother's embrace back in the day. Whenever I reminisce about that old rural house, I cannot help remembering our family dinners on its roofdeck. That deck was your grandfather Bou-Nejem's holy shrine and altar. You are too young to remember your grandfather Bou-Nejem. Oh, how he loved that roof-deck of his, and how he enjoyed savoring his dinners there, in the open air.

Your grandfather—God rest his soul—was the village schoolmaster. He was a teacher to two generations of students; parents and their children. I can still hear the elders' and old-timers' whispers whenever I returned to the village of my childhood: "is this the son of Master Bou-Nejem? May God rest his father's soul! He was our teacher when we were little lads. Funny how time flies!"

But your grandfather had been a peasant farmer long before becoming a schoolmaster. He loved the land and worshiped it with religious fervor. The fondness and devotion he had for his mulberry trees and olive groves were so profound, almost mystical, bordering on reverence.[95] He would often scrub his hands in the dirt of his fields, mumbling "the soil is pure and sacred." He dreamt of one day leaving his two-story home near the village square,[96] to go breathe the open air of "God's country," and build himself a modern house; three rooms in a single row, with two bedrooms flanking a living space in the middle. Things worked out the way he intended. He did build himself a secluded sanctuary near the *qalé'* dryland,[97] and he shrouded it with flowers, apricot and plum trees, and trellises of vines all around. But our secluded house was often crowded with throngs of friends of your grandfather's; people who took great pleasure visiting and savoring his company and the sights of flowers and the shades of vines that Bou-Nejem so lovingly brought to life.

Everyday at sunset, with almost religious devotion, your grandfather went up to the roof-deck of his well-covered and secluded house. To him, that place was his closest point from earth to the heavens. It overlooked the mountains and the valleys of the Lebanon, and your grandfather communed in profound intimacy with the flickering lights emanating from the hilltops and the bellies of the valleys. He used to say: "There is more intimacy in the spaciousness of the roof-deck! The roof-deck expands one's lungs and makes man loom larger!" At the beginning of summer, your grandfather used to lug his bed up to the roof, at which sight the neighbors of the nearby quarters would exclaim: "Summer is here!" Likewise, whenever they noticed that the bed was no longer on the roof, they sighed: "Autumn is upon us!" You could say that my father's bed was a barometer of sorts: Its ascent to the roof inaugurated the summer season, and its descent announced the arrival of autumn.

Your grandfather was a pious man, Rida! He knew both the Torah and the Gospels by heart. He also had a beautiful singing voice. Ask his former students if you don't believe me; the village in its entirety really, and all those who studied under him, would tell you what an exquisite singing voice your grandfather had as a young man. So magnificent was his voice that the bishop insisted he take holy orders and become a priest; that is, because he could read and write of course, but also due to his beautiful singing voice. I forgot to mention that my own grandfather was himself a village priest, and he had always fancied his own

son following in his footsteps and becoming a priest, thus rendering
the priesthood a hereditary family tradition. But your grandfather had
other plans: He fancied himself a teacher during the day, and a peasant
beginning at sunset, lasting through the night and until the first glim-
mers of daybreak. However, his renouncing the priesthood did not prevent him learning the rudiments of the religion, and mass service. He
sang church canticles particularly well according to the Byzantine rite.
Indeed, whenever I think of your grandfather, I picture him, in the summer, praying on the roof-deck of his house, and in the winter kneeling
on a sheepskin before the fireplace. He sang with almost angelic perfection the hymns and canticles of the Bible. And in the evening, he always
made sure to gather us children around his altar, atop his roof-deck
shrine, to partake of singing hymns and canticles and church choirs
in unison.

Ironically, just as much as your grandfather Bou-Nejem adored his
roof-deck, your grandmother Sharifé detested it. Of course she did not
dislike it because she disliked the stars. To the contrary, Sharifé loved
the stars and took pleasure in watching the constellations; specially the
ones that she could identify by name; namely Libra, the "Seducer,"[98]
Scorpion, and the Pleiades. No, she did not dislike the roof-terrace because the evenings spent there were wonderful; nor because the night
breeze, which, often wrapped around the rooftop, was rejuvenating and
calmed the worn out nerves bringing slumbers to the weary eyes. Nor
did Sharifé dislike the roof-deck because she disliked the religious songs
that we all sang in chorus there. To the contrary! She loved nighttime,
and she loved its starlit skies. She also loved singing and taking part
in our nocturnal family rituals. Except that your grandfather at times
would interrupt her and say: "Hey there, Sharifé! You are singing out of
tune! You either keep the tune, or better keep quiet!" But no, this is not
the reason your grandmother hated the roof-deck. She disliked it for
two main reasons.

She used to say: "Every year I have to redo Bou-Nejem's mattress
and comforter; the night dew and the sunlight of day wreck havoc on the
iron of the bedframe; can you imagine what they do to the bedding's cot-
ton and wool materials? And I be damned if Bou-Nejem took the pain to
put away or cover his beddings from the elements a single time."

The second reason your grandmother hated the roof was that it was her chore every night to haul dinner and dinnerware up the stairs to the rooftop; food, coffee tables, water pitchers, grape baskets, and all. After the hard toil of her day, it was no small burden for her to carry all of this dinner gear up the long wobbly wooden stairs leading up to the roof-deck.

"Eat dinner first, then go up to your roof-deck!" she often pleaded with your grandfather.

"Oh, come now," he often responded, "you're not going to refuse us the simple pleasure of dinner on the rooftop, are you?"

Truth be told, no one should reproach Grandma Sharifé for grumbling about the issue of the beddings. Refurbishing on a yearly basis both beds and beddings is a matter that could be draining to the most comfortable of budgets of the rural Lebanese household; especially in bad crop years. This is to say nothing of hauling dinner and all its trappings up the stairs, then bringing everything back downstairs, daily, when slumber had begun weighing on the eyelids. Not exactly what one would call a pleasant evening ritual to look forward to!

Rida! I don't know if I ever mentioned to you that our mothers of yesteryear toiled much longer and much harder than our mothers of to-day. Likewise, I don't think I ever told you what kind of "time keeping" our mothers relied upon to get up in the morning and keep up with the demands of their daily tasks. What do you think was their time-keeping method? An alarm-clock? No! A wristwatch? Not that either! A pocket watch? Certainly not! The first thing that your grandmother Sharifé relied upon to keep time was the position of the stars: mainly the "Deceiver" (or Venus), or else the Pleiades at their rising, or both the setting and ascendant Libra. Likewise, all of our mothers kept time at night by reading the stars. Yet Venus "the Deceiver" at times misled them. They believed that this star preceded daybreak by about two hours, and that these first lights of dawn lasted long. But that was because "the Deceiver" had led them astray. That is partly why most of our mothers did three-quarters of their day's work during the night, before first light: They kneaded the bread, did the wash, fed the sheep, watered the plants with water hauled from distant springs, and readied baskets of figs and grapes before the children awoke.

The second time-keeping method relied upon by our mothers was the roosters; that is to say the roosters' crowing at daybreak. But this was primarily the method of the lazy, mainly because the roosters of our village were well trained and extremely well behaved—unlike the cheeky roosters of Ras-Beirut![99] Our village roosters knew and understood well that night was night, and that God made it for sleep and rest and peace and quiet. And so, when the darkness of night fell, our village roosters slept soundly and quietly, like everybody else, and this until daybreak. Only then, at the break of dawn, did our village roosters unleash their melodious sonorous crowing, tearing apart the quiet of the night! And only then did the lazy mothers awake. As for the roosters of Ras-Beirut, I can tell you that they are the worst kind of roosters this world has ever seen: They crow pretty much all the time; in the early evening, at the cusp of midnight, at the break of day, and again some more after daybreak. They have no manners, no education, and no discipline! It is true that it is not always the rooster that is to blame in this case, but rather the people of Ras-Beirut themselves, whose lives are often lived topsy-turvy with nighttime taking the place of day, and daytime lived at night!

I feel badly for our mothers of old! They were the consorts of the night. All we children knew was that whenever we awoke with the first rays of sun, we always found our grapes and figs baskets waiting for us on the porch, under the arched stone entryway of our houses. Our poor mothers were the accomplices of the night. It is no wonder that your grandmother Sharifé could not care less about the roof-deck and its rituals at the end of her hectic day!

Your grandfather always told her: "The roof-deck is nearer to the heavens, and, sitting there, we are in the company of stars. Why would anyone choose to sleep under a roof when you can sleep on top of it? How can anyone close their eyes at night without having them kissed by the evening dew? How can man fall asleep before marveling at the greatness of God and his creation at nightfall? As for me, I would not be able to sleep a wink before I could count the stars."

Oh, how he loved the nineteenth Psalm, your grandfather Bou-Nejem: "The heavens declare the glory of God; the skies proclaim the work of his hands. Day after day they pour forth speech; night after night they reveal knowledge . . ." And he always insisted we memorize that Psalm, the way he had done. He used to say: "Fetch us dinner, sweetheart! Someone please bring me over the water jug and the basket of grapes and figs, so that they may have time to cool in the evening breeze! Why don't you come on up and keep me company, children?" And so, we'd all climb up the stairs carrying in tow dinner platters, pitchers, and fruit baskets.

I am unsure why I am mentioning those evenings to you, Rida. Whatever little food was laid on that small dinner table, it was always exquisite food when savored on my father's roof-deck. The water in the pitcher was always the freshest and sweetest. The cool clusters of grapes were always delectable. And sweeter than both the grapes and the water was the taste of those sacred hymns that your grandfather took pleasure singing after dinner. Byzantine chants are striking in their majestic beauty. This is music for powerful throats and mighty lungs. And this calmness of the night on the roof-deck, this breathtaking twilight that shrouded us almost entirely with its twinkling stars, only heightened the glory and splendor of those hallowed chants.

I was a child back in those days, and my mother's arms were my pillow and cradle. What I loved most during those sainted evenings, were the fleeting moments after dinner on the roof-deck, when I'd begin nodding off to the sounds of Byzantine chants, shrouded in my mother's warm embrace.

Israel and Palestine

Given that the authors under consideration in this volume are primarily figures generally affiliated with well-delineated internationally recognized states (at least that is still the case at the time of this writing, in the midst of a heaving Middle East "under reconstruction"), it has proven especially daunting to adequately fit Palestinian writers anywhere outside an "Israel-Palestine" chapter. Fawaz Turki and Samir el-Youssef, although outside the circle of those considered paragons of Palestinian literature, are exquisite—albeit contrasting—representatives of the Palestinian condition and the Palestinians' intellectual trajectories of the past fifty years. Yet, rather than being representatives of a single state, they are mostly ensconced in a state of liminality, straddling Israel, the Palestinian Territories, Lebanon, Syria, Jordan, and other areas of dispersion, both East and West. And so it seems that treating Palestinian authors within the context of their own geographic dispersion (or in-gathering) would most appropriately do them justice in the proposed framework of this *Anthology of Modern Levantine Literature*. Perhaps a separate chapter specific to the "Palestinian diaspora" would have been a way of striking a middle ground. Still, in the end, the Palestinians' lives, regardless of where they are lived, are more intimately twined to Israel and Israelis than to any other state representatives in the Levant. Ghassan Kanafani (1936–72) perhaps said it best, admitting that "the Palestinian people's future is with Israel; it is neither with Europe and America, nor with China and the Soviet Union, nor even with the Arab states—who, whether individually or together as a nation, were never concerned with the lot of the Palestinians, and never lifted a finger to accomplish anything decisive on their behalf."[1] Moreover, it is worth mentioning that two of Israel's most widely read Hebrew authors today, Sayed Kashua and Anton Shammas, view themselves as "Israeli-Palestinians"—the latter being Christian, the former Muslim. Although not treated in this volume, both Shammas and Kashua naturally warrant being classified as "Israeli authors," given their medium and milieu of expression; yet both are also Palestinians, arguably more intimately related to their Israeli adversaries than to their own Palestinian kinsmen in the diaspora and in the Palestinian territories, and therefore more Levantine in their "oddity" than either of them may be aware.

At least in theory, Israel as a "national-ethnic state" for the Jewish people ought not be in conflict with minorities in its midst, and should remain a democracy for all its citizens, Jews and non-Jews alike. Unfortunately, that is not always the case today, and Israel the "ideal" often comes crashing against Israel the "reality" of its neighborhood. From the point of view of the Jewish people, the creation of the State of Israel was an act of redemption two thousand years in the making; an act of self-defense and self-determination against the obstacles of historical injustice, dispersion, and dispossession. Yet, from the Arab point of view, the creation of the State of Israel was an act of betrayal, aggression, and injustice, denying the Arabs of British Mandate Palestine their own right to self-determination. Adding another layer of complexity, from the point of view of Arab-Israelis, "their people," the Arabs, seemed locked in a state of permanent war with "their country," Israel.[2]

One cannot understand the basis of Palestinian and Israeli literature without some grounding in Arab-Jewish relations, and except as a function of the Arab-Israeli conflict. To do this, one must go back to 1948, more exactly to the November 1947 United Nations Resolution 181 calling for the partition of British Mandate Palestine into a Jewish state and an Arab state, and to the Jewish acceptance and the Arab rejection of the resolution. Likewise, one cannot understand the basis of

Palestinian and Israeli literature about this conflict without a measure of empathy for the Palestinians' plight, for Israel's fears, and for the validity of both Arab and Israeli narratives.

In brief, the Arab-Israeli conflict can be viewed through two widely divergent prisms. From a Jewish perspective, the 1947 United Nations Partition Plan was embraced by the Jews of British Mandate Palestine and rejected out of hand by the Arabs—the Arabs of the British Mandate *and* the neighborhood at large. The Arabs subsequently attacked the newly established Jewish state (Israel). It was an unequal struggle pitting an "Israeli David" against a superior "Arab Goliath." Israel the underdog nevertheless overcame the Arab onslaught and won the war, taking possession of territories initially allotted to the projected Arab state. Arabs subsequently fled the Jewish and newly conquered Arab areas in droves. Some Arabs were expelled from their towns and villages, yet most left of their own volition and at the urging of Arab leaders promising a triumphal return on the heels of victorious Arab armies, after the Jews had been thrown into the sea. These events precipitated what became known as the Arab (later the Palestinian) "refugee problem," and prevented the creation of an "Arab state" in Palestine alongside the newly established "Jewish state"—or Israel, which was established with the "Declaration of Independence" on May 14, 1948, a few days before the onset of the 1948 war. Also part of this Jewish-Israeli narrative was the claim that not only did the Arabs reject the UN Partition Plan, stunting in the process the creation of an Arab state (in later iterations a "Palestinian" state) alongside a Jewish one; Israel nevertheless sought peace with the recalcitrant Arabs, but was met with their persistent intransigence—and the famous "Three Nos" of Khartoum.[3]

From the dominant Arab perspective, none of the preceding history was accurate, and none of the events as described in the Israeli narrative actually took place: The 1948 war did not pit "the many" against "the few"; the Jewish war and political machine was actually more powerful and organized and sophisticated than the Israeli narrative give it credit for; and Israel knew that the Arabs were inclined to reject the UN Partition Plan, and had therefore prepared in advance for it. Moreover, Arabs did not leave their town and villages willingly, as the Israelis claim; they were expelled and "ethnically cleansed." Finally, Arabs did sue for peace repeatedly with Israel, but were met with Israeli obstinacy and rejection.

This is, in a nutshell, the Arab-Israeli conflict from two opposing viewpoints. It was an outcome of the "reordering" of the Levant following the 1918 collapse of the Ottoman Empire. It was an era of "massacres," "expulsions," "population movements," and "ethnic cleansing"—long before that last term had even come into being. "The lands of the Levant were living the vilest times of their history" in the early twentieth-century, writes Amin Maalouf: "[The] Empire was dying in shame; in the midst of its ruins were sprouting out new hordes of runt countries, [new nations, as it were], with each praying to its god to stifle the others' prayers. And on the roads, there began spreading the first processions of survivors. It was the hour of death. Yet my mother was pregnant."[4] This is in short the background of a Levant "under construction" in the early decades of the twentieth century—in many ways one that is not all that different from a Levant "under reconstruction" in the early decades of the twenty-first century. This was also the substrate of the Arab and Israeli "literatures of dissent" examined in this chapter. A literature bringing to the fore authors and works that have generally been neglected—or that have not been given adequate mention—in the traditional canon of the conflict's intellectual history; works and authors that "did not make it" into the accepted history textbooks, as it were, because the "conventional" literature on the Zionist and Arabist narratives is one that apostatizes the "other," whereas the Levantines highlighted here celebrate diversity, humanity, and humanism.

JACQUELINE KAHANOFF (1917–79)

In a 2011 collection of papers and short stories by little-known polyglot Israeli essayist Jacqueline Kahanoff, Deborah Starr and Sasson Somekh suggest that Levantine fluidity and hybridity had their champions in the State of Israel. Kahanoff, wrote Starr and Somekh, in the early 1950s had already envisioned a solution to the Arab-Israeli conflict, a solution culled from the confines of her native Egypt, where Jews, Muslims, Christians, Greeks, Italians, Syrians, Arabs, and others had lived together for centuries, if not in peace and harmony, then at least side by side and in acknowledgment of each other's distinctive character and multi-ethnic heterogeneity, often partaking of each other's languages and cultural rituals without even being conscious of their differences. As a child in Egypt, wrote Kahanoff, "I believed that it was only natural for people to understand each other even though they spoke different languages, for them to have different names—Greek, Muslim, Syrian, Jewish, Christian, Arab, Italian, Tunisian, Armenian—and at the same time be similar to each other."[5] Like the Israel of her old age, the Egypt of Kahanoff's youth was a symbiosis of religions, national origins, languages, and histories that were all uniquely Levantine. It is nationalism, and in the case of once cosmopolitan Egypt, it was the Arab nationalism of the 1950s, that brought an end to Levantine diversity. Under Nasser, "the idea of a liberal, pluralistic Egyptian nationalism which included the non-Moslems and was accepted by them had died," lamented Kahanoff in 1973.[6]

From Kahanoff's perspective, the Middle East will know peace only by recovering the halcyon times of ecumenical Levantine identities, where Arabs, Jews, and others lived together in mutual acceptance, and where hybridity and pluralism were celebrated elements of unity and overriding parameters of selfhood. Likewise, Kahanoff intimated that Israel may never find peace unless Zionism, a conceptual bedmate of Arabism, comes to terms with its own Middle Eastern essence.

Born in Egypt to an Iraqi-Jewish father and a Tunisian-Jewish mother, Jacqueline Kahanoff was raised in the port city of Alexandria, and grew up proud of her hybrid Mediterranean pedigree. Like many Christian and Jewish minorities of her generation, issuing from Ottoman coastal centers like Izmir, Alexandria, or Beirut, Kahanoff was a gifted polyglot intimately acquainted with her city's maritime conflations, kissed by its fluidity, at home with several of its languages— wielding with native familiarity a number of Arabic vernaculars, speckled with French, Hebrew, Italian, Turkish, and English—and straddling multiple cultures and multiple religious traditions. And so, Kahanoff's intimation that Israel "become part of the Middle East" was a reflection of her background, the outcome of her upbringing and the human space in which she came of age. Most importantly, *her* Middle East represented the cosmopolitan ethos of her times, elements of which were already expounded by Lebanese, Syrian, and Egyptian precursors from the 1920s on. Like her Mediterraneanist elders, the language of Kahanoff's literary output avoided Arabic and Hebrew—although she did at times write in both—languages that she knew well, but which she deliberately avoided, given their nationalist stigma, and their exclusivist association with Arabist and Zionist political ethos.

Kahanoff's relevance is not in that she dared live and utter anti-nationalist, perhaps "postnationalist" nihilist precepts. Her relevance is in that her work, her thought, and the intellectual school to which she belonged are being excavated, rehabilitated, and valorized by both Israelis and Palestinians today. Israelis and Palestinians as an "integral part of the Mediterranean or Levantine universe" is not an unorthodox notion, despite the assumptions of twentieth-century nationalisms and the pieties of the Arab-Israeli conflict, which expect—perhaps demand—that the two adversaries remain adversaries. Reviving Kahanoff and her notions of the Levant is a way of communing with the true spirit of the Middle East and of coming to terms with its true essence: a twined, multilayered, pantheistic crucible of identities, rather than the prevalent image of a uniform preserve of Arabs alone—or for that matter Jews alone—which advocates of exclusivist identities still cling to.

CHILDHOOD IN EGYPT (1959)[7]

When I was a small child, it seemed natural that people understood each other although they spoke different languages, and were called by different names—Greek, Moslem, Syrian, Jewish, Christian, Arab, Italian, Tunisian, Armenian.[8] I was aware that Arabs were more numerous than other people, and poorer: they were servants, peddlers, and beggars who showed arms without hands, legs without feet, eyes without sight, called out to Allah to send them a meager *piaster*.[9] The children scavenged in garbage pails for something to eat. Rich Arabs were pashas, but then many of them were Turks, and the Turkish ladies were princesses. One only caught a glimpse of them when they passed in their carriages. They wore a little bit of white veil around their heads and chins, while the Arab women were all wrapped up in black.

Moslems prayed kneeling on small rugs when the muezzin called them to prayer from the top of a minaret; it was a sad, beautiful song that filled the sky when the sun fell and disappeared. But in the morning, it returned to shine on everything, and that was why one prayed to God: to thank him for the Light.

It was a friendly world, with something exciting always going on. Crowds milled about in their brightest clothes for *Bairam,* after the Ramadan fast, and peddlers sold them magnificent sugar dolls in bright tinseled paper clothes, with little bells jingling on their heads. There were processions when the Holy Carpet returned from Mecca, or when the King opened Parliament; then all the streets were covered with orange sand and decorated with banners and festoons of light bulbs that shone brightly at night. At Easter time some shops sold chocolate eggs. Later, the Greek grocery stores sold eggs dyed in the most beautiful dark shades of purple, orange, and green. There was one holiday, *Shamm al-Nissim,* the Feast of the Sun, when absolutely everybody celebrated the spring by having a picnic by the Nile.[10]

Mother said that before going to sleep, it was good to remember all the nice things that happened that day, and there were lots of them, even on ordinary days. Sometimes camels came into town, carrying bundles of fresh-smelling greens in the rope bats flung across their humps, and it was funny the way they twisted their mouths, always chewing on something. Often my uncle Nono would invite me to see the new toys they had received at the store, and he said I could choose anything I wanted, although Mother scolded him for spoiling me too much. Or there were uncles and aunts who came from Paris or Manchester for weddings or business affairs. There were days, late in summer, when Nono and Uncle David distributed among their married children the good things they had received from Tunis—olive oil, and delicious big green olives, dates, and muscat grapes that were so good, that when we had a party to eat them together, everybody, even the children, were tipsy.

On Sundays, old Maria, our maid, sometimes took me with her to early mass in St. Joseph's Cathedral, where fat little angels floated among the pink clouds painted inside the domed blue ceiling. Father said I could go because God was everywhere, but that I must never, never dip my fingers in Holy Water or make the sign of the Cross, because I was

Jewish. Every people had its religion, he said, just as every bird had its song, and God loved and understood them all. Our religion, he said, was to await the coming of the Messiah, who would bring the day when people could love one another almost as God loved them all. I hoped that the Messiah would come quickly so that everybody could enjoy everything about other people's religions, as well as their own.

Our religion was also a mysterious language of prayers, called Hebrew, which only the men recited and understood. But, what was being Jewish most of all was to visit my father's parents, far, far away in the Abbassiyah quarter, where they lived in a little house surrounded by jasmine and honeysuckle. My grandfather Jacob, who came from Baghdad, sat in a long robe, with a turban on his head. He intimidated me because of his white beard and the prayer books which lay on a table at his side. My father gave me a little push, and I knelt before this old grandfather, who was also like a priest, to kiss his hand as my father had done, and received his blessing. When grandfather Jacob's hand rested on my head, I felt that this blessing was something ancient and precious, a treasure, which the grandfathers of our grandfathers had received from God. Because of this blessing, I was in God's safekeeping and belonged to the people of the stories in the old prayer books.

There were no real pictures in this grandfather's house; that was forbidden, but there were two frames containing writing on the plain white-washed wall, which I always saw as I lifted my head after the blessing. Father explained that one was the Ten Commandments in Hebrew, which God had given to Moses when they waited in the desert before entering the Promised Land, and these commandments told people what was right and what was wrong. The other was the Balfour Declaration, in English, and it said that the time was soon to come when we would return to our Promised Land. This land was called Eretz Yisrael, Father said, but now it is called Palestine, for we had lost our Promised Land. But we should remember that the Lord God of Israel had promised it to the sons of Jacob.

"To the daughters too?" I asked, and, smiling, my father said yes, to the daughters too, for Israel honored its women, the daughters of Rachel and Sarah. I thought how beautiful it was that the people in my family had the same names as those in the stories.

My grandmother sat on a couch in another room, draped in gray silk, her legs crossed under her. She was religious, and wore over her black wig a kerchief decorated with many crocheted flowers which dangled on her forehead with each of her movements, and which made her look young. Although I was told she was not beautiful, to me, this ancient Jewish queen, who never shouted and before whom people lowered their voices, was more than beautiful. I wanted the years to fly quickly, till I became an old grandmother just like her. My father's parents were the only people I knew who were in total harmony with themselves, inwardly and outwardly, who accepted themselves as they were and did not want to be other than they were.

I remember one summer we were in a hotel in Alexandria, by the sea. It was full of English officers and their wives, and one lady asked me what I was. I did not know what to answer. I knew I was not Egyptian like the Arabs, and that it was shameful not to know what one was. And so, thinking of my grandparents, I replied that I was Jewish and Persian, believing that Baghdad, the city they came from, was in the country from which all beautiful rugs came. Later, my mother chided me for not telling the truth, and said that when people asked me such a question, I should say I was European. I suffered because I knew this was not the truth either, and I burned with shame when the English ladies who had been nice to me laughed about "the little girl who wanted to be Persian."

I knew that my father suffered too, but I could do nothing about it. The image of his parents became something precious and secret I kept locked in my heart. They were the pillars that supported the frail bridge which tied me to my past, and without which there could be no future.

Whenever we passed the Qasr al-Nil bridge, where the English barracks were, I thought of the desert far away where the past slept under the sand. This was the treasure I must find when I would be grown up and free, so that the past could come alive and become the future. Sometimes the bridge opened to let white-sailed feluccas pass on their way to or from the mysterious place where the river and the world began. I thought that if once I stood at the edge of the bridge, just when it opened in the middle, I would fall into a felucca and be carried to that beginning, or to that end, where the river flowed into God, which was like a beginning. But perhaps I would miss the boat, and drown, sucked in by the whirlpools. I was safe only when I stood on the bridge. I knew that the feluccas traveled between Aswan and the Delta, carrying onions and watermelons, but the mythical river was my real world, where no harm would befall me.

We moved to a different house, where the river flowed by my window, and beyond it the three triangles of the pyramids spoke mysteriously of the time when everything called history started, long, long before English tutors taught us to read *Alice in Wonderland* and French schoolteachers made us memorize all kinds of nonsense about our ancestors the Gauls. The Wonderland was here, where our ancestors had created what the books called "ancient civilizations" at a time when the Gauls were savages clad in the skins of wild beasts, whose flesh they ate raw.

We played by the river where Pharaoh's daughter had found Moses, and where He, who would be the Messiah, was perhaps already born, a little child sleeping amidst the reeds. The Messiah would surely usher in a time when there would be no Christians, no Muslims, and no Jews, no white, black, brown, or pink people, and no princes who rushed by in their big red cars, so hardened by the thick crust of their wealth that they could not see, hear, or smell the poor who crouched by the gates of the Qasr al-'Aini hospital, where the air was foul from the stench of their sores. Barefooted, the princes would then approach them, and the crippled, the sick, and the poor would rise, forgive them, and be whole again.

My friend Marie, a Catholic, said that the Messiah had already come, and that he was Jesus. I could not bear to think the Messiah had come, and failed, without God giving men another chance, as he had done so often since the time of the Great Flood. Perhaps, I thought, many false Messiahs had to come, to suffer and die before every person could open his heart to Him who would come last. Jews were people who knew that another Messiah had yet to come, and that was why they waited. No matter what happened they would wait. That was their faith, their hope, their belief, that the Kingdom of Heaven would and could be on earth, in every man.

Marie spoke constantly of charity but accepted poverty as something to be compensated for in heaven. She was a Syrian, and like me, was half-native Levantine. She, too, was humiliated by our embittered British spinster teachers, but she never dreamt of revenge. She spoke of turning the other cheek, of meek resignation, of enduring one's sufferings for the love of Christ. I admired Marie; she also troubled and infuriated me. Marie never got angry. She told me I sinned through pride, and that people were not able to tell good from evil without the guidance of the Church. She pleaded with me and prayed for my conversion; she loved me and did not want me to burn in Hell because the Jews had killed Christ. I would retort, "When *my* Messiah comes, He will save everyone, even those who do not believe in him. And if he doesn't come, I don't want to be saved while other people burn in Hell. It's too unjust."

I racked my brain to find these arguments. I had had no formal religious instruction and had fitted together, as best I could, the notions I had gleaned from books, from the English translation of the Haggadah my father had given me for Passover and from what he told me of my religion. I was grateful for his trying. But one thing would often remind him of another, just like when people told stories in Arabic, so that I didn't know exactly where a story began or ended, and what was important and what was not.[11]

When I passed by the English barracks, I would remember Gulliver, a sleeping giant, pinned down to earth by thousands of threads nailed to the ground by thousands of little people. It occurred to me that perhaps our thoughts were like those threads. If we kept winding them between our heads and our hearts every day for years on end, like an invisible spider spinning a web around the barracks, then one day, all of us could pull together, and the slumbering giant would awake. But alas, too late. The barracks would crack open, like the Philistines' Temple, and an avalanche of stones and pink-faced soldiers would be hurled into the Nile when its waters were high, and disappear forever, sucked in by the whirlpools. Then, when the English soldiers were gone, we would lock up our nannies and Misses in chicken coops, and parade them in the streets, lined with orange sand, like when the King opened Parliament, so that everyone on our street would have a good laugh before we shipped them back to His Majesty King George.

I wondered if other children had such thoughts, and feared that perhaps I was mad. I tried to reason with myself. The Messiah who would come would most certainly forgive even the British soldiers and the English Misses, so before He came perhaps I should forgive them myself, and if I did, perhaps they would just go away. But I couldn't forgive. I didn't really want to. The truth was that I loved hating them more than loving them, because it excited and thrilled me, while love was something tranquil and restful, like sleep. But, if people loved to hate, then there was no difference between the black, the brown, the white, and it did not matter whether or not the barracks were destroyed, because the Messiah who would come would fail, as Jesus had failed, as Moses had failed, and nothing would change, and if nothing would change, there was no sense even in being Jewish and waiting for the Messiah to come.

This riddle was in the Haggadah, which I loved because it taught me that we were the people who would be given the Promised Land. God himself had not been able to soften Pharaoh's heart, nor make him give up his wicked power over another people. God had had to force Pharaoh by threatening him with the Ten Plagues, and He hoped that after each one Pharaoh's heart would be filled with pity. But Pharaoh loved his power and his wealth, and rather than give them up, he let the crops which fed his own people be devoured by locusts, and the river which fed their fields be turned to blood, and the first-born die in the little mud huts which were like those of the fellahin.

After all that Moses had sacrificed for them, even his own people had worshipped the Golden Calf, which was very much like Tutankhamen's mummy case in the Museum of Egyptian Antiquities. Moses, who was the son of an Egyptian princess, died of sorrow, thinking of those who had perished en route and were refused entry to the Promised Land. We, his people, had not been worthy of the Promised Land, and would weep in exile until we learned to know what we had been chosen *for*. Then we would return to the Promised Land once more, the Messiah would come, and all would be peace and harmony. Everything would be different. We and the Egyptians would be free together, and no one would set us against each other.

To make this happy end possible, I had to find out why things had turned out so badly in Pharaoh's time. I could do this only by elaborating fantasies around symbols, because I did not know the words needed to express my thoughts. True, I was very young, but I also felt that none of the languages we spoke could express our thoughts, because none was our own.[12] We were a people without a tongue and could speak only through signs and symbols.[13] Our elders spoke of ordinary, everyday things, or about religion. Their religion was to say *maktub, inshallah,* "amen," "Our Father who art in Heaven," and to pray and fast some-times; but it did not say anything about the things that were so difficult for us in life. Whether, for instance, it was right to want the British to go, and wrong to hate them, right to learn so many things from them and from their schools, but wrong not to want to be like the British and French, or our parents, or the Arabs. We were searching for some-thing *within* ourselves which we had yet to find. Religion seemed to have nothing to do with how people lived, and this did not seem to worry them, although they said that religion explained life and told them what they must do.

At school, we learned other things, but there too, we learned noth-ing about ourselves or what we should do. We did not know how it had happened that Jewish, Greek, Moslem, and Armenian girls sat together to learn about the French Revolution, *patrie, liberté, égalité, fraternité.* None of us had experienced any of these things. Not even our teach-ers really believed these words had anything to do with our lives. They seemed to think it was right for us to want to be like French children, al-though they must have known that we could not really become French, and that they did not really want us to be their equals or their brothers, and that actually we were nobody at all. What were we supposed to be when we grew up if we could be neither Europeans nor natives, nor even pious Jews, Moslems, or Christians, as our grandparents had been?

It was impossible to question anyone about these things. One could not ask one's parents, who kept saying they spent so much money to give us an education and advantages they had not had (and this was true), nor our teachers, who would laugh at us without even trying to understand. I could not share my feelings and thoughts with anyone, not even the other children, because I had no way of knowing if they were really happy and if they really believed the world we grew up in was true and good, or if they only pretended, as I did, because they were frightened and could not speak out. It was only through fantasies that I could explain this inexplicable little world to myself, and be able to fit it into a larger world, where I could find my place.

In one such fantasy I imagined a ruby and a lightning rod. The ruby was an inheritance received from my grandfather. A gentle fire glowed in its depth, and whoever held it knew the answers to all questions, and was at peace. I would fall asleep, my hand clutching this imaginary treasure, but when I woke up at night, my hand was always open. The ruby was gone. I believed that a wicked priest had risen from a dream and stolen it. Nothing could check this priest's power once he possessed both the ruby and the lightning rod—except trickery and deceit.[14]

The rod was light and fire, but it was a cold, hard, white light, and whoever touched it died instantly unless he owned a magic glove. When its rays touched men it made them work to build pyramids and bridges, and when it pierced the ground, the earth surrendered its riches. The lightning rod was in the movement of machines, trains, ships, and airplanes. It did things without thinking, while the ruby which had knowledge of all things, did nothing. The Master of the World used the rod to make life, and it was good when the ruby directed its action. The ruby was the jewel at the center of Pharaoh's crown, and the rod was the staff in his hand.

Pharaoh grew weary of holding the rod, as the power in it always wanted to strike, and from this power the wicked priest was born when Pharaoh slept. He persuaded Pharaoh to let him lock the rod in his temple, and replaced it by a stick. Then he stole the ruby, which he in turn replaced by another red stone. Pharaoh then became a statue, a dead, motionless god. But the people, seeing him with the ruby and the rod, did not know that he was dead, and that the wicked priest ruled by the rod alone. That is why they did not understand their own misery.

Pharaoh's daughter knew these things but, being a woman, she did not have the power to change them. She found the child Moses, and told him the secret. He became a novice in the temple, where he learned to use the power of the rod, which he caught and held in his own staff. He found the ruby too, and hid it in the desert, thinking that he could always return to it after he had defeated the wicked priest. When Moses challenged the wicked priest, he had to make his plagues more powerful than those devised by the wicked priest, but he could not stop them because he did not have the ruby. Even God could not stop the plagues, because if He made miracles men would not learn the meaning of their deeds and He would have to unmake the world He had created, starting from when he made the apple so tempting in the Garden of Eden that Adam and Eve *had* to eat it in order to learn right from wrong.

In the Wilderness of Sinai, Moses knew that even if he had not trusted in the ruby, but only in the rod, he would have died of a broken heart. After he died, mankind would be divided into two parts, those who remembered the ruby, and lived only to seek it in themselves, and those who knew only the power of the rod. The first were the People of the East, and because they rejected knowledge of the rod, they worked only if driven, grew lazy, sick, and poor, and waited idly for something to happen.[15] The people of Europe know only the rod which coldly lit their darkness; and because they created machines and electricity, they worked and made others work. They ruled the earth, but without understanding. I thought the Messiah would finally arise from those people who kept the memory of oneness, with each person yearning for that part in himself which was lost. The Promised Land was where they would meet and be one, the people of the ruby and the rod, in whom all things would be united.

When I reached adolescence, the fantasies lost their grip on me, or rather they expressed themselves more deviously through rational thoughts and political sympathies. I was not entirely aware that I was pretending to believe in certain ideas because they were already clearly formulated, while I could not express my own, partly for fear of appearing absurd, and partly because a reflex of self-defense prompted me to keep secret what was my own. This measure of deceit and self-deception, which disguised self-doubt was—and still is—characteristic of my Levantine generation. We thought ourselves to be Socialist, even Communist, and in our schoolyard we ardently discussed the Blum Government,[16] Soviet Russia, the civil war in Spain, revolution, materialism, and the rights of women, particularly free love. The only language we could think in was the language of Europe, and our deeper selves were submerged under this crust of European dialectics, a word we loved to use.[17] We talked and pretended to act as we imagined the youth of French lycées in France talked and acted, without being fully aware that they were still within a traditional framework which we had lost, and for which we envied them. We blithely dismissed everything that was not Left as reactionary, and because we were culturally displaced and dispossessed, without yet being able to define our predicament, we did not fully realize that our motives were not those of French youth, and were neither as pure nor as generous as we had imagined them to be. Revolution, which would destroy a world where we did not have our rightful place, would create another, where we could belong. We wanted to break out of the narrow minority framework into which we were born, to strive toward something universal, and we were ashamed of the poverty of what we called "the Arab masses," and of the advantages a Western education had given us over them.

Our parents were pro-British as a matter of business and security, and we were pro-nationalist as a matter of principle, although we knew few Moslems of our age. We felt this nationalism was an inevitable step on the road to liberation and true internationalism and, sensing that we might be sacrificed to it, we accepted it as unavoidable and even morally justified. We hesitated between devoting ourselves to the "masses" and going to study in Europe, to settle there and become Europeans. In later years, many of us switched from one attitude to another, or attempted to achieve some compromise between them, the most usual being to help educate or improve the lot of the Arab masses either by social work or by preaching Communist doctrine. Some of us became cynics, bent on enjoying our advantages "while there was still time," but some of us were acutely aware of our dilemma and the difficult choices before us. We felt cut off from the people and the country in which we lived, and knew that nothing would come of us unless we could build a bridge to a new society. Revolution and Marxism seemed the only way to attain a future which would include both our European mentors and the Arab masses. We would no longer be what we were, but become free citizens of the universe.

There was in us a strong mixture of desperate sincerity and of pretense, a tremendous thirst for truth and knowledge, coupled with an obscure desire for vindication, from both the arrogant domination of Europe and the Moslem majority which, we did not quite forget, despised its minorities. We would be generous and get even with the Moslem masses by introducing them to hygiene and Marxism.

Few of us Jews were Zionists, because we believed that for humanity to be free, we had to give up our narrow individuality as other people were expected to or, at most, we argued that the Jewish people had a right to national existence as did all other people, as an inevitable preliminary to "international Socialism."

I said these things, as my friends did, but wondered if they too only half-believed and were biding their time before speaking up with their own voices. Our teachers expounded knowledge from on high, and most of us who sat, heads bowed, taking notes were Jews, Greeks, and Syrians, the Levantines, those whom the Moslems called with superstitious respect and suspicion, the People of the Book. We the Jews, and the Greeks, were always there, had always been there, changing the world more than we changed ourselves, remaining the same under our many guises. Other people passed us by, and we bowed our heads until their power spent itself. Our teachers, too, would depart, but we would pass on the ferment of knowledge, making history in our insidious, secretive way, without ever being totally undone by it.[18] Perhaps in our own time, we would witness and share in the undoing of Europe's dominion, the fall of all its barracks, and even, perhaps, a return to the Promised Land. What would we, the Levantines, do in that world which would be ours, as well? In any case this new world would have to wait for us—we who were still in the schoolroom—to give it a different color and shape.

Throughout our Mediterranean world, and the vast continents it bordered, other young people were imbibing this knowledge from their teachers, never suspecting that the dormant seeds would suddenly burst out from under the silt of centuries. The Arabs and the other colonized peoples were the crossbreeds of many cultures by accident, while we Levantines were inescapably so, by vocation and destiny. Perhaps our ways would part, but together, we belonged to the Levantine generation, whose task and privilege it was to translate European thought and action and apply it to our own world. We needed to find the words that would shake the universe out of its torpor and give voice to our confused protests. We were the first generation of Levantines in the contemporary world who sought a truth that was neither in the old religions nor in complete surrender to the West, and this, perhaps, should be recorded.[19]

In later life our paths sometimes crossed, and we could talk with our own voices, Greeks, Moslems, Syrians, Copts, and Jews; those who became Arab nationalists, and Zionists, Stalinists, and Trotskyites, Turkish princesses in exile, priests and rebels. We talked of our youth when our souls were torn, and were so divided within ourselves that we had feared we could never recover. Yes, we had mastered words, and language in which to frame thoughts that were nearly our own. We were moved to discover how close we had been to each other in our youth, although it was perhaps too late to make any difference. Our choices had commanded other choices, which locked us in a position from which, in the adult world, there was no retreat.

Today, when we can no longer meet and talk, we know that history is our childish fantasies come true, and that they sometimes turn into nightmares. In newspaper stories we recognize the names of those we knew, hear the echoes of things we said or thought long ago. We understand why each one of us chose his particular road, and at last we recognize ourselves in events which happen *through* us, and not only *to* us, even though we may grieve that between our dreams and our deeds, the wicked priest has cast his shadow to separate us, and that none of us can as yet turn about and start again.[20]

TO LIVE AND DIE A COPT (1973)[21]

In 1964 an Anglophone, Egyptian-Coptic writer, Waghih Ghali, published his first and only novel, *Beer in the Snooker Club*. Kahanoff first became aware of this book nearly a decade after its publication and several years after its author had committed suicide. Featuring a Coptic protagonist and a Jewish love interest, the novel, set in the 1940s and 1950s, moves between England and Egypt and traces the struggle of Egyptians to hold on to their disappearing cosmopolitan, Levantine world. Kahanoff's essay, published in April 1973, serves as both a belated review of the novel and a reflection on Jewish-Coptic relations in Egypt. Kahanoff was apparently not aware that Ghali had spent time in Israel from July to September 1967 as a freelance journalist for the British press.

DEBORAH STARR AND SASSON SOMEKH, *Mongrels or Marvels*[22]

A friend of mine lent me the book *Beer in the Snooker Club* (Penguin) by the Coptic-Egyptian writer Waguih Ghali and asked for my opinion of it. The author's name sounded familiar and brought back memories. The Ghalis were a very wealthy and influential Coptic family, owning large estates in Upper Egypt. A young girl called Mona Ghali attended the same French high school as I did and lived not far from us, in an apartment block on the other side of a small square, in the Garden City by the Nile—the neighborhood was called Qasr al-Dubarrah. One summer I discovered she had a brother. A tall, dark, very handsome young man would stand on the balcony of their house, dressed in an all-white linen outfit, a red tarbush set rakishly on his head. He would smoke as he waited for his friends who came to pick him up every day at five in the afternoon in their fancy sports car. I heard that the young man had just returned from England, where he had obtained an education that he was not prepared to do any work whatsoever, and that he led a rather extravagant life.

When I read *Beer in the Snooker Club,* I wondered whether Waguih Ghali was the same young man I remember. There are many similarities between him and Ram, the hero of the book. Like that young man, whom I recall quite clearly though I never spoke with him, Ram had lost his father and belonged to the poorer branch of the family; otherwise, he would have lived in a palatial villa, rather than an apartment block, and would have had his own sports car. If indeed the young man of my recollections is the author of the book—how strange, how symbolic of our particular situation, that both of us, wielding our pens in the night hours, lived so close to each other, both of us trying to put on paper our impressions of Levantine Cairo and our problems as residents, while neither knew this of the other. Would Egypt's cultural scene have been different if the members of our generation had been able to associate with one another? Communal-religious boundaries were not easily crossed in those days, and what one knew about a member of another community was mostly gossip, and usually negative. It would have been interesting to talk with that clandestine writer, who seemed as desperate as he was reckless and charming. The heroes in Ghali's book surviving from the pre-Nasser period, are so familiar.

Ghali's testimony seemed all the more valid when I was told he had taken his own life, unable to adjust to Egypt under Nasser, nor to England, where he saw himself as a foreigner. "I am an Egyptian," Ram declares in *Beer in the Snooker Club,* but Nasser's Egypt did not claim him as its own. The Copts are descendants of the early Egyptians, most of whom were Christian in the Byzantine era. Those who refused to convert to Islam after the Moslem conquest did not fully integrate with the Arab newcomers nor with converts from other communities. The Copts remained apart, but they were certainly Egyptian, members of the lower middle class, at least, and as highly skilled artisans they were hard-working and thrifty. Those with a higher social standing had considerable influence in the pre-Nasser period. As nationalists, they hoped that Egypt would develop into a liberal democracy and that religion would not be the factor determining national identity. But the time was past for that early form of Egyptian nationalism, which was personified in Sa'ad Zaghlul. Egyptian nationalism became a pan-Arab Moslem movement with which the minorities could not entirely identify, and which in turn shunned all the minorities, even if they were—like the Copts—indigenous. The phenomenon recently returned, when a zealous, frustrated Moslem mob set fire to Coptic churches.

SUICIDE AS A WAY OUT OF ETHNIC CONFLICT

Copts from the upper classes were often given the names of gods from early Egyptian mythology: Isis, Osiris, Horus. Some of the most talented among them committed suicide, like Ghali, because they could not find their place in Nasser's Egypt, and were not capable of living in another country. Perhaps they lacked the flexibility that Jews have acquired through necessity. The Copts are like the reeds on the banks of the Nile: they bend as the storm passes over them but are well-rooted in the mud and cannot easily be transplanted.

Despite the sadness, *Beer in the Snooker Club* is an entertaining book, overflowing with indefinable Egyptian humor. Its sharp-eyed author mocks everything, himself included, with a fascinating mix of acerbity and good-humored wit. A melancholy envelops Ghali's book the way Egyptian dust covers the landscape. Like the silent desert, the great stone monuments, and the dead gods that weigh upon human lives, the heaviness cannot be shaken off. There are those, like Nasser, who try to escape it by feverish activity and dreams of greatness—but the burden of eternity wears them down and makes every human endeavor pointless. Egypt is a country whose inhabitants find it hard to believe in themselves or their future; everything in it seems to turn to dust. Sometimes I wonder whether the most egregious errors committed by its political leaders might not derive, to a certain extent, from that same fatalism, a fatalism that overwhelms them when they act stupidly, believing as they do that nothing can really change.

But let us return to Ram and *Beer in the Snooker Club*. Ram is a well-read young man, a nationalist, easily offended, Socialist in his sympathies. His heart is in the right place, but when he has to act he is paralyzed, as if pulled in opposite directions by too many conflicting forces, feeling a constant despair and seeing all action as basically futile. Young Ram and his mother live comfortably, thanks to the wealthy branch of the family, which does not want the shameful burden of poor relatives but is not especially pleased at having to cover Ram's debts. The elderly uncle, who lives on his rural estate, likes to enjoy himself in the company of young women when he comes to town. His mean and snobbish daughter Mary, who speaks only French, insists that her cousin Ram should find work or marry a young heiress. Both matters can be arranged through the family's connections. But Ram prefers to go to parties, play cards, read, drink, and smoke. How to occupy himself during the minutes or hours ahead: that is the question liable to distress him most. Much of his time is spent at the Sporting Club, in the company of those who "belong," such as American diplomats and representatives of American firms—or in the company of their wives. They all exemplify the kind of life-style in which Nasser's democracy took shape. The author has a fine ear for the absurd, bombastic things people say to hide their intellectual inadequacy. Sometimes Ram gambles in the basement of the Snooker Club. There he meets those who do not "belong"—including cocky, downtrodden Armenian storekeepers, and his best friend, Font. Font withdrew from the university and from society and was selling vegetables from a cart before he agreed, with lofty contempt, to serve at the bar of the Snooker Club.

Ram is in love with a wealthy young Jewish woman of Communist sympathies who was tortured on account of the activities of her former husband after he fled to Israel. He is also friendly with the daughter of a rich pasha, who received her education at the Sorbonne and lives alone, with flowers and book-binding as hobbies. Ram and Font need a change of air, and Edna, the young Jewish woman, pays for their trip to England, then disappears. But once there, the two young men cannot get their visas renewed. Luckily for them, they meet some liberal British intellectuals, the sort who are always ready to help foreigners in trouble. Together, the young people, English and Egyptian, drink, argue, and make love. Their unexpected encounters are entertainingly described, with a fine feeling for dialogue and a sense of the absurdity inherent in certain situations.

Ram's conversation with a tough and passionate elderly woman who collects tickets on the tram, and his exchange of views with an English soldier who fought at Port Said[23]—these are gems of irony. The soldier's version of events is very different from that of the young Egyptian patriot, and both men try to remain polite despite being very drunk and acutely irritated. Each of them, of course, sees the Suez situation in an entirely different light.

A SOPHISTICATED MINORITY CULTURE WITH NO PURPOSE

Ram and Font return to Egypt. It is their home and they cannot adopt any other. But they are not the types who become involved in political struggles and risk arrest and torture. They were educated in the wealthy sector of society, where the privileged had no duties beyond the obligation to be charming. With the declining status of the class to which they belong, they are left with no grip on reality. Something in them breaks and will never be mended. They are without faith or vitality. A cultural aimlessness and exhaustion pervade the milieu of those who belong to the upper strata of the minority groups and who flee the phantoms of a shared heritage to meet on a more personal level. Hopelessness dogs their clever discussions on politics, as well as their gossip and half-hearted love affairs. Their exchanges have no anger and no enthusiasm.

Although they are still well-off, these people find themselves marginal-
ized, gradually pushed aside by Egypt's Moslem society, with its newly
privileged class of officers and bureaucrats.

Looking back, it seems a great shame that educated, talented people
like Waguih Ghali were wasted and lost. For it is as if the whole country
was silenced. Was it a failure on the part of society, which indulged its
children to the point where they believed in their ability to stand up
and fight, even though they had never attempted to do so? Is the flaw
to be found in the sophisticated minority culture, which led nowhere
for those who did not belong? Or was it the fault of history, moving at
too fast a pace? Egypt's problems had been neglected for so long that
perhaps it was impossible to believe in a gradual move toward modern
social structures, toward a culture that was both deep-rooted and at the
same time open to the world. In addition, the minorities were Egypt's
intellectual mainstay, but their formal, exclusively European culture
put up a barrier between them and the Egyptian populace. They were
unable to create a rooted, open culture, and the rift between the Moslem population and the European-educated minorities only deepened.
Those minorities, while sharing certain elements of European culture,
were constrained by their communal or religious loyalties, and hence
there were mutual suspicions, prejudices, and quarrels that prevented
them from coming into contact with each other, not to speak of creating
ties with society at large.

ANTI-SEMITIC CHRISTIAN MINORITIES

The Christian minorities—Coptic, Syrian, Lebanese, Armenian, and
Greek—were sometimes anti-Semitic. The Lebanese and Syrian Christians owned newspapers and on occasion waged aggressive, pan-Arab
campaigns with an openly anti-Semitic, anti-Zionist tone, thinking
this would give them an advantage over other minorities, especially the
Jews.[24] Egypt was different from most other colonial countries in that it
had many European cultures intermixed or living in mutual hostility.
In Iraq and Palestine, for example, English was the dominant foreign
language. In Egypt, cultured people from all the different groups spoke
both English and French, and there were also large Italian and Greek
communities with their own schools and other institutions, linked to

the mother country and reflecting the different political positions there. Fascism, for example, split the large Italian colony and even the Italian Jewish community. In other words, there was really no dominant group among the European-oriented minorities, which were separated from each other by religion, political inclination, and language. This phenomenon made Egypt a complex, fascinating place, but at the same time prevented the consolidation of a minority "Levantine" culture as an alternative to the Moslem-Arab culture.

The Moslem "revolutionaries" in Nasser's ruling group repressed all the minorities en masse. The question remains: was anything at all gained by such repression? Egypt does not seem to have improved as a result of Waguih Ghali's suicide, or as a consequence of many others giving to other countries all they had to give.

Those who did not have "other countries" were silenced or lost. The case of Waguih Ghali is especially symbolic and sad, since his talent was indisputable, and he could not stay alive to develop it.

He no longer believed in anything—and that was fatal, because a writer has to believe at least in his work. For the Egyptian Copt, not even that belief was possible.

Part of Ghali's tragedy was that he wrote in English and felt himself to be Egyptian. But there is another way of looking at the issue. After all, Tawfiq al-Hakim and Naguib Mahfouz write in Arabic,[25] and still Sadat has virtually silenced them, along with two hundred other authors and intellectuals. They not only expressed support for the student riots, but also dared argue that Egypt had to relinquish pursuit of the pan-Arab dream and perhaps, in addition, reach some agreement with Israel on the issue of opening the Suez Canal.[26] Waguih Ghali, too, though not exactly a supporter of Israel, claimed in *Beer in the Snooker Club* that Egypt had more pressing problems than the war with Israel. It seems, then, that the earlier version of Egyptian nationalism, which had found expression in Sa'ad Zaghlul, and which was more liberal and humane, open to Western culture, and not hostile to the minorities, is not yet altogether dead in Egypt. It has just been forcibly silenced. The war of attrition on the Suez Canal was not the only war Sadat lost: there is also a war within Egypt, and its losses are perhaps even greater. The canal may one day reopen, but the writers and intellectuals who have died—

whether in body or spirit—will not be easily replaced. Even with all the doubts that beset him, and with all his perplexities, perhaps Waguih Ghali could have given the Egyptians more than is offered by those who have silenced people like him.

∾

SAMIR EL-YOUSSEF (b. 1965)

Samir el-Youssef is an Anglo-Palestinian novelist born in the Rashidiyyé refugee camp in southern Lebanon and has been living in London since 1990. He is the author of several books and novellas, including *Illusion of Return,* and a collection of short-stories, *Gaza Blues,* coauthored with Israeli novelist Etgar Keret. An essayist and public intellectual, el-Youssef has contributed to various publications in Europe and the Middle East. In 2005, he was recipient of the (German) PEN Tucholsky Literary Award in recognition of his commitment to the promotion of peace and freedom of speech in the Middle East.

Samir el-Youssef is a brave articulate writer; a leading figure among young Palestinian authors and intellectuals who advocate for nontraditional, "spacious" Middle Eastern identity models. Although committed to the Palestinian people and to shedding light on their continued plight, Samir rarely writes in Arabic, and seldom interprets the Palestinian condition from the (predictable) orthodox purview. In so doing, he deviates from his culture's normative themes and traditional social, political, and intellectual exigencies, whether pan-Arabist, Palestinian nationalist, or traditional Islamist.

El-Youssef is sober, honest, and courageous, producing work of great originality and depth, betraying no nostalgia, no lamentation, no self-pity, no yearnings for olive trees or lemon orchards or old house keys. He calls for no revenge, no retribution, no rewards, and no resentment. One could say that he doesn't even advocate for "return," a prevalent theme in Palestinian literature of exile.

In fact, "people do not *return*," he wrote recently; *even* when they *do* go back to the places of their birth and early lives, people are *only* "moving on!!" "Life is a one-way journey," he insists, and "as for those who claim to return to a place where they never were, they are simply

confusing the symbolic and metaphorical with the possible and actual.
[. . . Even] the Jews who went to Palestine didn't [actually] 'return'
but [instead] emigrated to Palestine."[27] And so, Samir el-Youssef is an
advocate of shared humanity (and humanism); a voice for reconciliation, and for a twining of multiple (spacious) identities and histories
that are *always* elastic, fluid, and inclusive. The works produced in this
anthology are an attempt at bringing back to the center of academic
(and public) discourse the idea of the Levant as a rich mosaic of ethnicities, religions, languages, and cultural accretions.

The Levant: Zone of Culture or Conflict? (2012)[28]

I didn't read Philip Larkin until the publication of his *Selected Letters*
(1940–85) and the heated debate that they provoked. Larkin had been
seen as one of the most beloved contemporary English poets, but in
1993, the year of the *Letters'* publication, it was revealed that in some
of his private correspondence this great poet had expressed views that
could only be deemed to be those of a racist. Some insisted that Larkin must be seen as the good poet he'd ever been. Others thought he
should be dismissed. The intransigent question about Art and Politics
had managed to make its way into the centre of attention again.

My first reading of Larkin was more like a detective mission; thor-
ough text searching for clues, which could link his poetry to those few
offending letters. Larkin's poems are riddled with signs of nostalgic
yearning. In themselves such signs would have been deemed harmless
were they not issuing from an English writer. In them were also hints of
resentment towards anything modern or abroad. But there was no real
evidence, no proof as it were, of a racist expression that could be used or
brandished by way of indictment in any serious debate. My mission to
impeach Larkin, I'm happy to report, was an absolute failure.

Why happy?

—Happy because as I read Larkin's poems I came to enjoy quite a
good number of them. Indeed I enjoyed more poems now than when
reading many other poets whom I'd explored without the grudge of
a detective-reader. Enjoying so many poems in such a small output
made me come back to Larkin time and again, reading him with open

mindedness and with no other purpose than the pleasure of reading poetry.

Repeated readings over the years made Larkin one of my most favourite poets.

Still, racism is a serious matter, and when one's favourite poet is branded a racist, one must explain how it is possible to reconcile the irreconcilables. Some commentators and friends of the late poet tried the usual method of playing down the issue of racism. Some insisted that art and politics, especially politics expressed in private correspondence, are two separate realms that mustn't be confused. Others argued that those letters should only be seen within the historical and cultural context in which they were written. But none of these arguments holds water. Larkin is a bigot and there is no way of getting around this disgraceful fact. So how could one read him knowing what he is or what he was?

Larkin's poems are good, and like all good art they have the ability to make the audience forget the repugnant views of the artist and bypass his personality too. Reading Larkin poems, just like listening to Wagner music, one temporarily forgets what such artists might have said, in either the private or public spheres. The ability of art to induce temporary forgetfulness is what I would like to make use of in answering the question that is the title of this essay: "Is the Levant a zone of conflict or culture?"

When talking about the Levant, there are two important and closely connected issues one must keep in mind: memory and the attitude of each of the Levant's communities towards the "other."

Jews, Palestinians, Kurds and many other nations and minorities in the Middle East have had a past of grief and a history of suffering, and therefore memory is a very important and popular term in many Middle Eastern quarters. Indeed memory is so important that it seemed to be the major source of informing and goading a given community's political attitude towards the "other," and sometimes towards the "self." The trauma of the dark past is generated in deep fear and suspicion verging on paranoia. Accordingly the "other" is seen as someone who has no other wish and intention but that of defeating us, destroying us. Whatever statement and move the "other" makes is often seen as part of a wider, sophisticated, devious plot; an endless conspiracy within which whatever is prefigured years earlier is bound to take place. The "other's" group, the opposite group, is usually given too much credibility, suspected of being always cunning, skilfully organised and highly co-ordinated, or at least having the benefit of unshakable determination to keep on fighting to the end. Willingness to negotiate and reach a peace agreement is often viewed with suspicion that even those who participate seem to be expecting little besides their suspicions being confirmed and justified.

The protracted and farcical Palestinian-Israeli peace process is a good example of how such two aspects manifest themselves. In this context, any concession made, no matter how small and insignificant, is often considered the first of many other greater concessions to follow, leading eventually to the destruction of those surrendering to compromise. Indeed there were times when Palestinian and Israeli peace negotiators seemed to be waiting to see who is going to flinch first, who is going to fail to keep their part of the bargain. The desire to play the role of the tragic hero must have haunted the mind of those peace-makers and was ready to be animated on the world stage: "Look, we have tried everything to reach an agreement; we stretched our out hand to them but they turned it down!" I am sure that such attitudes and such discourse were rehearsed numerous times.

With such paranoia left unchallenged, no wonder peace remains illusive and very difficult, not to say impossible, to achieve. Reconciliation is doomed to remain a distant hope, so long as the "other" continues to be viewed with distrust. And so, it seems that the common assumption that the Levant is evidently a zone of conflict, and worse, might remain so until doomsday, doesn't lack justification. But is there a way to challenge such a seemingly fated and enduring assumption?

Let us mention another term, which is just as popular as Memory: Resistance, or *The Resistance*. This is a sacred cow in many parts of the Levant. "No voice shall rise above the voice of the Resistance!" is an oft-repeated slogan. Once a group anoints itself a representative of the "resistance," or wraps itself in the mantle of some "resistance," *any* "resistance," it will have earned the right to do pretty much as it pleases— with impunity, as is often the case with many a "sacred" or "divine resistance" in the Levant today! So let us learn from the practitioners of "resistance" and establish our own resistance: The resistance against memory and paranoia. Indeed, what better way to resist unremitting "resistance" than to encourage forgetfulness?

But let me first emphasize two points: First, that the attitude of suspicion vis-à-vis the "other" is peculiar to politics, or anything that is determined through politics. Secondly, that people are not necessarily enslaved to their dark memory. Indeed, whenever they can, they try to distract themselves from both memory and politics; the act of forgetfulness is not so strange to them. Indeed these two facts have encouraged me through the last two decades to challenge the assumption that the Levant is, or could only, be depicted as a zone of conflict. However, the temporary forgetfulness that I am talking about is not the same as seeking distraction from reality, or escaping reality, or being cynical.

Good art for me is that which combines pleasure with education, or simply an intelligent joke that makes one laugh and think and then laugh again. The chance to forget here is a chance to think, to discover something else, or something different, or at least to recognise the significance of something that one might have overlooked or dismissed. In other words, forgetfulness is a chance to unlearn an old lesson and learn a new one.

I enjoyed reading Larkin's poems, but I also learned a great deal from them; they taught me many things about the English language and post-war England, and how to distinguish between an attitude of disappointment and one of hostility, and between expressions of solidarity and appreciation, and hypocrisy and conceit. Within the Levant the moment of temporary forgetfulness might be a chance for learning how to pave the way for the imagination of peace.

People who followed the Peace Process through its visual aspect must have noticed how hesitant and reluctant participants in peace negotiations looked. Starting from the notorious Arafat-Rabin handshake on the White House lawn, peace negotiators looked as if they were doing a dirty job; something that they were undertaking out of sheer necessity and desperation. The private argument, which was often made, seemed to confirm the implication of the image on the White House lawn; "we have to be realistic—we can do nothing but negotiate and reach a peaceful agreement." "Nothing" here means "we couldn't get rid of them or destroy them, so we have to make a deal with them."

No wonder the peace process has always looked like a half-baked process. When discussing what went wrong with the peace process an annoying expression was repeatedly used; "there is no culture of peace," it was often said. This makes one imagine communities in the Middle East doing nothing all day long except digging trenches.

That is not true! The Levant is no poorer a place than any other in the culture of peace. But what has been lacking in the Levant is actually *the imagination of peace;* people for a long time have been living in one state of conflict or another; or a state of *no peace and no war,* that they have no idea how the world might look like without war or the expectation of conflict and violence. Indeed people of the Levant seem to have got used to such assumptions that the alternative appears to them as an unreal world.

In a literary event that brought together a group of Palestinian and Israeli writers, just before the failure of the Camp David Talks in 2000, I remember the late Israeli writer Batya Gur commencing her talk by reading Cavafy's famous poem *Waiting for the Barbarians.* There had been a moment of exaggerated hope at the time; a time during which a breakthrough in the Israeli-Syrian peace talks was expected. Such a breakthrough would have meant that the last major stumbling block before achieving total peace will have been surmounted. Yet, in spite of the exaggerated hope, as Gur explained, one could nevertheless still sense the feeling expressed in the last two lines of Cavafy's poem: "Now what will become of us without barbarians? / Those people were some kind of solution." Whenever there has been a breakthrough, the sense of "Now what will become of us without barbarian?" has spread. Why? Because imagination has failed to keep up with reality.

Imagination is meant to precede reality and to provide examples, models, and images of how the new reality, the world in a state of peace, would look like. Instead, when the time for peace arrived, imagination seemed to lag behind, stuck within an old world languishing in the tyranny of the memory of a dark past and an attitude of scepticism towards the "other." No wonder that every time a peace treaty has been signed, people felt that they were venturing into the wilderness or at least, like those who waited for the never-arriving barbarians, that they have been deprived from a source of consolation.

The question in the title of this essay, "is the Levant a zone of conflict or culture?" is an ironic one indeed. Anyone with a token knowledge of the Levant knows that the Levant is of both, conflict and culture; it is only that the people of the Levant need to be reminded that theirs is a land of great culture, and that they need pay more attention to it. I was born and brought up in Rashidiyyé—a Palestinian refugee camp in Southern Lebanon. Rashidiyyé was, and still is, as bad as a refugee camp could be. A mere fifteen minutes walk from the camp stood the ancient Phoenician port-city of Tyre; a harbour town housing the awesome vestiges of one of the greatest, most pacifist, most benevolent builders of civilization. The refugee camp (in its indigence), and the ancient city (in all its glory), standing side by side, is a stark example of the Levant being both a land of conflict and culture.

When Philip Larkin's offensive letters were published in 1993, some people suggested his poetry be struck off from school curricula. This reaction made me think back to the old school of my boyhood, back in the Rashidiyyé refugee camp. Our teachers then talked up a storm about politics, the conflict, the hopelessness and indigence of our situation. Yet I don't remember any of them suggesting a school tour to the nearby Phoenician port-city of Tyre, a living testament as it were, to the ancient Levant; a place where we could, even for a fleeting moment, forget the misery of our present days and learn something new, something different, something hopeful; learn how when looking at what lay outside the "prison walls," and when considering that which challenges prevalent assumptions, one might be able to see above the clouds of past traumas, and beyond the paranoia of present days.

RASHED'S DECISION (2012)

He was distracted by the sight of Rashed, by Rashed's story, the old story of a fatal confrontation, far away and a long time back: seeing him now, after having remembered all those people, remembering their stories

and misfortunes; after, above all, making his own confessions, Naji remembered the story that Rashed had told him months ago. "Now I'm
ready for you, Rashed; you and your confession are no longer a secret;
I no longer have an obligation to keep it a secret," he said to himself: "I
see you now and remember, no, I actually imagine you back there, years
back and thousands of miles away, crouching, hiding behind a thicket
of reeds or shrubs on the beach of Gaza, holding tight to your Kalash-
nikov, ready to open fire, you murderer; yes, you murderer—by your
own admission!"

Rashed was watching three soldiers within firing range.

"But, no. I didn't see them as three soldiers," he told Naji, in that
small café on the Gray's Inn Road, "no I wasn't looking at three soldiers.
Had I seen them as soldiers, I would've shot them right away. No, I was
looking at three young men, three boys, naked and foolish boys." They
were swimming; they were playing, talking, merrily and loudly, and
splashing each other with water. "Totally naked and distant from their
military vehicle where I assumed they'd left their clothes and rifles. Yes,
they were far away from their weapons as if to feel free from what would
otherwise have reminded them that they were actually soldiers involved
in a costly occupation."

Rashed was baffled. What sort of soldiers were those? Were they
fools? Did they want to get killed? He knew very well that he only needed
to pull the trigger to get them one by one. He didn't want to shoot but
the opportunity he was offered was too good to be wasted. He was frightened that the ease with which he could get them was too tempting, and
hoped that soon they would get out of the water, get dressed and leave.

"For a moment," he said in the tone of voice of someone who
couldn't believe what he was saying, even after all those years, "I thought
of calling them, shouting from my hiding place: 'What the hell do you
think you're doing? Do you want to die?'"

The temptation to shoot was getting stronger; just to open fire and
kill them, naked as they were, on that deserted beach. But he didn't, not
right away. The only thing he wished to do at that very moment was to
shout: "Where the hell do you think you are? In your own country? Get
out! Go on get out before you get yourself shot!"

"That's what I honestly wanted to do," he said.

And now, telling Naji the story, he was still puzzled by his own attitude; why didn't he open fire? Why did he hesitate?

"But you did eventually shoot them?" Naji interrupted him. He wanted Rashed to skip the details and come to the moment when he finally shot them.

Now, recalling the day when Rashed and he had gone to that café on Gray's Inn Road—and that was a time when he could still sleep easily—he didn't know whether he wanted him to do so because he was eager to get to the end or simply because he was getting sleepy and wanted to go back to bed. He was also aware of the owner of the café getting restless because they hadn't ordered anything apart from coffee, and he knew how much the man hated customers spending hours over one lousy order. Naji knew that he was waiting impatiently for them to finish so he could come over to pick up the empty cups and ask if they wanted something else.

Rashed however didn't notice anything. He was totally engrossed in his own story and certainly wasn't yet ready to reach the end. He didn't want to skip the details; the story wasn't about the moment when he eventually made up his mind and shot, no, the story was about his long hesitation in doing so; and it was precisely these details that showed his hesitation.

"Why didn't you shoot at once?" Naji went on asking, trying to assure him that he understood what he was telling him.

"That is the important question. Of course I could have done that right away," he said and added mockingly, after a pause, "I could have killed them, earning myself the title of a hero. After all it wasn't every day that one shot three enemy soldiers."

At one point he was ready and certain that he could get them. But again, he hesitated. "I tried, but couldn't," he said staring at Naji, expecting him to ask why. But before Naji had the chance to say anything he went on, "How could one kill three naked boys playing in the water? How could one kill three children playing? Yes, children?"

He repeated the word *children* as if he wanted to assure Naji that his first use of the word was not the result of a random choice. He meant it; they were merely three children: "Children who have run away from school, wanted to free themselves and went into the sea, that's it, that's what they were. That's what we did during our childhood, ran away from school with our friends and went to the beach."

He decided to leave the area straightaway, leave and forget the whole matter but he simply couldn't. He remained there, hiding behind the reeds thicket. He never knew for sure what exactly made him stay. Now, sitting with Naji, recalling what had happened many years earlier, he tried to remember, to make out an explanation. Now he knew, he realised, at last, that to his dismay he had stayed because he wanted to protect them.

"Protect them? They were enemy soldiers?" Naji asked. He thought he was expected to ask such a question.

"Call me crazy, if you like, but yes," he said, "that's what I wanted to do, to protect them, to protect three enemy soldiers. They were in imminent danger. You see, it would've been very easy for any armed person, any armed passer-by, to open fire and kill them without any hesitation. Such a person would have considered himself lucky to fall upon such an opportunity, hunting three enemy soldiers, and thus earn himself the title of hero. And so I decided to stay until they'd left unharmed."

But then he found himself wondering again whether he didn't actually want, after all, to grab the easy opportunity himself and become a hero. Perhaps he didn't, after all, wish to protect them, perhaps he only wanted to make sure that nobody else would shoot them and gain the title of hero; perhaps he was still tempted to become a hero. Why should he leave such a chance to another person? Why should he when it could easily be his?

"So, I decided to stay to prevent another armed person from gaining an honour and fame which I was, by precedence, entitled to. I was the first to see them and I was the one who was able to shoot them. 'I could shoot them any time I liked,' I said to myself as if to prove that I wasn't incapable of opening fire. Yes, I could do that, right away! And I pointed the gun at them, 'I'll shoot them before anybody else does. If I don't shoot them someone else will. Someone who would come after me; someone who has no right to deal with them the way I do. I've seen them first. They are mine and I'll shoot them.' I was hallucinating. I was

going mad but I decided to shoot. I'll shoot them and I shan't tell anybody. I'll shoot them and say nothing about it, I'll run away."

Pointing the gun at them he tried again to shoot but couldn't.
Quite determined, he was, but he couldn't. However, the hesitation, this
time, didn't generate entirely from inside. Something had happened; a
little episode, a joke. He remembered it after all those years and couldn't
help smiling, "They were just children, as I told you."

They were still in the sea, in the water up to their waist, talking
and laughing loudly. One of them got out and went to the jeep. Rashed
saw him rummaging through bags and clothes before returning, carrying bottles of refreshments. As he got near he threw a bottle to one of
his friends who promptly caught it. Another bottle was thrown at the
other soldier, but this one failed to catch it. He actually slipped falling
back and his two friends burst out laughing. He was angry and started
swearing at them, but then started laughing too; the three of them were
laughing; they were happy.

"It was funny," Rashed said, "But it wasn't the funny side that
stopped me taking aim at them, fully determined to shoot, no, it was
the innocence. Yes, the innocence. That's the word I've always wanted to
use but somehow wasn't sure that it was the right one. Innocent, that's
how I saw those three soldiers; those three school children who had run
away to the sea to play. Innocent, yes, that's the word. That's why I didn't
shoot."

He fell silent as if that was the end of the story.

"What happened next?" Naji wasn't sure that he should ask such
a question.

"I shot them and left."

Naji was shocked. True he had already guessed that Rashed shot
them, but to hear it stated so bluntly, so curtly, without any indication
of regret, made it sound as if Rashed were revealing a new shocking
secret.

"Why?"

"Why did I shoot them? Why after all the thinking and hesitation, after I'd reached the conclusion that they were merely innocent
children?"

He asked. He was talking to himself.

"Yes?"

He was silent for a while. He seemed as if he didn't have an explanation. "What can I say?" He paused, "What can I say? Because I couldn't leave them there. I didn't want to leave them on their own. I wanted to protect them, to take them with me." He wasn't explaining to Naji why he had killed them, no, he was recalling what he had felt at that moment.

"No doubt you think I'm mad. But I'm not. Nor was I then when I shot them. Believe me I wasn't. I simply believed that those three children belonged to me and I shouldn't leave them there on their own. I felt that they were mine, my responsibility and I had to take care of them. Of course I should've killed myself too. I thought of it, and ever since have been thinking of taking my own life, but I'm a coward. I knew that I could get away, I could run away. I was tempted by life and I left. I'm not mad, believe me."

Naji believed him.

∾

FAWAZ TURKI (b. 1940)

Born in 1940 in the port city of Haifa, which at that time was in British Mandatory Palestine, Fawaz Turki came of age in the abject humiliating universe of the refugee camps of Lebanon, where Palestinians arguably suffered more than in any other host "Arab" country. His work is reflective of those formative years of his life. Turki is unafraid, often obscene, in the way in which he depicts himself as a decadent, irresponsible *enfant terrible*. To him, that might have been the only way he could scream in the face of dispossession, and attempt to undo the repressive culture in which he grew up. Like Nizar Qabbani, Fawaz Turki seeks to offend in order to instigate change. As a novelist, he probes deeply with his characters, while at the same time leveling base attacks and making sweeping generalizations about the misogyny, the sexual and social repression, the corruption, and the prevalence of patronage in traditional Palestinian and Arab societies.

One particular incident from Turki's life, which has clearly influenced him and played a role in charting his future, was the killing of his little sister Jasmine by his domineering authoritarian elder brother Musa. It is this tragedy, which can be interpreted as a metaphor of the Palestinians' own slaying at the hands of their "Arab brethren," that constitutes the central (existential) allegory of the texts selected for this chapter, from *Exile's Return: The Making of a Palestinian-American*.

Jasmine's murder was the trigger as it were, goading Turki to go seek out the magic behind the mountains.[29] In Turki's telling, Jasmine's death symbolizes Arab society's sexual repression, and Turki, through his depravity and lewd confrontational behavior, clearly sought the undoing of that society. Nizar Qabbani, whose own sister committed suicide for related—albeit not entirely similar—reasons, initially embarked on a similar quest, though arguably not as scandalous as Turki's confrontational style might have been. Yet, like Qabbani, Turki believed that a people, a culture, a civilization, cannot be liberated, cannot advance, cannot embrace modernity, so long as its women remain shackled by tradition, patriarchy, and misogyny.

In his railings against Arab societies, Turki makes the claim that the Arab (and Palestinian) individual is unable to break out of the shackles of the past and embrace modernity and democracy—that is to say democracy, not only as a political system, but also as a social system and a set of social ethics—because "fear" is an overriding element in the Arabs' social ethos. How responsive can Arabs be, he asks, to an ethos of freedom of expression when people have for generations existed with an ethic of fear? Fear of originality, fear of innovation, fear of spontaneity, fear of authority, and fear of freedom. Arabs are hard-wired, argued Turki, to accept orthodoxy, dependence, and submission. That is why, in his view, the Arab world today remains a collection of disparate entities ruled for the most part by authoritarian regimes whose rule relies on coercion, violence, blackmail, intimidation, paternalism, parochialism, clientelism, and terror; systems that demand from their citizens submission, obedience, and conformity.

Turki's rebellion, like that of Adonis before him, puts him in a state of liminality; a phase in the process—or the rite—of passage that is halfway between the old and the new; a state of limbo as it were; a state of being "stalled between seasons," as Adonis called it. Being in two worlds, or in between two worlds, knowing both intimately, partaking of the happiness and pains of both, but belonging to neither.

As noted earlier, growing up as a refugee in Beirut, with no regular formal education and only episodic employment, Turki became a neighborhood thug and petty thief. But he was ultimately given the opportunity to get some schooling, and eventually spent four years studying in England. When he returned to the Middle East, he was more disillusioned, more embittered, and more dispirited with the place than when he had left it. He ended up traveling to Saudi Arabia, where he worked at Aramco. But soon enough, his irreverence got him in trouble, cost him his job, and returned him to Beirut even more embittered than before. He soon realized that "after twenty-five years of living in Exile, of growing up permanently reminded of my status as an exile, the Diaspora for me, for a whole generation of Palestinians, [became] *the* homeland. Palestine is no longer a mere geographical entity but a state of mind. The reason, however, that Palestinians are obsessed with the notion of Returning, though indeed there is no Palestine to return to [. . .] is because the Return means the reconstitution of a Palestinian's integrity and the regaining of his place in history."[30]

In *Exile's Return,* Turki describes his return to the "homeland," to Haifa, for a visit, after more than forty years of living in exile. "My book is the story of one Palestinian exile who tries to come to grips and, finally, to terms with his condition. [. . .] [The] book is both a backward glance at my life as a Palestinian writer, activist, and an unhoused wanderer, and an account of my visit to Palestine, on the eve of the Persian Gulf War, in which I reflect on the tensions that exist between Palestinians who have always lived in their homeland and those, who, like myself, have lived in exile."[31] Turki notes that whereas the English-speaking reader may find his book informative, his fellow Palestinians in the Palestine Liberation Organization (PLO) will no doubt find it scandalous, and others from among his people may be "shocked by its harsh critiques of Palestinian popular culture and its antiquated mores."[32] To be sure, Turki mercilessly attacks several aspects of social and political life in Palestinian society and the Arab world at large. Most notably, Turki rails against what he calls "formal literary Arabic." To his sense, educated Arabs have three different linguistic personalities, all of which referred to as Arabic, but each different from the other to the same extent that Chaucer's English differs from Churchill's, and to the same extent both Chaucer's and Churchill's English differ from the African-American English spoken on the streets of New York or Chicago. He describes one variety of Arabic, which he calls "formal Arabic"—what is commonly referred to as Modern Standard Arabic—as a language invented in the "age of neobackwardness," his ironic label for the Arab literary *nahda* (renaissance) of the nineteenth century. Turki's first variety of Arabic is "classical" (or Qur'anic) Arabic, and the final variety, which is in fact dozens of languages (or dialects), is dubbed the "language of the masses"; a speech form "whose vocabulary, chaotic grammar, structure and tonality reflect the mutilated world Arabs inhabit."[33]

During his excursion through the "homeland" Turki visits his birthplace, Haifa, but also Jerusalem and Ramallah and other places both within Israel proper and in the Occupied Territories. He seemed in a constant state of movement, in search of what he called the magic country behind the mountain. He speaks of encounters with high-ranking Palestinian politicians and activists, one of whom, like Turki himself, a perfect example of liminality, living astride two worlds but belonging to neither: "Shaath was addressing me in English. He spoke Faultless textbook English, but his archaic imagery was quintessentially Arabic. Like other Westernized Palestinian intellectuals, especially those who embrace Islam and reject the West as the Great Satan, Shaath is tormented by the dilemma of a man who has gone far—but not deep—into an alien culture to which he suddenly realizes he can never belong, and is now drawn back to an Arab culture to which he can never return."[34] As readers of Turki will no doubt realize, his characters, his themes, and his railings as narrator, are all his own in real life; the disillusionment, sometimes the rage, of a man, like most Levantines, torn between two or more worlds but belonging to none.

Exile's Return: The Making of a
Palestinian-American (1994)[35]

JOURNEY TO THE HOMEGROUND

Once, to celebrate the end of Ramadan, the Moslem month of fasting, my Parents packed a picnic lunch and took us by bus to the park at Mount Karmel in Haifa.

It was one of those days that fall between seasons, with no clearly defined identity, when spring was about to surrender itself to summer. I was a few months shy of my eighth birthday. In less than two weeks my sister, Jasmine, who was turning into a precocious child, would be six. My older brother, Mousa, somewhat aloof and conscious of his privileged status as the oldest son, was twice my age. And Mom was pregnant with Samir, who was to wait for another six months, until we all got to the refugee camp in Beirut, before he decided to come into the world.

After we ate our lunch, Jasmine and I ran around the park rattling a stick on fence palings and playing hide and seek. Mousa lay on the grass with his arms holding the back of his head. At his age, he would have surely looked foolish playing with us. Instead, he joined my parents in discussing the political situation in what was then called Palestine. At that time in 1948 it was slowly being devoured by a madness in its history, the kind of madness that robs men and women of their human compassion and children of their innocence.

I remember the day I asked a Jewish boy I know from the neighborhood if he wanted to play. Uri and I had been friends for well over a year—and that is a long friendship in the life of a child. He just looked at me level-eyed, face set, with his chin up, in the typical manner of a boy snubbing another, and said, "My mother told me I can't play with Arabs."

The next time I saw Uri, I asked him aggressively why he had his shirtsleeves rolled all the way up. "You some kinda tough guy?" I demanded.

"You wanna fight?"

"What about you, you wanna fight?"

We looked at each other and nodded, frowning all the while. We did not, finally, fight. We just moved away from each other, troubled by the inexplicable absurdity of it all.

I never got to speak to Uri again. His family and mine lived on Miknass Street in a neighborhood that was predominantly Arab. The madness in our history was not only propelling Arabs and Jews—later to become known to the world as Palestinians and Israelis—to turn their backs on each other but to live in their own separate enclaves. So Uri's family moved out. The day they moved, I stood on the steps leading to our house, leaning against the railing, both hands in my pockets, watching Uri get into his parents' car just before it screeched off violently into the distance. I found myself involuntarily taking both hands out of my pockets and waving at him, but I don't think he saw me. The scene was sad in the extreme, but I couldn't tell any adult about it. I would have been harshly lectured about "the enemy," just as Uri had been.[36] Adults cannot bring themselves to admit that children are special guardians of human truth.[37] So Jews and Arabs first turned their backs on each other, then moved away from each other, and finally proceeded to murder each other. Who started it? Who cares. History had already poured fire into our blood and ritual reference into our meaning.[38]

My uncle was killed as his car was ambushed while driving past a Jewish settlement on the coast road leading to Haifa. Mousa, my older brother, joined the *Mojahedeen,* the Arab guerrilla group of the day. When he came home it was with guns and hand grenades, but often he took off for days, even weeks, on end. Innocent Jews and Arabs caught on the fringes of their respective neighborhoods were stabbed and killed. And then the matchless cruelty of the massacres started— massacres whose perpetrators, along with their supporters on each side, would describe as heroic, as if their justification lay in some book of sacred law. Both sides soldiered on, a fierce madness at their heels.
[. . .]

I took another memory with me from Palestine as madness devoured the land. As we finally trekked north on the coast to seek refuge in Lebanon, with thousands of other refugees fleeing the carnage, we came upon a pregnant woman lying by the wayside, emitting the ghostly sounds of the pain of labor. Her husband was running up and down the road, flailing his arms and pleading, "Brothers and sisters, I beg of you, brothers and sisters, I beg of you. Is there a midwife in your midst? In the name of Allah, the Merciful, the Compassionate, is there a midwife in your midst?

People crowded around the young woman, among them my mother, who knelt to comfort her and wiped her face with a wet cloth, waiting for a midwife to be found among the refugees on the road. As we waited, those haunting sounds emitted by the woman in labor seemed to splinter their surroundings into raw wounds.

A midwife was finally found, and we moved on.

The image of that woman lying by the wayside may have diminished in time or choked on some inexplicable subconscious impulse, but the remembered sounds keep rattling around in every corner of my being. When I hear them, I give the world the bitter smile of a thousand sleepless nights. Those sounds had their mad echoes in everything destructive I have done to myself and to others in my life.

Out of the havoc of my early childhood, it was the memory of a single day—the last of Palestine's halcyon days, that I spent on Mount Karmel picnicking with my family—that has acquired an irrevocable tenure in my soul. Time has not excised it. Nor has my encounter with despair in later years. No one knows, save other exiles, the unutterable solitude that is the private fate of those severed from home and homeland, how they are forever haunted by images of themselves as unhoused wanderers, carrying on their backs what little cargo they bring with them from their past: a name, a memory, an inner echo, a kind of dark meaning, and always the weight of a nearness out of reach.

That is why I am back here today, at Mount Karmel, standing in the same spot where I had that picnic on that cloudless day four decades ago, and I feel its energy enfold me like my skin enfolds my body.

I am home.

Yet as I say that to myself, I know how facile and illusory that outcry is. It is tawdry, I tell myself, for me to be saying that. I cannot return here, after forty years in exile, with my alternative order of meaning, my comfortable notions about homelessness being my only homeland, and say that I am home. The house is no longer as habitable as when I left it. The toys are no longer in the attic. An awry force in history has changed the place, and my own sense of otherness has changed me. This place could not be lived in by anyone other than its new inhabitants, and they have already stripped it clean of everything but themselves. From time to time I come across something here and there, inherited from nature—the view of the Mediterranean below, the cloudless sky above, the richly green trees around—that had always independently declared their own form of being, but apart from that, Haifa no longer speaks to me.[39]

A few feet away, a man with a skullcap is holding a child on his shoulders. The child, a girl of five or six, is crying. As she cries, she leans so far out from his hold that I think she is going to fall. Her father sits her on his lap, claps her hands together, and begins to speak to her. In English. With a Brooklyn accent. Elsewhere, I would not have found this scene charged with any meaning beyond the touching sight of a father out for a walk with his child. Here it is a scene with the unlogic of dreams and reality turned on its hinges.

This land is so pervaded by symbols, so defined by them, that even the people who live here have themselves become symbolic. I could not even see a father and his daughter in a park but as a symbol of disruption in my life. He is from America, and this place is now his. I am from this place, and America is now mine. In between his trip and mine, as we changed places, something happened to me. People who live in exile guard their names the way they shield their eyes from the sun. In exile everything is excitable, like storms in wintertime, the only season you know there. Without your name,[40] without those lips from childhood's mirror, you will be forgotten inside the American dream. I'm a first-generation American, still covered with the blood of ancient wounds.
[. . .]

How could a little people like the Palestinians go on like that, expecting to be reborn from the shadows of a place that no longer waits for them? A place where they no longer live but that still lives in them?

I walked around Haifa all day. I had thought so often about doing it that I was convinced the experience was somehow going to enter my consciousness and catch fire.

It did not. I was a stranger in a strange city that under different circumstances I would have found boring, tacky, and uptight. I was angry at myself for having thought that the experience was somehow going to be existentially enriching, emotionally rewarding, and intellectually edifying, but I felt nothing.

[...]

I know, I said to myself, one day soon I will meet one of the children who survived [Sabra and Shatila], and I will tear off my skin with grief and ram my head against his eternity. Above all, I will cut my fingers off, for what is the use of hitting them on the dumb keys of a typewriter, in my comfortable diaspora dream, in order to write a poem, and play with my child on a carpeted floor, and complain to myself that the whole world is taking its revenge on the defenseless children of our exiled nation. It is so helpless a project—so vain and absurd.

They all died, even those who survived, and I died too. For when the fascists came, they came also looking for *me*. When they came to Sabra and Shatila, they didn't come looking for radical Palestinians or conservative Palestinians, Moslem Palestinians or Christian Palestinians, rich Palestinians or poor Palestinians, young Palestinians or old Palestinians. They came looking for *Palestinians*. I am a Palestinian. I was not there only by a trick of fate.

Why was I not there? God, I tell you now, I would have wanted to be there. Hell, why am I addressing God? I should be addressing the devil. God has nothing to do with us. Our pact was signed with the devil, a long time ago. At least the devil knows his job. He delivers. God does not. God has shown us nothing but indifference.

I had no desire to be an activist after that. I did not wish to speak to anyone anymore, to re-create myself in words anymore. How can you speak the unspeakable, imagine the unimaginable?

A group of officials from the PLO, headed by a man with a belly that looked like a drum, arrived in Washington and told the Palestinian community that we should "work on this thing" and "gain publicity" for the cause by capitalizing on the sympathy of the American public. "Don't worry about it," he assured us, "only hundreds died, not thousands. We only say that for public consumption."

Go away from me, you bastards, And if you will not go away
from me, I will go away from you.

I went away from them all. I wanted, literally, to die. Dying, no less than living, is an art. When you are prevented from choosing how to live, you seek the freedom of choosing how to die.

[. . .]

"I'm here," I tell Salem when he answers the phone.

"Thank the Lord for your safe arrival. Palestine shines by your light. The land is richer for your presence. Welcome, brother, welcome," he hollers his flowery Arabic into the Phone. "Thank God, I say, for your safe arrival! Or should I say your safe return?"

I sit and wait in the hotel lobby. The place is almost empty, except for the odd resident journalist, the odd visiting UN official, and the odd tourist. The last type of visitor would have to be odd indeed to be visiting this part of the world at this time. It is December 21, 1990. Kuwait has been occupied by Iraqi forces for almost five months and close to a million allied forces, half of them American, are gathered in the Gulf to enforce a UN Security Council resolution calling on Iraq to pull out by January 15—or else. Talk of imminent war—inevitable war would engulf the entire region, including Israel—is prevalent. One would have to be a truly unusual tourist to choose this part of the world for a vacation, like the black American lady in her midforties, sitting at a table next to me in the lobby, earnestly reading *The Golden Book of Prayer*. From time to time as she reads, she lifts her head and nods contentedly, as if she has just made a spiritual discovery. In the old days before the *Intifada,* thousands of such people came at this time of year to make the pilgrimage to Bethlehem and tour the Christian holy places in Jerusalem. Even during the *Intifada,* over the last two Christmases, many still came. But this year, with war seeming the inevitable conclusion of the Gulf crisis, few have decided to brave it.

Salem finally turns up, accompanied by Leila. Salem and I hug and kiss on both cheeks. That's customary. Leila and I . . . well, we just shake hands. Leila is now a professor of psychology at Beir Zeit University, outside Ramallah. Seven years before, when she was doing her Ph.D. at the State University of New York in Buffalo and I was a writer in residence at the Communications Department, we were lovers. But here you do not hug and kiss a woman, even an old lover. That is not customary. It is even less customary to let on that, God forbid, a woman has had a lover at any time in her life. A woman who does that sort of thing is a tart. And a tart is shot and killed by a male member of her family or, at best, is ostracized. So Leila and I shake hands, and she sits between me and Salem in the lounge, a demure, blushful woman comporting herself with the linguistic propriety and sexual reticence expected of any female Palestinian in social life. Never mind that she is a thirty-six-year-old career woman, a brilliant intellectual, and an economically self-sufficient person. Here she lives with her parents, and if she is late returning home, she may be challenged by them or by any male member of the family, including a *younger* brother, to explain where she has been and with whom. The daring, impetuous, erotic Leila I had known in the United States, the girl of twenty-nine who had flaunted the glory of her youthful sensuality, and her readiness to share it, now sits across from me at the American Colony Hotel trying to communicate her feelings about seeing me again in ways other than words. [. . .]

IN THE STREETS OF BEIRUT

[. . .] One day Jasmine came home and declared that she had been offered a job as a waitress in the coffee shop at the St. George Hotel.[41] The money was good, and there was a chance she could become a waitress in the restaurant where the tips were even better. That's where Salwa, one of Abu Rustum's daughters, worked, Jasmine hastened to add, and she had been assured that the environment was "honorable."

"You are not associating with the daughter of that son of whore, Abu Rustum, I say," he thundered.

"Abu Rustum has nothing to do with this, Dad."

May the lord pour acid on his soul, and on his name and on his honor."

"May it be thus, if you wish, Dad."

"How much money is involved?" he asks.

Jasmine tells him and his face lights up. Perhaps it would save us from having to live in the refugee camp and even help repay his many debts. Perhaps he could discontinue the unbearable practice of going to the depot each month to pick up our rations, for he hated that more than he hated anything else—standing abjectly in line for powdered milk, dates, flour, and canned meat.

Soon after Jasmine became a bread earner, she became a changed woman, throwing her weight around the house, complaining loudly if Mother did not have her dinner ready when she came home or hadn't ironed her blouse before she needed it. If Mousa was listening to a program on the radio that was not to her liking, she would turn the knob without asking his permission. She even took to going out with Abu Rustum's daughter Salwa, with whom she worked at the hotel, and with Samar, Adnan's plump sister, doing what independent bread-earning girls did on their days off: walk up and down the streets of the Basta[42] or the Corniche,[43] where boys their age would follow them, making remarks about how cute they were, while from time to time the girls would throw glances over their shoulders and giggle.

Jasmine even took to coming home after dark following these outings. And when Dad asked her where she had been, she would retort that it was none of his business.

"I buy the bread you eat, Dad," she would proclaim confidently. "no one gives me a hard time around here, do you hear?"

Jasmine had changed, and so had Dad. He had become a decrepit, confused, uncomprehending old man who wanted to die before more disasters overtook his life and destroyed the system of meaning that had governed his life and his people's from time immemorial. He no longer exercised his authority around the house. He surrendered that to Mousa. And Jasmine had jumped from childhood to adulthood, skipping adolescence on the way—an independent woman who was not going to let meaningless customs smother her life at the root. By the sweat of her forehead she earned her bread. And bread is *nimeh,* the most sacred of all God's bounty. She could fill her own cup when she was thirsty, unsay what was said about the Way of His creation, barter tradition for dreams. No one would gag Jasmine anymore.

But our society, our culture, our time was not ready for that kind of independence. There is a line you do not cross. Tradition is tradition. It takes as long to remove as it had taken to create. You challenge tradition, you pay with your life.

One day Jasmine kissed a boy. She was seen by a friend of Mousa, and he reported the sighting to my brother. When Jasmine got home,

Mousa pointed at my sister and howled like an animal: "She soiled our honor!"

He turned to my dad. "She soiled our honor," he screamed triumphantly. But Dad had already abdicated his power to Mousa. Mousa then proceeded to pummel Jasmine until she was semiconscious. Even after she cowered in the corner, he still kicked, slapped, and punched her.

Such is the power of tradition, so pervasive in its grip on our instincts that no one in the house, including my ten-year-old brother, Samir, who was terrified, moved a finger to help her. She had, after all, kissed, actually *kissed,* a boy! No one delighted in seeing a sixteen-year-old girl, one's own sister, one's daughter, get savaged this way, but then she had it coming, didn't she?

Within less than ten minutes, Jasmine's face began to swell like a balloon. Bruises showed all over her body.

What had to be done was done. Nothing unusual here.

Then we sat down to have dinner.[44] Samir refused to eat. Jasmine remained cowering in the corner. During dinner, mother explained that Aunt Hanan, who lived in Damascus, was going to visit soon. Dad grunted his approval. After the plates were cleared, we listened to the radio for an hour and drank tea in small glasses. Then, as if on cue, mother proceeded to take down our mattresses, pillows, and blankets, stacked neatly in a corner and spread them on the floor, by 11:00 P.M. we all went to sleep.

Things were expected to return to normal the following day. For the rest of us they did, but not for Jasmine. Something had snapped loose in her. To be sure, she returned to work and continued to go to her sewing and embroidery class, but her movements were increasingly inert and automatic. Still, the rebel in her had not been entirely crushed, for she now sought an instrument with which to avenge herself, to express her refusal to accept her world's traditions—even at the price of her own ruin.

So one day, less than three months after her beating, she went to bed with a boy from the neighborhood.

When Mousa found out, we all knew what a drastic fate awaited her. Her punishment was going to be a terrible, terrible one indeed. It was just a question of the manner in which she would receive it. My sister had committed an unspeakable act beyond all understanding. Since time immemorial, women guilty of it were returned to their Glorious Maker, for presumably only He knew how to deal with them. Even Jasmine herself seemed to see no injustice in the fate that awaited her. At the time, even I saw nothing despotic or venomous in the verdict passed on my sister. I did not turn away in nauseated disbelief. I did not flinch with horror. I did not try to stop it. Tradition has long since devoured our autonomy. We could no more get outside it than we could jump out of our own skin.

Mousa chose poison. He handed it to Jasmine in a cup.

Jasmine stood by the dining table assuming the bored stance of someone standing in line at a movie theatre, and drank the contents.[45]

Then she lurched forward and staggered around like a bull gored by too many picks and fell dead on the floor.

Dad was the first to react. He knelt over his daughter's body and howled: "I'll join you, I'll join you soon, Jasmine, I'll join you soon, my lovely darling."

Mom started ululating those God-awful Koranic incantations of distress. And Mousa went out on the balcony, took out a gun that he had acquired for the occasion, and began to shoot rounds in the air.[46]

Now the whole neighborhood knows that we have redeemed our honor, just as tradition dictated. And just as tradition dictated, the judge in whose court Mousa was tried gave him three years in jail. "This young man," the judge intoned, "saved his kith and kin from disgrace." Those are the brute workings of our way of life.

I intended to kill Mousa as soon as he was released from jail.

The memory of my sister preyed on my soul long after her death. I remembered when she was eleven, when we were all still in the refugee camp and she worked as a servant for a rich family in Hamra Street,[47] the fashionable street in the Lebanese capital, and how her employer's kids, knowing she was afraid of the dark, used to lock her in a room and turn out the lights as they stood outside doubled up with laughter.

Above all, I remembered when she and I would go up to the roof of our house and watch the Shoof Mountains east of the capital and play games with each other imagining what lay behind them. It was like a secret that we shared, what we imagined. "There is a land beyond the mountains where boys and girls run the government," she would say, and I would counter with: "I know what lies behind the mountains—a big country where people go where they please and they have no parents, no jobs and no rules." Once she told me: "When I grow up, I want to go there and find out what lies behind the mountains." Even into our teens we continued to play our mountain game. When Jasmine was angry at the world, she would say to me, in shared secrecy, "I want to go live behind the mountains," or, "Let's you and me run off and live behind the mountains."

Now I can no longer look at the mountains without thinking of Jasmine. I cannot understand Mom's babble about how God surely has already forgiven Jasmine, because I cannot understand who is going to forgive God. Sometimes I would be at the Corniche, sitting on a rock, watching the sea, where I would go to take my failure to understand, my call for an explanation, and the sea would thunder back at me with mute indifference.

Even after I destroyed Mousa's coop on the roof while he was in prison, and released his miserable pigeons to find their own freedom, they kept coming back to perch forlornly on the ledge, as if they too were captive to the workings of our way of life.[48] They kept coming back week after week, looking for their old home. And then one day they stopped coming. Maybe they found a different home behind the mountains.

Where is Jasmine?

I will live forever tangled in my sister's memory. I will forever remember that day at her burial, with the earth slit open like a kiss, poised for the timeless taste of her dream.

I curse God and His world. I want to set fire to His universe. It is only my word, not his, that can feed life into a stone.[49]

Soon after Jasmine's death, I felt a new consciousness grow in my mind. I wanted to distance myself from the moronic serenity that characterized our culture. I would swagger around the Basta with Adnan and his friends at all hours. I carried a switchblade. I took up the local argot. I affected, with impressive ease, the gestural repertoire that defined the young neighborhood toughs. I was making a lot of money working for Adnan, and I was feeling independent. In short, I was being, for the first time in my life, the only determining force of my destiny.

[. . .]

[. . .]

"We [the Palestinians] made the same mistakes in Jordan in 1970 where we were just as haughty, just as arrogant, and just as stupid as in Lebanon. You will remember that by 1970, directly after the battle of Karameh two years before,[50] a pivotal event that had given us the take-off, and earned us the popularity, for our movement, we had become literally a state within a state. But instead of using that power to gain the support of the Jordanian masses, we did everything in our power to alienate them against us. Again the checkpoints! Foolish armed men at checkpoints stopping cars and harassing pedestrians. They would stop a Jordanian soldier, ask for his ID, intimidate him, and on some occasions take his weapon away from him. You don't take a soldier's weapon from him, especially a Bedouin soldier. A soldier would rather you took his pants off than take his weapon. The Popular Democratic Front for the Liberation of Palestine, or so they called themselves as a Marxist group—Marxist my foot, they didn't know anything about Marxism—would hoist red flags over the minarets of mosques as a way of advertising their intention to turn Jordan into a communist state. These idiots were so ignorant of the ways of their own people that they had no inkling of the profound role Islam plays in Arab culture. They didn't know that that was one sure way to turn the people against them. Once they actually demanded that the Amman government declare Lenin's birthday a national holiday!

"So in Jordan the people finally, predictably, inevitably, turned against us. Our *own* people. Keep in mind that out of every five Jordanians, three are Palestinian. And our political leaders from the movement, ignorant as ever of the hostility they were generating by the irresponsible behavior of their cadres, would be up there giving speeches in Formal Arabic about liberation and struggle and sacrifice and martyrdom and the rest of it—speeches that would go on for two, three, or four

hours. I remember on my occasional visits to Amman in those days—I
was barely twenty then—I would attend these gatherings and listen to
these damn speakers, and in the end I would wrack my brains trying—
honestly trying—to fathom what had been said. They said nothing. Absolutely nothing. It was all like poetry, bad poetry to be sure, but like
poetry.[51] Meant to entertain. They would use these damn long words,
and meaningless phrases, about the heroism of our fighters, the honor
of our Arab nation, the imminent liberation of Palestine. I can't imitate the comical way of these rhetorical speakers, but you know what I
mean. They would shout and scream their rhetoric at the audience and
then bring their voices to a hush when they talked about the memory
of this martyr or that. And the people, brother, the people loved it all.
They loved the theatrics. The acting. They loved the action on the stage.
For that's all it was. The people just sat there and applauded madly, having a great time. All they were missing were their water pipes. [. . .] For
hours on end, speaker after speaker would hurl words at you. Words
flew all around you, wastefully, senselessly. How could our language,
any language, sound so ugly and meaningless and sterile? I can't believe
that we speak the same language that the Koran is written in, the same
language that Ben Khaldun wrote *Makadamat* in." Salem is referring to
an elegantly written seminal work on the philosophy of history by Ben
Khaldun, a classical Arab scholar, whose contribution continues to be
recognized by modern historians.

Salem's capacity to hold his liquor amazes me. The man has demolished three-quarters of his fifth of scotch, and he's still coherent.

"We screwed up in Jordan," Salem continues. "We made so many
mistakes there. Basic, elementary mistakes that we insisted on repeating in Lebanon. The same mistakes, the chaos. The lack of discipline.
The irresponsible disregard for mass sentiment. The blind obedience to
the word of your *massoul* [political commissar] and that of the *tanzeem*
[political factions]. The authority we follow, the language we speak, the
backwardness we are mired in and can't get out of are all issues that
are important to an understanding of why we have repeatedly failed
to score one single political victory during the last eighty years of our
struggle for independence. We Palestinians like to think of ourselves as
more progressive, informed, educated, heroic than other Arabs. That's

a joke. We are straitjacketed by obedience to authority like other Arabs. We speak our language as wastefully as other Arabs. We are held back by our backwardness—a backwardness whose existence we refuse to admit—like other Arabs. When we burst on the scene in 1968, after the battle of Karameh, the Arab world saw us as its revolutionary vanguard, but we turned out to be its jerks. And it took the Palestinians, our generation of Palestinians, a quarter of a century to acquaint the rest of the world with our identity, and through that mutual acquaintance the world discovered that we are not worth knowing." [. . .]

What is it about Palestinian history that has made failure to meet challenge preordained in it? Why has failure constantly dogged us? What's wrong with us?

Palestinians, like other Arabs, suffer from a multiple personality disorder. People who live in the Arab world have not yet resolved whether to call themselves Moslem, a name that their history gave them; or Arab, a name that their secular ideologies of the *nahda* movement—the nineteenth-century awakening—chose for them after the First World War; or names like *Lebanese, Palestinian, Jordanian, Kuwaiti,* and the like—the national names that colonial overlords had thrust upon them. To this day, the overwhelming majority remain locked in combat with themselves—and in places with each other—over what their name should be.

It all started with the *nahda*.[52] The figures who dominated that era were so gifted with self-deception that it was then believed that to break with the past, and thus effect a leap into modernity, the Arabs simply had to take Europe, and secular nationalism, as a model. The problem with the leaders of the *nahda,* who came from the three centers of activism in the Arab world at the time—Cairo, Damascus, and Beirut (Palestine has always been a marginal province in modern Arab history)[53]—was that they were a mimetic Westernized elite who lacked intellectual dash and operated outside the orbit of mass sentiment. They failed to grasp that the European ideas that they were so voraciously imbibing and transplanting to the Arab world—in politics and literature, in science and technology, in law and education—were rooted in the material conditions of European history. The European leap from medieval backwardness to the modernity of the Renaissance had occurred in response to decisive social changes triggered by internal and spontaneous forces. Aped by this Westernized Arab elite, these became tawdry ideas that *impeded* the Arabs' drift toward genuine social reform.

[...]

But the Arab is not in fact a citizen in his own country. He is an object that lives within a regimented social universe where the word of the authority figure has acquired attributes beyond those even of the Word of God. The individual's process of socialization reinforces this system of terror, for the various subsystems of society—the family, the school, the neighborhood, the ethnic milieu, the worship center, and the cultural environment—are microcosms of the vertical relationship that exists between the state and the individual.

[...]

Fear of retribution by the state and by the social milieu contributes to instilling in the individual, even encoding in his consciousness, the need to accept orthodoxy, dependency, and submission. This in turn triggers in him a permanent sense of fear—fear of originality, innovation, and spontaneity, fear of life itself. The Arab thus actively participates in perpetuating a broken-down society by accepting its stringent rules of self-discipline and its definition of him as a bane of creativity, not its source. Traditional social values, in effect, end up creating an individual who fulfills the basic needs of the power structure: absolute obedience to state authority, the sole arbiter of his allegiances, loyalties, and sentiments. A mass of people are socialized not only to believe in the supremacy of established power but to believe that they can be governed by a handful of rulers.

[...]

A whole people have, in effect, quietly acquiesced in the forfeiture of their powers of self-determination. All the while that Arabs called themselves Arabs, their identity as Moslems was surreptitiously outflanking them, and their national names—Lebanese, Palestinians, Jordanians, Kuwaitis, and so on—were bedeviling them. They belonged to all three names—Arab, Moslem, the national name. They belonged to one. They belonged to none.

The Arab peoples' linguistic currency today also expresses the temper of their age, for they communicate in three different tongues, three tongues that, though derived from the same source, are as different as Chaucer's, Churchill's, and African-American English are from one another. These are Classical Arabic, the language that Islam bequeathed; Formal Arabic, the one invented by the age of neobackwardness;[54] and Oral Arabic, the language of the masses, whose vocabulary, chaotic grammar, structure, and tonality reflect the mutilated world Arabs inhabit.[55]

Classical Arabic is a great language that drew on and was energized by the intellectual resources of a commonwealth of nations noted not only for the intellectual coherence of its Islamic heritage but also for the innovative weld of sensibility that characterized its Abbaside, Ommayad, and Spanish eras. Classical Arabic, at the height of its inventiveness between the ninth and twelfth centuries, was a living, breathing language that reflected, and helped create, the emotional intensities of the age. To the modern Arab, however, especially the Oral Arab, Classical Arabic is as mute, as incomprehensible, as the hieroglyphics in an Egyptian tomb. That is why modern Arabs always listen to, rather than read, their Koran: they have a limited perception of its symbolism and are totally disconnected from the verbal consciousness of its text. Differences in idiom, in resources of social feeling, between the world of classical Arabs and the mutilated world of modern Arabs render impossible any communication between the two.

Now enter Formal Arabic, whose emergence and development have taken place, significantly enough, roughly over the past 150 years, coinciding with the *nahda*, Westernization, "independence," and neobackwardness. The exclusive lingo of the ruling elite, the Westernized intelligentsia, representatives of state power, the bureaucrats, the *mokhabarat* sadists, and the effete literati, Formal Arabic (sometimes known as Media Arabic) is a kind of secondhand derivative of Classical Arabic, replete with pretensions and artifices imported from the West.

Unlike Classical Arabic, a tongue that derived from specific historical springs and unlike Oral Arabic, an adventurous creature, Formal Arabic is a bastard, the offspring of the times of neobackwardness. Its ambiguous jargon, stock similes, mechanical habits of expression, and complex rhetoric—not to mention the Western intrusions—lend it no sense of spontaneity or style. It lacks directness and intensity of feeling.

Like the ruling class that uses it, the language blunts and stultifies. It communicates but creates no communion. Formal Arabic neither lives nor is lived; rather, it is a lingo reflecting the deadness of spirit of a society and a class that possess formality but no form, rhetoric but no style, dissimulation but no grace.

It was in Formal Arabic, for example, that Nasser and Voice of the Arabs Radio from Cairo spoke to the Arab masses in 1967 on the eve of the June War, as did Saddam and the Voice of the Mother of All Battles Radio in 1991 on the eve of the Gulf War. If these broadcasts made absolutely no sense, that is because Formal Arabic has totally absorbed, and been absorbed by, the hysterics and buffoonery that characterize the Arab world today. It has the function of perpetuating the backwardness of Arab society, enforcing the brutalities of the regimes, and justifying the debauchery, waste, corruption, and decadence of its ruling elite. Used generation after generation by the ruling elite to intimidate, deceive, and control, its syntax has long since come to interact with and support the various instruments of domination in society.

The controlled puritanism of Formal Arabic, whose goal is standardized mediocrity and boorish conformity, has imposed substantial limits on the Arab libido.

It is not surprising, then, that Formal Arabs, whose language possesses no apparatus for swearing, obscenity, sexuality, or the merely sensual, often resort to the novel vocabulary of Oral Arabic. The balance in Formal Arabic is therefore constantly being shaken by inventive compositions imported from Oral Arabic that mock conventional constraints.

The relationship between language and sexuality in Arab society is a mirror of that between authority and freedom. Thus, the right to be loud, enjoyed by men, is denied to women when they are in the presence of men. Obscenity is profuse and condoned between men; but the sexual act itself, even in its privacy, is mute. Overt sexual expression in the conjugal bed is proscribed for the same reason that free discourse is proscribed between the rulers and the ruled in Arab culture. And just as the father, the teacher, the policeman, and the clergyman are socialized to represent state power in the home, the school, the street, and the mosque, so is the male its representative in bed. Thus, the repression of sexual fulfillment in Arab society is as much physiological as sociolinguistic.

It can be argued that individual freedom is either enriched or diminished by the quality of linguistic and sexual interplay. Take the youth revolt of the late 1960s in the United States. Recall how its primary aims were sexual and linguistic. The young assaulted social taboos by creating their own argot that was all but incomprehensible to the rest of society, and they created what came to be known as the sexual revolution. They were there "to do their thing" and "tell it like it is." Although the Sixties movement died, its legacies are still evident in American culture, and its impact on language and sexual mores is equally clear.

In the Arab world today, public discourse remains the domain of Formal Arabic. Embodied in the cant of this dead language, much of social and cultural reality exists as a set of obscure, irrational notions. There is an established set of rules beyond which nothing is admissible. How could a society produce a literature when it does not allow anything adversarial, critical, or innovative to be said? In other words, how could the language of the police bully, the government bureaucrat, and the mimetic intellectual, a language that demeans ideas, debases labor, and cheapens the value of human existence, produce a body of elevated thought and expression? Much of what passes for Arabic "literature" today should be remaindered as quickly as it is published.

The repressive constraints that Formal Arabic places on the soul of Arab culture are reflected in the flight of high school and university students to foreign languages, mostly English and French, as a mode of intellectual release. These other languages have become a means for young Arabs to seek a new window on life and draw on energies of spirit that may one day afford an escape from their social and cultural prison. Only when that transformation has taken place will young Arabs begin to speak their own language with force and elegance and find that their culture will speak back in kind.

Only in Oral Arabic do ordinary Arabs feel at home. They use it to spin tales about their heritage, to compose the lyrics of their own songs, to celebrate the wonders of the land, to speak of the mysteries of God's creation, to remember their fallen patriots, to narrate the exploits of their ancestors, and to speak of their historic meaning. It is zestful and lively but in the end it is as helpless and mutilated as the people who speak it. It expresses the terrors of the individual and his inward flight from the make-believe world he inhabits.

EPILOGUE: THE LAND BEHIND THE MOUNTAINS

When I left Palestine on January 14, a day before the Gulf War started, I believed that peace between Israelis and Palestinians would remain an elusive dream. Like most other observers, I was unaware of the shifts of political sensibility, already dimly at work, that would soon declare themselves with sudden force. The notion that representatives of the Israeli government and the PLO would, within less than three years, recognize each other and sign a peace agreement on the White House lawn did not seem to belong to our time. Even more remote was the possibility that, at long last, the Palestinians would soon be statehood-bound, or at least become a people *enracinés* in one form or another.

Palestinians and Israelis had demonized, fought, and killed each other for eighty years. Being an outright pessimist, I was convinced that they were destined to chew their nationalist slogans to the marrow and live out their flat and shoddy political lives in constant conflict for eighty more.

No one, at any rate, was much concerned then with the fate of the Holy Land and its two peoples.

In the middle of January 1991, the world's attention was focused on the Gulf War and Iraq, getting decidedly trounced. The allies were able, in a comparatively short time and with little cost to themselves, to crush Saddam's forces, expel his army from Kuwait, effectively disarm him, divide his country into three parts—two of which would remain outside his control—and bring him to total submission.

The mother of all battles was over for the Iraqi dictator, but not for his suffering people who would shoulder its disruptive and painful consequences for years to come.

[. . .]

Saddam was not a rhetorical bully like Adolf Hitler—Saddam could not even speak well publicly—but he was, like the other "brother strugglers," a polluter of language who delighted in creating a make-believe world for his people to inhabit. It is doubtful that after their

debasement at his hands words like *mother, celebrate,* and *heroism* would
ever recover a sane meaning in the Arabic language.

[...]

The Gulf War, like no other event in modern Arab history, shook
long-held assumptions about pan-Arab solidarity—wobbly notions to
begin with. In its wake, the Arab world stood divided and helpless.

In the Arabian Peninsula, the oil states were no longer rich. Their
stability had been undermined by unrestrained spending, huge military
purchases, bizarre banking practices, and enormous expenditures on
the war itself. Saudi Arabia, the richest among them, which had had
$121 billion in financial reserves a decade before, was now in deficit. In
the Fertile Crescent, the confrontation states bordering Israel, hit equally
hard by their loss of military, economic, and political support from a
collapsed Soviet Union, were in no position to confront anyone. The
Maghreb countries in North Africa were experiencing unprecedented
turmoil resulting from Islamic fundamentalism and economic disloca-
tion. Egypt, which had ceased to be a player in inter-Arab politics after
the signing of the Camp David Accords in 1979, was helpless in the face
of its own Islamic terrorists. And the PLO, ostracized by the Gulf Arabs
and denied financial aid, was broke and teetered on collapse.

The stillness that followed the Gulf War spoke directly to the
ruin of the Arab spirit and destroyed the Arab people's hold on long-
cherished ideals about both individual and national identity.

The Arabs, in effect, were being summoned to join the new world
order and to rethink their assumptions about confrontation with Israel.

Israelis too had no workable alternatives either. They also had
to rethink their assumptions about the enemy and try to reach an ac-
commodation. Otherwise, they were left with the nightmare choice of
dominating a people who would only be ruled by repression, followed
by revolt, followed by more repression and again by revolt. This was
a situation that, especially since the start of the *Intifada,* had taken its
psychological toll on Israelis.

[...]

A quarter-century after Golda Meir denied that a Palestinian people existed, while the Palestinian National Charter denied Israelis their
right to statehood, both peoples realized the biblical truth that you have

to know thine enemy to deal with him. How your enemy defines himself is important; how you define him is not.

It would be a long time before this agreement yielded its full political and economic fruits. But clearly, this was a reconciliation more than an agreement, the feast that comes after a long fast.

We remain too close to the fact to predict whether the Palestinians, as they begin to rule themselves, will go from "Gaza and Jericho first" to full-blown independence, or whether they will fail, as so often in the past, to embrace the turning points in their history.

Will the PLO, given its record of corruption, ineptitude, and cynicism, be equal to the challenge? Will it yield to the forces of modernity growing in Palestinian society, to the representatives of the Children's Crusade whose uprising was largely responsible for the groundswell that led to the ceremony on the White House lawn? If this Palestinian entity is to be democratic, as I understand young Palestinians, like Zakharieh and Mohammed (the boys from the underground) would want, can it deny Islamic activists self-expression and assembly and, potentially, political power? And what of other dissenters (not all of them rejectionists or fundamentalists) who will form an adversarial current in society? Will the PLO send its police after them, as any other Arab regime would do, to silence their voices and break their heads? Will we in other words, see yet another dreary Arab state where the night knock on the door, and dragging off dissenters to the gallows, would be all too common?

To go from Gaza, a grim, turbulent strip of land inhabited by 800,000 souls, and from Jericho, a mere dot on the map, a dusty outpost by the Dead Sea whose sedentary population was the last to join the *Intifada*, to a promised land of independence and stability is a trip that shakes our grasp of the "reality principle."

The whole experiment may go haywire. After all, it is the PLO that will be custodian and overseer of the Palestinian future in the West Bank and Gaza. And lest we forget, the Palestinians are a little people, unprepared for the challenges of modernity, a community that still moves around the treadmill of immemorial traditions and beliefs, which is one reason that no other people in the world has repeated its history as Palestinians have.

Yet we should not be given warrant to see nothing but a bleak future for Palestine. Young Palestinians in the West Bank and Gaza, who comprise the overwhelming majority, possess large reserves of political consciousness and new social habits honed by years in the underground. These will finally take root. I am convinced that in a future Palestine we will hear the *Intifada*'s shaping echo, not the strident voice of a tyrant "brother struggler."

Meanwhile, what is to become of the four million Palestinian exiles descended from the refugee exodus of 1948? The fact that they were not mentioned in the peace agreement, the shock of realizing that they will never go home, will profoundly alter the way they see themselves and the world around them.

While Palestinians in the West Bank and Gaza will be engaged in national building, Palestinians in the diaspora will lose much of their accustomed bearing. For years they will feel a loss too grievous to contemplate—and not only because, for the first time, they will no longer share a vision of the future with Palestinians who live on the Inside.

For almost half a century, the concept of the *awda,* the return to home and homeland, formed the pivot of an exile's inward life. The idea shaped the sensibility of Palestinians in whatever host state they happened to live. As the possibility of returning to Palestine faded over the years, the image of the *awda* still glowed vivid and real in their lives. If pressed, no sane exile would say that his expectation of returning to Haifa, Jaffa, or Lod was realistic. But Palestinians in the diaspora needed to believe that one day they would return. Not to believe would have torn up the roots of their identity. Like the square root of minus one, the *awda* was a big lie, an imaginary notion, a state of fancy. But just as this imaginary value is integral to the order of mathematics, so was belief in the *awda* necessary to the lives of Palestinians in exile.

Yet it is not inconceivable that diaspora Palestinians will learn to adjust, especially if the West Bank and Gaza are transformed from a mere homeground into an independent homeland. For then they will know that there is a tiny strip of land, a little corner of the earth tucked between the Mediterranean and the River Jordan, where they can go when the Kuwaitis kick them out, when the frenzied packs come to their refugee camps, when the bullies in their host states begin to snarl at their heels.

We in the diaspora will learn to live with the new realities. We will even learn to live with our memories—memories of a cloudless day on Mount Karmel and of God's rage on the coastal road to Lebanon; memories of exile and of mass graves at Sabra and Shatila. In our minds, these images are not frozen like statues. Every generation judges the past anew. It was the world of our being that created the world of our memories. And once that world is changed, so will our selective use of memory.

[...]

Now two million Palestinians in the West Bank and Gaza—perhaps more as the figure swells with the influx of exiles—will build their own homeland on their own bit of earth. Many more of us will stay in our adopted ones.

To me, the idea of a nation remains absurdly wrong. I find the idea of unrestrained, militant nationalism to be obscene. In the name of territorial integrity and ethnic purity, men have slaughtered one another for centuries.

Jewish nationalists who believe that the Jewish nation's boundaries include the territories stretching from the Mediterranean to the River Jordan and beyond, have their counterparts among the Palestinians. I met one of them in Washington soon after the White House ceremony. He was introduced to me as a former PLO fighter on his way to Jordan to be trained as a police officer. From there he would be Jericho bound. A man in his fifties, who wore his hair slicked back on both sides and curled on top like Cleopatra's diadem, he assured me that "in less than thirty years from now the whole of Palestine will be liberated and all the Jews will be gone from our country."

I have always sought to disassociate myself from that kind of venom. And that is why, though I am happy that Palestinians in the West Bank and Gaza will soon be free to determine their own destiny, I will not pick up and go to live in a Palestinian homeland.

Forty-five years of exile are homeland enough. Anywhere where one is free to watch one's favorite movies, reread one's favorite classics, listen to one's favorite music, support one's favorite unpopular causes, and, above all, do one's work without fear of retribution, is homeland enough.

I need not live in Nablus or Jericho or Gaza. I could live anywhere I am with my people—those from any part of the world with whom I share a commonality of values and a certain way of life. Paris, Sydney, or New York will do—especially New York, because New Yorkers are like Palestinians in many ways. They too are born of tragedy. Their ancestors landed at Ellis Island after escaping a czar who claimed to love them, a "brother struggler" who had anointed himself head of the national family, a tyrant who did not like their ethnic roots, a colonial oppressor who robbed them and couldn't care less about their famine. And there are other New Yorkers whose ancestors didn't land on Plymouth Rock; instead—as Malcolm X put it—Plymouth Rock landed on them. Like Palestinians, New Yorkers are a little mad, a little lonely, a little disgruntled. They live with no regard for the concerns of the rest of the planet and stare with murder in their eye if you dare to suggest that there is any place better than where they come from.

And I need not die in Haifa, Safad, or Jaffa. Washington will do. I have lived there longer than in any other part of the world. Nor, when I'm dust and forgotten, should it be of any consequence to anyone where my remains are buried.

Still, even to a hardened exile like myself, the emergence of a Palestinian state touches some covert longings in my soul. It will in any case compel me to rename myself. Palestinians in the homeground will laugh at those who continue to ascribe to their name attributes that predate the new Palestine. Believe us, they will say, we built a state because of our need for a safe haven, not for love of nationalism. Come over here and live with us. We will turn our soul's concern in your direction. May the Lord pour acid on your exile and destroy all the houses you've built in it. Come!

This idea of a [Palestinian] state is too fantastic. *A Palestinian state!* Surely this is the stuff of which dreams are made.

I can see myself, ten years from now, succumbing to the fantasy. In this dream, I fly to Palestine. My plane lands at Jericho airport. I am traveling light—some clothes, my notebooks, and a toothbrush. There is no need to bring anything else. This is a modern country, and I can buy everything I need here. I walk to Immigration and stand in line. Outside, the sun, as usual, shines brightly. Awaiting me is a life among the olive trees in a town by the River Jordan. The official greets me effusively and asks how I feel. I tell him I feel great, and it is the truth. He stamps my passport and says, "Welcome to Palestine." As I walk out of the airport, I repeat the name to myself. I want to test the sound of it, to make sure it is real. I repeat it, once, twice, thrice, then utter it as if in babble, like an infant who has not yet mastered words. I hop in a cab and am driven along a paved road hugging the river. The cabbie tells me the road was completed just four years before, after the PLO lost the vote in a democratically contested election, and the new president, whom everyone calls Brother Zakharieh, took on the task of eliminating corruption and building the economy.

The taxi driver turns on his car radio, and I hear Palestinian folk music, the lyrics simple and benign and not about struggle or death or sacrifice or steadfastness in the face of foreign oppressors. I reach out as if to touch the sounds, to grab them from the air, and rest them on my chest.

I ask the driver how far it is to my destination and he points ahead of him. Right there, brother, he tells me, just behind those mountains, in the distance.[56]

Egypt

Through the past century of its history, Egypt has vacillated between Arabism, Egyptian Pharaonism, and Islam, each tendency with an emphasis all its own and in different time periods. In comparison to the Fertile Crescent, Egypt's population is relatively homogenous, and in that respect can be said to be quite unique. Egypt is therefore more of a nation-state, or territorial state in the European sense, than say Iraq, Syria, or Lebanon. The people of the Nile are separated from their neighbors by a desert, and upward of five thousand years of uniquely Egyptian history and civilization *can* be associated with the present-day Egyptians. Being a flatland controlled by a traditionally strong central government, and being a hydraulic society (completely reliant on the Nile, its sole water source, its major artery of movement, and its main bridge between the north and the south of the country), Egypt was never attractive to persecuted minorities and never became a natural destination or refuge for minorities; at least not to the same extent that, say, the Lebanese or Syrian mountains were sanctuaries for persecuted minorities. In Egypt there are no people seeking shelter from powerful central governments—unlike minority peoples in the Levant proper. In fact, the Egyptians themselves have always *depended* on powerful central governments.

Landscape and topography in the Middle East (and the Levant region in particular) are a major component of the concept of minority and majority. That is why populations in places like Lebanon, Syria, and the Judaean hills between Israel, Jordan, and the Palestinian Territories are more complex ethnically, more richly textured and layered in terms of identity and self-perception, than is the population of Egypt. In that sense, the small Coptic Christian minority in Egypt (circa fifteen million by some estimates) can be said to be culturally, ethnically, and socially similar to the Muslim Egyptians—though they may more readily parade a historical connection to Pharaonic Egypt of antiquity. Still, Egypt is distinct, not only geographically speaking, but also in terms of its ethnic makeup and historic evolution; foreigners seldom ruled Egypt directly, and a local dynasty dominated during Ottoman times, so that the country would enjoy a modicum of autonomy unmatched elsewhere in the Ottoman dominions, and would develop the trappings of a state ruled from Cairo, *not* Istanbul.

From the beginning of the nineteenth century, one can witness the emergence of Egyptian identity with separate government and a well-delineated territory; this was the precursor of the Egyptian nationalist movement of the early twentieth century. Pharaonic remains and antiquities, readily accessible and visible to all Egyptians, acted as a visual foundation for a modern Egyptian identity, which in turn gave rise to Egyptian nationalism and eventually spawned a separate Egyptian state with a particular and unique Egyptian esprit de corps and mentality.

The progenitors of this Egyptianness or Egyptianism (also known as Pharaonism) were Westernized intellectuals par excellence; they advanced forms of identity (Pharaonism) that were utterly secular, and offered a clear departure from Islam and from Islam's and the Arab world's traditional forms of corporate identity. Egyptianists argued that Egypt was part of a wider Mediterranean cultural-civilizational ethnic pool; that Egyptians were part of the West, *not* the Arab region; and indeed, that they were progenitors of the West, Western civilization, and Western values. Arabness and Islam, they acknowledged, were a given in Egyptian identity, but they were not the major—nor even an important—component of it. Pharaonism, which was the main intellectual current advancing these notions, emerged around the same time as Phoenicianism and Syrianism—both emphasizing a non-Arab Mediterranean heritage, and both widespread and popular mainly among

Christian communities in Lebanon and Syria. What is intriguing about Pharaonism, however, was that it was a movement that was formulated, spearheaded, and espoused in the main *by* Muslim Egyptians, even as it appealed overwhelmingly to Coptic-Christian Egyptians.

Taha Husayn (1889–1973), the doyen of modern Arabic literature, and Ali Salem (1936–2015), a leading Arabic-language playwright, are considered two of the main avatars of Pharaonism; the former dominating the early decades of the twentieth century, the latter commanding influence in the early twenty-first. When he published *The Future of Culture in Egypt* in 1938 (explored in this chapter), Taha Husayn intended it as an outline for an Egyptian educational reform program, but also as a manifesto of his Pharaonic ideals. In this work, Husayn made the case for an *Egyptian* Egypt and an Egyptian identity separate and distinct from the worlds of Islam and Arab nationalism. Likewise, Ali Salem's work claimed Egypt to be a Mediterranean, not an Arab, place and space of world history. Salem's 2004 satire, *The Odd Man and the Sea,* presents a spacious notion of the Mediterranean as a sea of culture—fluid, inclusive, pantheist by its very nature, and of which Egypt is a vital current.

Over half a century before Salem, Lebanese thinker Michel Chiha, a contemporary of Husayn, summed up Mediterraneanism in words similar to Salem's own, saying that it is an identity construct made up of multiple identities, where fifteen centuries of Arab domination were scarcely valid justification for one to become "oblivious or disrespectful to the fifty centuries" that preceded the Arabs. "Even if relying purely on conjecture," argued Chiha, "the blood, the civilization, and the language of today's Lebanese cannot possibly be anything if not the legacy and synthesis of fifty centuries of progenitors and ancestors."[1]

Even Syrianism—as mentioned earlier, a non-Arab Syrian nationalism—advocated on behalf of a similar conception of the *Homo syriacus,* doing away with the "myth" that deemed the Syrians an Arab people whose destiny was somehow to be wedded to that of the Arabs. Likewise, as we have seen, intellectuals in Lebanon of the early 1920s, who referred to themselves as Young Phoenicians, promulgated similar notions that echoed among Egyptian contemporaries. One of the Young

Phoenicians' chief ideologues (the youngest poet in the group), Charles
Corm, maintained as early as 1930, and in the same vein as exponents of
a distinct Syrian and Egyptian identity: "From the remotest antiquity,
when they were still known as Canaanites, and later as Phoenicians, the
Lebanese people have created, preserved, defended, affirmed, and advanced an expansive and liberal civilization with universal impulses and
predilections so accessible to other peoples, to the point that some of
those, even the loftiest and brightest among them, had come to assimilate these attributes of Lebanese civilization as if they were their own,
adopting and identifying them with their own national genius."[2]

In 1937, another Lebanese member of the Young Phoenicians
group, Saïd Akl, writing mainly in Arabic this time, would declare that:

> Out of a vital, enlightened, and generous heritage, we have
> raised in these parts of the world, on these doorsteps of Asia,
> which penetrate deeply into the heritage of Europe, a father-
> land for the Truth. And we, its sons, have declared to the
> West, that admixture of light and war, that we possess a mis-
> sion to it, a mission to calm some of its recklessness and folly,
> to enrich its activity, and to set its eyes beyond immediate
> gain. Six thousand years of patience, thought, contempt for
> the material, self-denial, aspiration and careful examination
> of each point before accepting the whole, have led us to be-
> come custodians of this mission, this unique mission which
> entrusts us to Lebanonize the world.[3]

The Salem and Husayn selections of this chapter reveal precisely this
kind of Levant; the "doorsteps of Asia" as it were, wading deeply into,
and indeed molding, the heritage of Europe.

∾

ALI SALEM (1936–2015)

Before earning notoriety in the early first decade of the twenty-first century for his curiosity about Israel, and before being removed from the

Egyptian Writers' Guild on account of his repeated visits to Israel and
his collaboration with Israeli academics and literati, Ali Salem had been
one of Egypt's most prominent playwrights.

The author of dozens of books and plays, among them such Egyptian classics as *The Man Who Fooled the Angels, The Comedy of Oedipus,*
and *The Phantom of Heliopolis,* Salem was a mentee of Egypt's Nobel
laureate Naguib Mahfouz (1911–2006), and a committed secularist, reformer, and critic of the politics of hate, vilification, and dismissal of
"the other"—biases, as we saw earlier, that had been hallmarks of the
nationalisms and patriotisms of his generation, most prominently perhaps in an Arab nationalist context.

As an advocate of diversity and multiple identities, in tune with
Egypt's ancient Pharaonic past, Ali Salem's work offered a pungent indictment of insularity and the jingoist instincts of possessive nationalism. Instead—as the *Odd Man and the Sea* sampling of this chapter
will demonstrate—Salem provides for an ecumenical Egyptian Mediterraneanism as an alternative, celebrating fluidity, dynamism, and
openness. The *Odd Man and the Sea* satire describes an interrupted day-
dream sequence during which, depicting himself as a lover and disciple
of the Mediterranean, Salem's narrator spends long hours filling his eyes
and sating his hunger with refreshing vistas issuing from the Mediterranean Sea. But one day, his harmless reveries are intruded upon by
an imperious protagonist demanding he forget the Mediterranean and
embrace desert sands and the Red Sea. What eventually ensues is a duel
between an anthropomorphic Arab nationalism demanding "oneness"
and intent on curbing Egyptian diversity and individualism, on the one
hand; and on the other hand, a humanistic, humane Mediterraneanism
smitten by the *longue durée* of Egypt's millennial history and drawn to
a complex, capacious understanding of identity. In short, not unlike his
Levantine contemporaries who advocated for Mediterranean fluidity,
Salem rejected identity constructs predicated on a singular homogenous
exclusivist conception of the self. To be sure, he did not seem loath to
incorporating "Arabness" as a component of Egyptian identity. Yet he
rejected the notion of "Arabness" as a dominant, domineering complex.
The Odd Man and the Sea, in that sense, is an eloquent incarnation of

Salem's—and before him Taha Husayn's—benevolent, humanistic, patently Levantine vision of "other" and "self."

THE ODD MAN AND THE SEA: AN EGYPTIAN SATIRE (2004)[4]

I'm at a popular café in our street, the Nile Valley Street, which is a branch of the broad Arab League Avenue. I usually sit in this café sipping my coffee and playing the only game that suits me: the game of thinking.

One night, the people around me were immersed in playing dominos, cards and backgammon while I was flying far away on a board of my thoughts. I was thinking that I love the sea, the Mediterranean, in Arabic the "white sea." It was close to me when I was a child in my hometown of Damietta. And I was close to it—only some kilometers away. I used to go to its shore with my friends on bicycle. Several times, we went there on foot. You may consider me one of its followers or disciples, and definitely I'm one of its residents. I still remember that I used to stare at its surface looking for the far horizon, as if I wanted to see my neighbors there, in Italy, Greece, Spain and France. They are Europe and I'm Africa. We are neighbors, separated by two continents, unified by one sea.[5]

While I was flying above the clouds, he appeared in front of me. He was almost my age, but quite different. His face reflected deep feelings of piety and certainty, while my own betrayed puzzlement and fear of the unknown.[6]

He said:

"All the people around are engrossed in doing something useful, why do you sit around doing nothing?"

"I'm thinking, sir."

"Of what?"

"Of the sea, of the Mediterranean."

"Why don't you think of the Red Sea?"

"I don't know it. The few times I went there, I didn't feel any affection toward it. It's beautiful, however, yet something in it makes me feel desolate."

"But you feel affection for the Mediterranean?" he asked.

"Yes, it's one of the human rights to love the sea."

A cruel look crept upon his face, I felt restless. Once again he started asking questions:

"Do you feel that you belong to the Mediterranean?"

"Egypt itself is of the Mediterranean," I responded. "One day, thousands of years ago, this sea was just a lake, crossed by ships loaded by thoughts and art toward Greece, carrying the product of minds and souls, returning from there, loaded with other products of minds and souls."

"You didn't mention that you are an Arab," he pointed out.

"The Arabs are my fathers, but the Egyptians are my forefathers; do you advise me to inherit from my fathers and ignore the treasures left to me by my forefathers?" I asked him.

"I don't advise you, I order you."

"Who are you sir, to order me?"

"I'm the *mohtasib* (inspector) of the Nile Valley Street."

"Show me your papers."

"They are standing in front of you now. I'm the person and the document."

"Who gave you the right to . . . ?"

"I gave it to myself."

"What is it that you want sir?"

"For you not to think of the Mediterranean," he replied.

"I couldn't do that, even if I wanted to."

"You are thinking in a dangerous way. You don't belong to the Mediterranean or to Egypt or to Africa. You belong to the kingdom of God and you are one of His subjects."

"The whole universe belongs to His Almighty Kingdom, but I have an address, a place of residence, a location, a site, a history, laws, a constitution . . . I have rights."

"You have to forget the sea. Did you try to enjoy the charms of the sands?"

"Look sir, I love deserts, forests, lakes and valleys, but I'm mad about the sea."

"So I'm talking to a mad person."

"Yes, if that answer makes you happy."

"My job is to bring you back to your senses. A suitable number of lashes on your bare back will be useful in your case," he warned.

"Lashing doesn't exist in the Egyptian penal code."

"We are ecumenical; when I come, it must follow me."

"Oh, actually, I feel pain in my back."

"We didn't punish you yet."

"Either you want to eliminate law, or you intend to remove Egypt itself. Perhaps you want to cancel geography as well, obliterate history, so you can bring me back to a prehistoric phase when there were no countries, no borders, no identities, no human rights. So you think that I'm sitting now in a cave wearing a goatskin? I'm sitting in a café lit by electricity, among customers sipping tea that is made on a gas stove. This gas was extricated by tools imported from the West. Look, read that sign. It belongs to the clinic of a doctor who received his certificate in England."

"You are defending an infidel doctor who does not treat people by the words of God."

"On the contrary, the man listened carefully to the words of God and his prophets and knew that he must treat people with science."

"The science of the infidels."

"And you sir, Mr. Inspector, were you not invited to the countries of the infidels? Didn't they treat you in their hospitals in England and America?"[7]

"I only went there to study their conditions, not to learn anything from their ignorant knowledge. Yes, they treated me. But remember, it is lawful to gain from the infidels."

"You have spoiled my night sir. What exactly do you want from me?"

"Do you like the pharaohs?"

"I adore them. They are the lords of mind, thought, purity and a token of faith. They were the first to discover that there is a day of reckoning where people are judged for their actions. They were the first to arrive at the idea of human rights. How dare you ask me to repudiate my ancestors? Who are you, sir?"

"I told you, I'm the inspector of the Nile Valley Street."

For a moment, I felt confused; gradually I began to realize that I was afraid. I looked around me and saw people playing a very ancient game with small stones. The television disappeared; the gas stove disappeared; the owner of the café was using dry wood. The policeman regulating the traffic at the crossroad disappeared. The cars disappeared. The sign of the clinic disappeared. How could all this happen in a few moments? How could I fail to notice them? I must not lose my temper, I thought; it was always hard for me to be calm, but now I must be.

I said to him:

"Okay, sir, I'll show you that there's someone in Egypt who is going to protect me. Now, right now, I'm going to register a complaint against you before Mohammed Ali Pasha of Egypt."

To my right, I was shocked when I saw for the first time in my life a terminal station for donkeys and mules. I rented a strong mule, mounted it with the help of someone and ascended to Cairo's citadel. I was burning with anger. Luckily there was no traffic to slow me. I could see some workers uprooting traffic signs. I didn't see cars or trams; was the underground still there?

It didn't take much time to climb to the citadel. In front of the gate, I dismounted with the help of someone and cried out loud:

"Oh Pasha, governor of Egypt, Mohammed the son of Ali the great, I have a petition. The inspector of our street ordered me not to think of the Mediterranean, and has tried to force me to deny my ancestors."

Moments passed, then one of the Pasha's lieutenants came out on a white mare and shouted:

"Who is the caller?"

"It's me sir, Ali the son of Salem, one of the dwellers of the Nile Valley Street. I want to talk to the Pasha."

They let me in. The Pasha was sitting at a computer and one of his engineers was teaching him how to use it. Without looking at me he said:

"Speak!"

"The inspector of my street prevents me from thinking."

"Did he jump inside your head and hinder your train of thought?"

"No, but he scared me."

"That's your problem, not the problem of the state. What exactly do you want? To eliminate your fears, or to prevent the inspector from scaring you?

"Both, my lord."

"What? What is my interest in that?"

"I'm one of your subjects, my lord, and . . ."

"Let me finish . . . And one of your rights is to be protected by the state, by me."

"Exactly, Pasha, may God prolong the years of your reign."

"Why? How will I benefit from your freedom of thinking?"

"Your system will be strengthened and consolidated, Pasha."

"Ha, Ha. A deft phrase . . . But do you think that I reign by virtue of your thoughts? I rule by my tools."

"Okay, Pasha. Consider me . . . a beggar, begging a morsel of bread not for his stomach, but for his mind."

He turned to me for the first time and stared at me:

"You are spoiled thinkers, spoiled by totalitarian regimes. You all want freedom at the expense of the government. You want it for free, liberties without risks, without losses. Thinking in the Third World is a dangerous game."

"But beautiful my lord."

"Yes, beautiful to those who embrace beauty. But don't forget that this activates pathological jealousy in the hearts of those who are full or fond of ugliness. This brings us to a very important issue: People fight for freedom not because it's beneficial, but because it's beautiful. So, those who have a void in their hearts will fight to defend tyranny and slavery to their last breath. And now, what can I do for you sir?"

"I have something to say. Egypt belongs to the Mediterranean."

"And this belonging, what does it mean?" Pasha asked.

"It means that I am entitled to enjoy all the human rights that other residents of the Mediterranean have. And I'm ready and prepared to carry out all duties required for this purpose."

"For free?"

"I beg your pardon?"

"Do you want me now to issue a decree that Egypt is a Mediterranean country, and that life in it must be exactly similar to life in, let's say, Italy or Greece?"

"Yes, please, my lord."

"Do you think that the nations of the Mediterranean and the rest of Europe secured their human rights just because a decree was issued? Or because one or a group of people asked for it, or thought of it while sitting in a café inhaling their shisha? Listen thin thinker, can you be a Mediterraneanist without thinking of the price paid by its peoples? Your idea is right and your insight is correct. But in many stages of history people search for false ideas, are very happy with them, even chant and dance for them. Was anyone capable of convincing the German people that Adolf Hitler was a fraud who would lead their country to destruction? All thoughts conducive to leading us to hell are delicious and easily digested. People are easily tempted to abandon their freedom. Yet years after that the bills start coming in, so they pay up to restore their freedom. No one can give freedom to anybody. Are you still asking for the freedom of thinking?"

"Yes, my lord."

"Okay, feel free when you think, when you talk, when you write, but don't forward the bills to me; you pay the price, otherwise, you will be a shoplifter taking something from the grand mall of life without paying."

At that moment one of his courtiers came in as if he had decided to end our meeting. He called firmly:

"The Syrian delegation, Pasha."

I bowed preparing myself to leave, but the Pasha said:

"Wait, wait and see."

The Syrian delegation was made up of clerics, whom the Pasha welcomed with great respect:

"Welcome, welcome, respected dignitaries, men of justice, piety and people of faith, to what do I owe your generous visit?"

"We have a complaint Pasha."

"Your complaint is highly considered, your requests are orders to be obeyed and your demands are done. What is it?"

"Your great son Ibrahim Pasha, may God prolong his days and destroy his enemies . . ."

"Yes."

"After he blessedly invaded our country, he issued a decree that People of the Book, Jews and Christians, have the right to ride horses and mules, exactly like we do."

"What's wrong with that?"

"It's a dire violation of all our traditions and cultural heritage."

"Traditions and cultural heritage are changing for the best of people."

"But not for the best of us."

"How's that?"

"When the People of the Book ride horses, they may be higher than us, because we sometimes ride donkeys."

"And you want to be the highest all the time?"

"Yes my lord, by all means."

He sank into silence for some moments, then suddenly he cried out:

"I found the solution. If they ride horses, immediately respond by riding camels, so you will be the highest. Isn't it an inspired idea that can come only from a genius like me?"

Naturally, no one was bold enough to tell the Pasha that his idea was not that inspired. The Syrian delegation thanked him immensely and left, accompanied by tons of gifts that made for a very long caravan.

The Pasha smiled at me, playfully:

"This delegation came for another purpose: They wanted to know where I stood. In any society, in any stage of history, there are two main forces: The force of progress and the force of backwardness. The question in politics is: Where does the Pasha stand? If he stands firmly and clearly with progress, it will prevail. Now, my dear thinker, do you agree?"

"With what my lord?"

"On paying the price for your freedom?"

I asked to be discharged.

He said:

"It's out of my reach."

"Then allow me my lord, to join your era, the 19th century."

"But your people have already entered the 21st century. That is what the calendar says."

"Oh, once again you're trying to deceive me. People should struggle to live in the era they deserve and desire."

The Pasha was very generous with me; he gave me a small sack of money, a fine cloak, a secondhand concubine and a brand new stallion. I returned to our street. That same night, the inspector came to the café and asked me:

"Still thinking of the Mediterranean?"

"No, because I've just discovered that I can't afford it. But I now think of something good and attainable. I think of inviting you so we can smoke some hashish together."

"And I accept your invitation."

From that moment on, we became friends, I ceased to think, and he ceased to scare me. But I'm sure that there are others who can afford to think of the sea, of the Mediterranean.

∾

TAHA HUSAYN (1889–1973)

Deemed by many the doyen of modern Arabic *belles lettres,* Taha Husayn was born in the Minya Province, in Upper Egypt, on October 14, 1889. He was the seventh of thirteen children in a lower middle-class family. Due to a childhood illness, and inadequate treatment, young Taha was blinded at the age of three.

He studied the foundational elements of Arabic language at the local *kuttab* (a traditional school where children learned reading and writing, and memorized the Qur'an). He later attended Al-Azhar University, where he gained more solid understanding of Islam and traditional Arabic literature. But Husayn was dissatisfied with the rigidity and conservatism of that educational system, and would, by 1908, become one of the first batch of students to attend the newly established Cairo University. In 1914, he earned the first Ph.D. conferred by that school, before moving to Paris, as part of Cairo University's educational

mission. At the Sorbonne in Paris he would obtain a second Ph.D., this
time in social philosophy, as well as another postgraduate diploma, in
Roman civil code. Husayn was recipient of multiple honorary doctor-
ates from the universities of Rome, Madrid, and Oxford.

He became Egypt's minister of education in 1950, and made it his
crusade of sorts to make education accessible to all Egyptians, putting
into practice his personal motto, "Education is like the water we drink
and the air we breathe." His cultural and educational manifesto, *The
Future of Culture in Egypt,* excerpted in this chapter, and first published
in Arabic in 1938, was Husayn's platform and roadmap to Egyptian nationalism, Egyptian specificity, and Egyptian shared history with the
Levantine Near East and its Mediterranean backyard—in this sense
opposing Islamic traditionalism, Arab nationalism, and both their irredentist impulses.

Upon publication, and for many years thereafter, *The Future of
Culture in Egypt* instigated an outcry among Arab nationalists, and led
to a very public, often nasty, dispute on the pages of the arabophone
media, between Taha Husayn and Sati' al-Husri, the patron saint of linguistic Arab nationalism, whose stock in trade had been that "anyone
who spoke Arabic was perforce an Arab"—an assertion that Husayn
mocked and rejected out of hand. Ali Salem's *Odd Man and the Sea,*
treated earlier, was arguably a reworking of the Husayn-Husri duel, sati-
rizing Arab nationalism and lauding the humanism and spaciousness
advocated by Husayn's brand of Mediterranean Egyptianism. It is important, then, to read Husayn's *Future of Culture* and Salem's *Odd Man*
as complementary texts.

THE FUTURE OF CULTURE IN EGYPT (1938)

1.

The subject to be treated in this discourse is the future of culture in
Egypt, now that our country has regained her freedom through the revival of the constitution and her honor through the realization of independence. We are living in an age characterized by the fact that freedom

and independence do not constitute ends in themselves, but are merely means of attaining exalted, enduring, and generally practical goals.

Many peoples in various parts of the world have found their freedom and independence, to be meaningless and unproductive. Indeed, these qualities did not prevent them from being attacked by other peoples who also enjoyed them without regarding them as ultimates. They had a civilization built on the basis of culture and science together with the power and wealth engendered thereby. Had not Egypt neglected culture and science, willingly or unwillingly, she would not have lost her freedom and independence and would have been spared the struggle to regain them.

There is no use in regretting what is past, for we cannot do anything about it. Rather, we will sharpen our determination and strengthen our hopes for the future by reflecting on the triumph that climaxed the long and arduous struggle for independence, acknowledged by the civilized world in admitting us along with the other free peoples into the League of Nations. Exult and hope we may, but not to the exclusion of action. We must not stand before freedom and independence in contented admiration. Like all advanced nations, Egypt must regard them as a means of attaining perfection.

I know of nothing that causes me more worry than this newly won independence and freedom of ours. I fear that they may beguile us into thinking that we have come to the end of the road when in fact we have just reached the beginning. I am worried because we are now burdened with truly immense responsibilities toward ourselves, and the civilized world, which we may not fully appreciate. We may fail to make the progress we should, either through sheer neglect or insufficient determination. Such failure will be counted against us by Europeans in general and by our friends the English in particular, who will magnify our every shortcoming, however trivial, and say: they demanded their independence and struggled for it, but when they finally obtained it, they did not taste or enjoy it—they did not know how to use it!

Like every patriotic educated Egyptian who is zealous for his country's good reputation, I want our new life to harmonize with our ancient glory and our new energy to justify both the opinion we entertained of ourselves while we were seeking independence and the opinion held by civilized nations when they recognized our independence and cordially welcomed us to Geneva.

I do not want us to feel inferior to the Europeans because of our cultural shortcomings. This would cause us to despise ourselves and admit that they are not treating us unjustly when they are being arrogant. It is obnoxious for a man who is sensitive to dignity and honor to be compelled to acknowledge that he is not yet deserving of them. Let us keep this disgrace from ourselves and the nation. The way to do it is to take hold of our affairs with determination and vigor from today on, discard useless words for meaningful action, and establish our new life on a sound, constructive basis.

2.

I do not like illusions. I am persuaded that it is only God who can create something from nothing. I therefore believe that the new Egypt will not come into being except from the ancient, eternal Egypt. I believe further that the new Egypt will have to be built on the great old one, and that the future of culture in Egypt will be an extension, a superior version, of the humble, exhausted, and feeble present. For this reason we should think of the future of culture in Egypt in the light of its remote past and near present. We do not wish, nor are we able, to break the link between ourselves and our forefathers.[8] To the degree that we establish our future life upon our past and present we shall avoid most of the dangers caused by excesses and miscalculations deriving from illusions and dreams.

At the outset we must answer this fundamental question: is Egypt of the East or of the West? Naturally, I mean East or West in the cultural, not the geographical sense. It seems to me that there are two distinctly and bitterly antagonistic cultures on the earth. Both have existed since time immemorial, the one in Europe, the other in the Far East.

We may paraphrase the question as follows: Is the Egyptian mind Eastern or Western in its imagination, perception, comprehension, and judgment? More succinctly put—which is easier for the Egyptian mind: to understand a Chinese or Japanese, or to understand an Englishman or a Frenchman? This is the question that we must answer before we begin to think of the foundations on which we shall have to base our culture and education. It seems to me that the simplest way to do this is by tracing the complicated development of the Egyptian mind from earliest times to the present.

The first thing to note is that, so far as is known, we had no regular, sustained contacts with the Far East that could have affected our thinking and political or economic institutions.[9] The available archaeological remains and documents reveal little more than that Egyptians at the end of the Pharaonic period evinced some desire to explore the Red Sea coasts,[10] which they left only with great caution, chiefly for the sake of goods from India and South Arabia. Their attempts were tentative, unorganized, and ephemeral.

The contacts between ancient Egypt and the lands of the East scarcely went beyond Palestine, Syria, and Mesopotamia, that is, the East that falls in the Mediterranean basin,[11] but there is no doubt that they were strong and continuous and that they exerted an influence on the intellectual, political, and economic life of all the countries involved. Our mythology relates that Egyptian gods crossed the Egyptian frontiers in order to civilize the people in these regions.[12] Historians tell us that the kings of Egypt at times extended their sway over them. Ancient Egypt was a major power politically and economically not only in comparison with her neighbors, but with the countries that cradled the European civilization with which we are examining our kinship.[13]

It would be a waste of time and effort to set forth in detail the ties binding Egypt to the ancient Greco-Roman civilization. School children know that Greek colonies were established in Egypt by the Pharaohs before the first millennium B.C. They also know that an Eastern nation, Persia, successfully invaded our country at the end of the sixth century B.C. But we resisted fiercely until the Alexandrian era, having recourse at one time to Greek volunteers, and at another time allying ourselves with the Greek cities.

The meaning of all this is very clear: the Egyptian mind had no serious contact with the Far Eastern mind; nor did it live harmoniously with the Persian mind. The Egyptian mind has had regular, peaceful, and mutually beneficial relations only with the Near East and Greece. In short, it has been influenced from earliest times by the Mediterranean Sea and the various peoples living around it.[14]

3.

The mutually beneficial relations between the Egyptian and Greek minds in antiquity was acknowledged and lauded by the Greeks themselves both in poetry and prose. Egypt is favorably mentioned in the works of the story-tellers and dramatists.[15] Herodotus and later writers and philosophers give a great attention to her.

The Greeks before and during their golden age used to consider themselves the pupils of the Egyptians in civilization, particularly the fine arts.[16] History has neither denied this nor subtracted anything from it. On the contrary, the facts affirm an Egyptian influence not only on Greek architecture, sculpture, and painting, but on the applied arts and sciences as well, not to mention the various aspects of daily life, including political conduct.

We must note that Egypt was not alone in influencing Greece. Other Near Eastern nations, for instance, Chaldaea, had an abundant share in contributing to her civilization and progress.

The ancient Egyptian mind is not an Eastern mind, if we understand by the East China, Japan, India, and the adjoining regions. It developed in Egypt as a result of the conditions, natural and human, that prevailed there. It only exerted influence on and was in turn influenced by the neighboring non-Egyptian peoples, principally the Greeks.

From these clear and long since proven facts, Egyptians have deduced the weird and illogical conclusion that they are Easterners not merely in the geographical sense of the term, but in mentality and culture. They regard themselves as being closer to the Hindus, Chinese, and Japanese than to the Greeks, Italians, and Frenchmen.[17] I have never been able to understand or accept this shocking misconception. I still recall the astonishment I felt several years ago when I became familiar with the activities of a group in Egypt that called itself the "Eastern Link Association" and sought to promote contacts with the peoples of the Far East rather than with the peoples of the Near West. I clearly, indeed intuitively, understand our consciousness of the positive relationships existing between us and the Near East not only because of identity, of language, and of religion, but also because of geographical propinquity as well as similarity of origin and historical evolution. When we go beyond the Near East, however, these factors no longer obtain, except for religion and temporary considerations of a political or economic nature.

History shows that religious and linguistic unity do not necessarily go hand in hand with political unity, nor are they the props on which states rely. The Muslims realized this a long time ago. They established their states on the basis of practical interests, abandoning religion, language, and race as exclusively determining factors before the end of the second century A.H.,[18] when the Umayyad dynasty in Andalusia was in conflict with the Abbassids in Iraq. In the fourth century A.H.,[19] the Islamic world replaced the Islamic empire. Various national blocs and states emerged everywhere. They were built on economic, geographical, and other interests and differed in strength and stability.

Egypt was one of the earliest among the Islamic states to recover her ancient, unforgotten personality. History tells us that she violently opposed the Persians and Macedonians, the latter being eventually absorbed into the local population. Egypt yielded to the Western and Eastern Roman rulers only under duress and had to be kept under continuous martial law. History further relates that she acquiesced most reluctantly even to Arab domination.[20] The spirit of resistance and rebelliousness that followed the conquest did not subside until she regained her independent personality under Ibn Tulun and the dynasties that followed him.[21]

From the earliest times Muslims have been well aware of the now universally acknowledged principle that a political system and a religion are different things, that a constitution and a state rest, above everything else, on practical foundations.[22] This is definitely applicable to the Europeans who, when relieved of the burdens of the Middle Ages, organized their respective governments in accordance with temporal considerations, not Christian unity or linguistic or racial similarity.

Let us return briefly to the point I made above, that the ancient Egyptian mind was not influenced by the Far East either in small or large degree, a fact generally ignored by the Egyptians who tend to look upon themselves as Easterners, a term that they cannot satisfactorily explain.[23] The Europeans make the same mistake, even though their scholars have invested much hard work in verifying the connections between the ancient Egyptian and the Greek civilizations, the latter being the source of their own. In their general behavior and diplomacy they treat Egypt and the Egyptians as part of the East. It is neither important nor useful here to examine this European obstinacy, which is rooted primarily in political and practical considerations. What is important is that we demonstrate once and for all the utter absurdity of thinking that Egypt is as Eastern as India and China.[24]

4.

Until the time of Alexander the Egyptian mind influenced and was influenced by the Greek mind, sharing most if not all of its characteristics. After Alexander's conquest of the Eastern lands and the establishment therein of his successors, Eastern contacts with Greek civilization were multiplied, particularly by Egypt which evolved into a Greek or quasi-Greek state. Alexandria became a major Greek capital, in the strictest sense of the word, and perhaps the most potent outlet of Greek culture for the ancient world. It is an indisputable fact that this culture in all its ramifications sought and found a safe shelter in Egypt where it flowered and spread even more than when it was centered in Athens or in other Greek cities of Europe and Asia.

It would take us too far afield to discuss the Alexandrian philosophy that emerged from this strong link between the Egyptian and Greek minds, which had the profoundest effect on the course of civilization. Egypt's surrender to Roman power did not prevent her from becoming a refuge for Greek culture throughout the Roman period any more than Greece's subjection to Rome destroyed her Hellenism. On the contrary, she succeeded in impressing Hellenism upon the Romans themselves.[25]

5.

Islam arose and spread over the world. Egypt was receptive and hastened at top speed to adopt it as her religion and to make the Arabic of Islam her language.[26] Did that obliterate her original mentality? Did that make her an Eastern nation in the present meaning of the term? Not at all! Europe did not become Eastern nor did the nature of the European mind change because Christianity, which originated in the East, flooded Europe and absorbed the other religions.[27] If modern European philosophers and thinkers deem Christianity to be an element of the

European mind, they must explain what distinguishes Christianity from Islam; for both were born in the geographical East, both issued from one noble source and were inspired by the one God in whom Easterners and Westerners alike believe.[28]

How is it possible for fair-minded persons to see no harm coming to the European mind from reading the Gospel, which transports this mind from the West to the East, and at the same time to regard the Koran as purely Eastern, even though it has been clearly and straightforwardly proclaimed that the Koran was sent only to complete and confirm what is in the Gospels?[29]

If it is true that Christianity did not transform the European mind or eliminate either its inherited Hellenism or Mediterranean qualities, it must be equally true that Islam did not change the Egyptian mind or the mind of the peoples who embraced it and who were influenced by the Mediterranean Sea.[30] Indeed, we may go much further and say quite confidently that the spread of Islam into the Middle and Far East amplified the power of the Greek mind and extended it into regions where it had seldom reached before. The Europeans would certainly not have disputed or denied the fact if Christianity had recorded such an achievement.

Islam and Christianity came to resemble each other in another way. Christianity influenced and was influenced by Greek philosophy before the rise of Islam. Philosophy became Christian and Christianity became philosophical. The same thing happened when Islam came into contact with Greek philosophy. Philosophy became Muslim and Islam became philosophical. The history of the two faiths is one with respect to this phenomenon. Why does Christianity's association with philosophy make it one of the props of the European mind, while Islam's association with this same philosophy fails to make it a prop of the Muslim mind?

The essence and source of Islam are the essence and source of Christianity. The connection of Islam with Greek philosophy is identical to that of Christianity. Whence, then, comes the difference in the effect of these two faiths on the creation of the mind that mankind inherited from the peoples of the Near East and Greece?

When the barbarians attacked Greco-Roman Europe they dealt a dangerous blow to its civilization, almost extinguishing the torch of the

Greek mind which had glowed there before the collapse of the Roman
Empire. While it was barely able to flicker on in a few monasteries, Islam
was translating, enlarging, and propagating Greek philosophy, which
was subsequently transmitted to Europe. Here in Latin translation it led
to an intellectual revival that enabled the European mind to regain its
splendor in the twelfth century of the Christian Era.[31] Why is Europe's
connection with Greek culture during the Renaissance one of the props
of the European mind, whereas her connection with the same Greek culture through Islam is not so regarded? Can we seriously maintain the
existence of important differences between the nations living on the eastern shore of the Roman Sea and the nations living on its western shore?

Several years ago I heard a lecture by the great Belgian historian
Pirenne before a meeting of the Geographical Society of Egypt held
under the auspices of the Faculty of Arts. His discussion of certain matters that were overlooked at the time left a deep impression upon me.
He declared that the invasion of Europe by the barbarians would not
have doomed her to intellectual retrogression during the Middle Ages
had the sea lanes between East and West remained open. But the emergence of Islam and the ensuing rivalry with Christianity interrupted
communications for a time, with the result that Europe was rendered
economically prostrate first and then profoundly ignorant. When the
ties between East and West were restored, Europe cast off her shackles
of poverty and darkness.

This means, if I understand Pirenne correctly, that the cornerstone
of intellectual life in Europe rests on its connection with the East via the
Mediterranean Sea. How can this sea create in the West an outstanding,
superior mind and at the same time leave the East without any mind or
with one that is weak and decadent?

No, there are no intellectual or cultural differences to be found
among the peoples who grew up around the Mediterranean and were
influenced by it. Purely political and economic circumstances made the
inhabitants of one shore prevail against those of the other. The same
factors led them to treat each other now with friendliness, now with
enmity.

We Egyptians must not assume the existence of intellectual differences, weak or strong, between the Europeans and ourselves or infer

that the East mentioned by Kipling in his famous verse "East is East and West is West, and never the twain shall meet" applies to us or our country. Ismail's statement that Egypt is a part of Europe should not be regarded as some kind of boast or exaggeration,[32] since our country has always been a part of Europe as far as intellectual and cultural life is concerned, in all its forms and branches.

6.

Aggressions and misfortunes at times severed the link between the Europeans and Near Easterners, greatly weakening the latter's internal social structure. As a consequence, Europe was able to accelerate her Renaissance, while the Near East declined so rapidly and so far that it virtually lost its intellectual personality. When Egypt awoke along with the rest of the Near East, Europe had already achieved a great measure of progress and extended her power over most of the regions of the earth. The Turkish invasion of the Mediterranean basin halted the advances being made in the Muslim countries. It obliterated wholly or in part the markers of civilization and cut off for a long time Muslim ties with Europe.

Two things should be noted here. First, the barbarians inflicted a similar fate on Europe at the beginning of the Middle Ages. Why did not this even divest Europe of her Greek mind, and why is it alleged to have had this effect on the Near East? The Turks embraced the faith and civilization of the Near East just as the Barbarians did the faith and civilization of the West, yet the former are supposed to have altered the nature of the Near Eastern mind, while the latter had no effect on the European mind.

Second, the only country in the Near East that stood firm against the Turkish onslaught and preserved her civilization, mind, and Islamic heritage, although she suffered grievously in the process, was Egypt. Thus once again, as in the case of Greek philosophy and civilization, which she sheltered for more than ten centuries, Egypt may rightly claim the credit of having protected the human intellect.

The noted French author Paul Valéry once identified these three elements of the European mind: Greek civilization with its literature, philosophy, and art; Roman civilization with its political institutions and jurisprudence; and Christianity with its appeal for charity and its exhortation to good works. An analysis of the Muslim mind in Egypt and elsewhere in the Near East will yield comparable results: a literary, philosophical, and artistic component essentially related to Greek civilization; a politico-juridical component very much akin to the Roman system;[33] and a religious component, the noble Islamic faith, with its advocacy of charity and good works. Islam, no one will deny, came to complete and confirm the Old and New Testaments.[34]

In sum, wherever we may search, whatever line of investigation we may pursue, we shall not find any evidence to justify the thesis that there is a fundamental difference between the European and Egyptian minds.

7.

The development of modern communications has served to link Egypt closely to Europe, as indeed they linked all parts of the world. Although the renaissance of Egypt which began early in the nineteenth century is still unclear in some respects, its modern orientation is unmistakable. As far as the materialistic side of life—particularly among the upper classes—is concerned, it is purely European. The other classes more or less resemble their European counterparts, depending only on the capabilities and wealth of the various individuals and groups. We adopted and still retain the European attitude toward the external manifestations and embellishments of existence. Whether we did so consciously and deliberately or not, I do not know, but the fact remains that there is no power on earth capable of preventing us from enjoying life the way they do.

Like the Europeans, we have built railroads, telegraph lines, and telephones. We learned from Europe to sit at the table and eat with a knife and fork. We wear the same kind of clothes. All this we did without discrimination, without examination to know what is actually bad and what is unsuitable for us. So far has the European ideal become our ideal that we now measure the material progress of all individuals and groups by the amount of borrowing from Europe. Moreover, even the intangible aspects of life, surface differences notwithstanding, show the same influence. We did not hesitate, for example, to adopt the European system of government; and if we criticize ourselves for something, this is simply that we have been slow in following European administrative and political practices. Our political life in recent times has been in a state of confusion between absolute government and limited government, for which we have no precedent in our Middle Ages. I mean that our modern absolute government was affected by European absolutism prevalent before the rise of democracy; in similar fashion our form of limited government was shaped by the systems of limited government also existing in Europe. [. . .]

10.

[. . .] Europe is Christian. I do not call for the adoption of Christianity, but for the adoption of the motive-forces of European civilization. Without them Egypt cannot live, let alone progress and govern herself. The Europeans differ among themselves in many respects. Some follow various types and forms of Christianity, some are not Christian, and some are irreligious. Nevertheless, they all remain in basic agreement both as to the motive-forces of their civilization and the methods of obtaining and enjoying its fruits.

There is no doubt that modern European civilization has shown strong hostility toward Christianity. This proved very costly until an equilibrium between the two was finally established when honest Europeans began to realize that the true conflict was not between religion and civilization as such, but between the competing desires of those who control religion and those who control civilization.

God has spared us this misfortune. Islam knows no clergy, nor does it separate the men of religion from the other classes of society. It refrained from creating an intermediary between the Master and his servants. The evils that Europe witnessed as a result of the bitter struggle by the Church to defend its centuries-old vested interests will never befall us, unless we introduce something alien and intolerable into Islam.

Our good people should remember that as soon as Islam crossed the Arabian frontiers it came into contact with foreign civilizations whose relationship to the Muslims and Arabs at that time was the same as Europe's is to us now. The Muslim Arabs were not deterred by certain unpleasant features from adopting the motive-forces of the non-Muslim Persian and Byzantine Greek civilizations. Incorporating these

two into their ancient heritage, they produced the glorious Islamic culture of the Umayyads and Abbassids, which our conservatives are seeking to recreate.

The Muslims fought the atheists and mockers without rejecting
the alien civilization that produced them. Along with atheism, debauchery, and cynicism there are devoutness, asceticism, and piety. We were
doubly enriched in that we inherited both the libertine verses of such
men as Bashshar, Hammad, and Abu-Nuwas,[35] and the writings of
judges, theologians, and philosophers. No one, not even a man of religion, would urge the passage of a law to burn the works of the above-
mentioned poets.[36]

Europe today resembles the Umayyad and Abbasid Near East in
the richness of its civilization, which, like any human creation, possesses
good and bad aspects. Our religious life will not suffer from contact with
the European civilization any more than it suffered when we took over
the Persian and Byzantine civilizations. In practice, we are confronted
with the choice of either repudiating our ancestors, which I think we are
not prepared to do, or emulating their attitude toward Byzantium and
Persia by adopting in full measure the motive-forces of Europe. We have
actually been doing this last since we became acquainted with Europe at
the beginning of the past century, and the tempo, if anything, quickens
from day to day. A reversal of this process would mean our end.

My plea, therefore, is for nothing new.[37] I simply want the apprehensive to be reassured and to accept willingly rather than grudgingly
the inevitable. I know some fine men of conservative bent who depre-
cate Western civilization and yet are literally steeped in it. Many of those
who object to the unveiled face and the commingling of boys and girls
send their daughters to foreign schools where they dress in typically European fashion.

It would be absurd to pretend that I am the first to recommend
adopting the motive-forces of European civilization when the radio has
long since penetrated al-Azhar and has been used by the Rector himself
in addressing the Muslims throughout the world. Not only have the sciences and arts of this civilization come to al-Azhar, but the institution
has taken the initiative in sending special missions to the capitals of
Europe to learn at first hand from European professors. In passing, I

should like to refer to the irony that while al-Azhar, a citadel of conservatism in the East, has been frantically rushing toward this civilization, the Egyptian University, an offspring of this era, is inclining in the opposite direction owing to its belief that Egypt should progress at a measured pace using forethought and mature judgments.

In short, I want us to harmonize our words with our actions. Let us admit the truth and banish hypocrisy. Only by eagerly welcoming the modern civilization can we have realities of life. A sound philosophy, it seems to me, requires the frank acknowledgment of one's desires and a straightforward attempt to satisfy them. [. . .]

13.

[. . .] The foreign educational system prevailing in Egypt is not under the jurisdiction of the government and it does not respond to the needs of our people. The French, Italian, Greek, English, American, and German schools are concerned mainly with propagating their respective cultures and molding Egyptian students according to their own patterns. Unfortunately, these schools are superior in equipment and technique to our own so that Egyptians willingly enroll their children there. The result is that graduates of these institutions, no matter how much they love Egypt, think differently from graduates of native schools, as may be readily observed in their daily lives, sense of values, and judgments.

The independent Egyptian educational system pretends to follow the official curricula, but until recently it was not subject to state supervision. With a few exceptions, the practices of the schools led to corruption of thought and morality, public and private. They were founded everywhere by individuals and groups in response to acute local needs that could not be satisfied by the government. Since the number of children who attend these schools is very great, I fear we shall continue to feel the effects of the system for some time to come.

Al-Azhar and its subsidiary institutions scattered throughout the provinces form still another educational network not wholly under governmental control, despite the fact that their funds come from the Treasury and the Muslim pious endowments. Although nominally regulated by legislation, al-Azhar managed to keep aloof until recently from both normal life and state supervision. Its educational philosophy and techniques, derived largely from the Middle Ages, produce students very different in thought and behavior from secular-trained youth. The consequences would be far more serious than they are were it not for certain unifying elements in the national renaissance, principally the many newspapers, magazines and books read by Egyptian intellectuals of every persuasion, and to commonly-shared pains inflicted on many Egyptians now by the foreigners, now by their compatriots.

[. . .] It is an indisputable duty of the state to ensure that its boys and girls are provided with proper instruction in the national language. Language is both a vital component of the national personality and an instrument of communication among the people of a given country.[38] Thus, the state is not unjust or tyrannical if it requires the foreign schools in Egypt to teach Arabic and checks to see that this is done satisfactorily. Similarly, Egyptian history and geography should be part of their basic curricula.

The question of religious education in the school is complex. It is, of course, our right as well as our duty to ascertain whether or not foreign institutions are subverting the parental religion of the students and treating them as subjects for propaganda and evangelization. Egyptians differ with regard to religion in the schools. Some want education to be completely secular, with religious instruction being left to the family. Others consider religion as much a part of the national personality as language or history and instruction in it equally necessary. This undoubtedly represents the majority view and must, therefore, be reflected in the curricula of all the schools.

I know that many foreign school administrations will experience considerable difficulty in accepting the logic of this kind of thinking. But we must follow through if we are genuinely desirous of attaining national unity. Foreigners who dislike the idea of teaching Islam in their schools, which are by nature Christian or secular, should realize that it is equally difficult for Egyptians to tolerate the mere existence of these schools on their soil, however necessary they may be.[39]

My attitude toward the independent Egyptian schools is not wholly negative because any state that permits foreigners to found schools on its soil cannot prohibit its own citizens from doing the same. Moreover, I am eager to see the private enterprise of individuals and groups encouraged, not only in promoting education but in furthering all other types of civic endeavor. However, these schools too should be strictly supervised by the state in order to prevent the development of discordant elements at this crucial stage in our history.

No one should misconstrue my remarks and think that I want all the schools in Egypt to resemble each other or to cast their pupils in the same mold. On the contrary, I definitely favor differences in such matters as syllabus and method, provided that there be some agreement on the features that make up the national personality and instill in our children a readiness to defend Egypt's democracy and independence. [...]

32.

[...] Egypt influenced and was influenced by mankind, and this will be so in the future. Hence, from the practical as well as purely cultural points of view, knowledge of the past of other peoples besides Egyptians is a necessity. The above considerations apply more or less to arithmetic. Students must master the basic principles since they are a mind-builder and a useful tool for everyday life. They also serve as a ladder to the mathematical sciences, which constitute an integral part of general knowledge.

It may be appropriate here to discuss the question of when to start the study of foreign languages in general education. Egypt has followed the system, but not without some difference of opinion and confusion in theory and practice, of offering English, French, and other languages in the primary schools, i.e., the first stage for general education. It is my firm conviction that they should not be taught during the first few years of schooling, which should be reserved for concentrated attention on the natural culture, since all too soon they will be studying alien and unfamiliar countries.

There have been justifiable complaints that our children do not know their own Arabic language very well. Blame has been attributed to various sources—the language itself, the grammar, the teachers and their methods. However, what may well be the main cause is rarely mentioned, namely, that a child hardly enters school when he is rushed into the study of a foreign language which absorbs much of his time and energy. The fact that classical Arabic is unquestionably difficult for a youngster and remote from his needs because of its ancient and complicated grammar, system of writing, and improperly equipped teachers, is all the more reason for us not to deflect his attention toward a subject that he does not need at this period in his life.[40] Later on, with the growth of his mental and physical powers, he will be able to learn it at the same time that he is taking advanced work in his native language.

It was possible to justify the imposition of a foreign language upon the youth when the English controlled Egypt or when the language of instruction in the schools was English or French. But now that the English have nothing to do with educational affairs and Arabic has become the language of culture, it is no longer possible to defend and retain unchanged past procedures.

The example of Europeans who teach their youth foreign languages during the early years of schooling has been often cited, but is irrelevant for us, for two reasons. First, European children obtain from the older members of their families additional instruction in their mother tongue and national culture, which in many respects is more important and more enduring than what they learn in school. Our situation is completely different. The separation between home and school and between family and teacher is very great indeed. Many say that the Arabic taught in school is a foreign language compared to the colloquial; for it is not only not used at home or in the streets, but is not spoken usually or heard even during the Arabic language class itself, let alone during the geography, history, or science classes.[41] Secondly, European languages more or less resemble each other, a fact that facilitates and makes enjoyable the task of language learning for European youth and perhaps aids them in perfecting their individual native tongues.[42] Egyptians, on the other hand, experience considerable difficulty in learning such languages as French, Spanish, Italian, and German because Arabic is wholly unrelated to them in vocabulary and structure. Hence, until our children have developed their nascent linguistic and literary personalities and learned to express themselves freely and lucidly in Arabic, I deem it most inadvisable to expose them to the confusion and difficulties that result from a premature study of foreign languages.[43] [. . .]

34.

[. . .] The question at the core of the dispute was this: should the people be educated in science and specialized fields in anticipation of their all becoming leaders of thought and public affairs, or should a minority be given scientific and specialized training, while the majority are taught only how to cope with the problems of earning a living? If they are to become leaders, Latin and Greek as the foundation of science and specialization are certainly necessary. If they are just to be taught how to earn a living, vocational training and a modern general education that emphasizes living languages and experimental sciences should be provided, with Latin and Greek made compulsory only for those who are primarily interested in pure science. Phrased in this way, the question virtually answers itself: for it is clearly a senseless waste of time and effort to compel everyone to study languages that are of little value in most walks of life.[44]

[. . .] The practical conclusions to be drawn from my remarks are as follows: (1) the Faculty of Arts must have a strong Department of Classical Studies offering the B.A., M.A., and Ph.D. degrees, staffed with competent teachers. Students must be prepared for this in the general schools: (2) Latin, and in some cases Greek, should be prerequisite for would-be majors in the humanities; again, students must be prepared for this in the general schools; (3) our national pride and interest demands that we train Egyptians to take over certain of our basic institutions that have been directed by non-Egyptians since the beginning of our modern renaissance, e.g., Egyptian service of antiquities, which will doubtless have to remain under their present management until there are Egyptians who know Latin and Greek very well before starting to specialize in the field. It is painful to compel youths in the Institute of Antiquities to study Latin and Greek along with ancient Egyptian, Coptic, the various periods of Egyptian history, and archaeology. Again, students must be prepared for this in the general schools. Egyptian history, except for the modern phase, has been largely written by foreigners without any fruitful participation by Egyptians. We are still beginners in our ancient, Greco-Roman, and Islamic periods. Those who call for Egyptian historical studies, if they are serious, should at the same time advocate the use of such logical and indispensable tools as Latin and Greek. It is shameful to have to repeat over and over again the elementary facts that the relation between Egypt and Greece is very old, that the Greeks fashioned this relation through their writings and other creative works, that Egypt was subjected to Greco-Roman authority and institutions for ten centuries, an indelible part of our national history (the source material for which is in Greek and Latin), and that Egypt was linked during the Islamic period both to Byzantium and western Europe (the source material for which is also in Latin and Greek). The objectors to Latin and Geek should re-examine their position; for they are virtually condemning us to ignorance of our history except for what we can learn from foreigners. I cannot conceive of any proponent of Egyptian nationalism being happy about this patently disgraceful situation.

I have refrained from speaking about the value of the classics in training the mind for straightforward thinking since I should be understood only by those who already know them and are familiar with the benefits they confer. Scarcely a dozen Egyptians today possess this knowledge.

Although France, like other European countries, has in recent times become involved in a struggle between the partisans and enemies of the classics, the established and still universal practice there is to require all would-be teachers to have a command of Latin regardless of their field of specialization. Some of them are even required to learn Greek as well. I am sure that the situation is essentially the same in England, Germany, and Italy. At the educational conference held in Paris last summer I listened with great interest to the head of the School of Engineering in Zurich as he urged that Latin or Greek or both be made a prerequisite for students desirous of majoring in engineering.

Egypt's course of action to obtain her scientific independence is clear and simple. She will have to take it, unless she can continue to feel the humility she feels now in front of the Europeans.

35.

[. . .] Although the Ministry of Education will initially disagree with me, it will eventually accept the following classification of general school subjects into: (1) compulsory for all students, such as history, geography, Arabic, mathematics, and the experimental sciences; and (2) elective, such as foreign languages and literatures. Those who intend to major in mathematics or technical subjects in professional schools must study along with the basic background courses two modern languages, chosen from among English, French, German, and Italian. Those who intend to major in Arabic language and literature must take advanced work in Arabic, Islamic, a modern European language, and Hebrew or Persian. Those who intend to major in a humanistic discipline such as history, geography, philosophy, or any branch of European belles-lettres must take Latin, a modern European language, and Greek or another European language.

My plan will lead to a diversification of general education that will produce students of every type, all adequately prepared for university work. The Faculties of Sciences, Medicine, Engineering, and Agriculture will find men and women proficient in their native language as well as two foreign languages. The Faculties of Law, Arts, and Commerce will find various kinds of people: some who are trained for the practical world of business and who have proficiency in Arabic and two European languages along with a sound general education; some who want to go more deeply into the disciplines of belles-lettres and law and are well grounded in ancient and modern languages; some who want to study Arabic language and literature and master a European language and also Hebrew if they want to specialize in comparative or historical linguistics, or Persian, if they want to proceed to higher Arabic literary studies.

In short, we can invigorate the entire system of secondary education and spare the University the present expensive, time-consuming task of bringing its students up to the required level of preparation simply by adding to the curriculum two new modern languages, Latin, Greek, Persian, and Hebrew.

36.

My views on Arabic and the desirability of introducing several eastern languages into the secondary school curriculum are as likely to be attacked as those on Latin and Greek. I should like to clarify my position by asking at the outset this fundamental question: Why do we provide instruction in Arabic and train teachers for this purpose? There is just one answer. Arabic is our national language and as such constitutes an integral part of the Egyptian personality. It is the medium for transmitting to the younger generation the legacy of the past and serves as the natural tool by which we help one another realize our personal and societal needs. We use it every day both for mutual understanding and for self-understanding. When we think in a purposeful manner we become conscious of our existence, changing needs, emotions, and contradictory desires. We conceive of things only through word pictures which we either pass on to others or keep to ourselves.

We study and teach Arabic as an indispensable part of individual and group living in all its manifestations. We do so not merely because it is the language of religion or of our ancestors, but because it is our language and the language that we want the coming generations to know. There are many self-styled religious peoples on the earth who think as highly of their religion as we do of ours. They do not consider it unusual to use one language for everyday needs and another for their sacred books and prayers. Thus, while various Christians regard Latin, Greek, Coptic, or Syriac as their religious language, they all speak something else. Similarly, there are Muslims who do not speak or understand Arabic, even though it is their holy language, and whose piety and devotion to Islam are assuredly as intense as ours.

Those who assert that we study and teach Arabic just because it is a language of religion are deceiving the people. Although Arabic is a language of religion and a boon to those who speak it, it must be as free from narrowness and stagnation as religion itself. It belongs not to the men of religion alone, but to all the people, regardless of nation or race, who speak it. Each individual is at liberty to treat the language as any property owner does his possessions when he has fulfilled certain necessary conditions. It is absurd, therefore, to think that the teaching of Arabic is the inalienable and exclusive right of al-Azhar and its satellite schools. Absurd, because al-Azhar cannot be imposed on all speakers of Arabic—these include non-Muslims as well as Muslims. Absurd, because Arabic has been studied and taught in both Islamic and non-Islamic milieus. Absurd, too, because the various disciplines of Arabic

arose and flourished before al-Azhar was established, indeed before anyone even thought of it. None of the great grammarians and philologists
of the past like al-Khalil, Sibawaihi, al-Akhfash, al-Mubarrad, al-Kisa'i,
al-Farra', Tha'lab, al-Jahiz, Qudamah, al-Azhari, and al-Jawhari was re-
motely an Azharite.[45] Even the authors of the language textbooks used
by al-Azhar were rarely affiliated with the institution.

Those who assert that al-Azhar is or must be the sole guardian of
the Arabic language are uttering sheer nonsense. Religion does not support their arguments because it fails to restrict the protection of Arabic
to a single group of people; moreover, most of the founders and developers of the Arabic sciences were not men of religion. Nor does history
give them any aid because al-Azhar chanced upon these sciences after,
rather than before, they matured. Al-Azhar guarded them, for which it
is entitled to thanks, but it added nothing of importance. It has, to be
sure, the right to participate in their further development, but it must
not be permitted to monopolize them.

As long as Arabic is used in all situations of life, and not exclusively
for religious purposes, concern for it, as for anything connected with
the intellect, should be freely shared both by the state and by individuals. Hence, the state should feel no compunction about taking charge of
Arabic instruction and reorganizing the existing system to make it more
responsive to modern conditions.

The things I have been talking about would seem to be so basic and
so obvious as not to require any proof. However, even if the authorities
are aware of them, they cannot summon up the courage to take appropriate action if it means opposing al-Azhar, which they view as some
sort of monster standing watch before the Arabic language. Al-Azhar
nowadays lacks freedom of thought as well as familiarity with modern
science. It knows absolutely nothing about the evolution of foreign languages, ancient or modern, Semitic or non-Semitic, or anything else
about them for that matter. It does not have a mastery of even the Arabic language sciences. Yet there are important Egyptians who pretend
that al-Azhar's domination of the teaching of Arabic is a good thing
from the point of view of the language. They do this either because they
are afraid of being called irreligious—despite the fact that we are living in an age when such accusations made to serve worldly interests

should come to an end—or because they desire to support al-Azhar in the name of religion—despite the fact that we are living in an age when religion ought not to be used as a tool for intimidation or the attainment of material objectives.

The state, I repeat, should take over from al-Azhar and its satellite institutions the task of teaching Arabic and training instructors. The practice followed in other countries is worth pondering. The men of religion in Europe, for example, do not teach Latin (or Greek) on the grounds that it is the religious language of their people. Latin and Greek are taught in non-ecclesiastical schools, although they are not the languages of daily usage. How about Arabic, then, which is employed in both ordinary and intellectual life? We must banish forever the ancient myth, wiping it out as Lubad was wiped out, and treat Arabic forthrightly as the secular thing that it is.

If the state is as duty-bound to train teachers of Arabic as it is to train teachers of history, geography, physics, and chemistry, it must logically start their preparation in the secondary schools, not in the University or the College of Dar al-Ulum or the Institute of Education. Under the system I propose, provision will be made for two types of Arabic specialists: (1) linguistic—preparation to include work in a Semitic language begun in secondary school and continued through the University; and (2) belles-lettristic—preparation to include the study of Persian on both the secondary and university levels. Would-be Arabists, I have pointed out, should be required to study thoroughly one modern European language. I cannot conceive of instructors in any general education subject being ignorant of European life and unable to make direct contact with it through the medium of one of the principal languages.

We shall return to this topic again, but now we must deal with another vexing aspect of the problem.

37.

Just what is the Arabic language that we want to teach in the public and private schools and whose instructors we want the state itself to train? And in what way do we want to teach it? I should like at the very outset to reassure the conservatives in general and the Azharites in particular that the language which I am anxious to have taught to perfection

in the schools is classical Arabic, the language of the Koran and the
Holy Traditions, the language of our ancient prose and poetry, science,
philology, and philosophy. I am, and shall remain, unalterably opposed
to those who regard the colloquial as a suitable instrument for mutual
understanding and a method for realizing the various goals of our intellectual life because I simply cannot tolerate any squandering of the heritage, however slight, that classical Arabic has preserved for us. The colloquial lacks the qualities to make it worthy of the name of a language. I
look upon it as a dialect that has become corrupted in many respects. It
might disappear, as it were, into the classical if we devoted the necessary
effort on the one hand to elevate the cultural level of the people and on
the other to simplify and reform the classical so that the two meet at a
common point.[46]

I urge the state to undertake the training of teachers along the lines
sketched above and to encourage competent scholars to change the language and related sciences so as to put them in tune with modern life and
thought. I warn those who are resisting reform that we face the dreadful
prospect of classical Arabic becoming, whether we want it or not, a religious language and the sole possession of the men of religion.[47]

This may happen sooner than anyone thinks possible, for [classi-
cal] Arabic in Egypt is now virtually a foreign language. Nobody speaks
it at home or school or on the streets or in clubs; it is not even used
in al-Azhar itself. People everywhere speak a language that is definitely
not Arabic, despite the partial resemblance to it. Throughout the Near
East there are a number of cultivated people who understand, read, and
write classical Arabic well (in the main not Azhar graduates). However,
even of these the majority cannot speak it fluently. When you write a
book for the masses you have to simplify your grammar and syntax considerably in order to be fully understood. If we were to test the capacity
of so-called literates to understand the meaning of a chapter by some
contemporary author, the results would be painful and ludicrous.

The reactionaries seek to block progress in language reform and
simplification now by advancing religious arguments, now by asserting
the right of all the Arabs to participate in the process. They forget that
God gave us the Koran and the laws of religion before the language sciences were created, and that the creators of these sciences were inspired,

among other things, by the desire to prevent Arabic from becoming corrupted or lost, the very reason for our concern today. They are, or pretend to be, ignorant of the fact that the pioneers, recorders, and developers of grammar were Iraqi scholars with whom the Egyptian, Syrian, African, and Andalusian Arabs did not consult before they carried out their own scientific research and wrote their own books.

Which of the Umayyad or Abbasid caliphs or amirs of Iraq ever called a general conference to ratify al-Khalil's discoveries or Sibawaihi's "The Book"? Whereabouts in the Islamic realm was this conference held? Which one of the Muslim caliphs, amirs, or sheikhs presided and delivered the introductory address? And what did the conference decide with respect to the grammatical principles that were disputed by the scholars? Do you think it regarded the "five nouns" as inflected with consonants or with vowels? Or with vowels before the consonants? Or with vowels implicit in the consonants?

We might laugh at this sort of nonsense if the matter were not so serious, involving as it does the life and death of the [classical] Arabic language. Since the Umayyads and Abbassids did not threaten to punish the Basrans or Kufans when they established the language sciences and when differences of opinion impelled some of them to perform miracles of analysis, and since there were no meetings in Basra, Kufa, Damascus, Baghdad, or elsewhere to deal with the problem of grammar or its reform, why should anyone today advocate the holding of them among Egyptians and non-Egyptians? There is, naturally, no objection to people coming together as individuals to study and argue these questions. Quite the contrary, it would be an excellent thing to do. By the same token the state too has the right, if not the obligation, to initiate reform when the necessity is great.

The conservatives, Azharites and non-Azharites alike, must recognize the gravity of the situation which affects adversely almost every phase of life, including religion. If I did not hate to accuse Muslims of committing sins—and unlike others I do not arrogate to myself the right to pass judgment on the impiety or immorality of any Muslim—I could confound them with their own arguments. What more need be said than that young Egyptians are definitely ignorant of Arabic and thus unable to understand the Holy Book and Traditions. Those who are blocking reform are at the same time blocking its results. What verdict does al-Azhar pronounce on those who stand in the way of understanding God's Book and the Prophet's Traditions? Are they Muslims or apostates? Are they doing good or harm? Let us be done with this senseless farce and earnestly set ourselves to the task of furnishing the youth with a language that they can appreciate and enjoy instead of the useless hateful thing they now possess, which leads many of them to prefer a foreign tongue, as Dr. Hafiz Afifi Pasha has pointed out.

Various ideas have been presented from time to time to the Ministry of Education. The originators made it quite plain that they did not expect immediate acceptance. They wanted their views to be publicized and studied not only in Egypt but throughout the Arab world. If they stood the test of analysis and debate, the Ministry was to have them written up in book form and then circulated among educators and teachers. Only when they indicated their approval would the Ministry formally commission the preparation of textbooks and include them in the curriculum. What more could one ask of these innovators? Do the elite secretly fear that the spread of knowledge will destroy their present monopoly, which is comparable to the position enjoyed by the ancient Egyptian priests who maintained exclusive control over the various branches of learning and religion?

I believe that language simplification is prerequisite to a general reform of the educational system itself; for one cannot study effectively unless the language of instruction is clear and easily grasped by the mind and heart. Like almost everyone else, I should like teachers to use classical Arabic in every class regardless of the course, but I am reluctant to insist because they do not know the language well enough and, if required to speak it, would fail to communicate the subject matter to their pupils.

Although Arabic is part of the basic educational syllabus that is obligatory for everyone, very few people have been able to master its intricacies. Even fewer are prepared to spend years learning the rules of grammar only to find ultimately that their knowledge is imperfect. An educational system that does not teach the youth to read and write their native language well is a mockery.[48] Are the Azharites content to teach the youth not much more than the letters of the alphabet and have them forget even this little soon after they leave school? Do they believe that the present unsimplified Arabic grammar allows the pupils really to master the language within the limited period of compulsory education?

In addition to favoring a revised Arabic grammar and rhetoric, such as the committee appointed by the Ministry of Education has suggested, I hold with Bahi al-Din Pasha Barakat that we should do something about our system of writing which leads the people to make so many errors. He too says that the people should read in order to understand, not understand in order to read. The writing system must be made to serve the cause of clarity, to render sounds accurately and fully, with due regard for speed and economy of effort. I advised Bahi al-Din Pasha Barakat to proceed cautiously in this matter and begin by organizing a competition throughout the world, setting up technical committees to decide what reforms may be adopted lest it arouse angry opposition for that reason. The reform of Arabic writing is, however, a fundamental step in the reform of education.

Adoption of the most pressing reforms would relieve students of the vast amount of time-consuming drudgery involved in learning the minutiae of grammar and go far toward assuring them of relative freedom from error in reading and writing. It would also obviate the necessity for resorting to the solution found by the Turks, namely, replacement of Arabic alphabet with the Latin. Although many people approve this idea, I have resisted and always will resist the use of Latin letters for several reasons which I do not propose to take up here.[49]

Such resistance, however strong, will not be enough unless we hasten to modify the writing system and thus overcome the arguments of those who propose a radical solution. Suppose you were to order the Egyptians to use camels, mules, and sailing ships instead of automobiles, trains, trolleys, and steamships—do you think they would pay any attention to you, especially if they saw others availing themselves of these swift and sure means of transportation? So it will be with reading and writing. Either you simplify them or the people will turn to something easier and better. They will not prefer ignorance to knowledge or permit reading and writing to remain much longer the monopoly of a few. The world has changed and the masses are not so satisfied with their lot as they used to be. We shall be far better off if we stop fooling ourselves, and, by making a virtue of necessity, reform, not only grammar and rhetoric, but the system of reading and writing as well.

38.

Although I love grammar dearly—my friends can testify to that—I want only those majoring in the language and literature to go into it deeply. The vast majority of our general school teachers should be spared this burden. It is not easy to do, but we should make a determined effort to ascertain the indispensable minimum of grammatical data and convey it to the teachers by means of attractive literary texts rather than in purely scientific terms. Those who think that mastery of grammar leads to a mastery of language or that profound study necessarily enables one to understand its secrets are making a serious mistake. Grammar, which is simply philosophy, represents a luxury, primarily for educated people. It is an independent branch of knowledge and of concern only to specialists and ardent amateurs.

When I was a boy, al-Azhar believed that grammar and the wordy nonsense it called rhetoric constituted the very core of language, while everything else was the unessential rind. Literature, naturally, was unessential rind. All of us who took the courses of the late Sayyid al-Marsafi were the objects of criticism and scorn because we ignored the core for the rind. Our sheikhs plainly despised the "Diwan al-Hamasah," the "Kamil" of al-Mubarrad, and, of course, both the professor teaching them and his students. When not angry at the latter, they pitied them for preferring the works of Abu Tammam and al-Mubarrad to those of al-Bannan and al-Sabban. Azharites may recall the Sheikh Muhammad Abduh endured much vilification in the early years of this century because, after great effort, he succeeded in introducing the modern sciences and [Arabic] literature into al-Azhar. It astounded the people who were accustomed to regard literature as a religious heresy and to accuse those who study it of wickedness and apostasy.

Members of the literature course still joke about a letter sent by a very important sheikh to the governor of Cairo who did not understand it at all. He then referred it to the rectory of al-Azhar. The sheikh was summoned and asked to explain. He obliged with a paraphrase in the colloquial, while someone rewrote it in the official style and sent it back to the governor. Afterwards the professor used to boast in class of his incomprehensible, complicated style. When we insist upon students applying themselves to the minutiae of grammar, we practically force them to become like that distinguished Azhar professor, i.e., incapable of writing intelligibly.

I had an opportunity this year to read portions of the examination papers written by students of the special section of the secondary diploma. I was amazed and no little angered by the harm that the study of grammar and rhetoric had done to their capacity for lucid expression. They had obviously memorized entire sentences which the teacher himself had not understood when he uttered them, nor we when we read them. We can best overcome this danger by treating grammar and rhetoric as branches of literature rather than as independent subjects.

We must now give some thought to literature proper and the necessary textbooks. Under our old educational system secondary school pupils were required to begin the study of literature with the pre-Islamic writings and such ancient books as the "Kalilah wa Dimna" and the "Kitab Adab al-Dunya wa al-Din" which they recalled with indignation after they were graduated from school. The pre-Islamic writings are exceedingly remote from everyday life and not everyone likes the "Kalilah wa Dimna" or the "Kitab Adab al-Dunya wa al-Din."

During the regime of Nagib al-Hilali Pasha as Minister of Education some changes were instituted. The study of literature was initiated with the modern period and youths were spared the strain of having to listen to lectures on al-Nabigha, Zuhayr, al-A'sha, and Imru' al-Qays. Also, the reading material was somewhat diversified and a committee appointed to prepare texts in harmony with our times.

We are unfortunately still very far from realizing the purpose for which literature is studied in school. Literature is perhaps the most important element of general education because it disciplines the mind, stirs the heart and refines the taste, whereas other subjects only affect the mind. Ancient Arabic literature, despite its idealism, beauty, and profundity, is much too limited to be regarded as the sole means of achieving these aims; for it did not touch on all the phases of ancient life, not to mention modern conditions, which it naturally could not have foreseen. As a matter of fact, even our contemporary writings are incomplete in many respects.

School students must become acquainted with their own alien literature through the medium of Arabic, which is necessarily closer and more meaningful to them than any other language. It behooves us, therefore, to do everything in our power to make the youth love their language and realize that it is just as important and as flexible as any other.

Progressive nations like France do not require general school graduates to study all the languages of the Greeks, Romans, English, Germans, Italians, and Spaniards, but they are expected to become very familiar with the most important authors in translation before their formal education is terminated. It is as important for our boys and girls to study the various modern and ancient foreign literatures as it is for them to perfect their Arabic. Simple and attractive translations of desirable texts that are not available at present should be commissioned by the Ministry of Education. Otherwise, Egyptian students will continue to be inferior to their counterparts in Europe, shallow and superficial, incapable of discussing anything more profound than their schools affairs, and not always intelligently at that. It is useless to ask the holder of an Egyptian secondary school diploma about Homer, Pindar, Horace, Virgil, Dante, Cervantes, or Victor Hugo (Shakespeare, of course, is well known). However, his foreign counterpart can discuss keenly these literary figures as well as innumerable orators, philosophers, and historians.

I well remember my experiences in France where I went in order to complete my studies. Although I already had a doctorate from the Ancient Egyptian University, I found it necessary to review almost every secondary subject and even to read some very elementary books if I were to derive any benefit from attending the Sorbonne. [. . .]

Conclusion

From War to Hope

Turmoil in the past one hundred years of Middle Eastern history has driven a good number of Levantine authors to take refuge from their vexations and seek both outlet and solace in a peculiar bent of intellectual expression and cultural production. Literature, especially, offered both safe haven and transcendence of the Middle East's grim realities. The evocative texts explored in this volume—which, it ought to be repeated, remain a drop in the vast ocean of modern Levantine cultural production—reveal charming facets of the Eastern Mediterranean in its natural settings and its spiritual and intellectual dimensions; a Levant at once extoled and condemned by both its offspring and its gods; a Levant brimming with histories and rituals and civilizations that are at the same time exhilarating and exasperating, somber and cheerful, grim and hopeful.

Indeed, despite the gloom that their region and its problems might have otherwise inspired, the Syrians, Egyptians, Palestinians, Lebanese, and Israelis examined in this volume still managed to evince a buoyant optimistic disposition; the temperament of a diverse, multiform, polyglot blend of cultures and contrasted conceptions of identity, at peace with complexity, and exalting hybridity, fluidity, heterogeneity, and a repudiation of orthodoxy.

It was natural for some of the works probed here to have stemmed from a literature of exile, written by expatriates, refugees, vagabonds, and bohemians, who were often mavericks to their times and space and place, who did not always write what might have been expected of them, and who often used languages other than those corresponding to their presumptive identities. Yet even among the dispossessed Palestinians for instance, the works under consideration were hardly those of lachrymose lamentations and nostalgia, evincing no jeremiads over loss of homeland, no indictments of God and the heavens for inequities and betrayals. Rather, the exilic literature of this anthology revealed itself to constitute a rejection of roots and tearful attachments to unattainable pasts, proving to be forward-looking contemplations of better days at hand. Likewise the Israeli and Jewish samples of this volume may hardly fit the assumptions and predilections of those expecting a literature of strife and contest and rejection of the other's otherness.

More importantly perhaps, this is an anthology celebrating diversity in language, in attitudes, in ethnic and cultural belonging, and in historical perspective. In sum, the Levantine authors of this volume provide a critique of narrow resentful nationalisms, proposing instead a "Levantine hybridity" as a spacious parameter of selfhood; a "Levantine cultural space" as a legitimate historical, geographic, and cultural setting for identities that are dynamic, shifting, changing, never smug, resentful, or static: "an area, a dialogue, and a quest" in Philip Mansel's apt description.[1]

In that regard, francophone Lebanese novelist Amin Maalouf— who was a nomad in this work, traveling through the text with no chapter of his own, but who still provided bearings and inspiration for others throughout, intruding on their topics—described his little piece of the Levant as a conjugation between mountains and seas; rootedness and tradition and endurance and constancy, but fluidity and mutation and movement as well. Lebanon, which was used as a template for the Levant of Maalouf's literary creation (though Lebanon itself is seldom mentioned by name), was a jumble of cultures and languages and ethnoreligious groups. In this happy disorder, writes Maalouf in his 2012 novel *Les Désorientés,* "we belonged to multiple poles of attraction," and it had become almost a national duty of ours "to make light of ourselves and each of our respective communal identities, before gently mocking the ethnic communities of our counterparts."[2] Lebanon's diversity was the blueprint of humanity's future," wistfully affirmed Maalouf, "but alas this future was doomed to remaining a blueprint," trampled underfoot by resentful nationalisms.[3] Wars came and went and crushed in their wake Lebanon's ecumenism. It was "the end of the world," in Maalouf's telling; the end of a civilization; "our civilization," as he put it, "the Levantine civilization," which is "an expression that brings a scornful smile to the lips of the ignorant, making the partisans of triumphalist barbarity cringe; those children of arrogant tribes who make battle in the name of the One and Only God, and who know no worse enemy than our subtle, fluid identities."[4]

Levantines of Maalouf's generation proudly upheld these noble ideals of diversity and urbane multiculturalism; they proclaimed themselves the enlightened children of Voltaire, Camus, Sartre, and Nietzsche, disciples of surrealism and liberalism and Enlightenment; yet "they quickly faded back into the primordial Christian, Muslim, and Jewish molds" of old when trouble came knocking.[5]

Although written in the form of a novel, Maalouf's *Les Désorientés* was the real history and story of the Levant, its protagonists more archetypal than imaginary, drawn from dreams, regrets, aspirations, and remembrances of real lives and events; a Levantine mosaic, as it were, at once the expression of rootedness and attachment to the ancestral soil, and the longing for exile; "a sanctuary and a passageway," in Maalouf's telling,

a land of milk and honey, and blood and tears as well; neither Heaven nor Hell, but rather, Purgatory. . . . Many events had come to pass; [my] village had witnessed so many upheavals, so many destructions, so many bruisings, until one day I resolved to surrender to exile. I whispered my regrets to all the ancestors and [set out to leave]. At my back, the mountain stood near. At my feet lay the valley. . . . And over there, in the distance, I could see the sea; my cramped little plot of sea, narrow and distant, ever moving forward, ever rising toward the horizon, ever changing, like a never-ending road.[6]

In the end, there may be no "happy returns," no "Odyssey-like" homecomings, only roads and movement and peregrinations and exile; a humanist dynamism, as it were, celebrating fluidity and versatility and identity in motion. The future of the Levant is made up of nostalgia, writes Maalouf in *Les Échelles du Levant*, "nostalgia for a bygone era where men of all origins confused lived side by side on their Levantine ports of call, and blended all their languages together. Would this be a reminiscence of times past? Or is it a foretelling of the future? And what about those who persist in their attachment to this dream? Are they backward-looking reactionaries? Or are they visionaries?"[7]

Maalouf's narrator is unable to provide an answer. Yet he affirms that the children of the Levant still dreamed those audacious dreams, and were indeed still justified in doing so, in spite of current realities suggesting otherwise; that the capacious "humanism" and "universalism" of the Levant still made room for "Turk and Armenian to be brothers," and may indeed have room to spare for Arab and Jew, Christian and Muslim, arabophone and polyglot, to still mingle and mix and coexist.

Readers may wish to decide for themselves whether the preceding is truly humanism, or simply nihilism. But readers may also have noticed that the imagery of roads and seas and mountains in this volume— suggesting perpetuity, rootedness, *and* everlasting movement—are of paramount importance to anyone who is emotionally and intellectually invested in the Levantine Mediterranean culture of Egyptians, Palestinians, Israelis, Lebanese, and Syrians; a first offering of what remains an expansive (and largely unexplored) literary and cultural ocean. But an offering that challenges traditional assumptions about a Middle East still largely deemed uniform, homogenous, immutable—even exclusively Muslim, or Arab—when its historical and modern realities tend elsewhere.

It is hoped that this volume has offered a glimpse into *another* Middle East, largely suppressed but still bustling with life under the ashes of orthodoxy and the remains of shattered nations, pining to be rediscovered, restituted. Amin Maalouf dreamed and wrote about this world; a world, in his words, inhabited by courteous, generous men, *always* impeccably groomed; *always* sharply attired; *always* meeting others with reverence; *always* greeting women with ceremony and deference; *always* looking askance and with utmost disdain at all that is discrimination based on difference of race, language, creed, and opinion; *always* taking stock of the world with the passion, the wonderment, and the innocence of children.[8] And to Albert Hourani's malignant description of the Levantine as shiftless, sketchy, disoriented, Maalouf saw the Levantine as "authentic," "human," and "humanistic"; the child of multiple civilizations and successive occupations, "an Armenian and a Turk who can still hold hands in the midst of massacres," who can still—by their deeds and by their lives, not their words—say "no" to hatred and monocultural jingoist resentments.[9]

Perhaps an iconic scene of Maalouf's—already recalled elsewhere in this volume—is worth being summoned once more in the guise of a "conclusion" that may also be a prelude to another "beginning." A hundred years after its birth, the post-Ottoman, Arab-defined Middle East may be dying again an inglorious death; in its wreckage "new runt countries" are emerging; old-new nations as it were, with some beseeching their gods to silence the prayers of others.[10]

Columns of refugees, meandering around the world, are changing countries; it may be the hour of death! Yet there are also new souls being born, forlorn, yet alive, along new, foreign roadsides; it may be the hour of new beginnings.[11]

Notes

PROLEGOMENA

1. Albert Hourani, *Syria and Lebanon: A Political Essay* (London: Oxford University Press, 1946), 70–71.

2. Michel Chiha, *Le Liban d'aujourd'hui* (1942; repr., Beirut: Éditions du trident, 1961), 49–52.

3. Philip Mansel, *Levant: Splendour and Catastrophe on the Mediterranean* (New Haven: Yale University Press, 2012), 1.

4. Amin Maalouf, *Léon l'Africain* (Paris: Livres de poche, 1987), 2.

5. Amin Maalouf, *Origines* (Paris: Éditions Grasset, 2004), 7.

6. Labib Zuwiya Yamak, *The Syrian Social Nationalist Party: An Ideological Analysis* (Cambridge, MA: Center for Middle Eastern Studies, Harvard University, 1966), 83

7. Yamak, *Syrian Social Nationalist Party*, 80.

8. Yamak, *Syrian Social Nationalist Party*, 89.

9. Yamak, *Syrian Social Nationalist Party*, 89.

10. Adonis, *Al-kitaab, al-khitaab, al-hijaab* (Book, Discourse, Hijab) (Beirut: Dar al-aadaab, 2009), 65–66.

11. See for instance Reza Aslan's recent *Tablet and Pen: Literary Landscapes from the Modern Middle East* (New York: Words without Borders, 2011). An ambitious, much-needed encyclopedic compendium, Aslan's work was ultimately disappointing; a compilation without context or framework, at best cataloging modern Middle Eastern literature with not much knowledge of the themes or periods of the authors and works under consideration. For an anthology billed as "Literary Landscapes from the Modern Middle East," from Turkey to Afghanistan, *Tablet and Pen*'s scenery was puckered with omissions rendering it closer to a moonscape than a true landscape. Israeli and Jewish authors were curiously absent from a collection, which also remained silent on such

giants of modern Middle Eastern literature as Constantine Cavafy, Taha Husayn, and Nizar Qabbani. Moreover, its introduction of the work of Adonis, an author currently reflecting on questions beyond the jingoisms and precariousness of modern Middle Eastern identities, remained cursory at best. Oddly enough, the final poem in Aslan's compilation, Behnam's exquisite *Hanging from the Trees of Babylon*, indicts the monism of reductive identities, and celebrates diversity, hybridity, and the linguistic humanism that has defined the Middle East for millennia. "Ask me about the future," pleads Behnam, and, "I'll reply in Babylonian" was his majestic answer. Remarkably enough, Aslan provides no context and no explanation to this intriguing reply, which if anything, reads like a celebration of the Middle East's diversity and a validation of both its linguistic and cultural humanism.

12. Fouad Ajami, *The Arab Predicament: Arab Political Thought and Practice since 1967* (Cambridge: Cambridge University Press, 1992), xv.

13. Fawaz Turki, *Exile's Return: The Making of a Palestinian-American* (New York: Free Press, 1994), 8.

14. Turki, *Exile's Return*, 267.

15. Turki, *Exile's Return*, 272–73.

16. Turki, *Exile's Return*, 2.

17. Turki, *Exile's Return*, 4–8.

18. Turki, *Exile's Return*, 273.

19. Samir el-Youssef, *The Illusion of Return* (London: Halban Publishers, 2007), 12 and 152.

20. El-Youssef, *Illusion of Return*, 57–58.

21. Adonis, *Ra's ul-lugha, jism us-sahraa'* (The Language's Head, the Desert's Body) (Beirut: Saqi Books, 2008), 15.

22. Adonis, *Language's Head*, 15.

23. Adonis, *Language's Head*, 15.

24. Adonis, *Language's Head*, 15.

25. Adonis, *Language's Head*, 15.

26. Turki, *Exile's Return*, 4 and 273.

27. Amin Maalouf, *Le Rocher de Tanios* (Paris: Éditions Grasset, 1993), 276–77.

28. Fernand Braudel, *Memory and the Mediterranean* (New York: Alfred A. Knopf, 2001), 4–5.

29. Anthony Smith, *Myths and Memories of the Nation* (Oxford: Oxford University Press, 1999), 64.

30. See Amin Maalouf, *Discours de reception et réponse de M. Jean-Christophe Rufin: Réception de M. Amin Maalouf* (Paris: Académie française, June 14, 2012), www.academie-francaise.fr/discours-de-reception-et-reponse-de-m-jean-christophe-rufin (accessed July 4, 2014).

31. Maalouf, *Discours de reception*.

32. Rabih Alameddine, *The Hakawati* (New York: Alfred A. Knopf, 2008), 511–13.

33. Amin Maalouf, *Les Désorientés* (Paris: Éditions Grasset, 2012), 484–85.

34. Maalouf, *Les Désorientés*, 55.

35. Maalouf, *Les Désorientés,* 59.

36. Maalouf, *Les Désorientés,* 378.

37. Maalouf, *Les Désorientés,* 378.

38. Samir el-Youssef, "Levant: Zone of Culture or Conflict?" *Levantine Review* 1, no. 2 (Fall 2012): 203–4.

39. T. E. Lawrence, *Seven Pillars of Wisdom* (New York: Anchor Books, 1991), 33.

40. Efraim Karsh, *Islamic Imperialism: A History* (New Haven: Yale University Press, 2006), 7.

41. Karsh, *Islamic Imperialism,* 128.

42. Wheeler Thackston, *The Vernacular Arabic of the Lebanon* (Cambridge, MA: Department of Near Eastern Languages and Civilizations, Harvard University, 2003), vii.

43. Samar Farah, "So You'd Like to Learn Arabic. Got a Decade or So?" *Christian Science Monitor,* January 17, 2002.

44. Israel Gershoni and James Jankowski, *Egypt, Islam, and the Arabs: The Search for Egyptian Nationalism, 1900–1930* (New York: Oxford University Press, 1986), 220.

45. Bernard Lewis, *The Multiple Identities of the Middle East* (New York: Schocken Books, 1989), 53.

46. Isabel Burton, *The Inner Life of Syria, Palestine, and the Holy Land,* 2 vols. (London: Henry S. King, 1875), 1: 105–6

47. Gertrude Lowthian Bell, *Syria: The Desert and the Sown* (London: William Heinemann, 1919), 228.

48. Khairallah Khairallah, "La Syrie," *Revue du Monde Musulman* 19 (1912): 16.

49. Lawrence, *Seven Pillars of Wisdom,* 333–34.

50. Lawrence, *Seven Pillars of Wisdom,* 336.

51. Lawrence, *Seven Pillars of Wisdom,* 336.

52. Lawrence, *Seven Pillars of Wisdom,* 336.

53. Lawrence, *Seven Pillars of Wisdom,* 336.

54. Bassam Tibi, *Arab Nationalism: Between Islam and the Nation-State* (New York: St. Martin's Press, 1997), 187.

55. Tibi, *Arab Nationalism,* 189.

56. Adeed Dawisha, *Arab Nationalism in the Twentieth Century: From Triumph to Despair* (Princeton, NJ: Princeton University Press, 2003), 8.

INTRODUCTION

1. Cyrus Gordon, *The Bible and the Ancient Near East* (New York: W. W. Norton, 1997), 17–19.

2. Charles Corm, *La Montagne inspirée* (Beirut: Éditions de la Revue Phénicienne, 1987), 102.

3. Corm, *La Montagne,*102.

4. Corm, *La Montagne,* 106.

5. Maurice Dunand, *Byblia Grammata: Documents et recherches sur le développement de l'écriture en Phénicie* (Beirut: Imprimerie catholique, 1945), 6–8.

6. Humphrey T. Davies, s.v. "Ethnicity and Language," *Encyclopedia of Arabic Language and Linguistics* online edition, ed. Lutz Edzard and Rudolf de Jong, www.paulyonline.brill.nl/entries/encyclopedia-of-arabic-language-and-linguistics/ethni city-and-language-EALL_SIM_vol2_0005 (accessed January 18, 2017).

7. Selim Abou, *Le Bilinguisme arabe-français au Liban* (Paris: Presses universitaires de France, 1962), 157–58.

8. Abou, *Le Bilinguisme,* 166.

9. Abou, *Le Bilinguisme,* 32–33; Raymond Weill, *La Phénicie et l'Asie occidentale* (Paris: Librairie Armand Colin, 1939), 7–8.

10. Abou, *Le Bilinguisme,* 33; Étienne de Vaumas, "La Répartition de la population au Liban: Introduction à la géographie humaine de la République libanaise," *Bulletin de la Société de Géographie d'Egypte* 26 (August 1953): 29.

11. Henri Lammens, *La Syrie: Précis historique,* 3rd ed. (Beirut: Éditions Lahad Khater, 1994), 10.

12. Abou, *Le Bilinguisme,* 170.

13. Omar Farrukh, *Al-qawmiyya al-fusha* (Modern Standard Arabic Nationalism), Beirut: Dar al-'ilm lil-Malaayeen, 1961), 161.

14. Farrukh, *Modern Standard Arabic Nationalism,* 162.

15. Adonis, "Open Letter to President Bashar al-Assad: Man, His Basic Rights and Freedoms, or the Abyss," *As-Safir,* Beirut, June 14, 2011.

16. Adonis, *Al-kitaab, al-khitaab, al-hijaab* (Book, Discourse, Hijab) (Beirut: Dar al-aadaab, 2009), 65–66.

17. Adonis, "Open Letter."

18. Adonis, "Open Letter."

19. "The Voice of Freedom,"*Baghdad Times,* www.baghdadtimes.net/Arabic?sid =75390 (accessed June 6, 2011).

20. Abu Khaldun Sati Al-Husri, *Abhaath mukhtaara fi-l-qawmiyya al-'arabiyya* (Selected Works in Arab Nationalism) (Beirut: Markaz dirasaat al-wihda al-'arabiyya, 1985), 80.

21. Al-Husri, *Selected Works,* 80.

22. William Cleveland, *The Making of an Arab Nationalist: Ottomanism and Arabism in the Life and Thought of Sati-al-Husri* (Princeton, NJ: Princeton University Press, 1972), 127.

23. Michel Aflaq, *Fi sabiil al-Baath* (For the Sake of the Baath) (Beirut: Dar at-tali'a, 1959), 40–41.

24. Aflaq, *For the Sake of the Baath,* 43 and 68. See also Olivier Carré, *Le Nationalisme arabe* (Paris: Petite bibliothèque Payot, Fayard, 1993), 52.

25. Sylvia G. Haim, *Arab Nationalism: An Anthology* (Berkeley: University of California Press, 1963), 62–64.

26. Carré, *Le Nationalisme arabe,* 52.

27. Quoted in Haim, *Arab Nationalism,* 64.

28. Quoted in Haim, *Arab Nationalism,* 174.

29. Eirlys E. Davies, s.v. "Ethnicity and Language," *Encyclopedia of Arabic Language and Linguistics,* ed. Kees Versteegh (Leiden: Brill, 2011).

30. Labib Zuwiya Yamak, *The Syrian Social Nationalist Party: An Ideological Analysis* (Cambridge, MA: Center for Middle Eastern Studies, Harvard university, 1966), 89.

31. Quoted in Yamak, *Syrian Social Nationalist Party,* 83.

32. It is also likely that "Ispir" (or "Esber") may be an Arabized form of the Greek *spiro,* short for *spyridon* (Latin *spiritus*), and the namesake of the Eastern Christian Saint Spyridon (270–348 A.D.).

33. French Foreign Ministry Archives (Archives du Ministère des affaires étrangères, Paris-Quai d'Orsay), Correspondence Politique et Commerciales, Serie "E," Levant, 1918–40, Sous-Série: Syrie, Liban, Cilicie, carton 313, dossier 27, pp. 39–40.

34. Matti Moosa, *Extremist Shiites* (Syracuse, NY: Syracuse University Press, 1988), 287–288.

35. Moosa, *Extremist Shiites,* 288.

36. Fouad Ajami, *The Dream Palace of the Arabs: A Generation's Odyssey* (New York: Vintage Books, 1999), 120.

37. As reported in a conversation with the author, by Sadiq Jalal al-Azm, Boston, May 2000.

38. Al-Azm, conversation with the author.

39. Adonis, *Identité inachevée* (Paris: Éditions du Rocher, 2004), 21.

40. Adonis, *Ras ul-lugha, jism us-sahraa'* (The Language's Head, the Desert's Body), (Beirut: Saqi Books, 2008), 26.

41. Adonis, *The Language's Head,* 102.

42. Adonis, *Book, Discourse, Hijab,* 27.

43. Adonis, *Waqt bayna r-ramaad wal ward* (A Lull between the Ashes and the Roses), (Beirut: Dar al-'awda, 1972), 11.

44. Adonis, *A Lull,* 11 and 34.

45. William Harris, *The Levant: A Fractured Mosaic* (Princeton, NJ: Markus Wiener Publishers, 2003), xi.

46. Fernand Braudel, *Memory and the Mediterranean* (New York: Alfred A. Knopf, 2001), 96.

47. Braudel, *Memory and the Mediterranean,* 106.

48. Braudel, *Memory and the Mediterranean,* 127–28.

49. Kamal Jumblat, "La Méditerranée: Berceau de culture spirituelle," in *Les Années cénacle,* ed. Michel Asmar (Beirut: Dar al-nahar, 1997), 99.

50. Quoted by Camille Abousouan, in "Présentation," *Les Cahiers de l'Est* (Beirut, Lebanon: July 1945), 3.

51. Quoted by Abousouan, in "Présentation," 3.

52. Franck Salameh, *Language, Memory, and Identity in the Middle East: The Case for Lebanon* (Lanham, MD: Lexington Books, 2010), 45.

53. Charles Corm, *6000 Ans de génie pacifique au service de l'humanité* (Beirut: Éditions de la Revue Phénicienne, 1988), 7.

54. Corm, *6000 Ans,* 170.

55. Michel Chiha, *Le Liban d'aujourd'hui* (1942; repr., Beirut: Éditions du trident, 1961), 49–52.

56. Chiha, *Le Liban,* 49–52.

57. Michel Chiha, *Visage et présence du Liban,* 2nd ed. (Beirut: Le cénacle libanais, 1984), 49.

58. Chiha, *Visage et présence,* 49–52 and 164.

59. Amin Maalouf, *Léon l'Africain* (Paris: Livres de poche, 1987), 2

60. Amin Maalouf, *Origines* (Paris: Éditions Grasset, 2004), 7.

61. Amin Maalouf, *Les Désorientés* (Paris: Éditions Grasset, 2012), 61.

62. Maalouf, *Les Désorientés,* 61–62.

63. Maalouf, *Les Désorientés,* 59.

64. Taha Husayn, *The Future of Culture in Egypt* (1938; Washington, DC: American Council of Learned Societies, 1954), 4–5.

65. Husayn, *Future of Culture in Egypt,* 86–87.

66. Ali Salem, *The Odd Man and the Sea, Beirut Daily Star,* August 17, 2004.

67. Salem, *Odd Man and the Sea.*

68. Salem, *Odd Man and the Sea.*

69. Salem, *Odd Man and the Sea.*

70. Salem, *Odd Man and the Sea.*

71. See Alexandra Nocke, *The Place of the Mediterranean in Modern Israeli Identity,* (Leiden: Brill, 2009).

72. Benjamin Tammuz, *The Orchard* (Providence, RI: Copper Beech Press, 1984), 62.

73. Deborah Starr and Sasson Somekh, eds., *Mongrels or Marvels: The Levantine Writings of Jacqueline Shohet Kahanoff* (Stanford, CA: Stanford University Press, 2011).

74. Alexandra Nocke, *The Place of the Mediterranean in Modern Israeli Identity* (Leiden: Brill, 2009), 221.

75. Starr and Somekh, *Mongrels or Marvels,* 125.

76. Starr and Somekh, *Mongrels or Marvels,* 126.

77. Starr and Somekh, *Mongrels or Marvels,* xi–xii.

78. David Green, "Levantinism Finds Its Place in Modern Israel," *Haaretz,* August 25, 2011.

79. Ammiel Alcalay, *Keys to the Garden* (San Francisco: City Lights Books, 1996), 18.

80. Braudel, *Memory and the Mediterranean,* 4–6.

81. Albert Hourani, *Syria and Lebanon: A Political Essay* (London: Oxford University Press, 1946), 70–71.

82. Hazem Saghieh, *Wadaa' al-'uruuba* (The Swansong of Arabism) (Beirut: Dar al-saqi, 1999), 9.

83. Saghieh, *Swansong,* 9–13.

84. Adonis, "Open Letter."

85. Adonis, *A Lull,* 11 (emphasis in the original).

86. Adonis, *Language's Head,* 15.

87. Adonis, *Language's Head,* 15.

88. Adonis, *Language's Head,* 15.

89. Adonis, *Language's Head,* 15.

90. Adonis, *Language's Head,* 26.

91. Adonis, *Language's Head,* 26.

92. Adonis, *Identité inachevée,* 22.

93. Adonis, *Identité inachevée,* 22–23.

94. Ahmad al-Shuraiqi, "Adunis: Al-ana al-muta'aalia wa dimaa' al-suriyyeen" (Adonis: His Transcendental Ego and the Syrian People's Blood), *Al-Jazeera,* May 11, 2011.

95. Al-Shuraiqi, "Adunis."

96. Adonis, "Open Letter."

97. Adonis, "Open Letter."

98. Adonis, "Open Letter."

99. Adonis, "Open Letter."

SYRIA

1. Jacques Tabet, *La Syrie: Historique, ethnographique, religieuse, géographique, économique, politique, et sociale* (Paris: Alphonse Lemerre, 1920), 29.

2. Tabet, *La Syrie,* 99–100.

3. Quoted in Labib Zuwiya Yamak, *The Syrian Social Nationalist Party: An Ideological Analysis* (Cambridge, MA: Center for Middle Eastern Studies, Harvard University, 1966), 89.

4. French Foreign Ministry Archives (Archives du Ministère des Affaires Étrangères, Paris-Quai d'Orsay), , Correspondence Politique et Commerciales, Serie "E," Levant, 1918–40, Syrie-Liban, vol. 700, carton 354, dossier 7.

5. Matti Moosa, *Extremist Shiites* (Syracuse, NY: Syracuse University Press, 1988), 287–88.

6. Isabel Burton, *The Inner Life of Syria, Palestine, and the Holy Land,* 2 vols. (London: Henry S. King, 1875), 1: 105.

7. Burton, *Inner Life,* 105–6.

8. Gertrude Lowthian Bell, *Syria: The Desert and the Sown* (London: William Heinemann, 1919), 228.

9. Khairallah Khairallah, "La Syrie," *Revue du Monde Musulman* 19 (1912): 16.

10. Fouad Ajami, *The Arab Predicament: Arab Political Thought and Practice since 1967* (Cambridge: Cambridge University Press, 1993), 34.

11. *Ya leil* and *ya 'ein,* literally meaning "O night," and "O eye," are common Arabic musical phrases that begin the musical genre known as *mawwal;* a vocal warm-up of sorts, that precedes the actual song being performed.

12. *Tawashih* (singular *Tawshih*) are a traditional Arabic musical form where music is the vehicle of classical Arabic poetry.

13. Abu Zaid al-Hilaali was an eleventh-century Arab tribal hero whose life story is fictionalized in one of the masterpieces of classical Arabic storytelling; an oral genre that recount's Abu Zaid's travels from Arabia to Tunisia, and the challenges and heroisms he encounters along the way. It is a story with ongoing new beginnings, never

an ending, keeping audiences riveted, dependent on the narrator, preoccupied by what may crop up in the next installment, following repeated daily cliff-hanger climaxes. A modern analogue of Abu Zaid al-Hilaali's adventures may be the American Soap Opera genre, or similar suspenseful televised serials. Qabbani's reference to Abu Zaid al-Hilaali here is meant not as a compliment to his accomplishments but rather a condemnation of the indolence of generations of Arabs, intoxicated by stories of past, spent heroisms, and beholden to obsolete traditions inhibiting their progress.

14. Qabbani's directness and candor are both sobering and appalling: sobering because he speaks of failings that no other Arab social critic has dared to speak of head-on before him; appalling—scandalous even, not to say seditious—because he is not given to the Arabs' traditional innuendo and discursive intimations. He tells it like it is, to use an American expression; an approach deemed abrasive and impudent in traditional Arab and Muslim social criticism. Not only does Qabbani from the outset denounce a culture and its archaic ways; he goes strait to the heart of that culture's ills, indicting its language, the very foundation of everything Arab—from Arab identity to Arab art to the very essence of Arab "being." As will become clear a bit later in this poem, Qabbani is unforgiving when it comes to the Arabs' lack of initiative, indolence, stagnation, and cultural backwardness. But what is most damning is the way in which he attributes all those ills to the flimsiness of the Arabic language itself, and its attachment to form rather than content. His poetry is more often than not about annoyance and anger with Arab society and the way in which it has rendered language an object of veneration rather than an instrument of communication; a device for flattery and veiling one's inadequacies rather than an engine of dynamism and movement.

15. The reference here is to Qabbani's personal transformation from a poet associated early on in his career with ghazal poetry—that is to say poetry dealing primarily with themes of love, often illicit or unattainable love—to a harsh social critic.

16. This is in reference to the new waves of Arab refugees from the West Bank and Gaza, on the heels of Israel's 1967 conquest of those areas, following the defeat of the armies of Jordan, Syria, and Egypt.

17. Qabbani is alluding here to the Arabs' tendency to relegate all matters of life to Allah's will; be it success, failure, life, or death, all is fated and predestined in an Arab's telling, all is Allah's will, and little or nothing can be done through human agency.

18. Qabbani's Arabic original uses the exact words of Qur'anic surat *Al-Imran* 3:110, which reads as follows, "You are the finest nation that has been raised up for Mankind. You enjoin that which is right and forbid that which is wrong; and you believe in Allah. And if the Peoples of the Book had believed as you do, it would have been better for them. Some of them may have faith, but most of them are perverted transgressors." It is interesting that Qabbani, who never hid his Arab nationalist and secularist sympathies, uses a well-known Qur'anic quote describing Muslims as "the finest nation that has been raised up for Mankind," applying it to Arabs—suggesting perhaps the overlap between Arabism and Islam, despite Arab nationalism's otherwise secularist ostentations.

19. Quraysh, Aws, and Nizar are three of the major Arabian tribes affiliated with the Prophet Muhammad, himself a member of the prominent Hashem clan of the

Quraysh tribe. The tribe of Aws had settled the town of Yathrib (later Medina) by the time the Prophet Muhammad had begun his ministry, and its members were known among the first "Ansar," or those who allied themselves with the Prophet and accepted his ministry and message.

20. Getting beaten is already humiliating, in any social context. Getting beaten with a shoe, in Arab society, piles up insult and disgrace upon an already demeaning act. A shoe is a filthy object in Arab society, and although getting beaten may be a degrading act, getting beaten by hand may retain for the assaulted some semblance of dignity. Getting beaten with a shoe, on the other hand, denudes the victim of all dignity—with the pinnacle of indignity being making someone "eat their shoe" after getting flogged with it.

21. This poem is a double-edged sword indicting not only the Arabs' lack of initiative, but also lamenting their loss of language and, indeed, the banality of the Arabic language. This certainly speaks of Qabbani's despair at the Arabs after the 1967 defeat. But it also indicts the lack of initiative, the indolence, the stagnation, and the cultural backwardness that many of Qabbani's contemporaries sought to castigate—albeit none with his honesty and clarity.

22. As a former Arab nationalist lamenting the failures of an ideology that many of its children had much staked upon it, Nizar Qabbani, even when scorning it, could not help recalling some of its most recognizable slogans and symbols: "From the Gulf to the Ocean" is one of the jingles popularized by the Baath pan-Arab nationalist party, which envisioned Arab unity in a projected Arab state extending from the Persian Gulf (which the Baath refers to as the "Arabian Gulf") to the Atlantic Ocean. That unity, of course, was never to be. Hence Qabbani's earlier lament that "had we not buried 'unity' in the sand," things might have turned out otherwise.

23. The moon is a very powerful symbol of Islam and of Muslim piety. This is so perhaps primarily because Muslims adhere to a lunar calendar, and their orthopraxy and holidays are all completely reliant on lunar cycles. Shattering the moon in the context of Arab or Muslim culture can certainly be taken as an affront to religious traditions and religion itself, and this might have indeed been Qabbani's intent.

24. "Subject and Predicate" refers to one of the foundational grammatical structures in "classical" Arabic syntax. As mentioned in the introduction to Qabbani, his poetry sought to avoid the semantic "escapisms" of his contemporaries—the infatuation with language at the expense of content. Whereas poets of his generation tended toward literary euphemisms and opaque circumlocutions, Qabbani's work flowed with devastating clarity; a fluid, simple, pellucid language almost bordering on the dialectal, free from grammatical exigencies. His quip against the "Subject and Predicate" in this segment can be deemed an assault on Arabic grammar itself, the obsession of all Arabic writers of note, and a tradition that he sought to undermine and dismantle.

25. Quraysh is one of the major Arabian tribes of the Prophet Muhammad's era; an illustrious dynasty to which the Prophet himself belonged before receiving his revelations and beginning his ministry. Ironically, it was this same tribe that was the Prophet's chief opponent for most of his life—although it did also produce some of his staunchest allies.

26. Kulayb, from a diminutive of *kalb* (Ar. "dog"), is a notable pre-Islamic Arabian tribe, famous for its poets.

27. Mudar is also another illustrious pre-Islamic tribe of noble Arabian lineage. Bidding farewell to these illustrious tribes was Qabbani's way of dissociating himself from their modern descendants, the leaders and avatars of today's Arab world, and what he referred to as their dilapidated culture, archaic language, and outmoded value systems; in essence, modern Arabs—upstarts as it were—unworthy of their venerable premodern progenitors.

28. This segment recalls Qabbani's feminist engagements and his role as a pungent critic of Arab misogyny and the Arabs' hypervirile mentality. As mentioned earlier, although his post-1967 work would turn into an "anti-Arab" (or anti–Arab nationalist) vitriol indicting the causes of the Arabs' defeat in the 1967 Arab-Israeli war, Qabbani remained true to his feminist beginnings, and maintained his unrelenting assaults on patriarchy, even when his main themes did not explicitly lend themselves to feminist topics.

29. The biblical imagery in this stanza is taken straight from the Qur'anic tradition; the tone almost poking fun at the notion of a Garden of Eden as reward for life lived righteously, in austerity, perhaps even chastity in a Muslim context.

30. Ariha is the Arabic name of a town in central (present-day) Syria, north of the city of Idleb. It is the administrative center of the Province of Idleb, and is believed to have been founded in the third millennium B.C., at the site of the ancient city of Ebla. It is the site of many ancient *tels* (archaeological mounds) and more recent historical monuments dating back to Roman, Mamluk, and Ottoman eras. The town is one of the major commercial and agricultural centers in the vicinity of the northern city of Aleppo, and is famous for its olives and olive byproducts (soaps, olive oil, etc.).

31. Furat is the Arabic name of the River Euphrates. Qabbani is clearly lamenting the etiolation of culture and the Arabs' disorientation by mentioning these two centers of ancient civilization and their apparent desolation under the rule of Arabs and Arab nationalists.

32. Panegyric poetry is one of the chief and most admired genres of classical Arabic literature. Its aim was to extol the virtues of tribe elders, sheikhs, caliphs, and other men of power and influence, often in overwrought hyperbolic language, usually earning the poet enough riches to keep him in the service of the extoled master. Qabbani's criticism here is directed at poets of his generation—as at those of past generations—who composed poetry for their own fame and fortune, and not for literary or social value. A modern analog that comes to mind is that of a "hack writer."

33. The reference here is clearly to Arab rulers spawned beginning in the 1950s by so-called revolutions, led in the main by a collection of colonels and petty officers, some of whom—Gaddafi, Mubarak, and Assad—have survived into the early decades of the twenty-first century.

34. Again, this is another assault on what Qabbani deemed the Arabs "indolence and defeatism," driven by superstition and predestination, "Allah's will" as he called it—a common "amulet" and verbal talisman of sorts, recited by most arabophones

when faced with challenging circumstances. Instead of resigning themselves to "Allah's will," Qabbani's work was an attempt at awakening dynamism and free will and human agency among his readers.

35. This is one of the last poems of Qabbani's; his "swansong" as it were, the despairing *cri de coeur* of a broken despondent man; a willing prisoner of a culture and a language that he clearly loved and revered, like any Arab and Arab nationalist worth his salt. But this was also an indictment of a culture and a language that have failed their children and votaries, many times over. Qabbani labored feverishly to mend and bandage his broken society, but it was all in vain. And even as he raged against his people's failures and their language's inadequacy, and even as he set ablaze his verses, his old books, his clothes, and all that connected him to the Arabs, and even as he begged to be let go from the stifling embrace of the Arabic language, its literature, and its sounds, Qabbani remained tethered to all these facets of Arabic culture. This poem was his last remaining attempt to be set free.

36. A pre-Islamic Arabian knight-poet famous for his eloquence in poetry and fearlessness in battle; Amru Bnu Kulthum's *Qasiida* (Ode) is considered one of the masterpieces of pre-Islamic Arabic poetry, one of the celebrated *Mu'allaqaat* (Hanging Poems). A tenth-century tradition claims that the *Mu'allaqaat* were written down in golden-embossed ink, on scrolls of linen, and hung on the walls of the Ka'ba in Mecca.

37. A seventh-century Arabian poet, al-Farazdaq is best known as the panegyrist of the Umayyad Caliph al-Walid. A central Arab cultural figure and a noteworthy poet of early Islam, his being disowned early on in the poem speaks to Nizar Qabbani's despair, surrendering some of the most prominent symbols of Arab culture and history.

38. Qabbani is referring here to the Arabs' infatuation with vainglorious history, with past accomplishment, and with resting on the laurels of the past while living a present of destitution, stagnation, incoherence, and irrelevance. In subsequent verses, he indicts the Arabs for attributing their present failures to fate, all the while carrying on with their bombast about a past that no longer obtains.

39. Here Qabbani refers to a specific poem by pre-Islamic (Jahiliyya) Arabian poet Umru' al-Qays, titled *Qifaa nabki* (Halt, Both of You, and Let Us Weep). The poem is in classical Jahiliyya verse and is part of the *Mu'allaqaat* anthology, a peer of Amru Bnu Kulthum's *Qasiida* which Qabbani mentioned earlier. The *Qifaa nabki* uses a dual form of the Arabic imperative verb "to stop," addressing two companions, requesting, in the first hemistich of the first verse, that they "stop" alongside him and "weep over the remains of a beloved's abandoned campsite." This exhortation would become a standard trope of classical Arabic poetry, sometimes used even by modern poets who had no desert campsites to weep over—and often no deserts at all—but who still made allowance for such imageries as tribute and proof of attachment to the ways of the forefathers. Qabbani certainly had no patience for such histrionics and orthodoxies; hence his claim that he had tried to "uproot" the Arabs "from the sludge of history" and from the curse of "tedious" *Qifaa nabki*. For more on classical Arabic poetry and its importance and influence even in the corpus of modern Arabic literature, see the selection by Kahlil Gibran in the Lebanon chapter.

40. Adonis, *Identité inachevée* (Paris: Éditions du Rocher, 2004), 21.

41. Archives of the French Ministry of Foreign Affairs, Sous-Série Syrie-Liban, volume 266, carton 413, dossier 2. In a May 12, 1923, telegram from the Alawite government addressed to the French minister of foreign affairs, the Alawites expressed dismay upon hearing talk by the French Mandatory Powers about instating a possible federative union between the Alawite state and the states of Damascus and Aleppo. Such a union, argued the Alawites, would spell the end of Alawite freedom and autonomy. They saw Lebanon as a "citadel" and a testament to the French commitment to minority rights in the Levant; the Alawite state was a moral, geographical, and political extension of that "citadel." Attaching the Alawite state to a Syrian federation would sap the "citadel" of its meaning as a stronghold for freedom.

42. Fouad Ajami, *The Dream Palace of the Arabs: A Generation's Odyssey* (New York: Vintage Books, 1999), 120.

43. Ajami, *Dream Palace*, 120.

44. Spengler, "Are the Arabs Already Extinct?" *Asia Times*, May 8, 2007.

45. Adonis, *Waqt bayna r-ramaad wal ward* (A Lull between Ashes and Roses) (Beirut: Dar al-'awda, 1972),12 and 33; emphasis in original.

46. The Greek name Adonis has Semitic etymology. It is a Hellenized form of the Canaanite *adoni* (my Lord, Aramaic *adonai*). In this sense, in addition to being the name of a god, "Adonis" is indeed a theophoric name to the same extent that "Dorothy" (the bequest of God), "Abdallah" (the worshiper of God), and "Michael" (who is like God/El) are theophoric names.

47. Adonis, *Identité inachevée*.

48. Adonis, *The Blood of Adonis* (Pittsburgh: University of Pittsburgh Press, 1971), 54.

49. Adonis *Blood of Adonis*, 54.

50. Related by Sadek al-Azm in May 2000.

51. Albert Hourani, *Arabic Thought in the Liberal Age, 1789–1939.* (Cambridge: Cambridge University Press, 1997), 148.

52. Kemal Karpat, *Political and Social Thought in the Contemporary Middle East.* (Westport, CT: Frederick A. Praeger Publishers, 1968), 87. See also Hourani, *Arabic Thought*, 275–76.

53. Yamak, *Syrian Nationalist Party*, 80.

54. Ernest Renan, *Oeuvres complètes de Ernest Renan* (Paris: Calmann-Lévy, 1958), 304–10.

55. Karpat, *Political and Social Thought*, 95. *Kitaab al-ta'aaliim al-Suuriyya al-ijtimaa'iyya* is the title of Saadé's work in the original.

56. Yamak, *Syrian Nationalist Party*, 79.

57. Yamak, *Syrian Nationalist Party*, 79–90.

58. Yamak, *Syrian Nationalist Party*, 89.

59. Khalida Said, *Mawaaqif*, February 1970, in Roger Allen's *Modern Arabic Literature* (New York: Ungar Publishing, 1987), 36–37.

60. Adonis, *A Lull*, 39.

61. Some English translations of Adonis's *This Is My Name,* render the Arabic *Aaya* into a "sign" or a "miracle," even though Adonis's frontal assault on the Arabs' religious, social, and national orthodoxies is blatant throughout his work, and the use of *Aaya* in reference to a "Qur'anic Verse" would have been a more obvious choice in *This Is My Name*—especially in view of the poem's repeated reliance on biblical and Christian symbolisms and imagery. A reference to Muslim symbols would not have been out of the ordinary.

62. Adonis, *Identité inachevée,* 20–21.

63. Adonis, *Identité inachevée,* 21.

64. Adonis, *Identité inachevée,* 61–62.

65. Adonis, *Identité inachevée,* 61–62.

66. Adonis, *Identité inachevée,* 61–62.

67. Ajami, *Dream Palace,* 118–19.

68. Ajami, *Dream Palace,* 120–21.

69. Michel Chiha, *Le Liban d'aujourd'hui* (1942; repr., Beirut: Éditions du trident, 1961), 49–52.

70. Yamak, *Syrian Nationalist Party,* 89.

71. Charles Corm, *6000 Ans de génie pacifique au service de l'humanité* (Beirut: Éditions de la Revue Phénicienne, 1988), 7.

72. Adonis, *Identité inachevée,* 20–21.

73. See Khalil el-Khoury, in *Hadiqat al-Akhbar,* Beirut, December 22, 1958, 2.

74. Adonis, *Identité inachevée,* 21.

75. Adonis, "Language, Culture, and Reality," *Alif: Journal of Comparative Poetics,* no. 7, *The Third World: Literature and Consciousness* (Cairo, Spring 1987): 115; emphases and punctuation symbols in the original.

76. Adonis, "Language, Culture and Reality," 115.

77. Adonis, *A Lull,* 34.

78. Adonis, *Identité inachevée,* 61.

79. Adonis, *Identité inachevée,* 61.

80. Adonis, *Identité inachevée,* 61.

81. Adonis, *Identité inachevée,* 62.

82. Adonis, *Identité inachevée,* 13–14.

83. Adonis, *Identité inachevée,* 13–14.

84. Adonis, *Identité inachevée,* 13–14.

85. He has taught literature at the Collège de France, across the Seine from the Sorbonne, and traditionally a symbol of "antiestablishment" French higher education.

86. Adonis, interview with Dubai TV, March 11, 2007, retrieved from www.youtube.com/watch?v=H2Y2ZcfUIZU (accessed January 14, 2017).

87. Adonis, *Identité inachevée,* 14.

88. Adonis, *Identité inachevée,* 14.

89. Translation from Adonis, *Blood of Adonis,* 46–54.

90. The theme here seems to be 'Tyranny, Silence, and Exile," notions visited and revisited in most of Adonis's work, speaking of the extinction of the Arabs, predicting

a future reality which, from an early twenty-first century perspective, seems to have caught up with Adonis. Still, he seems to have predicted even that, already writing in the late 1960s that "whatever will come it will be old"; that the Arabs' destruction has already been foretold.

91. Again, this is Adonis despairing of tyranny's resilience among the Arabs, yet submitting to it. But this is also Adonis arguing that the Arabs' past, present, and future are all one in the same; old ideas, atavistic instincts and obsolete traditions in new packaging; a regurgitation of the past, as it were. Qabbani called this "donning the accoutrements of modernity but still clinging to the old." At any rate, it is frightening that the nightmarish apocalyptic imageries of this poem, invoking destruction, described Lebanon's civil war a decade before it took place, and Syria's civil war a full five decades before 2011; "whatever will come it will be old."

92. Exhorting silence out of despair, or out of fear, or out of acquiescence in the futility of opposing or indicting that which is deemed immutable in Arab society. For Adonis, by 1967—and as noted by Fouad Ajami, "through the irony of reruns by the early 1980s," as well as in today's Syria and Iraq—Arab society had depleted all of its myths, and what remained was empty bravado, rhetorical arm-flexing, and bragging about past achievements already surpassed by other societies. But in terms of what had remained concretely, the persistence of cruelty, confusion, tyranny, silence, exile, futility, and sterility are really the only concrete remnants of Arab society according to Adonis.

93. It is a fact that Adonis had not yet witnessed a civil war before writing those verses; yet his description is ominous in its accuracy and in forecasting what was to befall Lebanon and Syria many decades in the future.

94. "There is something amiss, faulty, defective, out of order in us," Adonis seems to be saying. There's an eerie feeling (in reading these first few lines of this poem) that Adonis is in a nightmarish setting, where he's sitting outside of himself, outside of his people, watching them and himself, moving as if in slow motion, as if in quicksand; moving, but not advancing; moving, but sinking deeper into the abyss, into stupor, apathy, immobility, paralysis; into a nightmare. From this perspective, Adonis captures the ambivalence of a defeated civilization in retreat: "we enter the modern world," he seems to be saying, "we fail, we retreat into our shells; we become fixated on a world (on the past, on a glorious past, on a golden age) on a world that once was, but is no more; yet we go on lamenting our loss."

95. Again, historical and religious (namely, here, Muslim) images and symbols that reflect the tragic past and present of the Middle East, being washed away, or purified, through time-honored (but perhaps futile) ritual, tradition, and cultic practice.

96. Tragic present and past have to bring some sort of soothing denouement (conclusion), a brighter future. But even the future rejects the poet; even exile and banishment rejects him. The "night weighs and weighs" like a nightmare; sucking the Arabs deeper into the abyss, crippling them with paralysis more dreadful than death itself.

97. Again, this nightmarish terrifying paralysis, which psychologists refer to as hypnagogia, in conjunction with the Arabs' stagnation and stupor, is a state which

Adonis is able to relay in frightening realism. So debilitating and distressing is the night-mare in this case, he suggests, that we are unable to scream, hard as we may try, re-flecting the state of one's body, in a hypnagogic state, stuck between awakening and slumber, where the brain is awaking, but the body is still asleep, causing one to feel as if immobilized.

98. A passageway, a doormat, a scapegoat for conquerors, invaders, and intruders who leave nothing but destruction and stagnation in their wake (as well as submissive tame vanquished and acquiescent subjects). Note that Adonis proceeds from a decidedly "universalist" Levantine tradition. And so his indictment is against *all* those who con-quered his land (Syria); *not* just modern conquerors, but Arab and pre-Arab and post-Arab conquerors as well. One must keep in mind that Adonis dismisses "race and blood and language" as the defining forces in Arab and Islamic history and as the sources of Arab identity (or any identity for that matter). Again, Adonis is a minoritarian! He can ill-afford indulging a narrow, radical definition of home, culture, and hearth. He hails from a polyglot multicultural millennial universe, and cannot be reduced and slotted into restrictive labels.

99. Again, this is the missive detailing the age-long history of Adonis's land; for-eign invaders (pharaohs) desecrating the land and ravishing its people, with the people themselves submitting to their bullies (applauding them), and acquiescing in their tragic fate.

100. No future without innovation, Adonis seems to be saying: The past (tradition) is a desert, barren, desolate, sterile; we continue to live in a cultural era which has died; we continue to face history with that which has become extraneous to history. Keep in mind what Qabbani said in that regard: "What value has the people who have no tongue?" "We are only good for verbiage and oration and rhetorical arm-flexing . . . but our language, our words, our assumptions and cultural references are hollow, irrelevant, trivial, like watermelon skins and banana peels. . . . Decayed like worn-out soles."

101. Again, that "crescent moon"; that "opium of the East" to use Qabbani's im-age, fostering indolence, resignation, reliance on Allah and religion, and acquiescence in predestination.

102. Our only call for help, naturally goes to the supernatural, to the moon, to Allah, Adonis claims. "What does the moon have for us, a bunch of idle indolent lazy tobacco chewers," asked Qabbani? But then again, it is perhaps *Maktub,* written that Arabs should continue wallowing in this sort of mediocrity; they are at the bottom of the abyss, from where the only way to go may be up. But for them, from where they are, all they smell is "ravens" instead of the hope of liberty, freedom, emancipation, better-ment, and motion. Note the significance of ravens in Near Eastern cultures is not all that different from that of Western traditions.

103. And so, they continue on the path of exile, wallowing in their anguish and pain and hesitation and agony, only to be stopped, stalled, at the gates of salvation. They stall, they cannot move forward, and they resolve to go back to the past; to business as usual.

104. In this perspective, Adonis captures the ambivalence of a defeated civilization, still clinging to its ruins, still praying for resurrection, still imploring a *Deus ex machina* for a bail out.

105. Despair from history, from the past, which itself despairs of the Arabs and rejects them.

106. There may be a touch of sarcasm in Adonis's reference to gazelles and antelopes here. The image is a familiar one in traditional (especially pre-Islamic) Arabic poetry, usually in reference to the beloved. A woman's eyes are often compared to those of a gazelle, a symbol of beauty in traditional Arabic poetry.

107. In the end, it is the Arabic language that binds and confines the Arabs to an obscure and cloistered universe wrote recently Adonis in *Book, Discourse, Hijab*. Arabic, he has claimed, is a language that restrains and incarcerates its users and turns them into wardens overseeing their own penal colonies, regurgitating Arab and Muslim pieties and rituals that no one dares challenge; "Arabic culture is the culture of that which is divinely sanctioned and *only* that which is divinely sanctioned; a culture of 'commands and taboos,' and 'dos and don'ts.'"

108. Emphasis and random punctuations and brackets in the original. This was one of the many ways in which Adonis plied his language, in both form and content, to reflect the fragmentation of Arab culture and the Arab self; textual and linguistic fragmentation emulating the social, cultural, and political fragmentation of the Arabs so to speak.

109. Adonis called this "being stalled between seasons," in his *Elegy for the Time at Hand*.

110. To the community of Muslims, or the nation of Islam.

111. In total opposition to the classic (Cartesian) conception of the self, Rimbaud professed a new conception, of both the self and artistic creation: to him, the poet no longer masters that which emanates from him. He wrote, "J'assiste à l'éclosion de ma pensée: je la regarde, je l'écoute [I am a spectator in the birth and blossoming of my mind ; I watch the process, I listen to it]."

112. Adonis, *Al-Hayat,* May 17, 2012, retrieved from www.al-maseera.com/2012/07/blog-post_21.html (January 14, 2017).

113. Could this be an indictment of religion? Could "the older the stone gets, the more youthful it becomes" be an allusion to religion; the foundations of mankind's belief systems, which, although old and transcended by science and reason, remains "youthful" and vibrant, and readily espoused and defended by uncouth superstitious humans?

114. The century of which Adonis speaks here is the century of the modern state-system in the Middle East; a century during which Arab intelligentsia and Arab leaderships promised and feigned working for the sake of freedom, liberty, prosperity, self-determination, coexistence, and peace, but harvested what became known as the "Arab Spring" in the second decade of the twenty-first century; a "spring" which Adonis in this poem deems an "autumn" and the early beginnings of an eternal twilight.

115. The "fortresses of words" could be an allusion to the bombast, sabre rattling, and rhetorical arm-flexing that Qabbani speaks about in his own work; the hol-

low words and empty promises of Arab nationalism and its avatars, who, in the end, wrought nothing but devastation, confusion, and lostness.

116. The Arabic word for "elephant" (*fil*) consists of three letters, whereas "mosquito" (*ba'uda*) consists of five. This is a recurrent issue in Adonis's work; indicting the Arabs' valorization of "quantity" and "size" over "quality" and "content."

117. Could this be in reference to Adonis's native Syria, and the new paroxysms of savagery and violence into which the Syrian civil war has slipped? If so, there is nothing new here. Adonis already foretold the carnage to come in the late 1960s, in his *Elegy for the Time at Hand,* also featured in this chapter.

118. Is this an image of grieving mothers (as Adonis often invokes in his work)? Or is it a reference to the Arabs' misogyny, which Adonis deals blow after blow in a number of his poems.

119. *Shahada* is the Islamic profession of faith and the first pillar of Islam based on Qur'an 3:18: "There is no god but Allah, and Mohammad is his Prophet."

120. Wedding Christian and Muslim symbolism in a single image is something uniquely Adonis.

121. Again, Christian (cross) and Muslim (moon) imageries in an attempt to flaunt Adonis's own syncretism, while at the same time issuing an indictment against religious dogmatism.

Lebanon

1. See for instance Daoud Pacha (1861–68), Franko Pacha (1868–73), and Ohannes Pacha (1912–15).

2. "Niyyéél elli 'indo mar'ad 'anzé bi Jabal-Libnéén," in colloquial Lebanese.

3. Kahlil Gibran, *The Prophet* (New York: Alfred A. Knopf, 1994), 9.

4. Gibran, *The Prophet,* 3.

5. Gibran, *The Prophet,* 4.

6. Gibran, *The Prophet,* 5.

7. See for instance Isaiah 23 and Ezekiel 27:12–25.

8. Gibran never uses the term *Arabs* (which might have been anachronistic) in reference to the peoples of the Middle East of his times. Instead, he adopted the more accurate and less essentialist "Easterners," which also means "Levantines"; a reflection of his own worldview, and the diverse ethnic and cultural nature of his contemporaneous Near East.

9. Note Gibran's clarity and perspicacity in this segment, speaking of "various nations" that make use of "the Arabic language," and *not* a "single Arab" nation as is often the case with Arab nationalists vaunting Arabic as the national nimbus of Arabness. As was the case with many Maronite Christians of Gibran's generation, who were active in the Arabic literary renaissance (*nahda*) movement of the late nineteenth century but who were not yet "Arab" or "Arab nationalists" and did not engage a specifically "Arab" nationalist discourse, the allusion here is to a belief that the Arabic language—and in this case Modern Standard Arabic—had strictly expressive, literary, and learned functions, not nationalistic or patriotic ones, and certainly no office as the exclusive language

of Arabs and Arab nationalists. Gibran, like many of his Lebanese contemporaries, was acutely aware of the Levant's long tradition of multilingualism, recognizing that monolingual nations like the Irish, the Scots, the Australians, and many others, *can* be native users of the English language without necessarily becoming "Englishmen." So can the users of the Arabic language throughout the Middle East be skilled engaged Arabists without becoming—and without being deemed—Arabs or Arab nationalists.

10. The author's reference here is to Syriac and Biblical Hebrew having ceased being both spoken and literary languages.

11. Gibran uses the Arabic verb *yatasha'ab* in this segment to express diversification and branching out into new topics among "Muwaladin" poets—that is to say Muslim poets whose native languages were not Arabic, but who composed Arabic poetry. The Arabic noun *Shu'ubiyya,* from the same verbal root, has a negative connotation among Arab nationalists in modern times, because it alludes to those non-Arabs making use of the Arabic language, and therefore diluting the purity of the language and the nation alike. Although it is true that Islam is an egalitarian religion, and therefore, all Muslim men, whether Arab or not, are in principle equal, there are known instances of "social snobbery"—if not outright discrimination—expressed toward those non-Arab Muslims who were considered newcomers and, therefore, upstarts vis-à-vis the language of the Arabs.

12. Here Gibran is making reference to those users of the Arabic language who transformed that medium into an object of veneration, sacrificing their writings and their creative instincts to the constraints of form and verbiage and traditional standards of grammar and style, rather than plying and bending the language to their creative needs. See for instance the Adonis and Nizar Qabbani sections for more detail on the modern iterations of this topic.

13. It is important to note the distinction that Gibran makes in his Arabic text between "nation" (*umma*) and "nations" (*umam*). He clearly does not consider the users of the Arabic language to a single nation (*umma*) and addresses them as a "collection of nations" (*majmuu' umam*).

14. Again, Gibran is attributing the future life or death of the Arabic language to the "nations" that make use of it—deeming that future the "sociological" decision of multiple societies and multiple "nations," *not* the province of a single (Arab) nation. He even likens literary (classical) Arabic to English, a language that belongs to Englishmen and non-Englishmen alike.

15. Without mentioning his source, Gibran quotes directly from the Arabic version of Matthew 12:12 in this segment. His subtle allusion is simply that much will be taken from the Arabic language until it whittles and disappears, given that it is hardly giving anymore. To use his preceding image, living "in the shade," in isolation, impervious to the outside world, only gives the illusion of living. And this illusion often crumbles when that which appeared to be living in the shadows is brought under the light of day. Gibran's conclusion in the following segment suggests that Arabic might have had its day, but that its better days remain behind it; that life and dynamism are now the province of other languages.

16. Note that Gibran does not name "Arabs" specifically as pioneers of innovation in times past, but rather speaks of "Easterners" in general, a term that also connotes "Levantines." This suggests a wider, more fluid, more capacious conception of the Middle East, spanning classical antiquity and modern times, at once preceding and succeeding Arabs as such.

17. Note that Gibran does not use an Arabic term even alluding to "Arab countries" as such, given that none existed in 1922. The Arabic term *qutur,* which Gibran uses repeatedly in reference to Arab-defined entities, means "quarter" or "region," and in the broadest connotation possible "territory" or "province," but never "country" or "state" as such.

18. The symbolism of the Book of Life is revelatory of Gibran's deep religious formation in the Syriac-Maronite Church of Mount Lebanon. Jews and Christians believe the Book of Life to be a list of names of those who will be with God, in heaven, for eternity. But the Book of Life in Arabic refers to the Bible, and clearly this is the book to which Gibran is referring here. When he notes that "darkness" or "nothingness is the first, not the last word of the Book of Life," he uses the Christian Arabic term *sadeem,* clearly in reference to the biblical chaos or "confusion" that preceded Creation.

19. The "Syria" of Gibran, in the context of 1922, was very different from the Syria of today—that is to say the modern Syrian Arab Republic. For one, in Gibran's times, and certainly in 1922, there was no distinct country or political entity referred to as Syria. This is discussed in more detail in the Syria chapter of this anthology. But to reiterate briefly, Syria as such was a term coined by Eastern Christians toward the end of the nineteenth century; a cognate of the "Syrian churches" (that is to say churches that use Syriac in their liturgy), used in reference to lands where Syriac-Christians lived, and connoting discrete conceptions of selfhood, distinct and separate from parameters of identity used by neighboring Muslims and Arabs. In a sense, *Syria-Syrians* was a term that Near Eastern Christians of Gibran's generation, both in the Near East and the diaspora, used as a cognomen specific to them and their identity, to be distinguished from strictly Muslim, Turkish, and later Arab identities. In the middle of the twentieth century, the term Syria was expropriated by Arab nationalists and it began being used interchangeably with the Arabic term *Shaam,* referring both to Damascus (the city-state of classical antiquity) and the Ottoman *vilayet* (state) by the same name. Like the Christian Syria itself, Shaam was a loose geographical concept with no concrete political or historical connotations. Initially, in southern Arabian languages, Shaam meant "North," and as such designated lands to the north of Arabia, thus giving the appellation the same political significance as, say, the "Mediterranean," or the "Balkans," or the "Alps," or, in an American context, "New England." In other words, Shaam, and later its Arabized form of "Syria" (*Suuriyya*) were vague amorphous geographical designations. Of course, as mentioned earlier, there had always been a Syria as such, from classical antiquity into Ottoman times. But this "Syria" remained at best a topographic concept, strictly confined to European—not in the least Arab—usage. Moreover, in today's Syria, more so than in Lebanon and Egypt—both of which benefited from some form of distinctly Lebanese and Egyptian political personality with some historical depth—there has never been a

uniquely Syrian territorial identity nor a Syrian entity as such until the middle of the twentieth century. Indeed, what became Syria in 1936 had previously been the Ottoman *vilayet*s of Aleppo, Beirut, and Damascus. The 1920 League of Nations Mandates assigned to France and Britain over the Eastern holdings of the collapsed Ottoman Empire gave birth to a "Levant Mandate" accorded to France, and the "Palestine Mandate" accorded to Britain. It should be stressed that the territories assigned a French Mandate (what eventually became Syria and Lebanon in 1936) were referred to in official French and League of Nations documents as the "Territories of the Levant"—*not* Syria, and *not* Lebanon. Some historians, unfortunately, gloss over this detail, oversimplifying it in favor of such anachronisms as "Lebanon and Syria Mandates"—appellations that reflect the current state system in the Middle East, *not* the one in place between 1920 and 1936. In fact, the French Foreign Ministry Archives, a stock of diplomatic correspondence and internal memos that inform much of today's historical writings on these areas, refer to the region as the "Mandate of the States of the Levant" (Mandat, États du Levant). What became Syria in 1936 had in effect been five distinct states during the Mandate period (reflecting an Ottoman administrative precedent.) Those states were the État de Damas (the State of Damascus,) the État d'Alep (the State of Aleppo,) the État Djebel Druze (the State of the Druze Mountain,) the État Djebel Ansariya or Alaouite (the State of the Alawite Mountain), and the État de Cilicie (or district of Alexandretta, later ceded to the Turkish district of Hatay in 1938). What became the Republic of Lebanon in 1926 had been another separate state under French Mandate, also reflecting an Ottoman precedent, in the form of the State of Greater Lebanon (1920). Syria as such, in the time of Gibran, was a term coined and used exclusively by Eastern Christians, toward the end of the nineteenth century, in reference to a distinct identity of those members of the premodern "Syrian" or "Syriac" national churches, whose languages were collectively known as "Syrian" (*Suryaani*, or Syriac *tout court* in Western usage). Arabs and the Arab nationalists who have ruled Syria since independence are newcomers to this name, and can only lay claim to it through semantic perversions. In conclusion, the "Syria" that Gibran speaks of in this segment of his text is the Syria that had populated the political fancy of Eastern Christians of his generation who were doubtful of Arabism's ability to divorce itself from Islam and integrate arabophone Eastern Christians as equals within "Arab" societies. Albert Hourani has argued that the name Syria, designating a geographic entity roughly resembling the modern Syrian Arab Republic began to be used only around the year 1861, and then only in the writings of Lebanese Christians, among them Gibran, intent on creating a political entity capable of resolving their *dhimmi* (second-class) status and repudiating their inferior position within the world of Islam (see for instance Hourani's *Arabic Thought in the Liberal Age*, 317).

20. Gibran is referring here to the French, American, and Russian missionary schools that dotted the landscape of Mount-Lebanon beginning in the sixteenth century. As an early advocate of a "Greater Syria" as a homeland for all Eastern Syriac Christians, Gibran was initially not in favor of a distinct Lebanese entity, nor a distinct State of Aleppo (as a largely Christian entity), or Damascus and the rest.

21. See earlier comments concerning what exactly it is that Gibran means by "Syria"; i.e., a secular entity where members of Eastern Christian national churches (like

the Maronites, the Assyrians, and the Greek Orthodox among others) would live in a "Syrian" national entity, and would no longer be subject to discriminatory *dhimmi* laws to which non-Muslims under the caliphate and the Ottoman Empire were confined. But as mentioned earlier, the secular pluralist non-Arab and non-Muslim Syria to which Gibran yearned had always been an ethnic conundrum. Isabel Burton, wife of British explorer Sir Richard Francis Burton, summed up the ethnic conundrum of her day's Ottoman *vilayet* of Damascus as "various religions and sects [living] together more or less, and [practicing] their conflicting worships in close proximity." Outwardly, noted Burton, one does not notice too many differences, but in their hearts, the inhabitants of the *vilayet* of Damascus "hate one another. The Sunnites excommunicate the Shiahs, and both hate the Druse; all detest the Ansariyyehs [Alawites]; the Maronites do not love anybody but themselves, and are duly abhorred by all; the Greek Orthodox abominate the Greek Catholics and the Latins; all despise the Jews" (*Inner Life*, 105). Writing along those same lines in 1907, another British traveler, Gertrude Bell, noted that Syria was "merely a geographical term corresponding to no national sentiment." (*Syria: The Desert and the Sown*, 228).This view was echoed by many Levantine contemporaries of Gibran, most of whom maintain that there has never been a distinct Syrian society historically speaking; that what Europeans and Near Eastern Christians refer to as Syria had always been a bevy of disparate groups and loose geographic entities brought together by conquest and ruled forcibly through terror and tyranny; in sum, "a society based on despotism and brutal force modeled on that of the ruler" (see Khairallah Kharallah, "La Syrie," in *Revue du Monde Musulman* 19 [1912]: 16). It bears repeating that only Westernized "Syrians" like Gibran—that is to say Arabic-speaking Christians and Jews from Beirut, Mount Lebanon, Aleppo, Damascus, and elsewhere in what later became "Syria" per se—who were familiar with the languages and geographical concepts of Europe, began describing the lands of their birth collectively as Syria, and began viewing themselves as Syrians—as opposed to Turks, Arabs, or Christians for that matter.

22. Gibran is clearly alluding here to the advocates of Lebanese particularism on the one hand (who were primarily graduates of Jesuit institutions in Beirut and Mount Lebanon), and proponents of Arab nationalism on the other (most of whom were products of the Beirut Syrian Protestant College, later the American University of Beirut, where the first stirrings of "Arab nationalism" were intellectualized). One may assume that the third category alluded to by Gibran, that of those with "narrow worldviews" and a "particular brand of knowledge," are those advocates of religious identities, more specifically perhaps the prevalent parameter of selfhood admitted under Muslim rule.

23. Could it be that Gibran is calling for introspection and self-criticism, rather than casting the blame for the Easterners' ills on the rapacious colonialist West?

24. See for instance Dante's *De vulgari eloquentia* (On Eloquence in the Vernacular; ca. 1302) an essay written in Latin, and in which Dante defends the eloquence of his spoken Florentine dialect, which eventually became what we refer to as the "Italian language" today. Dante's aim in the fourteenth century seems to have been the same as Gibran's in the early twentieth century; the valorization of dialectal languages, and their elevation (at least psychologically and perceptually speaking) to the level of literary languages like Latin and Arabic. Like Dante, Gibran argues that language is not

static, but rather a living organism that has birth, evolution, life, and eventually death. Without saying as much, Gibran makes the argument that "spoken dialects"—a taxonomy often oversimplified into "Arabic *vulgari*" (or *'Aamiyya/Daarija* in Arabic)—are evolved, not defective speech forms, which will eventually replace Arabic as literary mediums. Although this is a dilemma bedeviling language purists and Arab nationalists in the modern Middle East, it is a phenomenon as old as the idea of Arab nationalism, which essentially posits that anyone associated with anyone associated with the Arabic language is perforce an Arab, regardless of whether or not he deems himself an Arab. In fact, Sati' al-Husri (1880–1967), a Syrian writer and spiritual father of linguistic Arab nationalism, maintained that,

> Every person who speaks Arabic is an Arab. Every individual associated with an Arabic-speaking people is an Arab. If he does not recognize [his Arabness] . . . we must look for the reasons that have made him take this stand . . . But under no circumstances should we say: "as long as he does not wish to be an Arab, and as long as he is disdainful of his Arabness, then he is not an Arab." He is an Arab regardless of his own wishes, whether ignorant, indifferent, recalcitrant, or disloyal; he is an Arab, but an Arab without consciousness or feelings, and perhaps even without conscience.

See Abu Khaldun Sati' al-Husri, *Abhath mukhtaara fi-l-qawmiyya al-'arabiyya* (Selected Papers in Arab Nationalism) (Beirut: Markaz dirasaat al-wihda al-'arabiyya, 1985), 80.

This overarching conception of Arabness was as popular as it was despised, rejected, and debated in the early twentieth century, before and after Gibran. In 1928, Egyptian writer Tawfiq Awan was advancing ideas similar to Gibran's, suggesting that the Middle East's spoken languages were not dialects of Arabic, bur rather languages in their own right. "Egypt has an Egyptian language," wrote Awan, "Lebanon has a Lebanese language; the Hijaz has a Hijazi language; and so forth—and all of these languages are by no means Arabic languages. Each of our countries has a language, which is its own possession: So why do we not write [our language] as we converse in it? For, the language in which the people speak is the language in which they also write. See Israel Gershoni and James Jankowski, *Egypt, Islam, and the Arabs: The Search for Egyptian Nationalism, 1900–1930* (New York: Oxford University Press, 1986). 220

25. It may seem scandalous for one of the pioneers of the nineteenth century's Arabic literary renaissance (*nahda*) movement to compare one of the mediums of his own literary creation, Modern Standard Arabic, to a "mummified corpse." But many innovators, from other eras and in other languages preceded Gibran along this path. Egyptian writer Salama Musa (1887–1958), another contemporary of Gibran, wondered whether Modern Standard Arabic, the language inherited from the Jahiliyya Bedouins, is still an adequate tool of communication in the age of highways and high-speed automobiles. See *Ma hiya al-nahda?* (What Exactly Is the Nahda?) (Algiers: Mofem Publishers, 1990), 233. In a metaphor reminiscent of Musa's, an Egyptian intellectual writing in the twenty-first century compared users of Modern Standard Arabic to "ambling cameleers

from the past, contesting highways with racecar drivers hurtling towards modernity and progress." See Sherif al-Shubashy, *Li-tahya al-lugha al-'arabiyya, yasqut Sibawayh* (For Arabic to Live On, Sibawayh Must Fall) (Cairo: Egyptian Book Authority, 2004), 10–18. Even René Descartes (1596–1659), the father of Cartesian logic and French rationalism, integrated a French-Latin dualism in his work. His adversaries, Latin language purists, argued that using French as a literary and intellectual language was too divisive and too vulgar to be worthy of consideration. Yet Descartes was undaunted, defending his "vulgar" French vernacular in the introduction to his *Discours de la méthode* writing that, "if I choose to write in French, which is the language of my country, rather than in Latin, which is the language of my teachers, it is because I hope that those who rely purely on their natural and sheer sense of reason will be the better judges of my opinions than those who still swear by ancient books. And those who meld reason with learning, the only ones I incline to have as judges of my own work, will not, I should hope, be partial to Latin to the point of refusing to hear my arguments out simply because I happen to express them in the vulgar [French] language" (René Descartes, *Discours de la méthode* [Paris: Garnier-Flammarion, 1966], 95).

26. Ma'arri (973–1058), a "Syrian" philosopher, essayist and poet, and Mutanabbi (915–65), an "Iraqi" poet, were considered among the most eloquent of those who have written in Arabic.

27. Gibran is clearly taking a swipe at the keepers of orthodoxy in modern Arabic literature; wordsmiths rather than creative writers per se; people beholden to the strictures and structures of the classical language (and its Modern Standard Arabic permutation), given to the forms and outer cloaks of language, rather than substance and utility. This is a dilemma that still faces intellectuals and literati working with Arabic in the twenty-first century. Syro-Lebanese thinker Adonis for instance, writing through the second half of the twentieth century and the early decades of the twenty-first, lamented the "obsolete context" of the Arabic language's "modern" intellectual output, most of it conveyed by way of a dead and obsolete language; dead stuff transmitted by way of a dead idiom; "speculative, non-revolutionary, non-scientific" writing, "mired in polemics and out of touch with the experiences that [yield] honesty and relevance." See Ajami, *Arab Predicament,* 35.

28. See the Qabbani and Adonis selections for more on this topic.

29. This imagery is appropriated from pre-Islamic (Jahiliyya) poetry, unrelated to the time and space of modern users of the Arabic language; especially those instigators of the Arabic literary renaissance (*nahda*) of the late nineteenth century, most of whom were children of the Levant—and therefore the offspring of temperate climes and merciful topography, exposed to the conflations of a fluid Mediterranean universe, bereft of parched deserts and searing heat, and rich in lush sceneries, snow-capped mountains, and abundant water. Therefore, comparisons of the beloved to "gazelles" and "drawn arrows" and the rest, although faithful to the traditional poetry of desert bards, remained unreflective of the realities of Near Eastern and Levantine cultures shaped by histories and nourished by traditions and cultural accretions different from those of Arabs of early Islamic times. Ultimately, what Gibran was suggesting in 1922 was

that the Arabic language would indeed be salvageable and would indeed have a "future" if it were allowed to reflect its times' needs and exigencies—rather than be placed on a pedestal, to be hallowed and upheld in its arcane themes, symbolisms, and representations. See, for comparison, the Adonis segment on "gazelles" and "antelopes," and the urgency of bidding them farewell.

30. Gum Arabic.

31. More imagery pilfered from pre-Islamic, Jahiliyya poetry.

32. As mentioned earlier, premodern (that is to say pre-*nahda*) Arabic poetry was fairly limited to the themes of satire, panegyrics, and praise, and those were primarily the themes adopted by the early pioneers of *nahda;* motifs and references that were alien to the Eastern Mediterranean and its particular historical and geographic experience, but which those who sought to "revive" Arabic *belles lettres* overlooked with the aim of preserving the inheritance of Jahiliyya and post-Islam poetry. Note that just as Gibran during the early twentieth century was railing against those still beholden to the motifs and clichés of the past, so did someone like Nizar Qabbani (see the chapter on Syria) through the remainder of that century. Indeed, Qabbani lamented the dilapidated Arab culture and the Arabic language, which he referred to as the language of "abuse and depravity," and whose poetry he deemed recitations of "debauchery, defamation, and insult." Likewise, instead of oration, verbiage, rhetorical bravado, and imagery borrowed from elsewhere, Gibran called for authentic literary production, that is in accordance with its particular habitat and circumstances.

33. In the end, what was the future that Gibran foresaw for the Arabic language, and *did* he in fact foresee a bright future? Or are the themes and struggles and challenges of his day still extant in ours? Keep in mind that the proposition with which he had launched into this debate might have remained unanswered; namely that "the future of the Arabic language is wholly dependent upon the future of living—and departed— creative minds issuing from the various nations that speak this language," that "where creativity is extant, the future of the language will no doubt be as glorious as its past," and that "where creativity is extinct, the future of Arabic will come to resemble the present of its two sister languages, Syriac and Hebrew." Is Arabic ultimately like "Syriac and Hebrew," and perhaps even Latin? Is it, like its predecessors, ultimately a cultic ceremonial language that few are able to transform into a spontaneous speech form and a transparent intelligible literary medium? The United Nations' Arab Human Development reports—a series of studies written by Arabs and for the benefit of Arabs since 2002—seem to share Gibran's concerns from a century ago. For example, the 2003 report notes that the Arabic language is struggling to meet the challenges of modern times, and "is facing [a] severe . . . and real crisis in theorization, grammar, vocabulary, usage, documentation, creativity, and criticism. . . . The most apparent aspect of this crisis is the growing neglect of the functional aspects of [Arabic] language use. Arabic language skills in everyday life have deteriorated, and Arabic . . . has in effect ceased to be a spoken language. It is only the language of reading and writing; the formal language of intellectuals and academics, often used to display knowledge in lectures. . . . [It] is not the language of cordial, spontaneous expression, emotions, daily encounters, and ordinary

communication. It is not a vehicle for discovering one's inner self or outer surround-ings" (*Arab Human Development Report, 2003* [New York: United Nations Development Programme, 2003], 54).

In 1931, the year he passed on, Gibran was still seeking answers to questions many other decent Middle Easterners are still asking for our times, in the thick of the mis-named and ill-defined "Arab Spring." "There is in the Middle East an awakening that defies slumber," he wrote:

> This awakening will conquer because the sun is its leader and the dawn is its army. In the fields of the Middle East, which have been a large burial ground, stand the youth of Spring calling the occupants of the sepulchers to rise and march toward the new frontiers. When the Spring sings its hymn, the dead of the winter rise, shed their shrouds and march forward. There is on the horizon of the Middle East a new awakening; it is growing and expanding; it is reaching and engulfing all sensitive, intelligent souls; it is penetrating and gaining the sympathy of noble hearts. . . . There are today, in the Middle East, two men: one of the past and one of the future. Which one are you? Come close; let me look at you and let me be assured by your appearance and conduct if you are one of those coming into the light or going into the darkness. Come and tell me who and what are you. Are you a politician asking what your country can do for you, or a zealous one asking what you can do for your country?

See Gibran, "Ask Not What Your Country Can Do For You," in *The Treasured Writings of Kahlil Gibran* (Edison, NJ: Castle Books, 1981), 775.

34. Nadia Tuéni, *Juin et les mécréantes* (Beirut: Dar al-nahar, 1968), 63.

35. Note that the title in the French original, *Liban: 20 Poèmes pour un amour,* can be somewhat enigmatic, and ultimately misleading in English translation. The subtitle *20 Poèmes pour un amour* can have two meanings in English translation, suggesting both "20 Poems for a Beloved," and "20 Poems for One Beloved."

36. See Asher Kaufman, "Tell Us Our History: Charles Corm, Mount-Lebanon, and Lebanese Nationalism," *Middle Eastern Studies* 40, no. 3 (May 2004): 1–28.

37. Charles Corm Archives and Private Papers, Beirut, Lebanon. See for instance letters between Corm and Eliahu Epstein, dated January 25, 1938; February 22, 1938; March 3, 1938; April 26, 1938.

38. Charles Corm's Archives and Private Papers, Quartier Nazareth, Centre Cul-turel Charles Corm, Beirut; Letters from Eliahu Epstein dated May 6, 1935, and Janu-ary 25, 1938. In the 1938 letter, Epstein informs Corm that Nahum Slousch was currently "out of Jerusalem but is expected back next week. On his arrival I shall discuss with him the matter in a more definite fashion and will let you have details."

39. Rushdy Maalouf, "Yabisat Arza" (A Cedar Has Dried Up), *Al-Hikma* (Beirut: Hikma Institute) 11, no. 9 (December 1963): 463.

40. Maalouf, "A Cedar," 463.

41. Maalouf, "A Cedar," 463; emphasis in the original.

42. Short for Maison Blanche de Beyrouth (Beirut White House), the name under which Corm's residence (and the former Ford headquarters) was known locally.

43. Maalouf, "A Cedar," 463.

44. Quoted in Kevork Bardakjian, *Hitler and the Armenian Genocide* (Cambridge, MA: Zoryan Institute, 1985). It first appeared in Louis P. Lochner, *What About Germany?* (New York: Dodd, Mead, 1942), 1–4.

45. Charles Corm, *La Montagne inspirée* (Beirut: Éditions de la Revue Phénicienne, 1987), 47.

46. Corm, *La Montagne inspirée*, 104.

47. This translation is a rendition of the original French "Le Dit de l'enthousiasme" cycle of Charles Corm's Epic *La Montagne inspirée*."Le Dit de l'enthousiasme" chapter may translate roughly into the "Saga of Enthusiasm"—with the term *enthusiasm* here being in anticipation of the establishment of Greater Lebanon, under the auspices of French High Commissioner Henri Gouraud. This poem is therefore a celebration of the euphoric moment that September 1, 1920, represented for Lebanese patriots of Corm's persuasion—the date at which Gouraud declared the establishment of the new state. General Henri Gouraud, a graduate of the prestigious Saint-Cyr military academy, and the heroic leader of France's Fourth Army during the Great War, sustained life-threatening injuries during the 1915 Dardanelles Campaign. He subsequently lost his right arm and right eye, and had only limited mobility in his right leg. He would nevertheless go on to command the Western Front for the remainder of the War, and would gain renown for his distinguished service, his heroism, and his agility as a war strategist. After the war, Gouraud was rewarded with the command of the French Army of the Levant, and would eventually become the first French high commissioner to the States of the Levant—the name commonly used in reference to the former Ottoman territories that fell to the allies after the war. Consequently, out of the disparate former Ottoman provinces of Beirut, Damascus, Cilicia, and Aleppo, Gouraud would inaugurate the creation of five new states: the State of Damascus, the State of Aleppo, the State of Greater Lebanon, the State of the Alawite Mountain, and the State of the Druze Mountain. Subsequently, in 1936, the States of the Druze Mountain, Alawite Mountain, Aleppo, and Damascus would be stitched together to form a Syrian Federation, which would form the nucleus of a formerly nonextant Syrian state—today's Syrian republic. Only the State of Greater Lebanon would remain outside of the new Syrian entity, and would continue functioning as an independent—albeit not always sovereign—republic. This poem of the *Saga of Anticipation* is both a celebration of the establishment of Greater Lebanon in 1920 (and later the Lebanese republic in 1926), and a tribute to Gouraud himself; a maimed war hero who would bring unity and redemption of body and soul, and who would breathe health into the mutilated "Lebanese nation." Thus, on a bright day on September 1, 1920, standing imperiously before local and foreign dignitaries expressly gathered for this momentous occasion, Gouraud would declare the birth of modern Lebanon in the following solemn words:

Before all the peoples of Mount Lebanon now gathered here, people of all religions, who were once neighbors, but who shall from this day forward be united under the auspices of a single nation, rooted in its past, eminent in its future; at the foot of these majestic mountains, which through their endurance as the impregnable stronghold of your country's faith and freedom have shaped your country's strength; on the shores of this mythical Sea, which has been witness to the triremes of Phoenicia, Greece, and Rome, and which once transported through the world your subtle, skillful, and eloquent forefathers; today, this same sea is joyfully bringing you confirmation of a great and old friendship, and the good fortune of French peace. Therefore, before all of these witnesses to your aspirations, your struggles, and your victories, and in sharing your pride, I solemnly proclaim Greater Lebanon, and in the name of the French Republic, I salute her in her grandeur and in her power, from Nahr el-Kebir [in the North] to the gates of Palestine [in the South] and to the peaks of the Anti-Lebanon [in the East.]

Charles Corm Archives, "Text of Henri Gouraud's Speech," September 1, 1920, typewritten by Charles Corm. See also Adel Ismail, ed., *Le Liban, documents diplomatiques et consulaires relatifs à l'histoire du Liban* (Beirut: Éditions des oeuvres politiques et historiques, 1979), 19: 81.

Charles Corm was present on that portentous day, and he must have taken frenzied jubilant notes documenting its goings on—as his own euphoria can barely be contained in the poetic recollections of *Le Dit de l'enthousiasme*. Here, Corm celebrates not only the "rendering whole" of a dismembered nation, but *also* the exquisite act of "restoring," "rehabilitating," and "remending" an "assassinated nation"—by a "mutilated" war hero no less. Hence, the different body-parts that Corm invokes and gives voice to throughout the poem, recall the parts of a formerly dismembered Lebanon now being lovingly restored to its former self. But those very same tattered body parts that Corm brings back to life are also the limbs of Henri Gouraud himself. See the *Easter Story* selection in this chapter for a better understanding of Ottoman Lebanon during the Great War, the hardships suffered by its inhabitants, and consequently the rationale that drove Charles Corm and others from his generation to campaign for the establishment of a "Grand Liban" (the "Greater Lebanon" entity celebrated in this poem), and acclaim the French colonial officer (General Henri Gouraud) that brought that Lebanon into being.

48. This is a clear reference to Henri Gouraud, a war amputee.

49. The French original is "Capitale de ma pensée," which in Corm's telling refers to the famed Béryte of classical antiquity and Roman times, the "Béryte of the old stones" mentioned in Nadia Tuéni's work. It should be noted in this regard that by the third century A.D., the Romans had baptized Beirut "Beritus Nutris Legum," that is to say, "Beirut the City of Law." That sobriquet was earned on account of the city's famous law school, and its reputation in forming some of the Roman Empire's most illustrious jurists and magistrates. This Beirut, in Corm's telling, a shining beacon of knowledge

and the main intellectual capital of antiquity, was the worthy capital of the new republic that Gouraud was bringing into being.

50. See *An Easter Story.*

51. As mentioned earlier, this part of the first cycle of *La Montagne inspirée* may be dedicated to the French high commissioner and the role that he played in the establishment of Greater Lebanon. To the Phoenicianists of Corm's persuasion, this new state was the culmination of their dreams of statehood, which began with the events of 1860 in Mount Lebanon; a series of conflicts and civil wars that culminated in large-scale massacres and forced immigration of Lebanese Christians. Of course, the agonies of the 1860s preceded Corm's birth, by decades. But he had heard stories of the massacres during his childhood—as would have any child of his generation, socialized in the Christian environments of Mount Lebanon and Beirut. Most importantly perhaps were the memories of the Great War, and the near decimation of the population of Mount Lebanon—due to famines and blockades that the Ottomans had imposed on the mountain, amputating it from the Mediterranean coast and the fertile hinterland of eastern Lebanon, once considered the "Granary of Rome." These memories were still fresh in the minds of children of Charles Corm's generation. That is partly why the events of September 1, 1920, were such an auspicious occasion for Corm and his Young Phoenicians. And that is why it was crucial for them to have an independent Greater Lebanon restituted to its Mediterranean harbors, breathing the "boundless air of the open seas." This was important certainly because, in their view, it restored Lebanon to its "natural and historical frontiers." More importantly perhaps, Greater Lebanon provided an outlet to the Mediterranean and meant that the country would never again become amputated from the rest of the world, from Mediterranean Europe namely, and would therefore never be subjected to the horrors of hunger—described in Corm's *Easter Story.*

52. Again, the reference here is to the redeemer of Lebanon, General Henri Gouraud.

53. The biblical cedars of Lebanon are not only the national emblem of the modern Republic of Lebanon; given their biblical significance, they populate the logos, regalia, and symbols of the Maronite Church—the "national church" of which Charles Corm was a member, and a community that was instrumental in the establishment of the modern state of Lebanon, transposing its own motifs, symbols, and narratives, onto those of the nascent republic. More importantly perhaps, cedar wood, prized for its strength and durability, was a crucial component of the Phoenicians' shipbuilding industry, and ultimately the fundamental ingredient in the growth of their maritime empire. Planting cedar trees, in Charles Corm's telling, meant rekindling the glories of the Phoenician forefathers and bringing them back to life.

54. This bespeaks not only the affection that many Lebanese of the time held for Henri Gouraud and his "act" of establishing modern Lebanon; it is also powerful testimony of the "love story" that bound some Lebanese, namely the Maronite Catholics among them, to France.

55. In other words, no human endeavor, no words, and no art form can adequately express (or bless) the exquisite generous act of "creation" that was France's formation of

modern Lebanon. And therefore, no act of "recognition" or "gratitude" emanating from the Lebanese, genuine and delicate as it may be, can fittingly repay the French.

56. The image of the figures of Venus of Milo, the Winged Victory of Samothrace, and General Gouraud, all three of which charmingly maimed and disfigured, is as exquisite as it is moving. Each of these figures may be visually defective or fragmentary; yet in the power and glory that they inspire, they each are in their own right a pinnacle of perfection. The Venus of Milo, considered by many an epitome of beauty, is a representation of Aphrodite, the Greek goddess of love and fertility, and in her own right a "life giver." Born on the island of Cyprus, a renowned Phoenician possession, Aphrodite is the Greek rendition of the Phoenician Astarte, whose chief worship centers were mainly in Cyprus, but also at Byblos (Gebal, modern-day Lebanon), and Ashkelon (modern-day Israel). The transition of the cult of Astarte-Aphrodite from Phoenicia to Greece is attested to by Herodotus, and by inference the "act of transmission" from East (the Phoenicians) to West (Europe) is a theme that is recurrent in Corm's work. In the end, from Corm's perspective, Venus of Milo, the Winged Victory of Samothrace, and General Gouraud, are all three the product of Mediterranean (and therefore Phoenician) intercourse and exchange of ideas, goods, and values. Corm's choice of Venus of Milo in this final image of the poem was as historical as it was aesthetic and emotive in its inferences. Likewise with the Winged Victory of Samothrace—which in its current rendition (like Henri Gouraud himself) is an amputee—yet it seems well-equipped and ready to take flight. And just as Nike of Samothrace is the greatest masterpiece of Hellenistic sculpture in Corm's telling, so was the maimed Henri Gouraud an epitome of French beauty, elegance, and heroism; conveying not only victory and triumph against great odds, but also the dynamism of energy, motion, and creation—in this case the energy, motion, and "creation" of modern Lebanon.

57. Nahr el-Kalb (the Dog River or the Lycus River of classical antiquity), which meanders some thirty-one miles through the gorges of Mount Lebanon before emptying in the Mediterranean ten miles north of Beirut, carries significant historical relevance. See for instance *An Easter Story* for more detail. For forty centuries, conquerors and armies that have processed along the Lebanese coast, from classical antiquity to modern times, have often left their markings on monuments that they erected along the banks and at the mouth of the Dog River. Some of those conquerors included Nebuchadnezzar, Marcus Aurelius, Napoleon III, and in more recent times the French high commissioner, General Henri Gouraud. The conquerors mentioned by Corm, Ramsis, Caracalla, Asarhaddon, and Barkuk, who are also memorialized at the Nahr el-Kalb corridor, left a particularly bloody trail.

58. Following a drawn-out cry lamenting the loss of Lebanon's "authentic, native" language (be it Phoenician or Syriac-Aramaic), Corm concludes by reconnecting with a suddenly rediscovered "Lebanese language." Indeed, even in the darkest hours of despair over the "loss of language," Corm recognized and revealed a hidden vigor to his ancestral tongue, which he claimed to have fused and infused the modern languages currently spoken in Lebanon. It is worth noting here that Corm is not merely discharging fanciful linguistic romanticism and naïf hope in the imperishability of his language.

To the contrary, he seems to exude confidence in the claim that his native language, the language of the Phoenicians, was still pounding vigorously in his veins, and suffusing his voice, in the form of spoken Lebanese. To him, a national language was like a timeless, warm, hallowed maternal voice, surging up from a distant past, reverberating in the present, emitting shudders of national pride and tales of forebears and glory. Therefore, even when they seem to acquiesce in their proverbial polyglossia, Lebanese nationalists of Corm's generation still yearned for an "authentic" national language and recognized its endurance and its latent essence in their modern idioms. Their touted multilingualism was, in Corm's words, simply a palliative, a borrowed outer garment, and an artifice meant to ward off the dominance of any single intruder language. Yet, the "Lebanese language" that Corm spoke of—both an "internal" emotive language *and* an actual living one—impregnated, metabolized, and transmuted the *other* languages currently in use in Lebanon; namely Arabic, which like other idioms, Corm viewed to be an intruder on preexistent sui generis speech forms. Although written in French, and in the French medieval poetic tradition of the *chanson de geste,* chronicling local heroic exploits, *La Montagne inspirée* was, as stated by Corm, "traduit du Libanais"—that is to say "translated from Lebanese." The introduction of each of the poems' three "cycles," or "sagas" presented them as French translations of an original Lebanese, thus suggesting that although "speaking in tongues" as it were, and sounding as if uttering French, Italian, or Arabic for that matter, the linguistic reservoir of the Lebanese people remains a single authentic ancestral "Lebanese" language, a progeny of the ancient Phoenician tongue.

59. Written in 1919, this story was first published in 1949, as part of a collection titled *Les Miracles de la Madone aux Sept Douleurs* (The Miracles of Our Lady of the Seven Sorrows) (Beirut: Éditions de la Revue Phénicienne, 1949). Named for the Beirut Mater Dolores Church (in the Ashrafiyyé district) very near to where Charles Corm grew up and was schooled, this collection of "miracles" tells stirring stories of suffering, redemption, and salvation, and is in a sense a celebration of the human spirit, and of light and hope against darkness and despair. The book of *Miracles of Our Lady of the Seven Sorrows* contains four short stories: *A Christmas Story, A New Year's Story, A Palm Sunday Story,* and *An Easter Story.* All four narratives, written in the style and with emotions reflective of traditional Christian devotional literature, were penned (or, at least, were outlined) during the Great War, by a young Charles Corm profoundly stirred by the calamities that he was witness to—even though his stories were published at a much later date. They are essentially Corm's personal recollections of the atrocities, devastations, and tragedies suffered in times of conflict. All four stories are dedicated "To all mothers; all of whom suffer in times of war, for the sake of their children." Charles Corm provided the pencil and charcoal-on-paper illustrations of the *Easter Story;* drawings which were reproduced from a notebook in which the young poet had kept a diary of images and sketches commemorating the war. Finally, it should be mentioned that the "Seven Sorrows of Mary/The Madonna" (Lat. "Mater Dolorosa") are popular Roman Catholic devotional prayers and meditations over the Virgin Mary's sufferings. The Beirut church by the same name lay in the Ashrafiyyé district where Corm grew up, where he later built the Ford Motor Company headquarters of which he was the sole

agent for the Middle East, and where he is buried today, in the Ras el-Nabeh Maronite Cemetery where parts of the events of *Easter Story* also take place. Furthermore, the church of the Madonna of the Seven Sorrows was Charles Corm's own parish and the chapel of the Jesuit college (the Université Saint-Joseph) that he attended as a young man. His father David Corm (1852–1930), a pioneer of modern Lebanese religious art, is credited with the murals and other paintings inside the church. At the age of seventy-eight, David Corm was reported to have produced one of his most impressive master-pieces; the painting of Saints Sergius and Bacchus astride their horses; it was a feat of artistic and technical dexterity at once. Being frail and unable to reach the top of his three-meter-high canvas by ladder, David Corm asked that the painting be turned on its head, and he completed it thusly, by painting its top half upside-down. He died a short time thereafter, on June 6, 1930.

60. Batroun is both the name of a northern Mount Lebanon district, and the coastal capital of that district. The port city of Batroun itself was a famous Phoenician harbor in classical antiquity, mentioned in the works of Strabo, Pliny, Theophanes, and others. It sits on a promontory just north of Byblos, another Phoenician trading town, considered by many the world's oldest continuously inhabited human settlement, the home of the earliest systems of alphabetic writing (see for instance Maurice Dunand's *Byblia Grammata: Documents et recherches sur le développement de l'écriture en Phé-nicie* [Paris: Imprimerie catholique, 1945]), and a major papyrus and "writing" trading center—hence its classical toponym "Byblos," a name from which the word for "Bible" is derived. The highlands of the district of Batroun are famous for their Greek Ortho-dox and Maronite churches, attesting to the appeal of their rugged terrain to hunted-down minority communities. The coastal city itself is home to the "Puy du Connétable" Crusader castle, upon which Fakhreddine II, the seventeenth-century Druze prince of Mount Lebanon, built a fort to preserve his autonomy from Ottoman suzerainty, and guard his Beirut-Tripoli coastal trade routes.

61. See above note on the Phoenician port city of Byblos, a UNESCO World Heri-tage Site. Also known colloquially in Lebanon as Jbeil, a distortion of the original Ca-naanite Gebal/Geval (for "the well of the god El/Al"), Byblos was a major center of archeological discoveries during the late nineteenth and early twentieth centuries, il-luminating much of what we know today about the Phoenician inhabitants of ancient Lebanon and their contributions to Mediterranean civilization. It is natural for Charles Corm, one of Lebanon's most eloquent cantors of Phoenician glories, to have chosen Byblos as one of the settings in a tale of trials, desperation, hope, and renewal.

62. This is a clear reference to Homer's *Iliad* and its conception of the notions of masculinity and the ideals of honor, bravery, nobility, and duty—especially as concerns the protection of homeland and family. Describing the ruggedness and nobility of Leba-non's highlanders, likening them to "some warriors from Homer," and bestowing upon them qualities instilled by both society and topology, from a very young age, are part of a trope dominating Corm's corpus. In this story in particular, nobility and dignity and grace—human and humanist values par excellence in Corm's worldview—are used in juxtaposition to the indignities and horrors suffered during World War I.

63. Two major towns of Mount Lebanon delineating its extremities from the eastern highlands (Tannourine) to the western port cities (Jounié). Tannourine teeters on the edge of valleys and gorges, and is dotted with ancient Maronite monasteries. It is distinguished by its ruggedness, its inaccessibility, and its isolation high up in the mountains. Jounié on the other hand, dominating one of Lebanon's major Mediterranean seaports, symbolizes openness, fluidity, movement, and access to the Mediterranean world. The interconnectedness between "mountain" and "sea" is a theme dear to the hearts of young Lebanese nationalists of Corm's generation, who saw themselves as proud descendants of the ancient Phoenicians, a breed of mariners-mountaineers. It is therefore not surprising that Charles Corm should use those two emblematic Phoenician towns in his narrative.

64. "Emm-Farid" literally means "the mother of Farid." It is an honorific title, its prefix the feminine form of the more common masculine "Abu." Both "Emm" and "Abu" are prefixed to a proper noun, usually the name of a first-born male offspring. Thus, in patriarchal Middle Eastern societies, titles like Emm-Farid and Abu-Farid become the honorifics or nicknames of the proud parents of a male child, often replacing their own birth names.

65. A mukhtar (Ar. "the chosen one") is ordinarily a village elder who represents a country's central authority in rural areas, often taking on the role of mayor or town manager.

66. Tartej is a hamlet of Mount Lebanon situated in the Byblos district.

67. See earlier historical overview of modern Lebanon, and the dismantlement of the Mutasarrifiyya by the Ottomans at the outset of World War I.

68. This is in reference to the Règlement Organique regime, which France had helped broker for an autonomous Mount Lebanon in 1861, providing the mountain's population a measure of political freedom and protection from Ottoman meddling and molestation. This special regime was guaranteed by a concert of European powers—Russia, Prussia, France, Britain, and Austria—and granted Lebanon legal autonomy, which yielded a relatively long period of peace and stability—that is until the Ottomans stripped the autonomous province of its special status at the outset of the Great War and proceeded to punish and subjugate its populations in retaliation for their "collaboration" with the European intruders   namely France. Given that the Règlement Organique had emerged in the midst of devastating wars and massacres in mid-nineteenth century Mount Lebanon, and had the purpose of alleviating the suffering of the mountain's population, many early twentieth-century Lebanese of Corm's generation came to expect France and its European allies to rush once more to Lebanon's rescue during the dire hours of World War I. France was, of course, preoccupied with its own tragedies on its devastated home ground, and Lebanon as a result had to wait until the postwar peace settlement to regain France's attention.

69. See Charles Corm's report in "Rendons le sol au paysan" (Let Us Give the Land Back to the Peasants), La Revue Phénicienne (Christmas 1919): 271.

70. Beirut and Tripoli were two major Ottoman metropolises—with Beirut as capital of the vilayet by the same name. Although diverse and cosmopolitan population-

wise, like most of the Ottoman Empire's mercantile port cities hugging the Mediterranean (Alexandria and Izmir for instance), Beirut and Tripoli remained overwhelmingly Sunni, dominated by Sunni merchant classes that were close allies and accomplices of the Ottoman establishment. Even the most modest of Sunni shopkeepers in those two cities were able to amass vast fortunes during the war years, often purchasing foreclosed farmlands and Christian properties at rock-bottom prices, overnight becoming formidable landed proprietors in their own right.

71. Lebanon as a distinct political entity did not exist in those days. Neither did Syria, Palestine, and the rest of the modern states of the Levant for that matter. Instead, Beirut was the capital city of an Ottoman *vilayet* by the same name, ruled by an Ottoman *vali* (governor). Likewise, Syria and Israel in their current modern configurations did not exist. What is today Syria consisted of two *vilayets*; the *vilayet* of Damascus (which included parts of what are today Israel and Jordan), and the *vilayet* of Aleppo (which included parts of modern day Syria and Turkey). The Beirut *vilayet* stretched over the coastal region of what are today Lebanon, Syria, and Israel, and included Latakia in the north (in what is today Syria), as well as Haifa and Akko in the south (in what is today Israel), and large swaths of what is today the Republic of Lebanon. Mount Lebanon, where some of the events of this story take place, benefited from an autonomous status, as a *sanjak* (autonomous province) guaranteed by a concert of European powers, and ruled by an Ottoman Christian and aided by an administrative council of local (Lebanese) politicians. This would remain the case from 1861 until the Ottomans' entry into the Great War, at which time the special autonomous regime of Mount Lebanon would be revoked, and retribution would be meted out against the mountain's Christian populations—peoples then deemed treasonous by the Ottoman authorities due to their European, namely French, sympathies, and their autonomist impulses. This is a theme alluded to throughout Corm's narrative.

72. Jamal Pasha, commonly referred to in Lebanese history books as "al-Saffah" (the Butcher), was a member of a "triumvirate" of pashas who ruled the Ottoman Empire during the First World War. He was the effective governor of the *vilayets* of Damascus, Beirut, and Aleppo during the war, and is believed to have been the perpetrator of the Armenian and Assyrian genocides, as well as the systematic starvation of Mount Lebanon, as described here by Charles Corm.

73. Peter Chebly (1871–1917) was Maronite archbishop of Beirut and president of the Lebanon Congress of Bishops. He was also the rector of one of Beirut's most prestigious Maronite-Catholic schools (the Collège de la Sagesse), and a vocal opponent of Ottoman rule over Lebanon. He was banished to Adana—along with large numbers of the Maronite intelligentsia—by the Ottomans at the beginning of the Great War. The land that he donated for the Ras el-Nabeh cemetery was part of the endowment of the Maronite Archdiocese of Beirut. What became the Maronite Cemetery of Ras el-Nabeh, where Charles Corm himself is buried today, lies in the Ashrafiyyé district of East Beirut. It abuts the neighborhood's Jewish Cemetery and sits on the eastern side of the Damascus Road, which cuts the city of Beirut in half, and which was once the major artery linking the Ottoman *vilayet* of Beirut to the *vilayet* of Damascus—hence its name

"Damascus Road." Damascus Road was therefore a bustling commercial nerve center, used in Ottoman times by coaches and grain traders traveling between the two main Ottoman provinces of the Eastern Mediterranean, and connecting cosmopolitan Beirut (and its Western legacies and ostentations), to the sleepy, rural, Ottoman interior in the east. Peoples of all faiths and religious and ethnic backgrounds, Jews, Christians, and Muslims, mainly merchant families, but also laborers and members of less fortunate social classes, took residence along the eastern and western sides of the Damascus Road. The relevance of this artery to Corm's *Easter Story* is that it witnessed the demise and utter devastation of one particular Lebanese community (namely the Christian community), while other communities (namely the Sunnis, who were associates and often accomplices of the Ottoman authorities) would survive and thrive during the Great War. These events of modern Lebanon's history were foundational in molding young Charles Corm's worldview, and contributed to his subsequent intellectual and political activities on behalf of an independent, neutral, and diverse Lebanese entity, distinct and dissociated from the intrigues and the foul politics of identity, resentful nationalism, and selfish irredentism that gripped the Eastern Mediterranean following the demise of the Ottoman Empire.

74. Note Corm's earlier description of the children of the mountain as "sturdy and carefree, besieging strangers in their midst with their large sunny eyes, bickering like some warriors from Homer, trying to outdo one another offering visitors the hospitality of their neat and modest little hovels."

75. Miniyé is a Sunni coastal merchant-town just north of the Tripoli harbor.

76. A coastal town south of Byblos.

77. Many of the inhabitants of Mount Lebanon had been reduced to scavenging and subsistence living during that period, and as a result became—albeit reluctantly—full participants in the devastation of their country's natural resources. The Ottoman authorities had confiscated all of the country's capital and assets assigning them to the war effort. In the process, they decreed and enforced a systematic "deforestation campaign" to feed the "fuel shortages" that the Ottoman armies were suffering on the war fronts. The corvée-like "woodcutting" assignments to which some inhabitants of Mount Lebanon were appointed contributed to large-scale deforestation of the countryside, which in turn profoundly disrupted the country's ecosystem and further contributed to landslides, loss of arable land, crop failures, and generalized penury and famine. In this segment of the *Easter Story*, Martha seems to have been left with no choice but becoming a participant in this general devastation, if only to earn her wretched daily bread.

78. Not very far from Fidar.

79. Qantar is common unit of mass in the Middle East, arguably a remnant of the Islamic *kintar*, which comes from the Roman *centarius* (a unit of one hundred). One qantar equaled a hundred rotol, and approximately forty kilograms.

80. A rotol comes up to one-hundredth of a qantar, which meant that Martha would have ended up giving her entire five hundred pounds back to the mukhtar.

81. On the Nahr el-Kalb, or Dog River, the ancient Lycus River, see note 57 above. Legend has it that in ancient times a wolf guarded the mouth of the river, which sits at

the foot of a steep mountain gorge wading deep into the Mediterranean coast, howling whenever conquerors approached, thus alerting the highlanders overhead. More importantly, at least from Charles Corm's perspective, Nahr el-Kalb was a symbol of Lebanese resilience and tenacity, figuring prominently in his *La Montagne inspirée,* where he proudly writes:

> Many were the nations that charged our land,
> This tiny plot of land, which quelled them in the end!
> We have witnessed the passing, of Peoples and of Ages,
> Yet withstood and endured, in the glistening horizon,
> Steadfast on our peaks, peaceful sober and wise, since the early dawn of time!
> Many were the magi, poets, and princes;
> Many were the gods, pompous kings and tyrants,
> Who walked in procession, at the foot of our mountain!
> O Ramsis, Asarhaddon, O Barkuk, Caracalla,
> Transcending all your crimes, outlasting all your horrors,
> The mouth of Nahr al-Kalb, has kept but broken shards
> Of your gory passage, on its quiet peaceful shores.

82. Currently the seat of the presidency of the modern Republic of Lebanon, Baabda was the capital of the *sanjak* (autonomous province) of Mount Lebanon, which the Ottomans had revoked at the beginning of the Great War.

83. The Glass Café (Leb. 'Ahwet le-'Zééz) was an iconic downtown Beirut coffeehouse dating back to Ottoman times. There are many Glass Cafés throughout Lebanon (in Sidon, Tripoli, and the Gemmayzé district of Beirut for instance), owing their names to their large glass façades. But the one mentioned by Charles Corm in *Easter Story* refers to the original Glass Café near Martyrs' Square, which owes its renown and historical relevance to its very location. It is situated in a central area of downtown Beirut, which is called "Martyrs' Square" in reference to Lebanese patriots who were executed near that location by the Ottomans on May 6, 1916. Corm must have been marked by the gory images of those days, as his home was literally at a stone's throw from the square in question. His choice of this location as stage for his story was certainly to accentuate its relevance as a place of suffering and martyrdom—and perhaps eventually redemption and salvation. Yet, Martyrs' Square did not become a memorial only to those patriots executed by the Ottomans in 1916. It was also the final resting place of thousands of peasants from Mount Lebanon, flocking to the city of Beirut in search of food (or salvation), and who probably breathed their last on that very location. It should be noted that Martyrs' Square is also referred to as the Tower's Square (Sééhit el-Birj) in reference to the Tuscan-style palace and tower that Emir Fakhreddine II, prince of the autonomous Ottoman province of Mount Lebanon during the seventeenth century, had built on that location, making Beirut the capital city of his dominions—which extended from the Mediterranean in the west, to the gates of Damascus in the east, and to Akko in the south. Fakhreddine's Palace and its lush gardens were subsequently destroyed by the

Ottomans, and their stones were carted away to prevent the monument from ever being rebuilt. But the name "Tower's Square," and its significance remained—although it would be given new contents and trappings by the Ottomans in later years. During the Russo-Turkish wars of 1768–74, Catherine the Great was reported to have dispatched an armada laden with heavy cannons to the Beirut harbor, in an attempt to occupy the Ottomans with an additional war front and weaken their hold on the Crimea. The campaign to dislodge the Ottomans from Beirut failed, but that particular battle ended up being one of the costliest for the Ottomans, and one during which they sustained heavy losses. In 1773, the Ottoman governor of Beirut, Jazzar "the Butcher" Pasha, decided to commemorate those events by erecting cannon-towers on that very same location, affixing a new historical event to a preexisting name. The plaza earned a new sobriquet in the process; the "Place des Canons" (or Cannon's Square), which was often used interchangeably with "Tower's Square." Thus, the famous Glass Café ('Ahwet le-'Zééz), with its towering iconic glass windows, would come to represent a symbolic and actual "looking-glass" through which pivotal events of modern Lebanon's history would paly out, get witnessed, and recorded. It should be noted that Charles Corm grew up at a stone's throw from the Glass Café, on the western edge of the Damascus Road (mentioned earlier), near a street that now bears the name of his own father, the painter David Corm. Young Charles witnessed firsthand the devastation wrought on Beirut and its children during the Great War. He was an ambulant Glass Café in his own right, roaming the streets of his ravaged city and countryside, bearing witness to their tragedy, recording their desolation, and chronicling their humbling and their utter destruction. The characters of Corm's *Easter Story* were real; people he'd witnessed, touched, and many times comforted. In a way, he was unlike the patrons of the real Glass Café; Ottoman officials and sympathizers from among Lebanon's Sunni ruling classes, who remained heedless to the suffering reigning outside their hangout's stone-deaf windows. In a way, Charles Corm's *Easter Story* was as much an indictment of war and a celebration of human resilience, as it was an indictment of indifference—a human failing as much as resilience might have been a human virtue and a symbol of the triumph of the human spirit.

84. Today's "Martyrs' Square," in the heart of downtown Beirut (see the above note), was the site of utter devastation and death during the Great War, due mainly to food shortages caused by large-scale confiscations by the Ottomans, and compounded by swarms of locusts overtaking the countryside and allied ships blockading the littoral.

85. This is Martha crying out for her son, in dialectal Lebanese, using the sorrowful vocative *ya*. It is difficult to translate its emotions into English, especially when emitted by an afflicted mother. Although the plaintive "Ya" of Corm's text can be rendered "My son! My dear son! Oh Farid! . . ." it does not captivate the emotion, the grief, and the despair evoked by a mother bemoaning the loss of her child. It is a plaintive cry, similar to that of the Madonna of the Seven Sorrows, muffled and dignified and stirring at the same time. That is why, although writing in French, Corm opted to produce this mother's lament, with its raw and dignified emotion, only in the language in which it was expressed: Lebanese.

86. Charles Corm prefaced this collection with the plea quoted above, in his words at once "immodest and respectful." Incidentally, he also dedicated the collection "to the one who will be my wife one day," *and* to French erotica author Pierre Louÿs. Erotic as they may seem at first glance, these texts will ultimately prove to be profoundly spiritual; an adolescent's tributes to his life's first encounters with love, perhaps some of it "imagined" or "fantasized" love, but certainly lyrical hymns testifying to Corm's love of country.

87. Although this text appears to have been written between 1911 and 1912 (the manuscript is dated 1912), some of its references may suggest a later date—or perhaps later edits and minor rewrites that the author might have played around with. Although prepared for publication by Charles Corm, and subtitled "Variations sur le mode sentimental" (Variations on the Sentimental), the text of *Erotic Stories* will remain unpublished and in manuscript form until 2011. This collection plots the trajectory of young Charles Corm's growing pains, his "puppy love," and his reluctant departure from childhood. The *Phoenicia: An Opening Prayer* selection is clearly the story of his first love, perhaps his early adolescent's sexual experience. *Phoenicia* is also Corm's ode to Phoenician Lebanon, arguably his first and only love, as the conclusion of the text may reveal. Notwithstanding the erotic nature of the recollections recorded herewith, their sexual references remain subtle, discrete, and even mystical, often confusing the reader as to whether the author was extoling a beloved woman or a beloved homeland. Either way, the style and symbolism of the text, throughout *Erotic Stories*, brim with biblical imagery culled from both Christian and Hebrew traditions. This rhetorical device, often wedding the Judeo-Christian ethics and heritage (into which Charles Corm himself was socialized) to pagan Canaanite-Phoenician allegory, pervaded his literary production. Both monotheistic "puritanism" and pagan "sensuality" are valorized in Corm's work, even as an adolescent. Moreover, Judeo-Christian monotheism and Phoenician paganism, with the latter having alluded to the idea of a "compassionate" deity, are essential elements (in Corm's telling) of the liberal compassionate humanism that he advocated, and which was the bequest of the Phoenicians that he admired and deemed progenitors of the modern Lebanese. Youthful and clumsy in its innocence as this particular poem may appear, its Phoenician themes are unmistakable. This is all the more remarkable given Corm's age at the time that this adolescent supplication was written. Even at seventeen years of age, Charles Corm had already mastered the stylistic, thematic, and emotive hybridity (again, a fundamental Phoenician characteristic in his telling), which he would continue practicing and advocating later in life, as an older seasoned man of letters, and as doyen of modern Lebanese *belles lettres*.

88. The imagery of the red of "the blood of souls," here twined to the red of "an ancient carpet of Asia," seems to suggest the "color purple" or the crimson-red of the Phoenicians. This "red," what eventually became the "color of royalty," was one of the Phoenicians' most prized industries, and arguably the best-guarded trade secret of the ancient world. It made the Phoenicians rich and famous, and became both a source of admiration and envy among the peoples of classical antiquity.

89. One cannot help evoking the Phoenicians, or picture them braving the waves of the ancient world, when Corm's language blends crashing waves and seas with the

reddish-brown color of copper. Both maritime trade and "riding the waves," as well red-dye industries, were notable Phoenician trademarks.

90. This is an explicit nod to Maurice Barrès's *La Colline inspirée* (The Hallowed Hill), a novel published in 1913. Barrès's earlier work, often swelling with youthful energy and patriotic devotion, left an indelible mark on Charles Corm's own literary production. Indeed, Corm's elaboration of Phoenicianism in later years (ca. 1916–19), culminating in the completion of *La Montagne inspirée* in 1933, another obvious allusion to Barrès's *La Colline inspirée,* speaks to some Barrèsian impact. Incidentally, the first cycle of *La Montagne inspirée,* titled "The Saga of Enthusiasm" ("Le Dit de l'enthousiasme"), was dedicated to Maurice Barrès. Written in French, but "translated from Lebanese" in Corm's telling, it read "En mémoire de Maurice Barrès, qui a su nous comprendre parce qu'il nous a aimés [In memoriam, to Maurice Barrès, who was able to understand us [Lebanese] because he loved us]." As mentioned earlier, the references to Barrès in many of Corm's literary production, were certainly not fortuitous. They bespoke the "ancient spirit" of "ancient forefathers," which were foundational in Barrès's *La Colline inspirée,* and likewise in Corm's own attachment to the Lebanese mountain, where still lives the ancient Phoenician spirit. Mount Lebanon was the repository of Lebanese identity in Corm's telling; it is the origin and extension of Lebanese selfhood, and fulfills the mystical desires of a poet on a quest for the absolute.

91. The "mysteries" of the "human sound," and its endurance and eternal life in alphabetic writing, is a prevalent theme in Corm's work. In *La Montagne inspirée* and elsewhere, as well as in his public lectures and journalistic output, Charles Corm always celebrated the Phoenician alphabet, deeming it a stunning accomplishment, the pinnacle of humanism and human achievement. In fact, *La Montagne inspirée* describes alphabetic writing and its place of honor in the pantheon of human creation as follows:

Today, no one would fathom holding
The invention of writing, to be the greatest miracle of all,
One whereby human genius, raised us up mere mortals
To the status of Creator, God,
With a simple sleight-of-hand!
For, the simple act of writing, breathes life into otherwise fading words,
Granting them plain form, and an eternal face;
Indeed the act of writing yields a lucid image
To the sounds of our words,
And assigns a high altar to our fleeting thoughts!

. . .

For, the simple act of writing,
Is like gushing out of one's own empty twilights,
It is an act of defiance against nothingness

. . .

For, when God set out to redeem his own sinful creation,
The Word became flesh, so as to defy death,

Likewise, when our ancestors, spawned the miracle of writing,
The word was given form!

92. The word *alcarazas* here refers to the fresh water, wine, or Arak (anised al-cohol) clay pitchers common in rural Mount Lebanon. The French alcarazas used by Charles Corm is a loan from Spanish with origins in the Arabic *al-karraz,* which itself proceeds from the Aramaic *karzé.* In its nominal form, the Aramaic word *karzé* means sermon. Its transitive verbal form connotes "consecration" and "dedication," by way of "sermonizing" and "throwing holy water." Hence the later Arabization of *karzé* from the Syriac noun *karruz* (predictor, announcer, herald making consecrations, by way of holy water), connoting the container of holy water, or libations.

93. Charles Corm's beloved is clearly worthy of baby Jesus here, the innocent recipient of fragrant "musk, nard, and myrrh" as a newborn, and the consort and friend of prostitutes and sinners in his adult life. Namely, the image that comes to mind here is that of the "Sinful Woman" of the New Testament, anointing Jesus's feet with perfume, and wiping them with her hair. "Let him he who is without sin among you be the first to throw a stone at her," says the evangelist John (in John 8:7), describing Jesus and his reaction to puritans and practitioners of phony virtue. Corm's preface to the collection of poems from which *Phoenicia* is excerpted likewise reminds those of us who may be quick with judgments of their own to "Let him, the first among men, who has never experienced the ecstasy of carnal love, cast the first stone . . ."

94. Story taken from a collection by Anis Freyha, *Isma' ya Rida!* (Listen Up, Rida!) (Beirut: Naufal Publishing), 1956. He wrote this book in the form of "children's stories" intended for his young son, Rida, so he began each chapter with "Isma' ya Rida," or "Listen up, Rida!" just before beginning his narrative.

95. Freyha uses the Lebanese rural terms *awdé* to refer to nonirrigated land often reserved for mulberry trees, and *na'bé,* which is a newly cultivated plot of land.

96. The term used in the Arabic original is *illiyyé,* which is dialectal Lebanese for a "two-story" rural stone house.

97. The original Lebanese *qalé'* refers to a topography common to Mount Leba-non, distinguished by white steep boulders, usually teetering on the edge of an abyss as if breaking away from a steep arid hilly place.

98. The Lebanese dialectal term *ghérraar* (the "deceiver" or "misleader," or even the "seducer") is used in reference to the planet Jupiter, which sometimes happens to precede Venus, or meet her, and is thus often mistaken for her.

99. This is the common colloquial Lebanese term for the western tip of the Beirut bay that wades into the Mediterranean.

ISRAEL AND PALESTINE

1. Olivier Carré, *Le Nationalisme arabe* (Paris: Petite bibliothèque Payot, Fayard, Fayard, 1993), 166.

2. For the duration of the Arab-Israeli conflict, and at least until the 1993 Oslo Agreements, the Arabs of Israel (known colloquially as "the Arabs of the interior," "the

Arabs of forty eight," or "or the Arabs of sixty-seven") were often viewed as "traitors" by other Arabs.

3. This is in reference to the Arab League Summit Resolution of Khartoum-Sudan, which met in the wake of the 1967 "Six Day War," called for maintaining a state of belligerency with Israel, and enjoined Arab leaders to espouse what became known colloquially as the "Three Nos": no to peace with Israel; no to recognition of Israel; no to negotiations with Israel.

4. Amin Maalouf, *Les Échelles du Levant* (Paris: Éditions Grasset, 1996), 45.

5. Alexandra Nocke, *The Place of the Mediterranean in Modern Israeli Identity* (Leiden: Brill, 2009), 221.

6. Deborah Starr and Sasson Somekh, eds., *Mongrels or Marvels: The Levantine Writings of Jacqueline Shohet Kahanoff* (Stanford, CA: Stanford University Press, 2011), 126.

7. *Childhood in Egypt* © Copyright Jacqueline Shohet Kahanoff 1985, published in Starr and Somekh, *Mongrels or Marvels,* 1–13. All material by Jacqueline Shohet Kahanoff reprinted by permission of Ms. Laura d'Amade.

8. It is deliciously accurate—*and* untainted—that Kahanoff distinguish between "Muslim," "Syrian," "Christian," "Arab," and "Tunisian" etc. Although the term "Christian Arab" may be problematic in some quarters today, Kahanoff's listing of the various groups above, distinguishing among, say, "Arab," "Christian," and "Syrian," is a reflection of her times' parameters of identity; categories which may all be perfunctorily folded into the "Arab" label today. For our purposes here, and for the sake of bringing some discipline to taxonomy relative to the Middle East's multiple identities, it may be useful to note that a medievalist's and a modernist's view of what constitutes a "Christian Arab" are two different matters. A "Christian Arab" in premodern times (that is to say before the emergence of Arab nationalism in the early decades of the twentieth century) was somebody from the Arabian Peninsula who happened to be a Christian. Yet, it is doubtful that those Christians of the Arabian Peninsula even referred to themselves (or were referred to by others) as "Christian Arabs" at the time; they were in any case all but decimated under Islam; this is part of the reason why there are no "native" Christian communities today in places like Saudi Arabia, Kuwait, and the rest. Those erstwhile Christians either converted en masse to Islam, were expelled, or simply succumbed to the sword. Indeed, save for some of today's arabophone Greek Orthodox of the Near East, who may still claim descent from the illustrious "Christian" Arabian tribes of Ghassan or Lakhmid, arguably often out of political expediency and ideological puffery than credible historical evidence, no such verifiably "Christian Arabs" remain. That being said, there is scant evidence suggesting those supposed "Christian Arabs" of pre-Islamic times even referred to themselves in such terms. The common, more accurate, generic term, designating all Near Eastern users of Arabic who happen to be Christian, is "Oriental," or "Near Eastern Christians"—both renditions of the common French term "Chrétiens d'Orient." Absent that, all Near Eastern Christian communities already benefit from their own specific ethnonyms, reflecting their memberships in "premodern national Churches"—e.g., Chaldaeans, Copts, Maronites, Nestorians, Assyrians, and

the rest. Otherwise, the term "Christian Arab" remains a novel phenomenon, an over-simplification, and ultimately a misleading, subjective, ideologically-charged cognomen that misleads more than it may illuminate.

9. See the Qabbani selections for comparison; especially the following, from the *Marginalia* poem: "And we beg Allah to hand us victory and withhold it from our enemy," or, "Do not curse out the heavens for having forsaken you. . . . Do no curse out circumstances. For Allah gives victory to those who desire it."

10. This is arguably a Coptic holiday (literally "breathing the breeze," with the semantic connotations of "relaxing," "taking a break," or "taking a leisurely trip), which traditionally falls on the day after Easter. Yet it is a national holiday celebrated by all Egyptians, and can be traced to an ancient Pharaonic tradition.

11. See Qabbani's references to "story-telling" and "Abu Zaid al-Hilaali," and the explanatory note on the latter.

12. Compare this to Charles Corm's Phoenicianism and the polyglossia that it advocated, especially in the *Hallowed Mountain*, and the passage that reads as follows:

For, a people is orphaned
When it hasn't a tongue;
And the languages of others
Are borrowed outer cloaks,
In which one seems dubious,
Shameful, lifeless, frail,
Obnoxious and strange!

13. See for comparison Nizar Qabbani's *Marginalia* poem, especially the "What value has the people who have no tongue?" lament.

14. It would be interesting to consider this "wicked priest" euphemism, and what (or whom) it is in reference to, as a spoiler of dreams and despoiler of lands, nations, and identities.

15. Can any parallels be drawn between this image and the themes in Qabbani's poetry?

16. See the Syria chapter. Léon Blum, a socialist, was France's first Jewish prime minister, elected to the office in 1936. See also the conclusion, and Amin Maalouf's reference to a similar theme, in "Les désorientés," where he and children of his generation bragged about being imbued of Enlightenment, about being the proud progeny of Voltaire and Sartre and Camus.

17. Compare this to references (dating back to the same era) from Amin Maalouf's *Les Désorientés*.

18. See the chapter on Lebanon for Charles Corm's take on the endurance and resilience and timelessness of the "Levantine"—in Lebanese emanation in his case. "We were here first," claims Kahanoff's Levantine emanation; all others are transitory. Likewise, from this same time period, "all Egyptians are Copts" was a common Coptic slogan; "some of us are Christian Copts, others are Muslim Copts . . . but all Egyptians

are Copts." Again, this is bringing to the fore the issue of the "precedence" of "first na-tions" vis-à-vis "conquering nations"—i.e., the Arab nationalist narrative viewed from a Levantine angle.

19. Clearly, Kahanoff was imbued in the thought and writings of Lebanon's Phoe-nicianists of the 1920s, and *their* take on Levantine identities. See the chapter on Leba-non, and the Michel Chiha and Charles Corm entries; francophone works which cor-respond to a tee with what Kahanoff evinces in her own work almost a generation later.

20. What or whom does the "wicked priest" euphemism refer to?

21. "To Live and Die a Copt" © Copyright Jacqueline Shohet Kahanoff 1973, translated from Hebrew by Jennie Feldman, in Starr and Somekh, *Mongrels or Mar-vels*, 128–35. All material by Jacqueline Shohet Kahanoff reprinted by permission of Ms. Laura d'Amade.

22. Editors' note from *Mongrels or Marvels*. Waguih Ghali's *Beer in the Snooker Club* (London: André Deutsch, 1964) is a semi-autobiographical novel that tells the story of a Coptic Egyptian exile in Europe. In many ways, the novel was a celebration of Egypt's ethno-religious and linguistic diversity, a critique of British colonialism, but more importantly perhaps an indictment of Arab nationalism and the regime of Gamal Abdel Nasser, which ultimately put an end to Egypt's capacious, cosmopolitan, Levan-tine character.

23. The Anglo-Egyptian treaty of 1936 permitted the British to maintain troops in the Suez Canal Zone. In 1951 Egypt revoked the treaty, and clashes along the borders of the Canal Zone in and around Port Said broke out between Egyptian anticolonialist demonstrators and British troops. In the novel, Font is injured during one such skir-mish (Starr and Somekh's note).

24. This is an apt, accurate observation, and the behavior of some Christians—espousing anti-Semitic attitudes, in the main imported from Europe—can be said to be a function of the *dhimmi* mentality, whereby non-Muslim minorities attempt to ingra-tiate themselves with the Muslim majority by advocating on its behalf, even espousing its dreams and phobias and prejudices.

25. Tawfiq al-Hakim (1898–1987) was a prominent Egyptian dramatist; Naguib Mahfouz (1911–2006) was a leading Egyptian novelist who won the Nobel Prize in lit-erature in 1988 (Starr and Somekh's note).

26. This is an idea already elaborated by Taha Husayn and the "Young Pharaohs" during the 1920s and 1930s. See the chapter on Egypt, and both Taha Husayn's and Ali Salem's essays.

27. Samir el-Youssef, *The Illusion of Return* (London: Halban Publishers, 2007), 152.

28. "The Levant: Zone of Culture or Conflict?" *Levantine Review* 1, no. 2 (2012): 200–204.

29. The reference here is to the "mountains of Lebanon," which Turki and his sister could marvel at from a distance, from the indigence of their refugee camps, but which they could not reach, nor touch or tread.

30. Fawaz Turki, *The Disinherited; Journal of a Palestinian Exile* (New York: Monthly Review Press, 1972), 175.

31. Fawaz Turki, *Exile's Return: The Making of a Palestinian-American* (New York: Free Press, 1994), vi.

32. Turki, *Exile's Return*, vi.

33. Turki, *Exile's Return*, 123.

34. Turki, *Exile's Return*, 9.

35. Material in this selection has been edited, with passages and sections left out.

36. This is arguably one of the most poignant, sad aspects of this conflict; changing a child's universe beyond his comprehension; a theme that recurs in the work of Turki, but also in Samir el-Youssef's and Jacqueline Kahanoff's—all of whom yearn for the "golden age" as it were, when Muslims, Jews, and Christians lived side by side in mutual recognition and respect on the eastern shores of the Mediterranean. Turki the child could certainly not understand why he would have been rebuked had he waved goodbye to his departing (former) friend, or had he—as any child would have done—run chasing after the car. In today's semantics of the conflict, what Qabbani referred to as the "abusive word lists of debauchery, defamation, and insult," Turki would have been called a "traitor," for having even thought of waving goodbye to his Jewish friend, the enemy as it were.

37. Juxtapose this to Antoine de Saint-Exupéry's *Little Prince,* and the poignant accuracy of his "all grown-ups were children once . . . yet, only few of them remember it."

38. The refreshing aspect of Turki's narrative and analysis dwells in its valorization of "shared responsibility." He does not wallow—as has become common in the Palestinians' literature of dispossession—in blaming the "other," or blaming circumstances. Turki takes ownership of the Palestinians' plight, and casts an introspective eye on its historical causes, calling for self-examination and self-criticism before pointing fingers at others.

39. There is a poignant, heartbreaking hint of Marcel Proust's *A la Recherche du temps perdu* in this passage—as there may be throughout Turki's narrative, and indeed throughout the work of other Levantine authors explored here; Palestinians, Israelis, and others. Thousands of pages of recollections and fuzzy memories issuing from Proust's "search for times lost" yielded the same conclusion; that seldom do the places of our memories remain the way we've preserved them in our mind's eye. "Places that we have known as children," wrote Proust in the first volume of his *Recherche,* "belong only to spaces in which we have placed them. . . . And the memory of a certain image is but regrets over lost moments in our lives; and the homes, the houses, the roads, and the avenues of times past are, alas, elusive and fleeting, like the years of our lives" (Marcel Proust, *À la Recherche du temps perdu* [Paris: Bibliothèque de la Pléiade, 1987], 1: 573).

40. The question of one's name, the sound of one's name, is one that many of the authors from the Levant—and the "conflations" of the Levant—touched upon with agitating emotion. Francophone Lebanese novelist Amin Maalouf for instance, in his self-narrative *Origines,* described himself as an exile of illusive origins; "a child of a tribe of eternal vagabonds, wandering off endlessly in a limitless desert, wide as the universe is infinite; . . . dwelling in tents disguised in costumes made out of stone; holder of varied nationalities that are only a function of random dates in time, or another steam-

ship setting off on a new voyage; sharing only one common denominator . . . beyond the generations, beyond the open seas, and beyond the Babel of languages: the rustling sound of a name, an identity grounded in mythology that I know to be false, but a mythology that I revere regardless, as if it were my only truth" (*Origines* [Paris: Éditions Grasset, 2004], 8).

41. Jasmine is Turki's younger sister, mentioned earlier in his recollections of Haifa and Mount Karmel.

42. Basta is an historic central Beirut district, famous for its antique vendors, bazaars, and furniture stores. It's a mixed Sunni-Shi'a neighborhood, about a ten-minute walk from the former Ottoman Grand-Serail, today the seat of Lebanese government and the prime minister's office.

43. The Corniche is a seaside promenade in West Beirut, alongside the Mediterranean coast and the city's central district. It offers a splendid vista of the Mediterranean, overlooked by the snowcapped summits of Mount Lebanon (the Mount Sannin range to be exact) in the distance. The Corniche bands along the Beirut promontory for close to four miles, with its starting point at the Saint George's Bay at the north coast of Beirut (site of the Saint George's Hotel where Jasmine worked), and into the Avenue de Paris and Avenue General de Gaulle near downtown Beirut. The promenade is usually swarming with skaters, joggers, bikers, and an array of food kiosks, giving to the Zeitouné Marina district and its avenues lined with upscale restaurants, boating clubs, night clubs, cabarets, and high-end high-rise apartment buildings.

44. The banality of cruelty.

45. Her own way—her most eloquent, if not *only*, way—to get back at her misogynistic society; making her final stand, her final "curtain call" with her own obscene (digital) gesture.

46. A reader socialized outside of the "honor killing" context would have assumed Mousa might have taken out a gun to shoot himself in remorse for the heinous act that he had just committed. But no! It was a *baroud d'honneur* celebratory bursts that he had in mind.

47. Hamra Street was one of the swankiest avenues in one of the trendiest neighborhoods of the old 1960s to early 1970s Beirut. Crowded with sidewalk cafés, luxury apartment buildings, and diplomatic missions abutting the prestigious American University of Beirut, it was once dubbed Lebanon's Champs Élysées.

48. This is a disturbing statement on "voluntary servitude," recalling Étienne de la Boétie's 1548 work by the same name, *Discours de la servitude volontaire,* in which he excoriates the politics of blind obedience, noting that "the powerful appear to be big *only* because we are on our knees."

49. Clearly this is Turki's *cris de coeur* in the face of the patriarchy and misogyny of his society. But his underlying message was that patriarchy and misogyny were symptoms of more deeply-rooted pathologies ensconced in the brutality and imperiousness of language. It is the Arabic language and its linguistic authoritarianism, argues Turki, which breed the repressive conditions whereby Middle Easterners are forced into self-imposed mutism and are "devoured" by tradition. Even those opposed to these stifling

conditions, the Samirs and the other battered quiet majorities in the Middle East—often deemed minorities—are acquiescent and resigned to their own bondage. See Leila for instance, from earlier in Turki's story. Yet Turki dares scream his rebellion against this language in the final sentence depicting his sister's ordeal, promising to "set fire" to God's universe. It is true that cultures mold and nourish the languages of their practitioners and adherents. But that is not necessarily the case with Arabic in Turki's telling. Arabic is not merely the language of Qur'an and the liturgy of over a billion of Muslims. Arabic is God and Tradition incarnate. Hundreds of millions of Arabs and Muslims, even those with inadequate grasp of Modern Standard Arabic, believe Arabic to be the hallowed language of God and the angels, and therefore a pristine primordial idiom that must not be sullied or fiddled with. In Turki's Jasmine metaphor, Jasmine symbolizes those silent Middle Easterners, peoples upholding narratives and cultural references that ostensibly challenge the imperious unitary orthodoxies of the Arabic language and those keepers of its traditions. The emotional bashing of Jasmine and the savage physical punishment meted out against her are "nothing unusual," as Turki notes; her fate is that of those who dare raise so much as a whimper in the face of orthodoxy.

50. This was a day-long 1968 battle between the Palestine Liberation Organization and the Israeli Defense Forces in the Jordanian town of Karameh, with the Israeli aim of destroying the Karameh Palestinian "refugee camp." As often is the case when it comes to the Arab-Israeli conflict, both sides declared victory, even though Israel was credited with having achieved its goal in the incursion—at the cost of a very high number of Israeli casualties.

51. The Arabs' tendency toward, and indeed their fascination with, verbiage and flowery rhetorical language is a theme that Qabbani and Adonis have treated at length in their own work. But this issue of language, and the hollowness of this hallowed language is indeed dealt a devastating blow by Turki. In *The Arab Predicament,* Fouad Ajami writes that Sami al-Jundi, a former Arab nationalist reared in the tradition of bombast and linguistic sabre rattling that Arabists had turned into an art form, attributed the "bankruptcy and incoherence" of Arab nationalism to the rhetoric and verbal wizardry of its avatars. "Nearly three hundred pages of text" in Michel Aflaq's *Nuqtat al-bidaaya* (The Starting Point), writes Ajami,

> yield no insight . . . ; there is only the visible infatuation with words and Aflaq's summons to the party to renounce power and go back to its "pure essence." . . . This language, observed one social analyst, had provided catharsis and relief and had enabled the Arabs to run away from their weakness: "Our wars have so far been verbal wars"; Arab society was basically an "expressive verbal society." Another serious writer's inquiry into the renewal of Arab society took him straight to the Arabic language as the root cause and expression of Arab decline. Arabic, he observed, was not so much a means of expression but an end in itself; A great writer was not measured by the worth of what he said but by his mastery of the language. The language—its nuances, its rhythm—was an instrument of

entertainment rather than a medium for transmitting thought and information. Unless liberated from the spell of the language, the Arab would
remain a captive of a sterile system of thought. (Fouad Ajami, *The Arab
Predicament: Arab Political Thought and Practice since 1967* [Cambridge:
Cambridge University Press, 1993], 33–34)

52. Turki defined *nahda* earlier as "renaissance" *tout court.* That is not accurate.
Nahda was strictly speaking a literary, and I would argue a strictly "linguistic" renaissance, whereby a "new" form of the "Arabic language," Modern Standard Arabic, began
being used as a journalistic and literary language, where Turkish and other languages
had predominated earlier. This *nahda* was retroactively, in later decades of the early
twentieth century, recast as the early stirrings of "Arab nationalism" or Arab national
awakening, but that is simply inaccurate. None of the *nahda* literati made the case for
an Arab national awakening, or any form of Arab-defined nationalism for that matter.
Arabism was the work of later, early twentieth-century doctrinaires.

53. Indeed, and this bears repeating, what began being referred to as "Palestine" in
1920 was nonextant beforehand, and in fact was part and parcel of the Ottoman *vilayet*s
of Beirut and Damascus—not a distinct "Palestine" as such.

54. "Neobackwardness" is the nickname that Turki bestowed on the *nahda.*

55. Although Turki's commentary and classification of the Arabic language's
multiformity is useful, it is not entirely accurate. Put briefly, Gordon's *Ethnologue* defines Arabic as a "second language" to more than three hundred million nonnative
speakers, and as a competency that is "not a first language. Used for education, official
purposes, written materials, and formal speeches. Classical Arabic is used for religion
and ceremonial purposes, having archaic vocabulary. MSA is a modernized variety of
Classical Arabic. In most Arab countries only the well educated have adequate proficiency in Standard Arabic, while over 100,500,000 do not." As for the spoken varieties,
which Turki terms "Oral Arabic" in the singular, Harvard linguist Wheeler Thackston
has identified five dialectal clusters of this "Oral Arabic" classifying them as follows:
"(1) Greater Syria, including Lebanon and Palestine; (2) Mesopotamia, including the
Euphrates region of Syria, Iraq, and the Persian Gulf; (3) The Arabian Peninsula, including most of what is Saudi Arabia and much of Jordan; (4) the Nile Valley, including
Egypt and the Sudan; and (5) North Africa and [parts of] the . . . regions of sub-Saharan
Africa." Thackston further acknowledges that although these five major dialectal regions were speckled with linguistic varieties and differences in accent and sub-dialects,
there is almost complete mutual comprehension within each of them. That is to say, "a
Jerusalemite, a Beiruti, and an Aleppan may not speak in exactly the same manner, but
each understands practically everything the others say." However, continues Thackston,
"When one crosses one or more major boundaries, as is the case with a Baghdadi and
a Damascene for instance, one begins to encounter difficulty in comprehension; and
the farther one goes, the less one understands until mutual comprehension disappears
entirely. To take an extreme example, a Moroccan and an Iraqi can no more understand
each other's dialects than can a Portuguese and Rumanian." Wheeler Thackston, Jr.,

The Vernacular Arabic of the Lebanon (Cambridge, MA: Department of Near Eastern Languages and Civilizations, Harvard University, 2003), vii.

56. Jasmine.

EGYPT

1. Michel Chiha, *Le Liban d'aujourd'hui* (1942; repr., Beirut: Éditions du trident, 1961), 49–52.

2. Charles Corm, *6000 Ans de génie pacifique au service de l'humanité* (Beirut: Éditions de la Revue Phénicienne, 1988), 7.

3. Saïd Akl, *Cadmus* (Beirut: Cadmus Publications, 1947), introduction, 22.

4. Published in the *Beirut Daily Star,* August 17, 2004.

5. See earlier references to *Leo Africanus,* and his narrator's conception of his identity, an African who is not from African, nor Europe, nor Arabia . . .

6. This is clearly a juxtaposition of "national" or "religious" rigidity next to cultural and conceptual fluidity and spaciousness.

7. This may be a reference to Sayyid Qutb (1906–66), one of the major ideologues and writers of the Egyptian Muslim Brothers, who actually spent an extended period of time in the United States during the late 1940s. Many analysts suggest it was these encounters with America, and Qutb's brush with its individualism, materialism, superficiality, mixing of the sexes, and what he deemed to be loose mores, that solidified his Muslim identity, further persuading him of the veracity of the Muslim Brotherhood's conviction (and its slogan, emblazoned on its official seal) that "Islam is the solution."

8. Note and compare to Ali Salem's mention of the "forefathers" in *The Odd Man and the Sea.*

9. It should be noted that into Husayn's "Far East" is included the Arabian Peninsula and its Arab-Muslim culture, from which Husayn sought to disassociate Egypt.

10. See *The Odd Man and the Sea,* regarding the duel between the Mediterranean and the Red Sea.

11. See note above. This is in reference to the duel between the Mediterranean and the Red Sea in *The Odd Man and the Sea.* Ali Salem's satire was in many ways a modern, twenty-first-century rendering of a very public and very fiery earlier duel, during the 1930s, between Taha Husayn (an advocate of Pharaonic Mediterraneanism) and Sati' al-Husri, who refused to concede Egyptian specificity, opting for coercion instead, in an attempt to force Egypt into the Arab fold.

12. This is allusion to Egypt as "cradle" of Western civilization, an honor also claimed by other advocates of pre-Arab Levantine identities in Lebanon, Syria, and Israel.

13. Lebanon's Phoenicianists go beyond mere—and arguably passive—kinship. They argue that Lebanon-Phoenicia were the creators of Europe and its values; Lebanon evinced a sort of compassionate, benevolent monotheism in the midst of brutal atheist civilizations, and consequently gave birth to Christianity, and ultimately Christendom, Judeo-Christian values, and Western civilization.

14. See Ali Salem, "The Odd Man and the Sea." For a Phoenicianist predecessor to this 1938 Husayn claim, see Charles Corm, *6000 ans de genie pacifique.*

15. Again, Phoenicianists made similar claims.

16. See Saïd Akl, *Lubnan in haka* (If Lebanon Could Speak), 6th ed. (Beirut: NObless, 1991).

17. It is curious how Arabs are not mentioned in Husayn's definition of "Easterners," and it is very likely that Husayn was thinking "Arabs" while mentioning "Hindus, Chinese, and Japanese," and so on.

18. Eighth century of the Christian era.

19. Tenth century of the Christian era.

20. Further down, Husayn will tell us that Egypt was receptive of the Arabs and "hastened at top speed to adopt" their language and religion (Arabic and Islam). Yet Egypt remained distinctly Egyptian, even though its language became Arabic, and its religion Islam.

21. Ahmad Ibn Tulun was a Muslim slave-soldier of Turkic origins, who founded the Tulunid dynasty that ruled Egypt in the late ninth century.

22. This, of course, is not all that accurate an assessment. State and religion in the "East," are well-nigh indistinguishable, especially as relates to Islam. Husayn so wants to link Egypt to Europe and the Mediterranean that he is willing to fabricate a "separation of church and state" as a central element and quality of Islam—which, pleasing an image as it may be, is neither textually nor empirically nor historically tenable.

23. As Husayn uses the term *East* and *Easterner* generically to dissociate himself and Egypt from the Arabs and Islam, he does, in the same vein, pay lip service to the Arabs and Islam (as if beholden to, or intimidated by the perceived Arabness and Islamic identity of Egypt).

24. Husayn's refusal to associate Egypt with the Arabs, or "Arabia," a geographic space which he folds into the term "East."

25. This seems to have been a common theme of Phoenicianists, Syrianists, Pharaonists, Canaanists, and Lebanonists: that their cultures influenced and modified their conquerors. In this sense, for instance, Lebanon was not Arabized, but rather it "Lebanonized" the Arabs. Husayn seems to be making a similar argument.

26. Note how Husayn affirmed earlier how "history . . . relates that [Egypt] acquiesced most reluctantly . . . to Arab domination."

27. Husayn is evidently oversimplifying matters here, or else has a superficial grasp of Christianity and the history of its evolution from a simple sect of Judaism in the "East," to a full-fledged religion and system of social ethics, as nurtured and developed by a specifically European social and intellectual "ecosystem"—primarily and initially with Rome's conversion to Christianity.

28. Again, a rather superficial depiction of both Christianity and Islam. For, while it is true that Jesus (who, from an Islamic perspective, was the founder of Christianity) was born in the "East," he was hardly the founder of a religion, Christianity. At least he was not the "founder" of Christianity in the same sense that Muhammad was the "founder" of Islam. And while it is also true that there are many elements of

comparison between Christianity and Islam—and indeed even more so between Islam and Judaism—there is much that sets those traditions apart from each other. Husayn's attempts at overexaggerating the commonalities between Islam and Christianity stem from his desire to prove Egypt's "European" accretions, and her association with "Christendom" the civilization rather than "Christianity" the religion. Of course, that distinction—semantically and conceptually speaking—between Christianity and Christendom *can* be made from a Christian perspective; the same cannot be said with regards to Islam, and both "Islam" the religion and "Islam" the civilization are to a large extent semantically and conceptually tautological.

29. What seems to escape Husayn is that, while the Qur'an was written in Arabic—by Arabs imbued in the Arabic ethos and ways of life—the Gospels were written in Greek and Aramaic, by Jewish cultural and linguistic hybrids, intimately acquainted with "Western" values and languages (Greek and Latin) and very thoroughly attuned with their own mother tongues, Aramaic and Hebrew-Canaanite. Moreover, and again, pleasing as this image may be, the Qur'an did not so much aim at "completing" and "confirming" the Gospels as it wanted to "correct" them. Like Christianity vis-à-vis Judaism, Islam "rejected" Christianity. But whereas Christianity "rejected" Judaism because it claimed it to be imperfect, Islam "rejected" both Christianity and Judaism because it claimed them to be false.

30. It is clear here that Husayn wants to have his cake and eat it too. He wants to accept and reconcile the Islamic element in Egyptian culture, but in the same vein reject its Arab (or Eastern, i.e., non-European, non-Mediterranean) component. There is both a clear relativism, and an equivalency, between Christianity and Islam, both of which seem to elude Husayn—or both of which are deliberately ignored by him. Christianity did not try to eliminate Hellenism precisely because it was the product of a Hellenist ethos and socio-cultural milieu. Islam, on the other hand, explicitly and unapologetically wanted—and did—eliminate all that preceded it. Everything that came before Islam was viewed as the product of the age of Jahiliyya, ignorance, and was therefore not worth keeping; all that came and/or will come after Islam can never measure up.

31. It is worth remembering however, that albeit a Muslim Abbasid endeavor— the Baghdadi Beit al-Hikma for instance, founded by Caliph Harun al-Rashid (786– 809)—the actual translators who transmitted the classical heritage of Rome and Greece into Arabic sources were in the main Christians and Jews. Among those, the most notable is Hunain Ibn-Ishaq (809–73) a native speaker of Aramaic who mastered Arabic, Aramaic, Greek, and Persian.

32. Khedive Ismail Pasha, also known as Ismail the Magnificent, was the grandson of Muhammad Ali Pasha, who is viewed as the founding father of modern Egypt. Of Albanian extraction, Ismail had similar ambitions as his grandfather's, worked to maintain for Egypt an autonomous status within the Ottoman Empire, and embarked on far-reaching modernization projects. He is notorious for what was then deemed a scandalous statement, declaring in 1879: "My country is no longer in Africa; we are now part of Europe. It is therefore natural for us to abandon our former ways and to adopt a new system adapted to our social conditions."

33. This, of course, relegates Islamic law to a secondary status, which is not entirely—or even partially—accurate. But again, Husayn is clearly writing with a form of advocacy in mind.

34. Husayn is overexaggerating here, and may indeed be flat out wrong. Whereas Christianity might have aimed to "improve" the biblical message, it did not completely reject it —hence the "New" versus the "Old" Testament binary, and the important role that the Hebrew Bible played in the birth and formation of Christian thought and civilization. No suchlike can be said of Islam with regard to either of Christianity and Judaism. Indeed, rather than "completing" or "confirming" the Old and New Testaments, Islam sought to correct (what it deemed) their falsity, and indeed aimed to replace them.

35. Those are Abbassid poets of Persian origin, who wrote in Arabic, and who defined the canon of "erotic," "homoerotic," and "wine-drinking" poetry, treating themes and imageries often bordering on depravity and lecherousness, even from a modern (enlightened) perspective.

36. Unfortunately, such claims often lack accuracy. The destruction of the royal library of Alexandria by order of Caliph Omar (ca. 642 A.D.) is a case in point. As one of the ancient world's most venerable libraries, flourishing under Egypt's Ptolemaic dynasty (ca. 300–30 B.C.), the Bibliotheca Alexandrina suffered its fair share of devastation and vandalism and rebirth over the centuries. Yet the burning of "sacrilegious" manuscripts under Islam is not unheard of. Although disputed by some scholars, Caliph Omar is quoted to have responded as follows to John Philoponus's entreaties to spare the library's books: "If those books are in agreement with the Qur'an, we have no need of them; and if these are opposed to the Qur'an, destroy them."

37. Husayn advocates the adoption of Europe's ways, not out of a need for imitation of that which is foreign, but because he considers his culture and that of Europe to be one. He even goes so far as arguing that Islam itself, once it had left the confines of the Arabian Peninsula, got "Europeanized" as it were, by way of its contacts with—and acceptance of—Byzantine-Latin civilization.

38. How does this gel with what Husayn said earlier about "history show[ing] that religious and linguistic unity do not necessarily go hand in hand with political unity, nor are they the props on which states rely"?

39. In spite of his reformist, secular, "Westernizing" ostentations, Husayn seems incapable of divorcing religion—i.e., Islam, which in the European context that he so compellingly advocates for belongs in the private sphere—from the public sphere. He had argued earlier that Egypt was "European" through and through; European in its history, it its cultural references, in its religions and its attitude vis-à-vis religion. He had even made the case that religion and the state are separate in Islam—and his own reading of Islam and the history of Islam only confirmed that assertion. Here, he is arguing that it is impossible for Egyptians to separate themselves from Islam. Islam, he claimed, "is as much part of the national [Egyptian] personality as language or history, and instruction in it is . . . necessary."

40. Aside from the inherent difficulty of Modern Standard Arabic, and perhaps even the unavailability of qualified teachers—although that is arguable—Husayn fails

to mention the functionality (or lack thereof) of the MSA form. It is difficult for a pupil to acquire knowledge of a language—or any skill for that matter—for which there is no practical use outside the classroom. Where can one speak, practice, or effectively use MSA outside of the constructed classroom setting. If the pupil's parents are francophone, and the pupil studies French in school, the student has the opportunity to use and practice what he or she has studied, at home. No such opportunity is afforded by MSA.

41. Husayn seems fully aware of this quandary that is Modern Standard Arabic, but still tip-toes around it for fear of offending the orthodoxies of purists and the religious establishment keeping a close watch on him.

42. This is rather simplistic. But, let us follow this line of thinking and make the argument that various Near Eastern "colloquials" also "more or less resemble each other." Could we then classify them as languages, as had done Husayn's contemporary, Tawfiq Awan, who, writing in 1929, argued that "Egypt has an Egyptian language; Lebanon has a Lebanese language; the Hijaz has a Hijazi language; and so forth—and all of these languages are by no means Arabic languages. Each of our countries has a language, which is its own possession: so why do we not write our language as we converse in it? For, the language in which the people speak is the language in which they also write."

43. One wonders how the study, *any study*—not only the study of a foreign language—can be possibly "premature"?

44. Would Modern Standard Arabic qualify as one of those languages; a language that is "of little value in most walks of life" as Husayn himself noted earlier; i.e., "the Arabic taught in school is a foreign language compared to the colloquial; for it is not only not used at home or in the streets, but is not spoken usually or heard even during the Arabic language class itself, let alone during the geography, history, or science classes."

45. Note that a great many of them weren't even Arabs, namely the grandfather of Arab grammarians, Sibawayh, whose native language was Persian, not Arabic.

46. Compare this claim—as to the supposedly transient nature of dialects—to the claim made by Kahlil Gibran in the Lebanon chapter predicting their march toward codification, and noting the possibility of Modern Standard Arabic itself meeting the fate of languages such as Syriac and Hebrew (that is to say, becoming a "dead language").

47. Husayn seems torn here between a number of tendencies. On the one hand he wishes to reform the classical (Arabic) language, secularize it, eliminate the "monopoly" of the clerics who have confiscated it, empty it of its religious content, and simplify its grammatical rules and conventions—in order to democratize it and make it into a more accessible and flexible national language. On the other hand, he ostensibly wants to abandon the colloquial—which in his view does not meet the criteria of a legitimate "language," but which, curiously enough, possesses all that which Husayn wishes to imbue the "classical" language—suitability for speech, simplicity, accessibility, functionality, secularism, and so on. He foresees—or rather advocates—an eventual "melting" of the "colloquial language" into the "classical" one. He notes, "It [the colloquial] might disappear, as it were, into the classical if we devoted the necessary effort on the one hand to elevate the cultural level of the people and on the other to simplify and reform

the classical so that the two met at a common point." So in a sense, Husayn is advocating a linguistic policy to meld both languages—the classical and the colloquial—together, as is he calling for the democratization of literacy—in order to normalize the teaching and ultimate "use" of the classical language as a spoken vernacular. Ironically, Husayn also seems to fear that the continued encroachment of "colloquial" on the "classical" language could ultimately lead to the disappearance of the latter at worse, or at best its relegation to the level of a liturgical language; "I warn those who are resisting reform that we face the dreadful prospect of classical Arabic becoming, whether we want it or not, a religious language and the sole possession of the men of religion." Not only that, but Husayn, a realist and a courageous intellectual, admits that "Arabic" as a spoken language is no longer extant: "Arabic in Egypt is now virtually a foreign language. Nobody speaks it at home or school or the streets or in clubs; it is not even used in al-Azhar itself. People everywhere speak a language that is definitely not Arabic, despite the partial resemblance to it. Throughout the Near East there are a number of cultivated people who understand, read, and write classical Arabic well (in the main not Azhar graduates). However, [even among those,] the majority cannot speak it fluently. When you write a book for the masses you have to simplify your grammar and syntax considerably in order to be fully understood. If we were to test the capacity of so-called literates to understand the meaning of a chapter by some contemporary author, the results would be painful and ludicrous." In my view, Husayn is a true reformer, but one who still feels obligated to pay lip service to the purists and the keepers of the classical language. His style and demeanor suggest he is writing in an era where many have already begun calling for discarding the classical language, and its replacement by colloquials.

48. This suggests that the native language is spoken "colloquial" Egyptian, *not* standard or classical Arabic.

49. Those reasons remain a mystery, as Husayn has never elaborated on this point elsewhere in his work. Yet, one wonders how a reformation of the Arabic writing system would have any meaning without a Romanization process—that is to say introducing a "vowels system" to the script.

Conclusion

1. Philip Mansel, *Levant: Splendour and Catastrophe on the Mediterranean* (New Haven: Yale University Press, 2012), 1.

2. Amin Maalouf, *Les Désorientés* (Paris: Éditions Grasset, 2012), 34–35.

3. Maalouf, *Les Désorientés*, 35.

4. Maalouf, *Les Désorientés*, 34.

5. Maalouf, *Les Désorientés*, 35.

6. Amin Maalouf, *Le Rocher de Tanios* (Paris: Éditions Grasset, 1993), 276–77.

7. Amin Maalouf, *Les Échelles du Levant* (Paris: Éditions Grasset, 1996), 49.

8. Maalouf, *Les Échelles du Levant*, 59.

9. Maalouf, *Les Échelles du Levant*, 79.

10. Maalouf, *Les Échelles du Levant*, 45.

11. Maalouf, *Les Échelles du Levant*, 45.

Bibliography

ARCHIVES

Archives Jésuites. Vanves-Malakof, France.

Charles Corm Archives and Private Papers. Quartier Nazareth, Centre Culturel Charles Corm, Beirut.

French Foreign Ministry Archives (Archives du Ministère des Affaires Étrangères, Paris-Quai d'Orsay). Correspondence Politique et Commerciales. Série "E," Levant, 1918–40, Sous-Série: Syrie, Liban, Cilicie.

PERIODICALS

Alif: Journal of Comparative Poetics (Cairo).

Asia Times (Bangkok).

Baghdad Times (London).

Beirut Daily Star (Beirut).

Bustan: The Middle East Book Review (Tel Aviv).

Christian Science Monitor (Boston).

Haaretz (Jerusalem).

Hadiiqat al-Akhbar (Beirut).

Al-Hayat (London).

Al-Hikma (Beirut).

Al-Hilaal (Cairo).

Al-Jazeera (London).

Levantine Review (Boston).

Middle Eastern Studies (London).

Revue du Monde Musulman (Paris).

OTHER SOURCES

Abou, Sélim. *Le Bilinguisme arabe-français au Liban.* Paris: Presses universitaires de France, 1962.

Abousouan, Camille. "Présentation." *Les Cahiers de l'Est,* Beirut, July 1945.

Adonis. *The Blood of Adonis: Transposition of Selected Poems of Adonis.* Trans. Samuel Hazo. Pittsburgh: University of Pittsburgh Press, 1971.

———. *Identité inachevée.* Paris: Éditions du rocher, 2004.

———. Interview with Dubai Television, March 11, 2007. Retrieved from www.youtube .com/watch?v=H2Y2ZcfUIZU (accessed January 9, 2017).

———. *Al-kitaab, al-khitaab, al-hijaab* (Book, Discourse, Hijab). Beirut: Dar al-aadaab, 2009.

———. "Language, Culture, and Reality." *Alif: Journal of Comparative Poetics,* no. 7, *The Third World: Literature and Consciousness* (Cairo, Spring 1987).

———. "Open Letter to President Bashar al-Assad: Man, His Basic Rights and Freedoms, or the Abyss." *As-Safir,* Beirut, June 14, 2011.

———. *Ra's ul-lugha, jism us-sahraa'* (The Language's Head, the Desert's Body). Beirut: Dar al-saqi, 2008.

———. *Sewing Their Lips Shut in Threads Spun with Their Own Hands.* Al-Hayat, May 17, 2012. Retrieved from www.al-maseera.com/2012/07/blog-post_21.html (accessed January 9, 2017).

———. *Waqt bayna r-ramaad wal-ward* (A Lull between the Ashes and the Roses). Beirut: Dar al-'awda, 1972.

Aflaq, Michel. *Fi sabiil al-Baath* (For the Sake of the Baath). Beirut: Dar at-tali'a, 1959.

Ajami, Fouad. *The Arab Predicament: Arab Political Thought and Practice since 1967.* Cambridge: Cambridge University Press, 1992.

———. *The Dream Palace of the Arabs: A Generation's Odyssey.* New York: Vintage Books, 1999.

Akl, Saïd. *Cadmus.* Beirut: Cadmus Publications, 1947.

———. *Lubnan in haka* (If Lebanon Could Speak). 6th ed. Beirut: NObless, 1991.

Alameddine, Rabih. *The Hakawati.* New York: Alfred A. Knopf, 2008.

Alcalay, Ammiel. *Keys to the Garden.* San Francisco: City Lights Books, 1996.

Allen, Roger. *Modern Arabic Literature.* New York: Ungar Publishing, 1987.

Arab Human Development Report 2003. New York: United Nations Development Programme, 2003.

Aslan, Reza. *Tablet and Pen: Literary Landscapes from the Modern Middle East.* New York: Words without Borders, 2011.

Asmar, Michel, ed. *Les Années cénacle.* Beirut: Dar al-nahar, 1997.

Bardakjian, Kevork. *Hitler and the Armenian Genocide.* Cambridge, MA: Zoryan Institute, 1985.

Bell, Gertrude Lowthian. *The Desert and the Sown.* London: William Heinemann, 1919.

Braudel, Fernand. *Memory and the Mediterranean.* New York: Alfred A. Knopf, 2001.

Burton, Isabel. *The Inner Life of Syria, Palestine, and the Holy Land.* 2 vols. London: Henry S. King, 1875.

Carré, Olivier. *Le Nationalism arabe.* Paris: Petite bibliothèque Payot, Fayard, 1993.

Chiha, Michel. *Le Liban d'aujourd'hui.* 1942. Repr., Beirut: Éditions du trident, 1961.

———. *Visage et presence du Liban.* 2nd ed. Beirut: Le cénacle libanais, 1984.

Cleveland, William. *The Making of an Arab Nationalist: Ottomanism and Arabism in the Life and Thought of Sati al-Husri.* Princeton, NJ: Princeton University Press, 1972.

Corm, Charles. *Contes érotiques.* Beirut: Éditions de la Revue Phénicienne, 2011.

———. *Les Miracles de la Madone aux Sept Douleurs.* Beirut: Éditions de la Revue Phénicienne, 2010.

———. *La Montagne inspirée.* Beirut: Éditions de la Revue Phénicienne, 1987.

———. "Rendons le sol au paysan" (Let Us Give the Land Back to the Peasants). *La Revue Phénicienne* (Christmas 1919): 270–77.

———. *6000 Ans de génie pacifique au service de l'humanité.* Beirut: Éditions de la Revue Phénicienne, 1988.

Davies, Humphrey T. "Ethnicity and Language." In *Encyclopedia of Arabic Language and Linguistics,* ed. Kees Versteegh. Leiden: Brill, 2011. Online edition, ed. Lutz Edzard and Rudolf de Jong, www.paulyonline.brill.nl/entries/encyclopedia-of -arabic-language-and-linguistics/ethnicity-and-language-EALL_SIM_vol2_0005 (accessed January 18, 2017).

Dawisha, Adeed. *Arab Nationalism in the Twentieth Century: From Triumph to Despair.* Princeton, NJ: Princeton University Press, 2003.

de Vaumas, Étienne. "La Répartition de la population au Liban: Introduction à la géographie humaine de la République libanaise." *Bulletin de la Société de Géographie d'Egypte* 26 (August 1953): 5–76.

Descartes, René. *Discours de la méthode.* Paris: Garnier-Flammarion, 1966.

Dunand, Maurice. *Byblia Grammata: Documents et recherches sur le développement de l'écriture en Phénicie.* Beirut: Imprimerie catholique, 1945.

Farah, Farah. "So You'd Like to Learn Arabic. Got a Decade or So?" *Christian Science Monitor,* January 17, 2002.

Farrukh, Omar. *Al-qawmiyya al-fusha* (Modern Standard Arabic Nationalism). Beirut: Dar al-ʿilm lil-Malaayeen, 1961.

Freyha, Anis. *Isma' ya Rida!* (Listen up, Rida!). Beirut: Naufal Publishing, 1956.

Gershoni, Israel, and James Jankowski. *Egypt, Islam, and the Arabs: The Search for Egyptian Nationalism, 1900–1930.* New York: Oxford University Press, 1986.

Gibran, Kahlil. "The Future of the Arabic Language." *Al-Hilaal,* 1922.

———. *The Prophet.* New York: Alfred A. Knopf, 1994.

———. *The Treasured Writings of Kahlil Gibran.* Edison, NJ: Castle Books, 1981.

Gordon, Cyrus. *The Bible and the Ancient Near East.* New York: W. W. Norton, 1997.

Green, David. "Levantinism Finds Its Place in Modern Israel." *Haaretz,* August 25, 2011.

Haim, Sylvia G. *Arab Nationalism: An Anthology.* Berkeley: University of California Press, 1963.

Harris, William. *The Levant: A Fractured Mosaic.* Princeton, NJ: Markus Wiener Publishers, 2003.

Hourani, Albert. *Arabic Thought in the Liberal Age, 1789–1939.* Cambridge: Cambridge University Press, 1997.

———. *Syria and Lebanon: A Political Essay.* London: Oxford University Press, 1946.

Husayn, Taha. *The Future of Culture in Egypt.* 1938. Repr., Washington, DC: American Council of Learned Societies, 1954.

al-Husri, Abu-Khaldun Sati. *Abhaath mukhtaara fi-l-qawmiyya al-'arabiyya* (Selected Papers in Arab Nationalism). Beirut: Markaz dirasaat al-wihda al-'arabiyya, 1985.

Ismail, Adel, ed. *Le Liban, documents diplomatiques et consulaires relatifs à l'histoire du Liban.* Beirut: Éditions des oeuvres politiques et historiques, 1979.

Jumblat, Kamal. "La Méditerranée: Berceau de culture spirituelle." In *Les Années cénacle,* ed. Michel Asmar, 91–100. Beirut: Dar al-nahar, 1997.

Karpat, Kemal. *Political and Social Thought in the Contemporary Middle East.* Westport, CT: Frederick A. Praeger Publishers, 1968.

Karsh, Efraim. *Islamic Imperialism: A History.* New Haven: Yale University Press, 2006.

Kaufman, Asher. "Tell Us Our History: Charles Corm, Mount-Lebanon, and Lebanese Nationalism." *Middle Eastern Studies* 40, no. 3 (May 2004): 1–28.

Khairallah, Khairallah. "La Syrie." *Revue du Monde Musulman* 19 (1912): 1–143.

el-Khoury, Khalil. *Hadiqat al-Akhbar,* Beirut, December 22, 1958.

Lammens, Henri. *La Syrie: Précis historique.* 3rd ed. Beirut: Éditions Lahad Khater, 1994.

Lawrence, T. E. *Seven Pillars of Wisdom.* New York: Anchor Books, 1991.

Lewis, Bernard. *The Multiple Identities of the Middle East.* New York: Schocken Books, 1989.

Maalouf, Amin. *Les Désorientés.* Paris: Éditions Grasset, 2012.

———. *Discours de reception et réponse de M. Jean-Christophe Rufin: Réception de M. Amin Maalouf.* Paris: Académie française, June 14, 2012.

———. *Les Échelles du Levant.* Paris: Éditions Grasset, 1996.

———. *Léon l'Africain.* Paris: Lattès, 1986.

———. *Léon l'Africain.* Paris: Livres de poche, 1987.

———. *Origines.* Paris: Éditions Grasset, 2004.

. *Le Rocher de Tanios.* Paris. Éditions Grasset, 1993.

Maalouf, Rushdy. "Yabisat Arza" (A Cedar Has Dried Up). *Al-Hikma* (Beirut: Hikma Institute) 11, no. 9 (December 1963): 463.

Mansel, Philip. *Levant: Splendour and Catastrophe on the Mediterranean.* New Haven: Yale University Press, 2012.

Moosa, Matti. *Extremist Shiites.* Syracuse, NY: Syracuse University Press, 1988.

Musa, Salama. *Ma hiya al-nahda?* (What Exactly Is the Nahda?). Algiers: Mofem Publishers, 1990.

Nocke, Alexandra. *The Place of the Mediterranean in Modern Israeli Identity.* Leiden: Brill, 2009.

Proust, Marcel. *À la Recherche du temps perdu.* Paris: Bibliothèque de la Pléiade, 1987.

Qabbani, Nizar. *Bread, Hashish, and Moonlight.* Beirut: Nizar Qabani Publishing, 1954.

————. *I Reject You, All of You!* London: Nizar Qabani Publishing, 1997.

————. *Marginalia on the Notebook of Defeat.* Beirut: Nizar Qabani Publishing, 1967.

————. *Mata Yu'linuuna Wafaat al-'Arab?* (When Will Someone Finally Announce the Death of the Arabs?). London: Nizar Qabani Publishing, 1994.

Renan, Ernest. *Oeuvres completes de Ernest Renan.* Paris: Calmann-Lévy, 1958.

Saghieh, Hazem. *Wadaa' al-'uruuba* (The Swansong of Arabism). Beirut: Dar al-saqi, 1999.

Salameh, Franck. "Adonis, the Syrian Crisis, and the Question of Pluralism in the Levant." *Bustan: The Middle East Book Review* 3, no. 1 (Spring 2012): 36–61.

————. *Language, Memory, and Identity in the Middle East: The Case for Lebanon.* Lanham, MD: Lexington Books, 2010.

Salem, Ali. *The Odd Man and the Sea. Beirut Daily Star,* August 17, 2004.

al-Shubashy, Sherif. *Li-tahya al-lugha al-'arabiyya, yasqut Sibawayh* (For Arabic to Live On, Sibawayh Must Fall). Cairo: Egyptian Book Authority, 2004.

al-Shuraiqi, Ahmad. "Adunis: Al-ana al-muta'aalia wa dimaa' al-suriyyeen" (Adonis: His Transcendental Ego and the Syrian People's Blood). *Al-Jazeera,* May 11, 2011.

Smith, Anthony. *Myths and Memories of the Nation.* Oxford: Oxford University Press, 1999.

Spengler. "Are the Arabs Already Extinct?" *Asia Times,* May 8, 2007.

Starr, Deborah, and Sasson Somekh, eds. *Mongrels or Marvels: The Levantine Writings of Jacqueline Shohet Kahanoff.* Stanford, CA: Stanford University Press, 2011.

Tabet, Jacques. *La Syrie: Historique, ethnographique, religieuse, géographique, économique, politique, et sociale.* Paris: Alphonse Lemerre, 1920.

Tammuz, Benjamin. *The Orchard.* Providence, RI: Copper Beech Press, 1984.

Thackston, Wheeler. *The Vernacular Arabic of the Lebanon.* Cambridge, MA: Department of Near Eastern Languages and Civilizations, Harvard University, 2003.

Tibi, Bassam. *Arab Nationalism: Between Islam and the Nation-State.* New York: St. Martin's Press, 1997.

Tuéni, Nadia. *Beirut.* Beirut: Dar al-nahar, 1968.

————. *Juin et les mécréantes.* Beirut: Dar al-nahar, 1968.

————. *Promenade.* Beirut: Dar al-nahar, 1979.

————. *Textes blonds.* Beirut: Dar al-nahar, 1963.

Turki, Fawaz. *The Disinherited: Journal of a Palestinian Exile.* New York and London: Monthly Review Press, 1972.

————. *The Exile's Return: The Making of a Palestinian-American.* New York: Free Press, 1994.

Versteegh, Kees, ed. *Encyclopedia of Arabic Language and Linguistics.* Leiden: Brill, 2009.

Weill, Raymond. *La Phénicie et l'Asie occidentale.* Paris: Librairie Armand Colin, 1939.

Yamak, Labib Zuwiya. *The Syrian Social Nationalist Party: An Ideological Analysis.* Cambridge, MA: Center for Middle Eastern Studies, Harvard University, 1966.

el-Youssef, Samir. *Illusion of Return.* London: Halban Publishers, 2007.

————. "Levant: Zone of Culture or Conflict." *Levantine Review* 1, no. 2 (Fall 2012): 200–204.

Text Sources and Credits

An earlier version of this anthology's introduction, titled "Adonis, the Syrian crisis, and the Question of Pluralism in the Levant," is reprinted with permission of Penn State University Press, from *Bustan: The Middle East Book Review* 3, no. 1 (Spring 2012): 36–61.

Nizar Qabbani's *Bread, Hashish, and Moonlight* (1954); *Marginalia on the Notebook of Defeat* (1967); *When Will Someone Finally Announce the Death of the Arabs?* (1994); and *I Reject You, All of You!* (1997), Copyright © Nizar Qabani, are all used with permission of Nizar Qabani Publishing and Estate.

Adonis's *Elegy for the Time at Hand*, previously published in Samuel Hazo's *The Blood of Adonis: Transposition of Selected Poems of Adonis*, Copyright © Samuel Hazo 1971, is used by permission of Samuel Hazo and Adonis. Extracts from Adonis's *Identité inachevée*: Chapitres: 1. "Dieu"; 2. "Nuances Arabes"; 5. "Les Arabes et l'Occident"; 8. "Poésie"; 9. "Mes Origines," Copyright © Adonis 2004, as well as excerpts of *A Lull between Ashes and Roses* Copyright © Adonis 1972; and *Sewing Their Lips Shut in Threads Spun in Their Own Hands' Weaving* Copyright © Adonis 2012, are all used by permission of Adonis.

Nadia Tuéni's *Blonde Stanzas* (1963); *Promenade* (1979); and *Beirut* (1968) are all used by permission of the Nadia Tuéni Foundation, Beirut.

All extracts from Charles Corm, *The Hallowed Mountain* (1933); *Miracles of Our Lady of the Seven Sorrows* (1949); and *Erotic Stories* (1912), are used by permission of the Éditions de la Revue Phénicienne, Beirut.

Anis Freyha's *Dinner on the Roof-Deck* (1956) is reproduced by permission of Hachette-Antoine, Beirut.

Childhood in Egypt © Copyright Jacqueline Shohet Kahanoff 1985, and *To Live and Die a Copt* © Copyright Jacqueline Shohet Kahanoff 1973 are reprinted by permission of Laura d'Amade, and of Emmanuel Sivan of the *Jerusalem Quarterly*, and have

Index